The Vampire King's Detective Wife

A Dark Fantasy Vampire Romance

Feka BC

Copyright © 2023 Jeka BC

All rights reserved

The characters and events portrayed in this book are fictitious. Any similarity to real persons, living or dead, is coincidental and not intended by the author.

No part of this book may be reproduced, or stored in a retrieval system, or transmitted in any form or by any means, electronic, mechanical, photocopying, recording, or otherwise, without express written permission of the publisher.

ISBN: 9798396069916
Imprint: Independently published

Cover design by: Angelica Maghirang
Printed in the United States of America

Dedication

To my wonderful Mother and Sister.

Thank you, <3

The Map of the Three Kingdoms

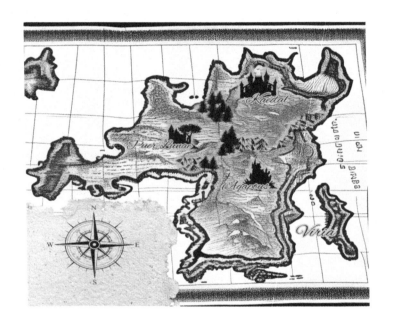

TEASER

Detective Inspector Naya Cirillo, renowned as the "Sherlock Holmes of the 21st Century," has earned her reputation despite her young age. Her name has become popular in her chosen field, attracting a lot of supporters, especially among young people who dream of following in her footsteps.

However, Naya's life takes an unexpected turn after receiving a letter from a mysterious admirer— one that reveals itself to be more than mere fan mail. Concealed within its words lies a cryptic message, a plea for help from an unknown sender.

Driven by her curiosity and sense of justice, Naya embarks on a journey halfway across the globe to find the sender. Little does she know that the letter she received is meant to lead her to a completely different world.

Trapped within a twisted tale of love, mystery, and betrayal, will she be able to solve the mystery behind the letter? Or will she suffer the same dreadful destiny as the sender?

Prologue

Naya

'Death is an unavoidable destiny that awaits all of us...'

Those words spoken by my father keep repeating in my mind as I press my back against the old willow tree. I'm currently sitting in the roots of it, patiently waiting for someone's arrival. A slight shiver courses through me as the cold breeze penetrates my denim jacket. The whole forest is draped in solemn silence, and the only sounds I can hear are the humming of the nocturnal birds and night insects.

A yawn escapes my lips as I stare at the silver moon that serves as my only light source in this dark forest. Most people are afraid of the dark, but not me. It makes me feel at ease and relaxed. It also makes me feel a bit curious about the secrets it might be hiding. Perhaps this attitude has something to do with what I do for a living. I am a detective, and curiosity is probably one of the most common traits that all detectives share.

I pull the sleeves of my jacket a bit to check the time on my wristwatch. It's close to 2 am already, which means I've been here waiting for more than 3 hours now. I let out a sigh of exhaustion. This stakeout is dragging on for far too long, and it is time-consuming. Furthermore, I have a flight to catch at precisely 10 am today. I huff in irritation. I am starting to feel a bit impatient.

That is when I hear the sound of a car stopping a few meters away from where I am, an audible sign that the person I am waiting has finally arrived.

A small smile curves on my lips as I rise from the root of the willow tree. Finally, the time has come for the monster to show himself, and it will be my job to raise the curtain and reveal his real identity to the world.

I hold my breath and listen as the car door opens and closes, followed by heavy footsteps. I can also hear the sound of metal being dragged through the pebbly ground. Then his footsteps halt, and from the sound of it, he starts digging. I wait for a few more minutes in the dark, waiting for him to finish his task and reveal the evidence.

"Yes!" I hear him exclaim with a hint of excitement in his voice.

That is my cue to reveal presence.

I dial my partner's number on the phone, wait for him to answer, before putting the phone back in my pocket. Stepping out of the shadows, I find myself face to face with the man I have been investigating for the past few days. He clutches a travel bag extracted from the hole he dug just moments ago. I am certain that the contents of that bag is the stolen money from the nearby bank he robbed around two months ago.

Our gazes lock, and I can see the flicker of recognition in his eyes. He knows he's been caught, but instead of fear, he greets me with a sly smile.

"Damn it. I'm busted, aren't I?" he says with a smug grin playing on his lips, his voice thick with sarcasm. He thrusts the shovel back into the ground and sets the bag down, taking a seat atop it.

Sweat trickles down the side of his forehead, and I can see the exhaustion in his eyes. His breathing is ragged. But despite his weariness, he seems almost amused by the situation. Without taking my eyes off him, I pull out the small journal from my pocket that

I always carry with me and begin to read its contents.

"You and your girlfriend orchestrated the robbery at the rural bank where she was employed, a heinous act that claimed the lives of five tellers and one guard," I narrate, then flip to the next page of my journal, scanning my meticulous notes. "You cunningly used her as a human shield to facilitate your escape, though deep down, she was your willing accomplice. However, after escaping from the authorities, you decided to kill her so that you could have all the money to yourself— that's selfish and greedy even for a criminal like you. Not a very noble move, is it?" I comment as I shake my head in disbelief.

The confident and amused smirk etched on his lips churns my stomach with disgust. His eyes reveal no trace of guilt or remorse, leaving me perplexed by the capacity of someone to commit such a heinous crime solely for the pursuit of wealth. Even after dedicating over five years to this field, I remain astounded by the depths humanity can plummet when it comes to money.

Since he hasn't responded to my previous comments, I turn my attention back to my journal.

"Considering the widespread news coverage of the bank robbery, it dawns on you that it would be unwise to conceal your girlfriend's decomposing body near your location. Additionally, you anticipate that the authorities will soon pay you a visit to get your statement regarding your 'missing' girlfriend that's been kidnapped by the bank robber. Therefore, you devise a plan to bury her remains in the woods alongside a clever scheme to conceal the stolen money."

My lips curl into a small smile as I read the last entry aloud. This is the last page of my journal. I guess this is fate's way of telling me that this is my last case as well. I close the notebook and tuck it back into my pocket with a sense of closure washing over me. I shift my gaze back to the man in front of me.

"You buried the money 6 feet below the ground. Covered it with dirt, put your girlfriend's dead body 4 feet up on top of it, and cover it again. Thus, when the authorities discovered her remains, they naturally assumed the robber had killed the girl and buried her body in haste. Nobody suspected that the money stolen from the bank was buried in the same spot where her remains are." I conclude and fold my arms firmly against my chest. "Did I miss anything?"

The man's smile widens as he slowly claps his hands in mockery.

"Great observations, Detective Inspector Cirillo. Just as I expected, the Sherlock Holmes of the 21st century never disappoints," he remarks as he rises from his seat. "I'm curious. How did you arrive at the conclusion that I buried the money beneath my dead girlfriend's body?" There is a hint of sudden interest in his tone of voice.

I shrug nonchalantly, and allow myself a small smirk.

"You maintained an unnerving calmness during the interview with my colleagues regarding your missing girlfriend. I decided to discreetly follow you, and it became apparent that you had an obsession with pirates," I reply in a steady and measured voice. "Based on this observation, I reckoned that if you were indeed the thief, you might have chosen to conceal the stolen money beneath a dead body of a person, much like how pirates buried their treasure to deter further digging. It was a hunch, an intuitive leap." I pause briefly, and assess his reaction. "However, the challenge lies in the absence of concrete evidence to legally incarcerate you. You're smart and played the part of a grieving boyfriend well when the police found her body."

"That's impressive. Your evidence is right here," he says and kicks the bag of money on the ground. "I waited for the heat of her death and the news about the bank robbery to subside before coming back to get my money. I'm guessing you figured out tonight would be the time I'd retrieve the bag since I have a flight scheduled later this afternoon."

I nod in agreement. "It's a perfect tragic story— you leaving the country to move on from your dead girlfriend when in reality, you killed her and are now trying to escape with the stolen money."

To my surprise, the man suddenly pulls out a gun from his waistband, and before I can react, he is already pointing it straight at my head.

"I thought this hole," he gestures to the hole he dug mere minutes ago, "would remain vacant. But it appears that I have one more body to dispose of before I make my departure."

Despite the danger, an amused smile dances across my lips.

"Scary," I scoff and lift my hand to inspect my impeccably manicured fingernails. "I actually have an appointment at the nail salon later before my flight. Just so you know, you're the 27th person to pull a gun on me. You guys seriously need to come up with a new idea. Repetition makes our lives boring."

With that, I swiftly retrieve a small knife concealed on the left side of my denim jacket and hurl it towards his hand, aiming to disarm him. His scream reverberates through the forest as he clutches his wounded hand, my blade deeply embedded in his flesh. I close the distance between us with a long and purposeful stride and kick the gun away from him before he has a chance to use it.

Without wasting any more time, I extract my phone from my pocket and bring it to my ear.

"Got him. Where are you?" I inquire on the phone.

"We're on the road now, Sherlock. Do you think you can keep him down for five more minutes?" Michael asks from the other line.

I grin confidently. "Five minutes? Easy," I retort and cast a glance at the man who is still on the ground, seething with rage

I quickly pull out a pair of handcuffs and secure his wrists, making sure they're tight enough that he won't be able to escape. Moments later, I heard the sound of a police siren approaching. Michael and two other officers step out of the car, all with big smiles on their faces.

"Another case closed, thanks to my favourite detective. Great job, Naya," Michael praises, giving me a tap on the shoulder.

I nod in acknowledgement, basking in the satisfaction of a job well done. I bid goodbye to my comrades and stride toward my faithful motorcycle hidden among the thick bushes on the other side of the forest. This baby has been my partner in crime for years now. A pang of sorrow grips my heart at the thought that this ride may mark our final journey together, or maybe not. Who knows?

I decided to take a long way home on my journey back to enjoy the scenery of my town one last time. This town has been my home for 25 years now, and

I can't believe that I'm going to leave it all behind because of my curiosity.

As I park my bike in front of my modest one-story house, a wave of contentment washes over me. But it's tinged with sadness, knowing that this will not be my home for much longer.

I walk inside and make my way to my room. Messy papers, newspaper clippings, and a few pictures of the people I'm investigating are scattered all over the place. On my bed, there's a box and a large backpack.

I march to my bed and open the box, revealing a letter and two other items I received not more than three days ago.

I let out a heave and read its content over and over again.

To my little lamb,

I hope this letter finds you well. I've been a long-time fan of yours, someone who's been following your work since I first heard of your name. This is a very long letter, but I hope you take the time to read it.

I have always been impressed by your dedication and skill. Your ability to solve even the most complicated of cases is truly remarkable. I always dream of being like you, and I wish to have your courage and dedication to protect the weak.

Beneath your strong personality hides a soft heart full of passion, dedication, and the courage to help those who are in need — something I envy about you. Some people wear lamb's clothing to fool others around them and to hide their monstrous works. But you, my darling, are different. You are a lamb hidden in wolf's clothing.

I cherish the moments every time I see your name again in the newspaper, and I eagerly anticipate more of your exceptional work in the future. However, I am aware that there will come a time when I will no longer have the privilege of reading news about your achievements. It pains me to know that I won't be able to follow your journey any longer. Though, it's okay. I already accepted my fate; after all, death is an unavoidable destiny that awaits all of us.

That's why I summoned all the courage within me to write you this letter. As someone who has admired you for a long time, I want to give you something that will remind you that there are people who genuinely value your work.

As my final goodbye, I'm leaving you this ring and this key. These are the two most precious possessions I have. I wish for you to keep them on my behalf.

Keep going, my little lamb.

Sincerely yours,

n.

"Death is an unavoidable destiny that awaits all of us..." I read the part that catches my attention aloud.

Initially, I thought that this letter was just a simple mail from an admirer, and the items included were

13

her gifts to me. However, upon closer inspection, I realize that there is a pattern to it. This is not just any letter from an admirer; it is a plea for my help.

For what reason? I don't know. I can't tell.

I don't have a clue who she is aside from the initial at the bottom part of the envelope— 'N'. Who is this N? And why is she asking for my help? Why did the letter she sent me contain the words my father used to tell me when he was still alive? I have so many questions that need answers. I figure that the only way to find the reason behind this disturbing letter is to travel halfway across the globe and pay a visit to the return address.

I pull out my journal from my pocket and place it on the table beside the newspaper that bears my name. That's when one of the newspapers on the table caught my attention. It has a headline about missing inmates. The news piques my interest slightly, but I have more important matters to attend to at the moment.

I pick up my phone and dial the number of one of the few people I trust with my life. After a few rings, he answers, and I hear his voice on the other end.

"Commissioner Faison. I want to follow up on the two months' vacation I requested," I inquire.

"Of course, it's been processed now. Michael just arrived at the station five minutes ago with the man. The case is officially closed. You can leave without any problems," he responds.

I let out a victorious smile at his confirmation, excited about the fact that I am finally set to leave this small town soon.

Once the sun starts to shine this morning, the newspaper will herald the news of a renowned detective who has triumphantly cracked the case of a bank heist and multiple murders. My name will once again echo through the streets, as it has so many times before. But the people don't know that this will be the last time they read about me in the local newspaper.

Little do they know that this will be the last case I am going to solve for this town.

Chapter 1

Naya

The bus I'm riding comes to a stop in front of the old wooden signboard. The rusted metal that serves as its post leads me to believe that the signboard is at least a hundred years old. I can't even make out what's written on it.

"Are you sure this is the correct location?" I give the driver an inquisitive look as I stand near the door.

The driver nods to answer my question, and I am left with no choice but to get off the bus despite the fact that I find it quite hard to believe that the letter I received really came from this place.

I survey my surroundings as the bus starts to drive away. The vegetation is quite lush in this area. The road is undeveloped, which is quite surprising, especially since we are already in the 21st century. Roads are supposed to be all asphalt by now, not made of dirt and mud.

I take out my phone from my pocket to check the GPS, only to be disappointed to see that there is no reception in this area. I look around me and sigh. As time passes, this is starting to feel like one of those wrong-turn movies.

I shrug and put my phone back in my pocket. If this is really where the fan mail came from, then all I need to do is look around. With that in mind, I tighten my grip on the strap of my backpack and start walking. In a forest full of hundred-year-old trees, I'm sure it's not that difficult to find this Moonblade Manor, right?

As I tread along the barely noticeable human path, my surroundings becoming increasingly lush and overgrown. The dense vegetation makes it difficult to see more than a few feet ahead of me. I have never been thankful that I'm dressed warmly in boots, thick pants, and a denim jacket. This place is wet, muddy, and I don't have enough patience to deal with all of that.

Whoever this 'N' is, he or she should have a good reason for sending me that letter. I didn't travel halfway across the globe to play Tomb Raider in a lush forest a thousand miles away from civilization just to be disappointed.

I take a deep breath and wipe the sweat from my brow with the back of my hand. I tilt my head to look at the clear sky. It's still mid-day, but I know it is important for me to find that manor, or else I'll be spending the night in the middle of this forest.

I know that my decision to follow the clues given by the sender of the letter may sound stupid to some people, but I have my reasons for doing so.

To begin with, my intuition is urging me to go. There is something about the letter's contents that has piqued my interest and convinced me to pursue the leads it offers.

Moreover, as an inspector detective, it is highly unlikely for me to receive a letter suggesting that the sender is on the brink of death while referencing a phrase my father said before he was murdered and not investigate it further. It has to be some lead to something deeper.

Finally, the key that is included in the letter is a crucial piece of the puzzle. It indicates that there is a lock somewhere that only this key can open. All of those convinced me that what I received was not just any letter; it was an invitation to embark on a quest for answers, and I believe it's up to me to accept the challenge and uncover the truth behind the mystery sender or not. Of course, there's a chance that I could be mistaken, but what is the worst that could happen here?

I sigh and look around me. Given the current situation, I think I now understand that the worst that could happen would be— me being stuck in this forest forever, or worse, becoming the lunch of any wild animals that are roaming the area.

After nearly two hours of walking, something strange finally comes into view. I let out a sigh of relief and my lips tug into a smile.

It seems that I'm not going home empty-handed after all.

I take a step towards the massive gate. The manor appears to have been long abandoned, and it looks like it came straight out of a Dracula film. But that doesn't stop me from feeling hopeful.

I don't even bother to call for anyone. The mansion exudes an aura of desolation, as if untouched by human presence for over a century. With a sense of ownership, I thrust the gate open and step inside. The resounding clinks and grinds of metal disrupt the once-pervasive silence, signalling my intrusion into the solemnity of the surroundings.

I survey the place with amazement, completely enthralled by the beautiful medieval mansion that stands before me. Its peculiar charm defies my expectations, casting an air of mystery over the entire place.

I walk towards the front door and knock. I know it is a bit crazy for me to do that, given that I highly doubt someone still lives here. Just as I expected, I received no response. From the looks of it, this manor has been abandoned for years. But if that's the case, who sent the letter to me?

That's when I remember something.

The key!

I place the bag on the porch's dusty floor and unzip it to get the box containing the gifts and the letter I've received. I take out the key and put the box back neatly inside my bag.

A victorious smile forms on my lips upon seeing that the key matches the doorknob's keyhole, an indication that I am indeed in the right place. Good. That means I can confirm that whoever sent these items has a connection to the old mansion in front of me.

I insert the key into the keyhole and turn it to the right, only to be disappointed when it doesn't work.

"Oh, come on!" I hiss in annoyance as I pull the key out. I am starting to feel a little impatient. I'm exhausted and hungry, and this door won't even open.

I kick the door out of irritation, creating a loud cracking sound, but it still doesn't budge.

I take another look around the house, searching for anything that could help me. Suddenly, my eyes land on a peculiar sight— a large birdcage-shaped shed located on the side of the house. Despite its unique design, it seems to be in excellent condition compared to the rest of the manor. The wall of it is made of solid brick stone, preventing me from seeing what is on the inside.

'Weird,' I thought to myself.

My brow furrows, and my gaze shifts to the key in my hand, wondering if it's meant for the shed instead of the house. Intrigued, I pick up my bag and make my way to the shed. Its design is simple but eye-pleasing, with a few vines and flowers crawling up the walls, adding to its charm.

I stop in front of the shed's door and insert the key into the keyhole, praying to God for it to work. This is my last chance; otherwise, I'll have to force my way inside the mansion and risk being sued for destruction of property.

My eyes brighten when I hear a clicking sound, a clear indication that the key did work.

Excitement courses through my veins as I push open the door of the shed. "Yes!" I exclaim, punching the air in triumph.

Darkness greets me, and my vision automatically starts to adjust to the small room. I retrieve the key from the keyhole and put it back in my pocket before stepping inside, the sound of the door closing from behind me with a silent creak. I fumble around in my backpack and retrieve a small lamp. With a flick of the switch, a soft glow emanates from the lamp, casting its warm light across the space.

The room is a sight to behold—a miniature library frozen in time. Dust particles dance in the air, and cobwebs cling to forgotten corners. The faint aroma of aged books tickles my senses, invoking a sense of nostalgia. Before me stands a small table in front of a solitary white metal chair.

My detective instincts immediately kick in. I place the lamp on the table and look around curiously. This is exactly why I am here. I know the letter I received isn't just fan mail but rather a message, a puzzle that

I need to solve even though none of it makes sense right now.

I quickly scan all of the books, careful not to disturb anything. Judging by the dust blanketing the whole library, I can tell that this place had been untouched for years.

However, after looking around for a minute and not seeing anything peculiar, my hopes start to dwindle. I let out a sigh and combed my fingers through my hair out of frustration. I am here at the place where the fan mail came from. I can recognize the pattern, but what the heck am I missing? I don't see anything that connects me to the letter I receive.

I stare at the books on the shelf and start counting to ten to calm myself and regain my focus.

"One... Two... Three..." I count aloud, my voice echoing through the quiet library. "Four... Five... Six... Se—"

The rest of the numbers get stuck in my throat when I notice something unusual about the books. I blink twice to make sure my eyes aren't playing tricks on me and take a closer look at it. For some reason, the writings on the spines of the books bear no resemblance to any alphabet in any language I am familiar with, which I find really odd.

Without wasting any time, I take out my phone and launch an app that allows me to search for all kinds of alphabets known to humanity, including ancient writings and hieroglyphs. I scan one of the spines of the books and wait for a few seconds for the app to read the writing. I hold my breath while staring at the three dots, waiting for the results. Suddenly, the three dots stop moving, and the app reveals the results.

"No results found," I whisper in a very low voice, feeling a mix of excitement and confusion.

A smile forms on my lips at my discovery as I once again scan the books around me. It's confirmed. The books on these shelves were written by people who have never been known to humanity.

CHAPTER 2

Naya

I take a closer look at the book I'm holding and let out an irritated sigh. The letters and writings in it are too complicated for me to decipher. It's weird because the letter I received was written in English.

It is now clear to me that the letter I received was not fan mail. It's a message asking for my help. And as a person with high morals, it was hard for me not to answer the call.

I am aware that what I did is a gamble, but it is something that I can't ignore. I feel like it has a deep connection to me. What puzzles me the most is how the sender knew the phrase my father used to tell me when he was still alive.

My father was murdered when I was 15. He was a great detective of his generation. I followed in his footsteps and became a detective with the hope of bringing justice to his death. However, after five years of searching, his case remains unsolved. The police department assisted me and gave me all the evidence they had, but even a genius detective like myself couldn't solve the case. I couldn't find evidence that would help me figure out who was responsible for his death. You can imagine my surprise when I received the letter three days ago, which contained the words my father used to tell me when he was still alive.

I'm hoping to find something useful here that will help me with my investigation. However, now that I have these books in front of me, I realize that it was all false hope. Those letters will not lead me to the person who murdered my father. Instead, they lead me to an old abandoned manor filled with books I can't read.

I close the book and return it to the shelf. It will take months to decipher these books. It won't be an easy task, but that doesn't mean I can't do it. It looks like I will need to camp here for the next few days if not weeks.

Also, I need to find a source of food nearby. All I have are a few instant foods in my backpack. I don't think that'll be enough if I plan on staying here for a few days.

I turn towards the door of the shed and reach out to open it, only to freeze in my spot as the doorknob refuses to budge. Fear slowly creeps up inside me, quickening my heartbeat and dilating my pupils. Annoyed, I grumble and try to twist the knob again, but it stubbornly remains stuck.

"What the heck?" I mutter to myself, growing increasingly irritated at the situation.

I kick the thin metal door in exasperation, not liking the fact that I am now trapped in a birdcage. I let out a short sarcastic laugh. If this is a joke, then it's not funny. I'm going to die if this door doesn't open.

I take a deep breath and try to push my fear aside, and focus on finding a solution. Panic is the last thing I need right now. I need a clear mind to get out of this place. I begin to carefully inspect the door for any sign of a keyhole or other mechanism, but my search is in vain. It becomes apparent that the door can only be opened from the outside. I let out a defeated sigh and leaned back against the table.

It looks like this is where it all ends.

After following a clue from the fan mail sent to me, I ended up being locked in a birdcage-shaped library.

If someone were to write my life story, I'm sure the last book would be titled 'The Mysterious Disappearance of Great Detective Naya.'

I wince at the thought of it. That title sounds awful.

I take one last look around, hoping to find something that will help me get out, but it is hopeless. This small room is just a library filled with books I cannot read. I slump into the chair and sulk. Is this really where it ends for me?

I am lost in that thought when my gaze is drawn to the small drawer beneath the table. On instinct, I pull the drawer open, revealing a small envelope that is identical to the one I have received. I frown. It seems that it was placed inside the drawer on purpose for me to see.

I take it out of the drawer and tear the envelope open. The letter inside is neatly folded in two, just like the other letter I have.

> To my little lamb,
>
> If you are here, that means you answered my call. For that, I am grateful. You and I share the same name and face, but we do not share the same fate. If you are wondering who I am, I am the future Queen of Puer Lunae. A Kingdom that is soon to fall apart. As the future Queen, it is my duty to protect my Kingdom to my last breath. I am far from saving, but my Kingdom won't go down with me. Detective Naya Cirillo, I know that what I am asking you is too much, but this is my only chance. You are my only hope.
>
> Sincerely yours,
>
> N.

My head tilts to the side as I examine the letter, trying to understand its message. Puer what? Kingdom what? What the hell is going on? It doesn't even give me a hint as to how I can get out of this birdcage. I am her last hope? Well, that's a shame because I am hopelessly stuck in this shed right now.

I take another deep breath to calm myself. This is a prank; this is all a joke, and I am stupid for falling for it.

Annoyed, I place the letter and envelope on the table. That is when I hear a clicking sound coming from it. I grab the envelope and take a look to see what's inside, revealing a gold necklace with a pendant on it with the word—.

"Naya..." I murmur and frown.

My eyes turn towards the letter on top of the table. This letter sounds like it's straight out of a fantasy novel. However, looking around me right now, if the letter sounds like it came from a fantasy novel, so do these books around me. The fact that these books are written in a language unknown to humanity means something, right?

I put the necklace around my neck before turning my attention to the books before me.

"Okay, I'll bite. Let's say that this is not a prank. What am I supposed to do now? Where can I find the Kingdom you're referring to?" I speak loudly.

I pray to heaven that there's someone out there listening to me. It will be much scarier to think that I am all alone in this place. I imagine my death to be heart-stopping, not because of hunger and dehydration. That's boring, not to mention pathetic.

As if on cue, one of the books on the shelf falls to the floor. I pick it up and open it. When I don't see any clue from it, I place it on the table and examine the space where it fell from. My eyes brighten in excitement upon seeing a tiny keyhole in it.

Finally, damn it!

I quickly take the key from my pocket and insert it into the keyhole. I tilt it to the right and smile when I hear a slight click, indicating that it has opened something. I remove the key and wait to see what happens next. I feel the room begin to shake, and I end up grasping onto the table to keep my balance. The bookshelves in front of me move back and divide themselves into two, revealing a stone tunnel.

My forehead creases while surveying it. So, there's a secret door? Fancy.

I make my way across the stone tunnel. Surprisingly, it leads me to the living room of a house, making my brow furrows in total confusion.

"This is getting weirder and weirder. Seriously, where am I?" I ask myself while looking around the house. The furniture looks medieval, not primitive, but it seems like it came straight out of the Victorian era. Is this the interior of the Moonblade Manor?

I glance over my shoulder as I hear the tunnel leading to the library start to close from behind me. Panic sets in, and I sprint towards it, desperate to reach the opening. However, my efforts prove futile as the passage seals shut with a snap, seamlessly blending back into the wall. It now appears like an ordinary surface, concealing any hint of the hidden door that once existed.

"Well, I suppose this is preferable to being in that birdcage." I shrug and turn my attention to the room I'm in. Looking out the open window, I can tell that I am not in the same place as before. The medieval and glamorous houses outside are far from the lush forest where I was stranded a moment ago.

I stride towards the nearest door, disregarding any potential consequences of trespassing. I swing it open without hesitation, paying no mind to the possibility of being caught. Yet, what lies on the other side is far from what I anticipated. My eyes widen in disbelief as I come face-to-face with a wounded woman who bears an uncanny resemblance to myself.

"Oh my God!" I rush up to the maiden to check on her.

Is she the one who sent the letter to me?

She's slumped against the bed, a silver knife embedded in her chest. Her eyes are closed, but the gentle rise and fall of her chest indicate that she's still alive.

"Miss, miss. What happened? Please tell me you are okay!" I frantically scan the room, berating myself inwardly for the absurdity of my own question. There's a silver knife lodged in her chest. Of course, she's not okay!

The woman opens her eyes, a pale smile gracing her lips as she lays her gaze upon me. Blood trickles from the corner of her mouth, and my throat tightens as our eyes lock. It feels like I'm peering into my own death like I'm staring at my own reflection.

"Who are you?" I mutter, my voice escaping me in a bewildered whisper.

"You've come..." she breathes heavily, her hand reaching up to gently stroke my cheek. There's a glimmer of amusement and astonishment in her eyes as she looks at me.

I stay frozen in my spot, my mind reeling with disbelief and confusion. We're not merely identical; she is me, and I am her. How is this even possible? I reach out to hold her hand, but before our fingertips can make contact, her hand slips from mine and falls limply to the floor. Panic surges through me, and my eyes widen in horror as I witness the light in her eyes flicker and fade.

"No, no... Please don't leave me like this. You can't die, you called out to me, and I came," I plead desperately, clutching her hand tightly.

I don't know who this woman is. It's the first time I've laid eyes on her in this lifetime, yet it feels as though I'm losing someone incredibly dear to me at this very moment.

As I gaze at her lifeless, pallid face, tears well up in my eyes, only to be abruptly halted by astonishment when her body begins to transform into ashes, slowly disintegrating before my disbelieving eyes.

The silver knife clatters onto the stone floor, its impact shattering the heavy silence that enveloped the room. Tears stream down my cheeks as my gaze fixed on the dagger that was used to kill her.

Why did she have to die? Was this the purpose of her summoning me here, to witness her tragic death? What role am I meant to play in all of this? Yes, I am a detective, but her body has vanished, leaving me with only questions and the silver knife as tangible evidence.

Lost in contemplation, I hold the silver knife in my trembling hands, examining it closely as I attempt to make sense of the bewildering events that have unfolded.

Time eludes me as I linger in that contemplative state, thoughts swirling in my mind. The abrupt sound of the door opening and closing jolts me back to reality, snapping me out of my reverie.

"Lady Naya, are you ready now? King Atticus is growing impatient. The carriage that will take you to the church is waiting," the person says but abruptly halts, seemingly taken aback by the situation unfolding before them.

I look over my shoulder to the source of the voice, discovering a pair of mesmerizing deep blue eyes fixed upon me. The newcomer is garbed in a suit reminiscent of the Victorian era. Determined to compose myself, I hastily wipe away my tears, preparing to face this unexpected presence.

The man standing before me possesses a handsome face, and for a fleeting moment, I find myself captivated by his physical appearance. However, the atmosphere swiftly shifts as his face darkens, his once deep blue eyes morphing into a fiery red hue. In an astonishing display of speed, he materializes directly in front of me, causing my eyes to widen in shock. His hand clutches my neck, threatening to break it if I dare to provoke him.

"What have you done to her?!" he bellows in a menacing tone, his voice laced with a combination of shock, rage, and defeat. I notice the tears welling up at the corner of his eye, mirroring his turbulent emotions. His grip on my neck tightens, his lips parting to reveal razor-sharp fangs. As his eyes darken, they transform into an abyss of pitch black.

At that moment, I am paralyzed with fear, confusion, and disbelief. The person before me is unmistakably not human. Questions start to swirl in my mind. Where am I? Who the heck are these people?

"Answer my question! Who sent you, and why did you kill her?!" he roars once again, his eyes blaze with unbridled fury, demanding an explanation.

The man or creature before me believes I am responsible for the woman's death. I cast my gaze upon the trembling knife clutched in my hand. Of course, I'll be his primary suspect. He has found me holding the silver knife in the room where her ashes are scattered.

I open my mouth to defend my innocence, but my words only come out as a gurgle because he is choking all of the oxygen out of me. His grip on my neck tightens even more. Each passing moment intensifies the struggle for air, while my futile attempts to break free from his vice-like hold prove fruitless.

In the midst of this life-or-death struggle, my hand clings to the silver knife with unwavering determination, as if my very existence depends on it.

'Please forgive me for this...' I silently plead, mustering every ounce of strength within me as I drive the knife forcefully into his arm.

A resounding hiss reverberates throughout the room, and as anticipated, he releases his grip on my neck. I gasp for precious air and crumple to the floor while the man clutches his wounded arm in pain.

His eyes transform into a fiery red hue as he glares at me with unabated hatred. My grasp on the knife tightens, its blade pointed firmly in his direction.

"I am innocent until proven guilty! Yes, I am holding the weapon that killed her, but it doesn't mean I am the murderer!" I vehemently defend myself, the words tumbling out in a rush.

Suddenly, a resounding knock echoes from the other side of the door, causing both of us to turn our attention towards it.

"Is Lady Naya ready? King Atticus has dispatched another warrior to fetch her. The wedding was scheduled to commence hours ago," a woman's voice calls from the other side of the door.

Our gazes lock, and a fleeting moment of panic settles between us as we both realize the predicament we are in. He is nursing his injured arm, and I am clutching the knife that took Lady Naya's life— an unmistakable evidence of a grave crime.

"Fuck!" we both curse simultaneously knowing that this is not going to end well for both of us.

Chapter 3

Naya

"If you are not the killer, then who are you?" The man's gaze narrows in anger as he scrutinizes me. However, I notice a gradual return of his eyes to a normal blue hue, an indication that his rage is subsiding.

"I am Naya," I reply in a quivering voice. I press my palm against my chest, while my other hand tightly grips the knife. I refuse to let my guard down. This person standing before me is far from human, and I need to be prepared for anything.

His expression darkens as he strides purposefully toward me, each step measured and deliberate. He stops exactly in front of me. His imposing stature makes me feel small and vulnerable. Tension fills the air, and I can feel my heart pounding in my chest.

"Are you seriously going to continue your act?" he hisses with fury lacing his tone "You and Lady Naya might have the same face, but I can tell that you are a fraud!"

A sharp gasp escapes me as I witness his expression transform into pure rage.

"Listen," I immediately interject, attempting to maintain composure. "I never claimed to be her." I gesture towards the ashes scattered on the bed and floor. "You asked me who I am, and my name is Naya."

My grip on the knife tightens. If this man tries to harm me again, I am going to cut off his arms completely...

I remain frozen in place as he leans closer, his warm breath grazing my skin. A lump forms in my throat as I struggle to swallow. Before I can react, a searing pain surges through my neck, and I realize he's biting me. Shock overtakes me, my eyes widening as I feel my life force being drained. Dizziness and disorientation take hold, and I know I must fight back if I want to survive.

Summoning every ounce of courage within me, I forcefully push him away, causing him to stumble back, his piercing gaze fixed upon me. He wipes the blood from the corner of his lips, never breaking eye contact.

Instinctively, my hand rises to my neck, anticipating a wound, but to my astonishment, I find nothing there.

I take a cautious step backwards, putting some distance between us. It suddenly dawns on me the kind of creature I'm facing.

"Vampire," I whisper, the word barely escaping my lips.

"Human," he responds simultaneously.

A chilling realization washes over me, finally grasping the true danger of the situation I find myself in. An involuntary shiver runs down my spine as I contemplate the horrifying possibilities of what could have occurred had I not managed to push him away in time.

"Good heavens," I exclaim and smack my forehead. "The Kingdom the letter mentioned... it's a kingdom inhabited by vampires."

This isn't good. How did I end up here? Vampires are supposed to exist solely in books and the realms of imagination, not in reality.

"You're a human..." the man remarks, regarding me as if I am some kind of a mythical creature that shouldn't exist.

Well, it's reassuring to know that we share the same sentiments regarding each other's existence. I look up to meet his gaze. This man seems to be a loyal companion of the woman who died a few minutes ago. Lady Naya is the one who summoned me here. I'm sure this man is not an enemy. At least, I hope so.

I take a deep breath to regain my composure. "Yup, human. Detective inspector Naya Cirillo." I introduce myself, extending my hand towards him for a handshake.

"You are the detective she's always blabbering about..." he mutters with a mix of recognition and disbelief flickering in his eyes. "I am Lady Naya's personal butler. You can call me Samuel," he finally introduces himself.

He scrutinizes me from head to toe, seemingly unable to believe that I am standing before him.

"So, she did know me. But how?" I furrow my brow, my gaze shifting to my extended hand before lowering it. It seems that handshakes are not customary etiquette in this place.

Lady Naya seemed to know a lot about me. She even knew my father's favourite phrase to tell me when he was still alive.

But the question remains: How?

My eyes dart to the spot where she lay just moments ago before her body turned into ashes. Countless questions flood my mind, and only she holds the answers. However, she's dead now. I release a sigh of despair. If I had known this was going to happen,

I should have remained within the confines of the birdcage. It would have been a safer choice.

"Lady Naya is a—."

His words were abruptly interrupted by a knock on the door, drawing our attention to it.

"King Atticus awaits Lady Naya. The ceremony has been postponed for far too long," someone says from the other side of the door, sounding a bit impatient.

"Lady Naya will be out in exactly ten minutes," Samuel replies loudly, making me frown in confusion.

I turn to look at him with a 'what the heck are you thinking' expression on my face.

"Are you out of your mind? She's dead! You have to tell them the truth!" I hiss at him in a voice that was just above a whisper. Concealing a murder is a criminal offence, even if you're not the killer.

"No, listen. Once you inform them that Lady Naya is dead, you and I are going to die today. King Atticus will have our heads for the unexpected death of his future queen. And I am not planning to die until I kill that coward who dared to lay a hand on her." He turns his back on me and makes his way towards one of the doors.

I shake my head in disbelief and follow him from behind. The future queen is dead, and I am considered one of the suspects.

Though I managed to convince this man that I am not the killer, I know it will be a different case with the King. Besides, I'm pretty sure that being a human in vampire territory is never a good thing.

"Even if you don't tell them that their future queen is dead, they will figure it out anyway. Who will you present to them after ten minutes?" My voice is filled with worry. Heck, I am confused and worried. I'm still trying to wrap my mind around the idea that I am in a place filled with vampires.

The man doesn't answer my question. Instead, he opens the massive door of the closet, revealing one of the most beautiful wedding gowns that I have ever seen in my lifetime, its exquisite design and intricate details captivating my gaze.

Turning to me, a mischievous smirk plays on his lips, his eyes gleaming with a hint of mischief.

"I don't know about you, but I believe I have a Lady Naya to present to them in ten minutes," he says as he takes the white wedding gown and pushes it towards me.

Confusion contorts my face momentarily, but in an instant, disbelief washes over me as I finally understand his plan.

"Oh no, you don't..."

"Oh yes, I can, and you will."

***

Some books possess plot twists that will set your heart racing with anxiety, while others will leave your mind spinning in confusion. If my life were to be written as a book, I am certain the plot twist would fall into the latter category.

"Stop frowning, Naya. Lady Naya always has a smile ready to offer everyone," Samuel whispers.

My palms clench into fists as I try to control the urge to punch him. I take a sharp inhale and remind myself of the gravity of the situation. I need to go along with this charade, or both of us will face the wrath of the vampire king reigning over this kingdom.

"Well, I am not her. I am about to marry a man I have never met in this lifetime, and he happens to be a vampire king. If he discovers our scheme, we are both going to die!" I hiss at him in a low voice to make sure only the two of us can hear my words.

"Trust me, if the people here discover that you're a fraud, we will meet our demise right where you stand," he retorts sharply.

I can't help but roll my eyes in annoyance, but I quickly adjust my expression to a forced smile. How did I end up in this place and situation again?

I hear the music begin to play, and the children in front of us start to move forward. I take a deep breath, exhaling slowly to calm the tension in my chest and prevent myself from fidgeting.

The church is adorned with elegant wildflowers and opulent gold silk curtains. It's undeniably a wedding straight out of my dreams, except for the fact that it's happening against my will and the groom is a vampire gives this event a spicy twist, turning it into a nightmare.

The gazes of the people inside the church are fixed upon me, filled with admiration as if I am the most stunning woman they have ever laid eyes upon.

Observing the aristocratic appearance of the individuals surrounding me and the grand mansions we pass on our carriage ride to the church, it becomes evident that the Kingdom is prosperous. Yet, this realization only adds to my confusion.

"I don't understand..." I blurt out, causing the man beside me to look at me.

"Don't understand what?" he questions as we begin our walk towards the altar.

"Lady Naya said in the letter that this Kingdom is soon to fall apart. It doesn't look like it's about to fall apart to me."

I shift my gaze to Samuel. His eyes are now solely focused in front of us, but I feel him tense up in response to my comment.

"Don't be fooled by what you see. Just because this Kingdom appears prosperous on the surface doesn't mean it's not bound to fall into mishap anytime soon."

That makes me frown. I want to ask him more to clarify what he meant by that, but he already let go of my hand. My attention is drawn back to our present situation. I swallow hard as my eyes land on the man standing before the altar, patiently awaiting my arrival.

I'm about to marry the king of this kingdom, a vampire king.

I let out a sharp exhale the moment our eyes meet, my blue orbs locking with his hazel-brown ones. In that instant, I find myself immobilized, captivated by the sheer authority exuding from him.

I'm about to wed a man who possesses an aura of power that makes me instinctively want to yield. After all, he is a king, and such dominance should come as no surprise.

A tender smile graces the man's lips as he gazes upon me with adoration. Despite my better judgment, a blush spreads across my cheeks. My heart begins to race erratically, and I struggle to tear my gaze away from him.

The warmth emanating from his eyes engulfs me, creating a sense of safety and reassurance. He's making my heart flutter with a bewildering mixture of emotions. Am I being hypnotize? After all, don't vampires possess the ability to ensnare the minds of humans?

"Ahem..."

The forced cough from the priest breaks my trance, diverting my attention from the mesmerizing gaze of my soon-to-be husband. I shift my gaze to the man in the white coat, offering him an awkward smile. It's evident that he isn't amused by my absent-mindedness as he directs his gaze towards the extended hand of the King.

A pang of embarrassment washes over me upon realizing that I've been so enthralled by the King's divine appearance that I failed to notice his hand extended towards me. The sound of laughter ripples through the church, likely indicating that the onlookers assume I'm deeply infatuated with the man I'm about to wed.

'Great acting skills, Naya.'

I close the remaining distance between us and firmly grasp his hand. It radiates warmth against my palm, sending a wave of pleasant sensations through me. He lightly squeezes my hand, and in that simple gesture, the butterflies in my stomach awaken, causing a riot of emotions that push aside any lingering fear.

"You may proceed with the ceremony, Cassius," my soon-to-be husband instructs the priest standing before us.

Cassius, the man he addressed, nods and begins reciting from the book. After a few moments, he raises his gaze to meet my eyes, as if waiting for my response.

I lift my gaze to meet his and offer him an uneasy smile. Truth be told, I'm not fully attentive to his words. Nerves have taken hold of me, making it difficult to comprehend what he just said.

"I suppose this is where I say, 'I do'?" I murmur just enough for the three of us to hear.

The man beside me lets out a soft chuckle, finding my comment amusing, but the priest wears a disapproving expression. Cassius gives me a bored look as if telling me that he's tired of my antics. What is his problem with me, really?

"I do," I respond before letting out a sharp exhale. There's no turning back from here anymore.

The King turns to face me with a smile on his lips. That's enough to make my heart skip a beat. The love that is vividly written in his eyes while looking at me both excites and pains me. That love was not meant for me. That was for a dead woman. I am nothing more than a replacement, a substitute for Lady Naya.

I offer a bittersweet smile, feeling a pang of sorrow for the King. I can already envision the pain he will suffer once he discovers the truth. I will do my utmost to conceal it, but as an old saying goes, there are three things that cannot be hidden for long: the moon, the sun, and the truth.

"King Atticus and Queen Naya, I now pronounce you husband and wife," declares the priest. "May the bounties of the universe, the joy of love, the peace of truth, and the wisdom and strength of the great spirit be your constant companions, now and forever. You may now kiss the bride."

A gasp escapes my lips as I realize what comes next.

Before I can fully process what is happening, my husband tenderly draws me closer. Our eyes meet fleetingly before he lowers his head, capturing my lips in a gentle kiss. I squeeze my eyes shut, feeling the warmth of his lips against mine. It's as if fireworks explode in a burst of sweet sensations, coursing through my veins. The next thing I hear is the resounding applause and cheers from the crowd, congratulating us on the beginning of our journey together.

CHAPTER 4

Naya

I close my eyes, relishing the gentle caress of the cool breeze against my skin. I take a sharp inhale before opening them and fixate my gaze upon the glass of wine cradled in my hand. It is one of the sweetest wines I have ever tasted, yet I find myself unable to fully appreciate its flavours. I exhale heavily, my breath mingling with the surrounding air. My gaze meanders to the captivating view before me, drinking in the sight of the resplendent Victorian houses that surround the castle.

Until now, I still can't believe that this is really happening. I am now a queen. Not just any queen, but the Queen of vampires. Seriously? It sounds sick, I know. It's undeniably terrifying, yet somehow, I find it strangely cool. How many people can say they've experienced the honour of being hailed as the 'Queen of Vampires'?

I'm certainly not complaining.

"Are you enjoying the view of your kingdom, my Queen?" That voice grabs my attention, compelling me to glance over my shoulder.

A beautiful woman with blonde hair and green-gem eyes approaches me. She takes the space right beside me, invading my personal bubble. I furrow my brow. Is she Lady Naya's friend?

The newcomer sips from her glass of wine, the golden liquid glistening under the ambient light. She then turns to face me with a wicked smile playing on her lips. I can't help but notice the sharpness of her features and how her eyes sparkle with malice as she looks at me.

"You may have won for now, but not for long. Enjoy your reign while it lasts," she declares, her voice laced with a hint of venom. With a gesture of mock salutation, she tips her glass in my direction.

Okay— definitely not Lady Naya's friend. Got it!

I will add her to my list of suspects. In fact, she will be at the very top of that list.

A smug grin gradually spreads across my lips as I observe the unmistakable hatred lurking within her eyes despite her smile.

"Of course, I will." I retaliate, my tone dripping with sarcasm. "I mean, seeing you dying of jealousy right now, I'm certainly enjoying this," With a mocking gesture, I raise my glass in a toast. "Cheers, then?"

The woman's eyes widen in shock, taken aback by my audacious response. I arch an eyebrow. She certainly doesn't expect me to talk back.

I've come to the conclusion that Lady Naya is a sweet woman who doesn't know how to fight back. Well, too bad because I am a police officer, a detective inspector, and being weak is not my thing. You don't need that in my line of work, especially when dealing with criminals who kill and torture people for pleasure.

The shock in her eyes gradually dissipates and is replaced by a darkened expression. My smirk widens, relishing the knowledge that I've successfully managed to provoke her. The fact that she is a vampire does not intimidate me. After all, I am a queen. I highly doubt she would be foolish enough to raise a hand against me.

She turns her back on me and strides purposefully toward the exit of the balcony.

I can't help but shake my head as I follow her with my eyes, the smile of amusement still dancing in the corner of my lips.

"I rushed here because I was scared that you might not be able to handle Harriet, but it seems you are more than capable of holding your own," Samuel's voice prompts me to shift my attention towards the secluded section of the balcony.

"That woman is going on my main suspect list," I tell him.

"I don't think it's her. Harriet might be a little bitch, but I doubt she'll attempt something as dangerous as assassinating the future Queen on her wedding day."

I take a sip of my wine and lock eyes with Samuel. "As a detective, you should know the first rule: anyone with a potential motive for killing the victim becomes a suspect. Therefore, she is a suspect."

"If you put it that way, then you have tons of people to put as a suspect," he counters.

That makes me frown.

"That complicated, huh?" I sigh, and I lean towards the stone railing of the balcony. It appears that this is not going to be an easy puzzle to solve.

I raise my eyes to the expansive sky above us, its darkness juxtaposed with its awe-inspiring beauty. Shifting my gaze, I fixate on the glass of wine I'm holding, only to frown when I remember something.

"Naya already knew that someone wanted her dead..." I whisper absentmindedly. "But if she knew there was a plot to assassinate her, why didn't she inform the king or you?" I question.

Samuel's face darkens, and his eyes start to change colour, giving me a window into his emotion.

"As her butler and a close friend, she knew I would stand by her side, no matter the circumstances," he utters in a voice tinged with anger. He forcefully punches the stone railing, causing me to flinch involuntarily. "How did I not see it? Lady Naya lives in constant fear for her life, and I failed to notice! Damn it!"

I don't dare to say another word. My gaze remains locked on the glass of wine clutched in my hand. Samuel is suffering internally, and I can sense the combination of pain and regret emanating from him. But none of us can grieve right now. We both need to keep our guards up. No one can know that the real Naya is dead.

If I am going to use the last letter I received from her as a reference, Lady Naya believes that she will be the downfall of this kingdom. It was her intention from the very beginning for me to take over the role of Queen. But why? Why couldn't she save Puer Lunae and evade her own demise? Why do I sense that there is a crucial piece of the puzzle missing?

"I hope I'm not interrupting anything. May I have a moment with my beloved?"

A lump forms in my throat as I recognize that familiar baritone voice. My gaze shifts toward Atticus, my husband. I force myself to smile even though my heart is now starting to pound like crazy. Never before in my entire life have I felt intimidated by anyone, not even a deranged killer responsible for over twenty deaths in a single year. Only the King possesses the power to evoke such emotions within me.

"Of course, Your Majesty," Samuel bows first, displaying his respect before exiting the balcony, leaving me alone, vulnerable in the presence of his King.

A smile curves on Atticus's lips as he closes the distance between us. I have the urge to step back, but the railing already presses against my back. I've got nowhere to escape.

"I've been searching for you everywhere..." he whispers, his words intended solely for the two of us to hear.

He places both of his hands on either side of me, effectively trapping me between his strong, muscular frame and the unyielding stone railing. After all, he is my husband now. He has every right to be affectionate and romantic with me. My palms grow clammy, and my knees start to weaken.

This man is dangerous.

"Well... I kind of get a little captivated by the view from here." I reason, offering a half-truth intertwined with a lie.

His brows furrow slightly, yet the playful smile lingers on his lips.

"Is that so? I assumed you were here to reminisce about the time we first crossed paths..." He tenderly caresses the side of my cheek with the back of his hand, gently tucking a few strands of my hair behind my ear.

Our eyes lock with each other. Somehow, I find myself unable to tear my eyes away from him. My reaction towards him is starting to get really confusing. It's as if I've lost control over my own body.

He leans in closer, drawing nearer to me. Initially, I anticipate a kiss, but instead, his lips merely graze mine before descending to the sensitive skin of my neck. A gasp escapes my lips upon realizing what he is trying to do.

No! I can't let him do it!

The logical part of my brain tells me that I need to find a way out of this situation. However, for some reason, I can't seem to find the courage to shove him away. Instead, my hand glides across his broad shoulder, trailing up to the nape of his neck as if involuntarily encouraging his actions. My eyelids shut of their own accord as if it is the righteous course to take at this moment. Deep within me, panic begins to swell.

What the fuck am I doing? Damn it!

I hold my breath in anticipation upon feeling his fangs graze against my skin. Once he tastes my blood, this is going to be the endgame for us. I shudder with a mix of fear and anticipation as his tongue caresses the most sensitive spot on my neck. A moan escapes my lips, and my breath grows heavier with each passing second.

His left arm slithers around my waist, and just as I believe it to be the end for me, a distinct cough resonates from a few meters away.

Atticus swiftly distances himself from me, and we both turn to see an elegant woman standing several meters apart. A pleasant smile graces her lips, but for some reason, all of my senses are giving me a warning sign

"My King, if you don't mind, may I have a word with my daughter?" the woman asks with a sweet smile on her lips.

The King releases a frustrated sigh before stepping back from me. He gazes at me and tenderly strokes the side of my cheek.

"I'll be back shortly. If you need anything, don't hesitate to call my attention," he assures me before planting a gentle kiss on my lips.

I touch my lips, still feeling the lingering warmth from his kiss, as he turns his back and walks away, granting my 'mother' and me some privacy. Judging by the King's reaction and my gut feeling, I can safely assume that this woman standing before me is someone I should be wary about. However, I won't voice any complaints because, in a twisted turn of events, she has just saved me from being murdered by the King.

The woman closes the gap between us, drawing near.

"My darling, you are truly exquisite. Who would have imagined that you would become the beloved of the King?" she remarks and takes the space that was occupied by Samuel mere moments ago.

"Believe me, I never expected it either," I shrug.

"Now that you are the Queen, it will be easier for you to persuade the King to appoint your father as the Minister of Finance. The house of Nardelli needs to have control over the kingdom's trade and finance," she suggests.

My mood sours upon hearing her words. Seriously? I'm impressed. I've been here for less than twenty-four hours, and already I'm being entangled in political matters. I release a sigh and cast her a bored glance.

"You know what? Why don't you convey that message to the King directly?" I retort in annoyance, then turn away from the balcony and stride off.

I hear a gasp of surprise from the woman behind me, but I refuse to glance back at her. I won't allow myself to be used as a pawn by anyone. Lady Naya appears to be a pushover. While I don't know her personally, I can gather from how others treat her that she's the type of person who fails to assert herself. I refuse to be like that.

"Her expression is priceless,"

I turn to my left upon hearing Samuel's voice. There's a proud smile on his lips while looking at Naya's mother who stands not far from us. Samuel closes the distance between us and stands right by my side.

"Do you think I should consider her as a potential suspect?" I ask.

Samuel shrugs in response. "I don't think so. Elizabeth Nardelli is greedy in position and power. She's capable of killing someone, but she won't kill her daughter. Especially that Lady Naya is set to bring her so much power." he smiles. "So, how do you find this place so far?" He asks, averting the topic in a completely different direction.

My lips twitch in annoyance. He's right. The woman appears to be consumed by greed, and I believe she views her daughter as a means to an end. She wouldn't have a motive to kill Lady Naya.

"Medieval but fancy," I reply and let my eyes wander across the hall. This place is exactly what you can imagine during the age of Dracula. It's ancient, yet the architectural beauty is breathtaking. "Anyway, earlier in the balcony, the King made an attempt to... to..."

I feel my face heat up in embarrassment upon remembering what happened a moment ago in the balcony before Lady Naya's mother barged in. I bite my lower lip in annoyance. I can't even finish my damn sentence.

"He attempted to bite you," Samuel finishes my sentence for me. "I saw that, and I almost interfered, but I'm glad your mother decided to butt in."

I exhale deeply and clasp my hands together.

"I keep telling myself to push him away, but it's like my body... I feel as though I have no control over it," I say with confusion in my tone.

My confession prompts a smirk from my butler.

"That's to be expected, considering you are the King's beloved. It's in your genetics to submit to him. Atticus thirsts for your blood, and as his beloved, your body naturally responds to satisfy that thirst."

My eyes widen in surprise, and I stare at him in disbelief.

"What do you mean I'm his beloved? Naya is his beloved!" I scowl at him.

"Yeah, and you are Naya," he says as if it were the most obvious thing in the world.

"That's not funny."

"Good, because I'm not joking either. You are Atticus's beloved. You may not have realized it, but when you accepted the vow earlier, it bound your soul to the King's soul."

My forehead creases deeply in confusion, completely baffled by what he is trying to explain.

"What do you mean? Isn't being beloved supposed to be determined by destiny?" I ask.

He lets out an amused smile and shakes his head.

"Where did you get that information? To be someone's beloved, there needs to be an agreement between both parties. What do you think is the purpose of the wedding ceremony?"

"Oh, fuck!" I exclaim in frustration. I rake my fingers through my hair in frustration. My eyes narrow into slits as I give him an accusing glare, feeling like he deceived me in some way. "You never told me anything about being the King's beloved!"

Samuel leans forward. He crosses his arms in front of his chest, still with a smug smirk on his lips.

"Don't give me that look, my Queen. I haven't had a chance to explain it to you," he says in a voice laced with amusement.

I let out an irritated sigh.

It's not like I have any other choices now. It has already happened, and I surely can't undo my vow from earlier. Damn it!

"Anyway, let's go," he continues, "The King has given me orders to prepare you for the wedding night."

"Wedding night?" I ask with a confused expression on my face, even though I already have an inkling of what he means.

"Honeymoon,"

CHAPTER 5

Naya

There's a loud banging on my chest as I try to make myself more comfortable in the bathtub overflowing with crimson-red roses. I inhale deeply multiple times to calm myself, emptying my mind to keep myself from panicking.

I let out a bitter smile. I have faced dangerous criminals back in the human world, but this is the first time I have felt this kind of terror. I am not afraid of death, nor of the people who bring death to others. It's my job to hunt them. However, the thought of being alone with the King on our first night terrifies me.

Samuel told me that I needed to trust him on this. He won't do anything that will put both of us in danger, but I don't know what his plan is to stop this. Biting is often associated with vampire mating, and we cannot allow Atticus to bite me. Once he tastes my blood, he will know that I am human, and if that happens, then this game is over.

A knock on the door causes my gaze to shift in its direction. I perceive the sound of the door being opened, and soon after, a woman enters the bathroom, clutching a towel and lingerie in her other hand.

I bite my inner lip in anticipation. So that's what I am going to wear for this occasion?

I step out of the tub, and she quickly wraps the towel around my body.

If possible, I would prefer to spend the entire night within the confines of this bathroom. However, memories of the books I have read resurface, reminding me of the recurring theme where men tend to intrude into the bathroom when their partners are bathing. The thought alone makes me feel uneasy and fidgety. It seems that readers often perceive the invasion of personal space as romantic, but the mere idea of the King stumbling upon me in this vulnerable state is far from enchanting. Trust me, that kind of encounter would lead to anything but romantic.

After drying off, the woman hands me the garments, including a very tiny nightdress and a black silk robe that accentuates my curves. And when I say "tiny," I mean it. The silk undergarments are too cheeky and too narrow to cover my private parts. Goodness.

"Your mother chose this nightdress for tonight," she explains upon seeing my troubled expression.

An annoyed huff escapes my lips.

Great, a greedy mother who's pushing her own daughter towards the King for the sake of connection and influence. This type of scenario never gets old.

I have no choice but to put on the garments she gave me. Samuel better be quick, or else I'm going to snap his head for good. After securing my robe, I take a seat in front of the large vanity mirror. The helper takes a comb and begins to brush my ginger-coloured hair.

I can't help but stare at my own reflection. The black night dress does nothing but emphasizes my pale white skin tone. My warm-coloured hair and ocean-blue eyes accentuate my features so perfectly.

A smile slowly graces my lips. Who would have guessed that putting on a nightgown would bring out the woman in me? Back in the human world, I always wear a denim-on-denim outfit. Wearing this kind of attire is not appropriate in my field of work. It's hard to hide a weapon in this outfit.

"You look like a seductress, my Queen," the woman says with a genuine smile as she glances at my reflection in the mirror.

The sincerity of her tone warms my heart. Well, at least there's one person in this world who genuinely likes me.

"What is your name?" I ask softly, my eyes fixed on hers. It's not true that vampires don't have a reflection. Or maybe this mirror isn't the same as the one in the human world.

Instead of a verbal response, the servant's melancholic smile is her only reply. She shakes her head gently, diverting her gaze to my hair, her delicate fingers gliding through the strands of my ginger-coloured locks with tender care.

I frown, puzzled by her reaction. "Did I say something wrong?" I inquire, hoping to understand her reluctance to answer.

"I'm a servant, my Queen," she replies while purposely avoiding my gaze. "It's not customary for nobles and royals to ask for our names."

Her words caught me by surprise, but I didn't bother saying anything about it. This Kingdom sure has a tradition.

"Well, as your Queen, I order you to tell me your name," I try to make it sound as friendly as possible.

A warm smile lit up on the girl's face. "If you insist, my Queen. You can call me Minna."

"And you can call me Naya." I offer. I know I should get used to it, but it still makes me uncomfortable when people address me as their Queen.

Minna's expression turns a bit serious at that. "You shouldn't show too much kindness. People tend to take advantage of that. It will only invite disrespect."

My smile widens. That is indeed true. Showing kindness to others is a good thing. However, it also tends to invite those who want to exploit it.

"You can call me Naya if we are alone." I negotiate.

Minna smiles and nods at me in agreement. The worry that is evident in her eyes a while ago disappears. I can't help but wonder if this woman has a close relation to Lady Naya. She seems to genuinely care about her well-being.

Minna takes a step back away from me. "I believe it's time for you to get inside the royal chamber now. The King is waiting."

I wince.

Right, honeymoon. I almost forgot about that.

I force myself to leave the chair. Minna walks towards the door and opens it for me. I let out a harsh exhale to calm my senses. This situation was far more terrifying than I had anticipated.

I feel my knees starting to wobble. Fear and anxiety start to consume me from the inside. I keep reminding myself that I am a detective, someone who has faced the most dangerous criminals and murderers with full confidence, without fear. But now, I'm terrified of my own wedding night.

I step into the expansive room, its spaciousness engulfing me. The initial sensation that greets me is the cool, gentle breeze wafting from the open balcony. I take a deep breath to calm my racing heart.

"Enjoy the night, Your Highness..." Minna adds before making her way out of the royal chamber.

I turn to her with a hesitant smile but she is already closing the door of the room, leaving me on my own to face the King. I wince. Well, if things don't go according to plan, I'm pretty sure this will be my last night, so I might as well enjoy it.

A shiver courses through my body as I contemplate what lies ahead tonight. I step to the centre of the empty room as I anxiously anticipate the arrival of the King. I expected Atticus to be here by now, waiting for me while drinking wine, perhaps?

My gaze shifts to the bedside table, where two wine glasses and a bottle caught my attention. I approach the table and reach out to grasp the untouched bottle. Its undisturbed state assures me that the King has yet to set foot in this room.

A sigh of relief escapes my chest. I'm praying that Samuel has a great plan for me to get out of this alive. I open the wine and pour myself a glass of it. I know that wine is an aphrodisiac and is not good for me in a situation like this, but I need something to soothe my nerves and divert my thoughts away from what is about to happen.

Taking the wineglass in hand, I make my way towards the open balcony. The cool embrace of the fresh night breeze envelops me, and my eyes are treated to the exquisite sight of the timeless and graceful architecture adorning the buildings that encircle the palace.

"It's beautiful." I murmur, my gaze fixed upon the ethereal expanse of the distant, shadowed horizon.

This Kingdom is nothing short of breathtaking, especially on a night illuminated by the radiant glow of a full moon. It possesses a charm reminiscent of a bygone era. It looks like something straight out of a vintage postcard.

"Loving the view of your kingdom?"

The voice behind me jolts my heart into stillness as if time itself pauses. I can almost sense the warmth of his breath brushing against my left ear, sending a shiver down my spine. I swallow hard, feeling my throat constricting. How did I fail to notice his presence or catch the sound of his footsteps? Was I really so engrossed in my own thoughts that I didn't feel him approaching?

His arms encircle my petite waist, urging me to face him. My fists instinctively clench, my knuckles turning white as I reluctantly turn my gaze towards him.

Perhaps this is precisely why I am so afraid of him. I am confident in facing my enemies back in the human world because I know I am in control. I carefully studied each of those criminals and devised the best strategy to put them behind bars. However, with this man standing before me, everything becomes a whirlwind of chaos. My thoughts and emotions intertwine in disarray. It's not him that I fear; I fear losing control because of him.

"You are so beautiful, Naya," he strokes my left cheek with the back of his fingers.

I muster a smile in response to his compliment, but my fear and anxiety distort it into more of a wince.

Meanwhile, Atticus gazes at me with a sense of admiration. In some peculiar way, I find myself grateful that he hasn't seemed to perceive the depths of my fear. Or perhaps he does notice it, and in light of the impending circumstances, he deems it a natural reaction.

"I can hear your heartbeat, my love. We are husband and wife now, but it seems like your reaction towards me hasn't changed a bit," he states.

My smile swiftly dissipates. Damn it! He did notice it. It just so happens that Lady Naya and I share a similar reaction in his presence. I bite down on my lower lip, summoning the courage to lift my gaze and meet his eyes. Admiration and longing unmistakably shimmer within those captivating hazel orbs.

"I hate to admit it, but your presence is enough to make me want to run and flee as far as I can," I confess, allowing my vulnerability to show slightly.

Atticus's lips curl into a mischievous smile as his gentle touch grazes the side of my cheek. The pounding in my chest intensifies, almost stealing my breath away.

"Trust me, my love. I don't mind the chase, especially when it involves you," he suggests, and without warning, he effortlessly lifts me off the ground with his robust arms, causing a gasp of panic to escape my lips. "How about we do something to lessen that fear and make you more comfortable around me?"

My grip on the wineglass slackens, making it slip from my hand and shatter into countless fragments upon the unforgiving stone floor. Yet, the King doesn't even pay attention to it.

He carries me inside the room to the waiting bed with red petals scattered on top of it. I remain still in his hold even though I'm on the verge of breaking down. What does he mean by making me comfortable around him? I don't care what his plan is. I'm pretty sure I'll be everything but comfortable with him. That is not going to work. Damn it!

What the heck happened to Samuel? He promised that he would help me get out of this situation.

Atticus gently places me upon the luxurious silk sheets, rendering me utterly vulnerable to any of his advances. A whirlwind of anticipation and trepidation envelops me. So, this is how I'm going to die? On the night of my honeymoon? That sounds tragically romantic.

The King's gaze, brimming with admiration, locks onto mine as he lowers his head, bestowing a trail of tender kisses upon my cheeks, gradually descending to the delicate expanse of my neck. A flush of warmth creeps up my cheeks, intensifying the colour upon them. He captures my hands and firmly secures them by my head. My body begins to stiffen in fear against his. Involuntarily, a gasp escapes my lips, capturing his attention and prompting him to look at me in my eyes.

"I hate how you look so beautifully captivating even in your most vulnerable state," he whispers, his words laced with a mixture of adoration and torment as he gradually withdraws from our intimate proximity.

He gently takes hold of my hand, guiding it to rest upon his chest. Confusion furrows my brow as I sense the forceful thumping of his heart against my palm.

"It's okay if you're afraid. I'm good at hiding it, but you have the same effect on me," he murmurs in a soothing tone, attempting to alleviate my apprehension.

"I'm scared, Atticus," I confess, averting my gaze and directing it downward. "Not only of you but of everything in front of me,"

I'm in a place I am unfamiliar with, bearing the title of Queen in a kingdom whose existence I was previously unaware of. I am about to have sex with a stranger I only met today. Even the toughest person I know will surely cower if placed in my shoes.

I inhale deeply and push him a bit, making us both sit on the bed. I want to run away from him until I am back where I belong, in the human world.

Lady Naya called me here for a mission which I have no idea how and where to begin. I don't think she understands that apart from solving the mystery of her death, I must also strive to ensure my own survival and evade the clutches of death. To say that my current situation is complicated is an understatement. It's a wild chaos.

"Wearing the crown is never easy but trust me when I tell you that I'll be with you in every step. You'll get used to it," my husband reassures me with a gentle smile, completely misinterpreting the reason behind my fear.

His hand extends toward the delicate ribbon that secures my robe, his touch leisurely unravelling it, unveiling the scanty silk fabric that barely veils my form. A sharp intake of breath escapes him as the robe glides down, coming to rest upon the bed. Lust taints his eyes, transforming them into a deep, fiery crimson hue.

I feel a different type of anxiety wrapping around me upon seeing his reaction. Vampires are known for their primal aggression, a fact I should bear in mind after perusing several books about them.

"Let's not get too caught up in the future and focus on the moment. I badly need you right now, my Queen," he murmurs, his head dips down, and I feel his lips on my neck, peppering it with tender kisses and bestowing gentle suction upon my sensitized skin.

CHAPTER 6

Naya

Atticus's lips glide from my collarbones up to my neck, making me shudder with anticipation. Goosebumps rise upon my skin as his fingertips delicately graze the clingy fabric that embraces my form, gradually unfurling it. With each unveiling of my skin, vulnerability and exposure intertwine, intensifying the flame of desire within me. Involuntarily, my body arches towards him, silently pleading for more. I bite down on my lower lip, suppressing the urge to release my fervent cries.

My chest tightens in panic, but I cannot deny that this situation is so hot that it makes me feel delirious. It's as if I am in heat.

Samuel informed me that my body would respond accordingly to my beloved's needs, and that is what I am afraid of. I cannot allow the King to feed on me. The invisible mask that I am wearing will undoubtedly fall off if that happens.

A gentle, cool breeze brushes against my exposed skin, a telltale sign that he has successfully divested me of my garments.

Atticus's hand caresses my cheek as he leans in to capture my lips. His kiss is electrifying, igniting a fire within me that I never knew existed. This time, his kisses are more insistent, more demanding, as if he wants to consume me entirely. His tongue explores the depths of my mouth with a possessive hunger, leaving me breathless and wanting more. It's as if he's staking his claim on me, declaring me as his own.

If I were in the right state of mind, I would probably push him away and use the krav maga techniques I learned during my military training. However, I am not thinking clearly at the moment. I respond to his kisses with equal passion, as if there's nothing wrong with our situation.

This whole ordeal is driving me insane, and I am on the verge of losing my mind. This is not me. This is not the detective who swore to fight for justice in front of her father's grave. This is not the woman who fearlessly confronted countless criminals on her own.

As our lips continue to collide, the intensity of our kiss grows stronger. His hands explore my body with desperate hunger, and I find myself responding in kind. My mind, once racing with conflicting thoughts and fears, shuts down, and I give in to the heady pleasure of his touch. The taste of him upon my lips, the beguiling scent of his skin that fills my senses, and the sensation of his body intimately pressed against mine all meld into an all-consuming experience.

But just as I believe the flames of desire have engulfed me completely, an abrupt knocking at the door startles us both. We freeze, our bodies still entwined, as we listen for any further sound. The momentary interruption breaks the spell, and Atticus pulls back, his eyes dark with frustration and longing. A part of me mourns the loss of his touch.

I inhale deeply to gather my scattered thoughts and pull the comforter up to cover my body. Atticus turns to look at me with a glint of annoyance in his eyes.

A smile tugs at the corners of my lips.

"It seems someone doesn't appreciate interruptions," I playfully tease.

"This better be important, or else I might end up murdering one of my subjects on our first night," he mutters through gritted teeth.

I can't help but giggle at his frustrated expression. The King surely hates being cockblocked.

It's funny to think that I'm no longer afraid of him. Maybe he's right. The more time I spend in his presence, the more at ease I feel.

Atticus gets off the bed to greet the unexpected visitor. I'm grateful for whoever is behind the door. What just happened was a close call for us.

I can hear the annoyance in my beloved's voice as he speaks with Samuel. I can barely make out what they're saying, but I see Samuel hand Atticus a bottle of wine. The King accepts the bottle of wine and slams the door close. The scowl on his face remains as he makes his way back to our bed.

"So? What was that for?" I ask.

"Your butler said that your mother sent this to congratulate us on our wedding," he explains, lifting the bottle of wine for me to see.

My brow furrows in confusion. My mother sent us a bottle of wine? That's odd. If I had to guess, this is what Samuel is referring to. I hope it is because if it's not, I'm pretty sure this will be my last night in this world. My gaze never leaves the bottle of wine as the King puts it down on the bedside table.

Now it's all up to me to make Samuel's plan work.

A cheeky smile slips through my lips as my beloved takes the space beside me.

"Aren't you curious about how sweet that red wine would be?" I purr, attempting to infuse my voice with a seductive allure. This is my only chance. I can't afford to let it slip away.

The King raises an eyebrow at the sudden shift in my tone, but before he can think further, I pull him closer and passionately kiss his lips. I release the comforter, exposing my half-naked body and enticing him to feast upon it. Then, with a slight push, I create a small space between us and disengage from our passionate embrace, grasping the bottle of wine from the bedside table.

"We have the whole night to ourselves. How about we take it slow?" I suggest with a smile that I know he won't be able to resist.

Atticus takes the bottle of wine from my hand and rises from the bed. He retrieves the corkscrew from the table and effortlessly opens the bottle. His eyes lock onto mine, a dangerous gleam dancing within them.

A surge of anticipation courses through me as he closes the distance between us. Excitement and apprehension intertwine, creating a whirlwind of emotions in my stomach. I push aside my fear, laying myself back on the bed, ready to be consumed by his desire.

"Just remember, you are the one who asked for this," he says as his eyes feast on my body.

Embarrassment tinges on my cheeks, but I refuse to let it consume me. The instinct to shield my chest is strong, yet I resist the urge, keeping my hands firmly planted at my sides to prevent myself from acting so timid in front of the King. This is not typical of me, but I need to remember that I am doing this to stay alive.

It's funny because I have no idea how this will end for both of us, but I'm already risking everything. We're only at the beginning, but I'm already losing so much of myself that I know I won't be able to get back. I'm praying it'll all be worth it in the end.

I involuntarily closed my eyes as the cool sensation of the expensive wine caresses my skin. Its fruity, sweet aroma permeates the room, intoxicating my senses and leaving me feeling lightheaded. The next moment, Atticus's tongue glides across my skin, tracing the path where I can feel the wine.

His tongue continues to explore my body with fervour, making the heat within me rise to a boiling point. Every touch is like an electric shock, sending waves of pleasure through every nerve ending in my body. The fruity sweetness of the wine mixed with his warm breath against my skin is a sensation that I will never forget. It's like every inch of my body is on fire, and he's the only one who can quench it.

"Atticus..." I let out a deep moan as he takes his time with each stroke of his tongue, making me arch my back and offer myself more to him. It's like he knows exactly what to do to make me feel alive and yet helpless at the same time. I have never felt so consumed by desire, and I never want this moment to end.

The silk sheets beneath me provide some relief as my grip tightens on them, my fingers digging into the fabric. It's the only thing anchoring me to this reality as I lose myself to the pleasure he's giving me.

Lust has overtaken my head completely, and I have already forgotten the real score between us.

Finally, unable to take the torture any longer, I reach Atticus's shoulders and bring him up so our eyes can meet. I seize his lips in a frantic, deep kiss, tasting the subtle sweetness of wine on his tongue. I put my hands between us and pushed him down on the bed, changing our position. In just a snap, I'm already on top, eager to be in control.

Atticus, on the other hand, seems more than willing to relinquish control. He's clearly enjoying this as much as I am. His arms tighten around my waist, pulling my body closer to his. Then suddenly, I feel him still under me. He stops responding to my kisses. My forehead contorts in confusion as I distance myself from him. I gasp for air as I see him in an unconscious state. I can't help but frown upon realizing that he just fell asleep on me, leaving me hanging and sexually frustrated.

I massage my temples, trying to calm the swirl of thoughts in my head as I recall the purpose behind the wine Samuel brought. Yes, Atticus falling asleep after consuming it is certainly part of the plan, but the lingering feeling of disappointment and dissatisfaction in my chest as I gaze at his slumbering form sure isn't.

I run my fingers through my thick curls and pull my scattered brain cells together. I stand up from the bed and gather my clothes from the floor, folding them neatly. After that, I adjust the King on the bed and drape a blanket over him.

That will do for now, I guess.

That's when I hear slow clapping emanating from the dark corner of the room. I instinctively turn my gaze in its direction, hastily crossing my arms over my exposed chest.

As if on cue, the man takes one step forward to reveal himself. I frown. How the heck did he manage to get in here?

"What the heck, Samuel? Do you want me to charge you for voyeurism?" I hiss at him in a low tone, not wanting to disturb the King.

"Oh, please. I've seen better." he scoffs, rolling his eyes at me, causing my jaw to drop in astonishment.

He'd seen better?

"I stayed to ensure that if anything went wrong, I'd be able to help you. However, it appears that you are more than capable of handling yourself, my Queen." He continues with a proud grin playing on his lips.

"Yes, I survived this night, but what about the next night? And the night after that?" I state and turn my back on him while shaking my head. I swiftly slip into my nightdress in my lame attempt to regain some modesty. "This mission is suicide."

"Judging by how you handle the situation tonight, I am confident that the next nights will be so much easier for you to survive," he replies nonchalantly as if it's not a big deal. "Anyway, I came in here as well to bring you this."

I turn to look back at him, only to have my eyes widen with amazement upon seeing him holding my bag. It's the only thing I brought from the human world. I was forced to leave it in Naya's bedroom in haste when Samuel rushed me to prepare for the wedding.

I close our distance and take my bag from his hand.

"Thank heaven!" I exclaim. "I thought I wouldn't be able to see it anymore."

"I figured that you'd need it for your investigation, so I decided to bring it here. Just make sure to keep it securely hidden from the King, or else that'll blow your cover," Samuel stresses as I go through the contents of my bag, checking each item to make sure nothing is missing.

I let out a sigh of relief after making sure that all my stuff was in here, including the blade that was used to murder Lady Naya. These are my clues to find the murderer. I can't lose any of my evidence.

"I'll begin my investigation tomorrow. I guess the sooner I can solve this case, the sooner I can leave this world," I state as I put the items back into my backpack.

I may not admit it, but I'm terrified. The way my body responds to Atticus is far from normal. It's too easy for me to lose control when I'm around him. It's too easy for me to feel vulnerable in his presence, and that's what frightens me the most.

"It's your decision, not mine. You're the detective here. My job is to assist you with the investigation and kill the murderer once we figure out who it is," he informs me as he heads towards the door. "I'll be taking my leave now. Rest well, my Queen. You had a long and exhausting day."

I let out a heave when the door shuts behind him. I shift my gaze to the bed where Atticus is sleeping soundly.

Rest well?

I let out a bland smile. That is easier said than done.

I make my way to the bed and settle beside my beloved. I close my eyes and rest my head on his chest, finding solace in his embrace. The future remains uncertain for both of us and at this moment, I can't shake off the fear that lingers within me, anticipating what awaits us at the end of this story.

CHAPTER 7

Naya

I wake up to the sensation of pressure on my abdomen. My eyes flutter open, and my forehead creases as I take in the opulent ceiling of the unfamiliar room. It's a far cry from the plain white ceiling of my own bedroom. The gentle sunlight passing through the curtains covering the windows and the enthusiastic singing of the birds from outside let me know that the sun is already starting to rise.

My eyes scan the entire room with a puzzled expression on my face before finally resting on the man who is peacefully sleeping beside me. One of his legs is draped across the lower part of my body. He lies on his side with one arm flung over my waist, his chest rising and falling steadily with each breath like the gentle waves of the ocean.

A heavy sigh escapes my lips as I recall the events of the previous day. I reach up to massage my forehead. It all seems like a blur to me. The letters, the murder, the unexpected wedding, and the honeymoon where we had poisoned the King. Why do I feel like I am digging my own grave right now?

"Good morning, my Queen," a raspy voice from beside me pulls me back to reality, forcing me to turn my gaze back to Atticus.

He is looking at me with a loving and satisfied expression on his face. The sunlight coming from the window reflects on his eyes, giving them a subtle glow. I put on a sweet smile on my lips, praying to heaven that he won't see the truth beneath my mask.

"Good morning," I greet him back.

Atticus sits up on the bed. The smile on his lips slowly vanishes, and it's replaced with a frown. He reaches out for his temple and massages it a bit.

I can feel my chest start to race with anxiety at the thought that he might remember that nothing really happened between us last night.

"Having a terrible headache?" I question, trying to turn his full attention to me and the present. I make sure that the smile on my lips is fully intact.

"Yeah, last night—"

"Last night is the most special night for me," I interrupt him. "Thank you for making me feel like the most beautiful woman in the world, my king," I whisper in a sultry voice and lean closer to him, putting a sweet peck on the side of his lips.

My words and sweet gestures work like magic. The frown on my beloved's face vanishes as he returns my smile. If there were an Oscar award in this world, hands down, I would get it.

"Anything for my beautiful queen," he responds, slipping his arms around my waist.

Before I can even react, Atticus's lips capture mine. My palms curl into fists as I try my best to prevent myself from pushing him away. I can't mess up. The King needs to believe that I am Lady Naya, the woman who is hopelessly in love with him.

I mirror the movement of his lips, feeling their softness against mine. His strong arms secure my tiny waist as my body moulds perfectly with his. Did I ever mention that we are both naked beneath this sheet? Because we are. I need to make my pretentious act as convincing as possible.

His kisses are too damn addicting for me to deny him. However, I am well aware that I need to get a hold of myself, or else this will be a tragedy for both of us. I push him away from me before I completely lose control.

Atticus releases me from his hold and caresses my cheek.

"How about breakfast in bed, my queen?" His voice dances between playful and suggestive, teasing my resolve and coaxing me to surrender.

The mischievous gleam in his eyes makes me want to say yes and submit to him, but the last thing I need right now is to let my emotions dominate me. My relationship with Atticus is just getting started, and knowing that it was built through lies and deception doesn't make anything easier for me. What we share now is fragile, liable to shatter at any given moment. If I am going to be honest with myself, I'm scared of what's waiting for us at the end of this.

"Nope, I'm sore in all places. Give me a break, my King. Otherwise, other people in the palace might end up thinking that you're abusing me behind closed doors," I respond, a playful glimmer dancing in my eyes as I rise from the bed, making sure to pull the blanket with me to hide my nakedness.

"Come on, it was our first night together. What did they expect me to do? Play poker with you?" He counters, reclining on the bed.

I can't help but smile as I tread towards the bathroom. People are probably expecting us to mate the whole day. However, I need to find a way to convince Atticus to leave this room.

After taking a refreshing bath, I extend an invitation to the King to join me for breakfast with his trusted people. However, he insists on having our meal inside our room to prolong our intimate time together. I politely declined, telling him that I would like to learn more about my royal duties by conversing with his advisors and ministers during our breakfast.

Despite his initial reluctance, I successfully persuaded the King to accompany me to the palace's dining area. He asks for a few minutes to freshen up before we leave the room together, but I inform him I'll be waiting for him in the dining room instead, to which he agrees without a problem.

As I step outside the King's chambers, Samuel is already waiting for me. It turns out that after the wedding last night, a few guests chose to stay behind. All of them are nobles, including Harriet and my mother.

As we approach the dining hall, the buzz of the guests' conversations grows louder, and the aroma of sumptuous delicacies wafts in the air.

We enter the grand hall, and immediately all eyes turn in our direction. I take a deep breath and straighten my back as I take in the place. The room is lavishly decorated with intricate tapestries, chandeliers, and elegant furniture. The high ceiling, adorned with elaborate frescoes, gives the room an air of grandeur and majesty.

Some people gave me a warm smile and greeting, showing their respect, but I didn't miss the wicked smile on my mother's lips and Harriet's eyes throwing daggers at me.

"Your Highness, we didn't anticipate your presence at the breakfast table today," Harriet states, causing my gaze to shift in her direction. A subtle smirk plays at the corner of her lips, a wicked smile that I know is meant to insult me. "Has the king grown tired of you so soon?" She jeers, her words laced with a bitter mockery.

See? I told you. Insult. I take a deep breath, mustering all the patience I can summon to endure this shit. With practised composure, I raise my left eyebrow in response, mimicking her smile.

"Well, I certainly didn't anticipate your company at breakfast either, yet here you are," I retort, gracefully flicking my hair as I stride towards the seat where the King and I had occupied the previous evening.

Harriet has every reason to want to murder Naya. She's envious of her. However, I don't believe the reason behind Naya's death is that shallow. There's more to it than meets the eye, and that is what I need to know. What happened is not just a simple murder. I'm pretty sure it has something to do with the kingdom itself and with the fact that she's the future Queen. I can't see the connection yet, but that doesn't mean that there's no connection at all. All I need to do is find the right thread that will connect all of the dots flawlessly.

Harriet shoots me a deathly glare, but I simply ignore her presence. My stomach grumbles with hunger, and all I want is a peaceful breakfast before I dive into my investigation. It is not easy to play the part of the Queen, the prey, and the investigator at the same time. I am a detective, not an actress.

Just as I am about to take my seat, the King enters the dining room. His eyes immediately scan the room, searching for me. A smile curls onto his lips as our eyes meet, and he strides towards me with purpose.

Suddenly, it feels as though the entire world around us dissolves into nothingness, leaving only the two of us in the opulent dining hall. Without a moment's notice, he closes the distance between us, capturing my lips with his own in a fervent, passionate kiss, heedless of the gazes of his subjects. My hands instinctively find their way to his chest, revelling in the sensation as he boldly showcases our love and the undeniable ownership we have over one another.

I respond to his kiss with equal fervour, relishing the stolen moment of bliss. But I'm fully aware that I'm also doing this to irritate a certain woman in the room who seems to take pleasure in provoking me.

A phoney cough from Samuel pops our romantic bubble. I quickly push my husband away and return my attention to the table. Some folks are looking away, while others are looking down, but I can't help but notice the annoyance written in their eyes. It appears that most of the people at this table are not so fond of Lady Naya being a Queen, or perhaps they are not just fans of public displays of affection.

Atticus takes the seat next to me, completely unconcerned about the other individuals at the table. He even assists me by putting food on my plate and making sure that I am enjoying the meal. It's as if he doesn't see anyone else aside from the two of us.

The love in his eyes is unmistakable, making me feel loved and guilty at the same time. Somehow, I know that once this is all over, this pretend relationship will leave a wound in my heart deeper than I can ever heal.

I trust you both enjoyed the bottle of wine I sent to your chambers last night," my mother speaks with a warm smile, breaking the stillness that envelops the room.

Her mention of the wine causes me to flinch, and I exchange a fleeting glance with Samuel. So, it is true that my mother had indeed sent the wine as a gift. However, I highly doubt she is aware of the sleeping poison it conceals within.

"Yes, the wine you sent is of the finest quality. Its sweetness surpasses any I have ever tasted," the King replies with a knowing smile on his lips while his eyes were not leaving mine, subtly reminding me of what we did to the poor wine.

I focus my attention on the food on my plate to avoid his taunting eyes. I can feel my cheeks heat up from the memories of last night. Does he really need to remind me of that?

An involuntary shudder runs through me as memories of his lips exploring my body, tracing the path of that sinful wine, surge into my consciousness. I don't think I will be able to look at the wine the same way again. Last night has permanently tarnished my innocence.

"How about you, my Queen? What did you think of the wine last night?" My mother shifts her gaze towards me, prompting me to quickly swallow the food in my mouth.

A series of coughs escape my lips as some of the food enters the wrong tube, drawing the entire table's attention. Atticus extends a glass of water to me, which I gratefully accept, emptying it in a single gulp.

Once I regain my composure, I turn to face my mother.

"It was absolutely exquisite," I answer, mustering a forced smile. "The breakfast is great as well. Thank you for the meal."

I take the napkin from the table and pat it on my lips. I'm done. I don't think I can still handle all of this unnecessary attention on this table.

I turn to face the King and offer him my sweetest smile.

"Since this is my first day as an official queen of the kingdom, may I have permission to visit the library? I want to learn how I can be of help as your wife," I inquire of my husband.

"The only thing you need to do as a queen of this kingdom is stand beside your King and bear the next successor. Other than that, you surely don't have to worry about anything else," my mother's voice interjects, causing my smile to fade into oblivion. To say that I am speechless is an understatement.

"Bearing the King's heir is one of the highest honours I can have as a Queen. However, the future of Puer Lunae rests on how I raise my child, and I believe being knowledgeable in all aspects of leadership will help me raise a leader worthy of sitting on the throne," I assert, causing the table to fall silent.

My mother's eyes narrow in my direction, but there's no way I am going to cower. She's Naya's mother, not mine. My mother would never say such a thing. That is not how you support your daughter.

At that moment, Atticus reaches for my hand, capturing my attention. Our eyes lock—his amber gaze meeting my deep blue one— and I become aware of the tension coursing through my body, my hand unconsciously clenched into a fist. I take a deep breath, centring myself and seeking solace in his presence. The women of this kingdom sure have an uncanny ability to test my patience.

"You don't have to ask me for permission to do anything you wish to do for the day. You're not my captive; you're my other half. But make sure to take your butler with you wherever you go for your own safety," my husband remarks with a warm smile gracing his lips, and I'm grateful for his understanding and support.

"Thank you." I lean down a bit to give him a peck on the lips before leaving my seat.

I can feel all eyes following me as I walk out of the dining hall, but I refuse to care. I may be a fraud, but that doesn't mean I will allow anyone to insult me—not even my so-called mother.

CHAPTER 8

Naya

"You need to teach me how to read these books," I flip the book in my hand to the next page. Then my gaze darts towards Samuel, who is currently sitting at the window nook of the library.

To my irritation, Samuel doesn't even bother to look at me. He seems lost in his own thoughts, oblivious to my presence. His eyes are focused outside, but I can tell that he's not really looking at anything in particular. I can see the pain and sadness engraved deeply in his eyes— the kind of pain I've been very familiar with after the unexpected death of my father.

I sigh and put the book back on the shelf. I cross our short distance and gently tap his shoulder.

Samuel shifts his gaze to me, his eyes blank and devoid of any emotion. The grief that I saw a while ago has disappeared.

"I know it's not easy to accept that she's gone. I didn't get a chance to say this to you yesterday because we were both occupied with things we suddenly needed to deal with. But I'm so sorry about Lady Naya. I rushed into this world hoping to save her, but..." My eyes turn to the floor, unable to meet his gaze and see the pain embedded in it.

"It's okay. It wasn't your fault. It was my duty to protect her," he says before turning his gaze back to the open window. "But I failed to do that."

I can feel the weight he carries in every word he has said. I look at his clenched fist. I don't know how close he is to Lady Naya, but the hatred written in his eyes right now is enough for me to know that they had a very close relationship.

"This library isn't really a good place to sulk, is it? How about we go somewhere peaceful? We never got a chance to bury Lady Naya's ashes, but that doesn't mean we can't make a tomb for her or something," I suggest, hoping it will be enough to ease the heavy atmosphere.

Samuel shifts his eyes back to me and lets out a forced smile.

"You're not allowed to leave the castle, my queen," he reminds me, emphasizing the fact that I am indeed a prisoner in the castle.

"Well, if they find out, I'm not allowed. Who says we have to inform them?" I reply.

A lopsided grin forms on his lips, this time a genuine one.

"This is perhaps one of the things that sets you apart from Lady Naya. You're dauntless, and you're not afraid to speak up even when you're at a disadvantage," he says as he rises from his seat.

"I'm a detective," I reply. "If you've spent the last five or six years dealing with criminals, being weak isn't an option. It's all about intimidation, and you need to show them that you're the authority."

I am the kind of person who would always run straight into danger and would not even blink if there was a gun pointed at my head. It is vital for me to have the courage to face danger when it arises and the ability to dodge it before it lands. I suppose that is something I've mastered over the last five years as a detective.

"Hey!" I squeal in surprise as my body is lifted off the ground, held in Samuel's arms in a bridal-style embrace. "Samuel! Put me down," I demand, attempting to wriggle free from his grasp, only to discover that his strength surpasses my own.

"Stop squirming. You mentioned wanting to find a location to lay Lady Naya's ashes to rest, didn't you?" His words cause me to cease my futile struggles. I remain motionless, lifting my gaze to meet his.

"You don't have to carry me," I remark, my brows furrowing as I cross my arms defensively over my chest.

Samuel pays no heed to my complaints, opting instead to gaze down at me with a knowing smile adorning his lips. His confident demeanour rises as he steps towards the window with me cradled in his arms, making my eyes widen in terror. My heart races as I realize what he intends to do. I open my mouth to protest, but no sound escapes my throat as he leaps into the air.

The sensation of weightlessness overtakes me as we ascend into the sky. My breath catches in my throat, and I instinctively cling to Samuel's shirt for assurance. The wind whips past us, tugging at our hair and clothes as the world below us shrinks into a blur of colours.

Finally, we touch down on the roof of the nearest mansion with a soft thud. My breath comes out in ragged gasps as I try to steady my shaking nerves, my heart still pounding in my chest.

"At least give me a heads up before jumping to our deaths!" I yell when I finally managed to redeem myself.

Samuel grins as he stares down at me. "C'mon, where's the fun in that?"

My eyes narrow at him in irritation. "You leapt out of a window of a castle 35 feet above the earth. How is that meant to be fun?" A harsh sigh escapes my throat. I'm not scared of heights, but I could use some warning.

To my annoyance, Samuel only lets out a faint laugh. I shake my head in disbelief and allow him to carry me to whichever part of the Kingdom. I have no idea where we are heading.

I lean on his broad chest and make myself comfortable. If there's one person I can trust with my life in this world, it will be Samuel. Our life depends on each other, and we are both fighting for the same reason, justice.

When he finally came to a stop, I took the opportunity to survey our surroundings. Gently, he set me down on the ground. For a few moments, a slight dizziness overcame me, causing me to lean on him until I could regain my balance. It feels as if I just got off a wild roller coaster ride.

"It's stunning," I breathe, taking in the breathtaking view before us.

We stand on a high vantage point, overlooking the entire Kingdom of Puer Lunae. The grandiose castle looms in the distance, a testament to the vampires' wealth and power. The peacefulness of the scene around us is a stark contrast to the chaos of our lives.

A smile spreads across my lips as I take in the sight of the Kingdom's old and classic architecture. Never in my wildest dreams would I have imagined that a parallel universe existed, let alone one inhabited by vampires. It all feels too surreal like I'm living in a dream.

"We're on a hill that also serves as the capital's border. This is Lady Naya's favourite spot in the Kingdom," he explains.

I turn to face him and see that he is standing in front of a willow tree. That's when I notice a cluster of white roses neatly placed at the roots of the tree. Drawing nearer to him, my eyes fixated on the slightly disturbed earth surrounding the tree's roots, indicating that someone had recently dug in this spot. I assume that this is the spot Samuel chose to bury Lady Naya's ashes.

My gaze shifted back to the cluster of white roses, and I couldn't help but notice a few petals starting to wither. "You and Lady Naya were so close. I'm a bit jealous," I confess. "She had people who genuinely cared about her well-being. But what I don't understand is why she didn't ask for help."

"We grew up together. I was hired to protect her by her father. At first, I thought she was one of those self-centred nobles, but she proved me wrong," Samuel says as he takes a seat in front of the grave. "Lady Naya is the sweetest and kindest woman I have ever met."

His palms clench into tight fists. I can feel the rage in his voice as he speaks. His expression is grim, and although I do not see any traces of tears in his eyes, I can tell that he is suffering.

"You're in love with her..." I blurt out of the blue.

Samuel doesn't respond to my statement. His expression remains blank and unreadable. My eyes land on the ground, feeling his pain and sorrow despite his stoic expression. His eyes might be blank, but there's a darkness in them that I can see beyond the calm front he is showing. I had seen that darkness before, in the eyes of a father who killed three men to take revenge for his daughter. That was the very first case I managed to solve.

"Naya is so lucky to have you by her side. I still don't understand why she didn't reach out or ask for your help and why she allowed herself to get killed. If only I had followed her lead much earlier. She's probably still alive until now." I lament. A part of me feels guilty upon remembering the first and last time I met Lady Naya. If only I had been an hour earlier, maybe I could have saved her.

Samuel shakes his head in response. "Even if you had arrived earlier, I don't think there's anything we could have done to prevent her death," he lets out a deep sigh and faces me. "You said it yourself. Lady Naya knew someone was going to kill her, but she didn't say anything to me. She feigned normalcy as if all was well..."

I nod at him in agreement. He has a point there. Lady Naya seems convinced that her death is necessary to save the Kingdom. I need to dig deeper into this. This is definitely the most difficult case I've ever handled in my more than five years as a detective.

Investigating in the human world is a lot easier because people know that I am a detective. They allow me to question and interrogate them for the sake of the investigation. However, in this case, I need to be as discreet as possible. The investigation needs to be done in secret, and I need to gather substantial evidence in order to convict the murderer.

"That's actually the reason why this is really confusing. Lady Naya knows her killer. She knows that he or she is coming to kill her. She mentioned in the letter that she's far from saving, but her Kingdom won't go down with her. 'As the future Queen, it is my duty to protect my Kingdom to my last breath...' A

Kingdom that is set to fall apart." Confusion etches across my face as I turn to Samuel, seeking answers. "Does that mean that her death saved the Kingdom? It sounds to me as if she died to take the fall on behalf of the Kingdom."

Samuel's jaw clenches at my conclusion. I can see the hatred lacing his eyes as they slowly turn a deep crimson colour. I don't know much about vampires, but I think I've seen enough of those red eyes to understand that it means they are starting to lose control of their beastly side.

"She didn't die to save the Kingdom. If there's really turmoil happening around, her death will never be enough to save Puer Lunae." He lets out a deep sigh to calm himself. The veins on the side of his forehead are beginning to show, indicating that he is beginning to feel agitated about the situation.

I know he is just as frustrated as I am. This feels like almost a hopeless case, but I refuse to give up. There are no witnesses, and there is not enough evidence. But I haven't really started my investigation yet. I'm pretty sure that sooner or later, I will be able to connect the dots.

I am missing one major piece of the puzzle, and that is the motive behind her death. Why would someone assassinate a future Queen? Jealousy? Power play? There are numerous possibilities, but I need something related to the letter she sent me.

"Just a question, my Queen. Did you notice anything unusual when you entered her room yesterday?" Samuel interrupts, breaking the solemn silence between us.

I shift my gaze towards the breathtaking castle in the distance, admiring the picturesque horizon behind it. My brow furrows as I attempt to recall if there was anything peculiar about the incident yesterday. However, apart from the silver dagger piercing her chest, I don't recall seeing anything out of the ordinary in the room.

"The dagger that was used to kill her has a silver handle, which means that whoever killed her is not a vampire or simply wearing gloves to protect their skin from being burned. The room is all neat. Her blood is only in one place where I found her body. That gives me the impression that she didn't try to fight her attacker." Those are the small things that I noticed amid the chaotic events I had with Samuel yesterday. "Also, she is not wearing her wedding gown. You find it untouched in her closet."

Both Samuel and I frown at the last part of my statement.

"It will take a few minutes for our body to decompose into ashes after being stabbed in the heart with a silver dagger. This suggests that when you entered the room, the killer had just left the room. Why is she not wearing her gown?" he ponders aloud.

I lock eyes with Samuel, his expression now tinged with confusion. I click my tongue and bring my hand to my forehead and think deeply.

"Lady Naya was aware that she would die on her wedding day. She didn't wear her wedding gown because she knew I'll show up to take her place. She manipulated us so perfectly. My conclusion is that she either killed herself to escape from the wedding and trap me in this world to take her spot, or she predicted that someone wanted her dead and prepared for it."

"Lady Naya would never take her own life. She is not suicidal," Samuel asserts firmly, his expression stern.

"I'm going to take your word for it. Let's move on to my second conclusion. Lady Naya knew someone was going to kill her on her wedding day. The fact that she was able to anticipate the timing and warn me suggests one thing: she was receiving death threats, whether through verbal communication or other forms. Whatever it is, we need to find it."

Samuel nods in agreement. I can see the interest in his eyes as to where our conversation is going.

"If that's the case, then the person responsible for her death either knows that you are a fraud," he concludes. "Or... if they are convinced that Lady Naya survived the assassination, they'll plot something to get you killed sooner or later."

I grin. I've been expecting an attack since last night and am kind of surprised no one has tried to kill me yet.

"They didn't witness Lady Naya's death. I'm certain they believe she survived and will send someone to finish the job. When that moment comes, it will be our opportunity to expose the identity of the murderer and reveal the truth to the King," I assert confidently.

Samuel regards me with a worried expression, clearly concerned about the precariousness of the situation. I know it's not a good idea to use myself as bait, but we don't have much choice. It's a waiting game now. Either they will kill me, or I will catch them. This is probably the most complicated case I've ever handled, but I must admit that this is also the most exciting and heart-thrilling.

CHAPTER 9

Naya

Apparently, my escape with Samuel did not go unnoticed by the King. After spending almost an hour on the hill, a group of soldiers arrived to escort us back to the palace for my safety. As we make our way towards the grand entrance of the palace, an elderly man catches my attention as he steps towards us. His lips stretch into a warm smile, revealing the wrinkles at the corners of his eyes and his hair adorned with delicate streaks of grey.

"My Queen, the King is looking for you. He requires your presence in the library." The elderly man speaks with gentleness and respect.

Samuel and I exchange puzzled looks, and a wave of unease washes over me as I worry that I angered my husband for leaving the castle grounds. I nod to the old butler and proceed to the palace library.

Given that this is our first day as husband and wife, I know I should spend the whole day with him and act like a newlywed lovebird, but I don't think I can do that. It's not a good idea.

Samuel follows me from behind and opens the library door for me. I pause for a moment and take a deep breath before entering. Whatever the reason for his wanting to talk to me, I hope it's not about Lady Naya's death or me pretending to be his dead fiancée.

My palms begin to sweat when I hear Samuel close the door behind me, giving my husband and me privacy to talk.

I scan the vast room filled with bookshelves, my eyes sweeping across the space in search of the King. Finally, I spot him standing in front of the open window, the same spot where Samuel had been sitting earlier. Determined, I make my way towards him, letting my presence known.

As I approach, I maintain a sweet, innocent smile on my lips, masking the inner terror that resides within me. It's a complex mix of emotions that consumes me whenever Atticus is near. Fear and comfort intertwine, creating a bewildering contradiction that leaves me questioning the very nature of my feelings.

He senses my approach and turns his gaze in my direction, a warm smile illuminating his face.

"I thought you wanted to spend your first day as Queen in the library, learning more about how to rule our Kingdom. I came here to see if there was anything I could do to help, only to discover that my Queen had decided to flee with her butler," he remarks, raising one of his eyebrows at me. However, the warmth of his smile assures me that I'm not truly in trouble.

I come to a stop in front of him and tilt my head back, meeting his gaze with my own as our eyes lock. His eyes, a captivating shade of amber, hold a myriad of emotions within them.

"What? Are you telling me you're jealous of Samuel?" I playfully tease, a mischievous tone lacing my words.

His smile widens at my question. His strong arms envelop my waist, pulling me closer to him. I notice how much he loves doing this. It's as if he is staking his claim on me by holding me close. It's only my first day in this Kingdom, yet the King has already managed to carve out a special place in my heart, and that realization fills me with a sense of unease. Deep down, I know that I cannot allow myself to fall in love with this man before me because one day, I will have to leave this Kingdom. I don't belong here, and my destiny lies elsewhere.

"And what would you do if I were?" Atticus's tone is playful, almost suggestive.

I tilt my head back, feigning contemplation as I gaze up at the ceiling, pretending to consider his question. Then, with a mischievous grin spreading across my face, my eyes return to meet his.

"Nothing," I reply, playfully pinching the tip of his nose. "Besides, you're adorable when you're jealous, so just keep it up."

I tiptoe a bit and place a soft kiss on the side of his lips. Then I take a step back to create distance between us, removing his hold on my waist in the process.

Turning away from him, I walk towards one of the bookshelves, pretending to peruse the titles. In truth, I have no idea what the words on the spines say. I need to learn these writings as soon as I can. Otherwise, this is going to be the reason for my downfall. I can't afford to stumble until I unravel the mystery surrounding Naya's death.

"You've changed," Atticus observes, his statement causing my hand to pause mid-air, suspended in the act of reaching for a book whose spine design had caught my eye.

Uh oh. Busted. Am I in trouble now?

"Change is a constant thing in the world, my King, and I don't think that's a bad thing," I reply as I turn to face him.

Atticus leans against the window, his expression inscrutable, which in turn makes me feel uneasy. I can't discern the thoughts swirling in his mind, and that uncertainty adds to my nervousness.

The King acts as a sweet husband to me, and I don't know if that is a good or a bad thing. He seems too perfect, almost too good to be true. A handsome and affectionate ruler, completely smitten with his Queen? It feels like a fantastical tale spun from imagination.

"I didn't say that it's a bad thing. I appreciate the person you're becoming. I'm always worried about you. What if I'm not there to protect you? What if Samuel isn't by your side? Your vulnerability troubles me, and the instinct to safeguard you is always present," he states, straightening his posture as he moves closer towards me. "This morning at the breakfast table, it was the first time I witnessed you standing up against your mother and assert yourself."

I nod in acknowledgement, the memory of the breakfast event fresh in my mind. Today was my first day as a queen, and I had already raised a lot of suspicions.

"I didn't intend to disrespect her. It's just that as your Queen, I must make decisions that are not solely influenced by my family's opinions but rather based on what I believe will be beneficial for the Kingdom in the long run," I explain, striving to convey my perspective.

Atticus's smile widens upon hearing my response. He halts in front of me, his touch tenderly caressing my cheek.

"I'm glad to hear that from you," he says, yet the lack of enthusiasm in his voice betrays his true sentiments about my perceived 'sudden' changes.

"Your expression tells me differently," I tell him with all honesty upon seeing the uneasiness in his eyes.

He shakes his head while maintaining eye contact. "I hate how you become too observant after our wedding. Is that the result of our souls being connected to each other?"

I give him a dubious look. I don't like it when people try to steer the topic instead of answering my question. It is my job to steer the conversation to gain more information from someone.

Closing the gap between us, I extend my hand and lightly grip his collar, a flirtatious smile playing on my lips. "Perhaps. Or maybe I'm simply striving to prove myself worthy of the crown I now wear. Tell me, my King, do you prefer the version of me from before?" I adopt a playful and alluring tone, utilizing my charm in an effort to get the answer that I want.

He catches my palm that is playing on his collar and drops a light kiss on the back of my hand.

"No, my Queen. You are exactly the perfect woman this Kingdom needs," Atticus pulls me closer to him and cages me inside his arms as he buries his face on my shoulder. "Don't force yourself to act strong every time to prove yourself worthy of the crown. Remember that you are allowed to be weak in front of me. You can always lean on me when everything gets too tough and overwhelming for you. Give me a chance to prove to you that I can also be strong for both of us."

I feel him take a deep breath, taking in the scent of my hair. For a second, it feels like a light feather touches my heart. I am a talkative person, but his kind and loving words are more than enough to render me speechless. Even though I know those words aren't meant for me, I can't stop myself from being hopeful.

I reciprocate the embrace, pressing myself against his chest, and surrender to the comforting scent that emanates from him, reminiscent of the deep woods in the midnight hour. But instead of instilling fear, it envelops me in a sense of tranquillity.

"I promise to keep that in mind, my King," I say as I look up to meet his eyes and tiptoe to capture his lips.

***

"So, how did your conversation with the King go?" Samuel asks, his voice filled with curiosity as he patiently guides me through the process of deciphering their scripts and delving into their books.

It's amusing how it transports me back to my early years, reminiscent of kindergarten when my mother patiently taught me how to recognize letters and form words. The experience brings a sense of delight and excitement. Learning new things, whether it's a new hobby or a new language, always brings joy.

"That's none of your business," I reply, returning my attention to the book I'm reading.

This book holds crucial information pertaining to the politics of Puer Lunae. According to its contents, there are five Ministers who serve as advisers to the King, each hailing from the most influential houses in the Kingdom.

They are the Minister of Trade and Finance, the Minister of Agriculture, the Minister of Peace and Treaty, the Minister of Health, and the Minister of Defense. If Naya's death had anything to do with her engagement to the King of Puer Lunae, I suspect that at least one of these five Ministers bears a direct connection to the murder case.

"Is that so? I thought I was your partner in crime here. I want to know if I'm going to die or not," Samuel insists, drawing my attention to him once more.

"I am a detective. My role is to investigate crimes, not to commit them. Now, kindly be silent and allow me to study in peace," I assert, rising from my chair and making my way to another table, carrying the book to resume my reading.

It is essential for me to study the function of each minister as well as establish connections with them to gather information. This is where I am going to start my investigation.

This is probably the best thing about my job. Starting from scratch and gradually piecing together the puzzle, slowly revealing the complete picture— it requires patience, a sharp intellect, keen observational skills, and a great deal of courage. Pursuing criminals is not a task for the faint-hearted.

"Very well then, if you insist on keeping your conversation with your 'husband' confidential," he grumbles, placing his foot atop the table. "But could you at least share some details about the crimes you have previously solved?"

The interest in his voice catches my attention, and I put down my book to meet his curious gaze.

"Why the sudden interest?" I furrow my brow.

"Lady Naya is your big fan, and she's quite proud to tell me that you look exactly the same as if you're her human counterpart," Samuel explains.

I can't help but smile at his response. Who would have imagined that I had a vampire fan? Now that I ponder upon it, how did Lady Naya discover my existence?

"That got me thinking. How did Lady Naya find out about me, and more importantly, can I still return to the human world?" I question, voicing the ponderings that occupy my thoughts.

I've been so caught up with everything that's happening in this world and the unexpected role thrust upon me as a queen it never occurred to me that I need to go back to the human world once all of this is over. I'm sure that by the time I return, the book titled 'The Mysterious Disappearance of Great Detective Naya' has already been published.

Samuel's lips curl into a smile, perhaps amused by my question.

I cock my brow at him. "And what is that smile supposed to mean?"

"You think you can still go back? Trust me, once you successfully unravel the mystery behind Lady Naya's death, you won't be able to go back," he replies with certainty in his tone.

My forehead creases as I look at him, not really understanding his words. "And why exactly is that?"

"You're underestimating the pull of the beloved," Samuel asserts, his voice tinged with conviction. "You share an unbreakable connection with the King. Your heart and soul are intricately woven into his being and the very fabric of his Kingdom. Even if I were to open the way to send you back to the human world right now, you wouldn't be able to leave."

My frown deepens, morphing almost into a scowl as scepticism settles within me. Sure, I am attracted to the King, but I don't think I am 'that' drawn to him to forget that I don't belong to this world.

"The only reason why I can't leave is because of my duty as a detective." I counter, attempting to rationalize my stance, although a part of me acknowledges the falsehood embedded within my words. "A detective cannot abandon an unresolved case; it is my obligation to bring closure to it."

"All right, you can keep convincing yourself of that. But you know what? I'm willing to bet my neck that you won't leave this Kingdom even after uncovering the mystery behind Lady Naya's death,"

Instead of dignifying his statement with a response, I roll my eyes in exasperation. It's pointless to argue with someone who is blinded by their own beliefs.

Returning my focus to the book I hold, I delve back into its pages, seeking solace within the written words. However, the tranquillity of the library is abruptly shattered as the door swings open with a forceful momentum. Both Samuel and I instinctively turn our attention towards the intruder. It is Minna, her features betraying a sense of urgency, and she hastily shuts the door behind her, taking a few laboured breaths as though struggling to regain her composure.

"Is there a problem?" I question, my voice laced with concern, acknowledging the obvious signs of distress emanating from her.

Minna's eyes brim with sheer panic as she closes the distance between us.

"My Queen, the Duke of Caceres has arrived," she manages to say, her words punctuated by gasps for air.

My brow furrows as I take in her words, a mixture of confusion and concern flooding my thoughts. Seeing the worry on her face makes me feel confused. Am I supposed to be bothered by this?

I shift my gaze to Samuel, hoping for insight or an explanation. Yet, my breath catches in my throat as I'm confronted by a startling sight. Anger and hatred burned fiercely in his eyes, his fists clenched tightly, and his irises now transformed into a deep crimson hue.

A subtle ache begins to throb at my temples, prompting me to reach up and massage my forehead in an attempt to alleviate the discomfort. Another name, it seems, finds its way onto my suspect list, further muddling the already intricate puzzle before me.

CHAPTER 10

Naya

I regard the man before me with unabated curiosity. Sitting across from each other, a round table acts as a physical barrier, dividing our spaces. We find ourselves in the grand receiving area of the palace, a space designed not only to extend a warm welcome to visitors but also to showcase the opulence and splendour of our kingdom. Stained glass windows bathe the room in a kaleidoscope of colours while exquisite paintings adorn the walls, their value unmistakable. Elaborate metalwork accents the room, serving as intricate embellishments, testaments to the skilled craftsmanship cherished in this world.

My gaze narrows at the man that's been introduced to me just a moment ago. At first glance, he doesn't look suspicious as he talks to my husband about some issues in our kingdom. I'm not going to lie; the Duke is quite attractive. However, for some reason, he gives off a dim aura that almost makes me uncomfortable. I don't like him.

When I asked Samuel about the Duke's connection to Lady Naya, he didn't respond. But his warning was clear— to avoid being alone with the Duke at all costs.

"My Queen, I apologize that I couldn't attend your wedding yesterday. There's an emergency in Caceres that requires my attention."

The man offers a friendly smile, but that only makes my insides churn, telling me not to get close to him. My protective instinct suddenly kicks in, wanting to shield the vulnerable lamb in wolf's clothing.

My eyes narrow in suspicion as I return his smile. "Don't worry about it, Idris. I didn't even notice you weren't in the ceremony."

The smile on the duke's lips fades, and a hint of anger flashes in his eyes. But then, it is only for a few seconds. In just a snap, the trace of anger in his eyes vanishes, and the warm smile returns to his lips. But in those few seconds, I saw the wolf hiding behind his harmless appearance.

I don't know why Samuel acts so hatefully towards this Duke, but I know it is for a justified reason.

My loyal butler stands just outside the door of the receiving room, patiently waiting for me. Never before have I witnessed Samuel assume the role of a strict bodyguard until this man entered the picture.

"It appears to me that being the King's beloved has wrought notable changes upon you, my Queen. You exude newfound confidence, a sense of self-assurance," Idris remarks, his observant tone laced with a touch of feign admiration.

"Indeed," Atticus agrees with pride sparkling in his eyes. "That is precisely what our kingdom requires—a strong queen."

I turn towards the King, a genuine smile gracing my lips, before redirecting my attention back to Idris. While I may not be familiar with him, two distinct emotions surge within me in his presence—fear and anger.

Idris is like a wolf cloaked in the garb of a lamb. He bides his time, waiting for the right time to strike. I have met a few criminals in the human world who use the same tactic, masquerading as gentle entities while concealing their true predatory nature. They are experts at deception, projecting an air of reasonability when in the company of others, only to reveal their darker intentions when alone with their unsuspecting prey.

"Power has the ability to transform an individual in an instant. It should come as no surprise," I remark, my gaze unwavering as it remains fixed on Idris. I'm not sure what he did to Lady Naya, but I am going to play his game. I'll be his prey, and I'll show the world what kind of demon he is hiding. I will make sure that I will be his downfall.

"You never fail to surprise me. I had no idea you had so much more to offer. Just when I thought I'd seen you at your best," Idris nods in approval as his eyes scan my body. His action sends chills down my spine, but not in a good way.

Atticus doesn't seem to notice the threat beneath Idris's voice, but I do. If he thinks he can scare me with that, then he has got it all wrong.

"Well, rest assured you will be seeing more of my 'best' in the near future," I respond with a polite smile adorning my lips as I shift my attention towards my husband. "I have a few matters to attend to in the library. May I be excused?"

My husband responds with a compassionate smile and nods in understanding. I offer him a small, grateful smile in return. I rise up from the chair that was crafted from solid narra wood and make my way towards the door to exit the room.

I exhale a sigh of relief, feeling a sense of respite as I firmly close the door, giving Idris and my husband privacy to continue their conversation.

Without delay, Samuel swiftly makes his way towards me, his voice tinged with concern as he speaks. "What happened? Did he say or do anything to you?" His gaze sweeps over me as if anticipating that the duke would dare to inflict harm upon me in the presence of my husband.

My brow furrows in response to Samuel's intense reaction, a mixture of confusion and curiosity taking hold within me.

"I am with my husband, Samuel. I don't think he would try anything funny in front of the King," I assure him, offering him a perplexed gaze.

He exhales a sigh of relief. I shake my head at his actions before turning away from him. I prefer to have our conversation in the royal chamber instead of a hallway where anyone could hear us. Samuel follows me without question. I don't know what the deal is between Lady Naya and Idris, but I am pretty sure it will be useful for my investigation.

I step into the royal chamber, my butler following closely behind. The golden rays of the setting sun penetrate through the glass windows and open balcony, casting a warm, luminous glow that envelops the room, but it does nothing to calm my racing nerves. As I make my way towards the walk-in closet situated on the opposite side of the room, I hear the door close behind me, momentarily sealing off the outside world.

Rows and rows of perfectly arranged suits, dresses, and shoes welcome me, but my gaze immediately turns towards one particular corner. I make my way towards it and pull my backpack behind all the lavish gowns where I have placed it to hide it from the King. I take out a medium-sized box from the backpack that contains the two letters and gifts Lady Naya has sent to me.

Samuel is waiting for me in the room, standing right beside a plush couch while still looking so tense. I make my way in front of him and place the box on the top table, facing the vanity mirror.

I open the box, revealing the letter I received from Lady Naya and a platinum ring adorned with a vibrant red ruby at its centre. When I first laid eyes on this ring, I was left in utter disbelief. Who would be stupid enough to send someone a gift as expensive as this ring? The ring's cost is probably enough to purchase me another Harley.

I used to wonder why this ring seemed a perfect fit for my ring finger. Now I know why. The original owner is basically another person who happens to look exactly like me.

"Beneath your strong personality hides a soft heart full of passion, dedication, and the courage to help those who are in need— something I envy about you. Some people wear lamb's clothing to fool others around them and to hide their monstrous works. But you, my darling, are different. You are a lamb hidden in wolf's clothing." I read a portion of the letter, then lifted my gaze to meet the intense stare of my butler.

"That's quite beautiful," he remarks.

"It truly is," I concur, nodding in agreement. "This is the letter Lady Naya sent me, and I believe we both know who she was referring to regarding the people who wear lamb clothing."

My eyes narrow, forming slender slits as Samuel averts his gaze, refusing to meet my piercing stare.

"Who is Idris? What has he done to Lady Naya?" My voice slices through the air, resonating with sharp authority, commanding his attention.

If Samuel persists in his reluctance to divulge the connection between Idris and Lady Naya, how am I to gather the vital information necessary to unravel this perplexing case? Among all the individuals within this kingdom, Samuel's cooperation is paramount. As Lady Naya's closest confidant, he possesses invaluable insights that can aid me in identifying potential suspects.

"Trust me, you don't want to know," He runs his fingers on his hair. Samuel shakes his head and begins pacing in front of me.

I can discern a mingling of panic and guilt in his expression, and for a second, I feel remorseful for pressuring him to speak. However, I have no other options.

"I need to know," I insist firmly, folding my arms across my chest to assert my determination.

As anger consumes him, crimson veins begin to surface on the whites of his eyes, transforming the royal chamber into an atmosphere of almost suffocating intensity. His eyes well up with tears, and his fangs elongate. He is livid, and I can understand his reaction. What I cannot comprehend is the guilt evident in his expression. Why would he feel guilty about what happened to Lady Naya?

After a prolonged and uneasy silence, he finally succumbs to the weight of the moment and decides to speak. "Idris is Lady Naya's former fiancé."

"And?" I prompt, urging him to provide further information.

"Lady Naya's mother betrothed her to that bastard, and..." He turns his gaze away from me, unable to meet my eyes.

"Damn it, Samuel! I am not as vulnerable as Lady Naya. If you truly want to help me bring justice to her death, don't leave me hanging and tell me what he did to her!" I erupt in frustration. Impatience surges within me as I grow weary of his treatment as if he doubts my ability to handle the harsh reality.

"He... he raped her," his voice quavers, a blend of sorrow and anger evident as if he relives the trauma of the past. With a defeated demeanour, he distances himself from me and slumps onto the bed. Rubbing his palms over his face, he appears drained, as if he has just emerged from a gruelling battle with a malevolent demon that has consumed his very soul. "He broke her repeatedly," he adds, his voice barely audible, as if whispered through the weight of immense pain.

A surge of pain and anger courses through my veins upon hearing his revelation. I take a seat before the vanity table, seeking stability and striving to maintain composure amidst his anguish.

In some way, I had already anticipated this response, yet the confirmation still inflicts a piercing ache. Lady Naya has been sexually assaulted. Her mother sold her off, basically.

Disgust churns within my stomach as I recall that it was her very own mother who placed her in such a harrowing situation. Heat prickles at the corners of my eyes, and before I know it, tears cascade down my cheeks. I never fathomed the extent of Lady Naya's suffering— a victim of an abusive, power-hungry mother who callously traded her own flesh and blood for the pursuit of power.

Now I completely understand why I hate that woman. How could a mother be so self-centred, so devoid of empathy and love?

I take a deep breath to calm the raging storm inside my chest. I place the letter back in the bag and stand up from my seat to go to the closet. I brushed off the stray tears that decided to fall down my cheeks without my consent.

After ensuring that my backpack is safely hidden, I walk out of the closet with my palms clenched in tight fists. The audacity of that Duke to show his face in front of me! That fucker is going to regret what he did. I will strip him of his title, and I'm going to make sure he pays dearly for the sin he has committed.

I make my way towards the door, ready to destroy the face of that Duke with my bare hands. I'm going to play his game. Let's see who will have the last laugh.

"My Queen, where are you going?" Samuel queries, noticing that I don't plan to stay inside that room after what I had learned.

I halt my steps and turn to face him. "I'm going to do what you have failed to do. That man doesn't deserve his title. He deserves to be in prison!"

I turn my eyes back to the door, but in just a snap, Samuel is already in front of me, ready to stop me from all the crazy stunts I plan on doing. He stands between me and the door, preventing me from opening it.

"I may have failed to protect Lady Naya, but that doesn't mean I'm going to let you run straight towards the fire. You're not going after him. That man is a dangerous person. You have no idea what he is capable of," his tone is stern and full of conviction.

An empty chuckle escapes my lips as I fix him with a piercing glare.

"You know who I despise the most, aside from criminals? Those who lack the courage to stand up for what is right," I growl with seething anger, causing him to freeze in his tracks. "You did nothing to aid Lady Naya. You simply stood by and watched."

The tone of my voice lacks vigour. However, even a shabby knife is enough to destroy someone's heart if you plunge it with enough force. Now, the reason behind the guilt haunting his eyes becomes clear. It's because he didn't do anything to save Lady Naya from the demon. He did nothing to protect her.

Samuel's jaw tightens with anger. He swallows the lump in his throat, and I can almost perceive the quiver in his lips.

"I am a butler, Naya," he gestures to himself. "He is a Duke! If I were to oppose his will, he has the power to strip me of my position. If that were to happen, Lady Naya would be left without anyone to lean on. She will be alone at his mercy."

Samuel turns his gaze away from me, and tears start to roll down his eyes. I know it's wrong to blame him, but he shouldn't stay silent about it. He could at least try to find a way to help Naya. At times, it falls upon us to be the voice for those who lack the power to speak for themselves. We must raise our voices, for that may be the sole means of saving them.

"That time, the only way I know I can do to protect her is by staying by her side. To be someone she can cry on," he adds in between his silent sobs. To my surprise, Samuel kneels before me, locking eyes with mine. "If you think what I did is a crime, then punish me, my Queen."

My eyes narrow to slits as I gaze at him, my anger intensifying. He lowers his gaze to the floor, signifying his surrender. My jaw clenches tightly, and I yearn to unleash my fury upon him for his insolence.

However, after a moment, I exhale sharply and shake my head.

"Carry that guilt to your grave," I seethe, my anger carefully restrained as I stare down at him. "That will be your punishment."

I stride past him and forcefully push open the door, exiting the royal chamber.

A rapist, huh? Let's see what that poor excuse of a duke can offer.

A dangerous smile curves upon my lips as I stride purposefully back to the library of the palace, determined to delve deeper into the hierarchy of the kingdom and gather evidence to condemn the duke. My heels create loud stomps with every firm step I take. I'm going to make sure that Idris is going to regret that our paths have crossed in this lifetime.

CHAPTER 11

Naya

My second day as a queen arrives rather slowly. I wake up in the arms of my loving husband, whom I don't even remember coming back inside the room last night. After dinner, I immediately went back to the royal chamber to call it a day while Atticus still had a few things to deal with. I fell asleep waiting for him.

A smile curves on my lips while staring at the peaceful slumbering form of my husband. He looks so rugged and handsome even in his sleep. Lady Naya is so lucky to have him in her life. The King is head over heels for her, and that only makes me curious as to why she never confessed to the King. Judging from how protective my husband is of me, I know he will do the same for Lady Naya.

My gaze shifts toward the glass window in the room. The morning sunshine streaming through it is almost blinding, signalling that I have woken up much later today compared to yesterday. A lazy yawn escapes my lips as I quietly slip out of bed, mindful not to disturb Atticus. I don't know how late he came into the room last night, and I don't want to disturb him.

My eyes fixate on him as I stand right beside the king-size canopy bed. He is lying on his stomach with the white sheet covering his lower body. My throat tightens upon realizing that the King is definitely the kind of man I would fall for if we were not in this situation right now. The urge to curl up right beside him and relish in the feeling of being in his arms makes me want to return to bed, but I know I can't do that. I can't do anything to tempt my husband to consummate our marriage, no matter how strong our physical attraction is.

A frustrated sigh escapes my lips as I turn my back on him and make my way toward the bathroom to freshen up a bit. I'm not sure how long my husband will be asleep, but from the looks of it, I'll be having breakfast in the dining hall alone.

Like yesterday, Samuel is waiting for me right outside the door the moment I step out of the royal chamber. A small forced smile is on his lips as he greets me good morning without enthusiasm in his voice. I haven't seen him since we argued yesterday about Idris. I had a suspicion he left the castle on purpose to calm down.

"Idris still hasn't left the castle for some reason. Do you have any plans for today, Your Highness?" he asks in a calculated tone as we make our way across the lavish hallway decorated with expensive paintings, stained glass windows every five meters, and metalwork hanging on the walls.

I halt my step and turn to him with a sigh, prompting him to stop in his tracks as well. "I want to check out the armoury," I announce.

Samuel's forehead contorts into a frown as he gives me a questioning look. "Why?"

"I need a weapon to protect myself, and I want to see if I can find one that is similar to the one that was used to kill Lady Naya," I reply.

"I don't think that's a good idea," He straightens his back with a look of disapproval on his face. He lowers his voice a little as if he wants to make sure that I am the only one hearing his words. "It will raise a lot of suspicions, especially since most people in this Kingdom are aware that Lady Naya has no interest in the Kingdom's weaponry. As long as you remain within the castle grounds, rest assured that our warriors are more than willing to sacrifice their lives to protect you."

That makes me frown. "I don't know about you, but I'm not fond of the idea of someone dying on my behalf," I contest. While I know that my actions might raise suspicion, I need to do something to protect myself. Once our warriors learn that I am a fraud, I highly doubt any of them would be willing to wield a weapon to protect me.

"You have to get used to it," he insists without tearing his gaze from mine.

I let out an exasperated sigh, frustrated that Samuel and I were having this argument when it was clear as the blue sky that someone was waiting for a chance to kill me. "Why are you so against it, Samuel? All I'm asking for is a weapon to protect myself when needed," I ask him.

Samuel's face darkens at my question, and his voice grows serious. "Because I know the weapon is not for you to protect yourself. You need a weapon to go after Idris, and I can't let you do that. I won't let you run straight into danger."

His words catch me off guard. I never realized that this was what was going on in his mind.

"I'm a Detective Inspector, Samuel. I am not a criminal. I'm not going out there to try to murder Idris myself if that's what you're most afraid of," I retort with a sharp hiss, wounded by his lack of trust in my judgment. I turn away from him in a mixture of annoyance and hurt, determined to distance myself from the conversation. I make my way toward the dining area of the palace, the clack of my heels echoing in the corridor. "Just when I thought you knew me better than that."

***

"What are we doing here?" I ask my butler who is standing tall right beside me.

After my breakfast, I found him in the library waiting for me. He had invited me to the castle's courtyard to show me something. So here we are, standing in front of one of the massive four towers that served as the foundation of the castle wall.

Rather than providing a direct response, Samuel turns his attention to the two guards stationed by the metal door of the tower. "Open the door for the Queen," he commands with authority.

The two guards exchange glances before pushing the door open, revealing to me what's hidden behind it. A gasp escapes my lips upon seeing what's on the other side. I turn to Samuel with a grateful smile on my face. I am about to thank him, but he beats me to it.

"Someone is waiting for you inside. I'll be waiting in here, my Queen," he politely says before nodding at me, giving me the go-signal to enter the armoury of the castle.

I nod and take a deep breath before stepping inside the tower. Anticipation fills my chest as I make my way across it, admiring a few pieces of long-range old-style firearms on the walls, swords, and various types of armour. For a medieval kingdom like Puer Lunae, this weaponry is extremely impressive. It's not much, but they have guns, implying they've already made huge advancements.

I hear the faint sound of the metal door closing behind me, but I am too engrossed in my surroundings to focus on it.

An audible cough to my left grabs my attention, drawing my gaze towards the staircase leading up to the second floor of the tower. I come face to face with a beautiful woman with strong facial features, probably half a foot taller than I am. One look and I can already tell that she is a pure-blooded warrior. Her physique is formidable, possessing a solid and well-built frame. Clad in a sleek all-black suit, her hips bear the weight of a sword.

The woman offers me a friendly smile.

"My Queen, it's unusual for you to take an interest in the palace's armoury," she says and makes her way towards me. "How may I be of service to you today, Your Highness?" The woman inquires as she halts right in front of me.

"Who are you?" I ask in curiosity instead of answering her questions.

A soft chuckle escapes her. Amusement is evident in her eyes. I inwardly cringe upon realizing my error. I shouldn't have asked that question so abruptly. What if Lady Naya knows who this woman is? It was a tactless move on my part.

"Please forgive me. I forgot to introduce myself formally," the woman takes a step closer towards me. "My name is Celestine, the Minister of Defense."

My mouth hangs open as her introduction slowly sinks in.

"The Minister of Defense is a woman?" I exclaim in surprise, my eyes widening as I stare at the woman before me with newfound admiration.

Celestine snorts at my reaction. I immediately slap my palm on my lips upon realizing what I just said. That was stupid of me to say.

"I-I didn't mean it in a negative way. It's just... unexpected, but not in a bad way," I quickly clarify, not wanting her to take my words negatively.

"No need to explain further. I understand your reaction. I fought tooth and nail to prove myself worthy of this position to the entire Kingdom," she responds, her gaze sweeping across the room filled with medieval swords, shields, and various contraptions that are beyond my understanding. "It took me years to earn the respect of my fellow warriors."

"I think you are more than qualified for this position," I respond with a warm smile. Knowing that this Kingdom has a woman as the Minister of Defense means a good start for me. If she's not an enemy, I can rely on her. "Anyway, I came here to look for a weapon."

"A weapon?"

I nod at her.

"Yup, a weapon. I need something that I can use to protect myself. Something that is lightweight and can be carried around without getting too much attention." I explain to her.

Celestine's smile broadens with approval, and she nods in agreement. It seems she appreciates my straightforwardness.

"I like women who know exactly what they want. Wait here. I have the perfect weapon fit for a queen," she states before turning her back on me.

The side of my lips curls upward as I follow her steps with my eyes. She makes her way towards the stair that leads to the second floor of the tower.

As soon as Celestine disappears from my line of sight, I find myself entranced by the surroundings, my curiosity ignited like that of a seven-year-old child. The room captivates me with its array of medieval weapons, each one telling a story of the Kingdom's history and the artistry of its blacksmiths. Each of the armour, swords, and shields has intricate designs. It showcases not only the strength of the Kingdom but also its wealth.

If I were to bring any of these weapons to the human world, it would surely fetch me a massive amount of fortune. Each one of these is priceless, not only because they are well-made but also because of their intricate design.

I reach out and gently pick up a long-range shotgun from the shelf, drawn to its unique presence. This vintage piece from the armoury collection is something I had only ever dreamed of, yet here it is, right before my eyes. The shotgun is a masterpiece, intricately crafted with meticulous attention to detail. Its handle, made of metal, is adorned with an exquisite engraving of a dragon head.

The metal feels cold against my fingers, yet it gives me a warmth that I cannot explain.

"For a woman, you seem so fascinated with weapons," Celestine's voice makes me look over my shoulder towards the direction of the stairs.

"This is the first time I've entered an armoury. It's overwhelming," I reply as I place the gun back on the shelf. My eyes turn to the box she's holding. It's an average-sized box, probably half a foot long.

"What is that?" I inquire, curious about what could be the weapon inside it.

"Oh yeah, I'm confident that you're going to love this," Celestine says and crosses the short distance between us, handing me the box.

I accept the box with a thankful smile and open it, revealing the beautiful silver blade hidden inside. The handle, crafted from gleaming metal, is designed with intricate details resembling delicate wings that gracefully overlap the blade. Beside it, a leather sheath rests, ready to protect and house the blade when not in use. Examining the length, I estimate it to be about one and a half palms long, the perfect size for me to conceal it discreetly at the side of my waist.

"It's beautiful," I murmur, completely overwhelmed to own such a beauty.

"Indeed. The blade is made of silver, so be careful touching it. The handle is made of metal. It's small but deadly. It's a weapon I crafted with my own hands. It's been stuck in this tower for a long time now as a display. I'm glad that it finally finds its partner." Celestine looks proud while looking at the blade in my hand.

"You made this yourself? That's amazing," I exclaim in amazement and meet her gaze. I can hardly take my eyes off the blade. This is perfect. This is precisely what I need. "I promise to take care of it."

I feel honoured and grateful for the gift. I pick up the blade from the box, being careful not to touch the silver part. I don't want to accidentally reveal that I am not a vampire.

I carefully insert the blade into the leather sheath, ensuring it is securely in place. Celestine then hands me a small black belt, which I fasten around my waist, allowing me to wear the weapon comfortably.

"That's perfect for you. But do you know how to wield it?" Celestine inquires, her eyes filled with genuine curiosity.

Good question. Of course, five years in the Police Academy helped me master how to wield blades of all kinds, but I can't really tell her that.

"I don't have much experience with this particular type of weapon yet, but I can always seek guidance from Samuel. He can teach me how to use it," I respond, weaving a lie to maintain the illusion. "Thank you again for entrusting this to me."

"It's my pleasure to serve you, my Queen." Celestine bows her head towards me to express her respect.

The smile never leaves my lips as I look at her. This Kingdom has many hidden gems in it, and I can't help but wonder what kind of people I am set to meet in the next few days. I can't wait to uncover the dark secret behind Lady Naya's death, and at the same time, I am excited to meet more people like Celestine.

I bid her farewell, expressing my gratitude once again, and proceeded to leave the tower. A sinister smile gradually spreads across my face. Now I'm ready to play with that bastard who dares to address himself as a Duke.

CHAPTER 12

Naya

I step into the royal chamber and discover my husband in the process of putting on his pants. Based on the damp locks of his hair, it's evident that he has recently emerged from the bathroom before my arrival.

I lean against the door behind me and watch the King getting dressed. I can't stop the smile of approval from forming on my lips as I take in his almost naked appearance, with his muscles flexing in every movement he makes. He must have noticed my presence because he looks over his shoulder and meet my gaze.

"Good morning, my Queen," he greets as he starts to button his inner shirt. He looks dashingly handsome and tempting with those bright hazel-coloured eyes of his smiling at me.

"It's already almost noon, my King. I don't think your greeting is still appropriate," I approach him without breaking our eye contact. His arms automatically snake around my waist when I'm already within grabbing distance, his palm settling on the small of my back. I reach for his shirt to button the rest for him.

"Is that so? Am I slacking now?" he playfully inquires, placing a tender kiss on my forehead.

His lighthearted aura immediately captivates me, drawing me in effortlessly. With the last button in place, I release his shirt and lift my gaze to meet his, finding his eyes fixed on me with unwavering intensity.

"Yep, but fret not. I believe your subjects would not mind if you chose to slumber through the day. They will understand that we are still basking in the glow of our honeymoon phase," I playfully tease, leaning in closer to plant a swift kiss on the corner of his lips.

But Atticus is having none of that as he quickly tightens his arms around my waist, pulling me close to him to deepen our kiss. I close my eyes and let go of my inhibitions, feeling the warmth of his lips against mine.

I despise how comfortable I'm becoming in his presence, yet I can't stop myself from falling deeply for him. Is it some kind of vampire thing? Is it because I am his beloved? Samuel did mention something about my soul being bonded to the King's soul after the wedding.

However, no matter what I feel, my relationship with Atticus is not something that I can keep forever; it is set to end the moment I solve the mystery behind the Queen's death. I hate to admit it, but there's a part of me that wants to play Lady Naya's identity forever. Is that selfish? Can I be Naya? His Queen? His wife? His lover, for real?

Atticus carries me effortlessly in his arms, and I feel weightless as we move towards the waiting bed. He places me down gently, and in an instant, he's on top of me, our lips meeting in a passionate kiss that leaves me breathless. The sensation of his body pressed against mine is electric, and I feel his lower region pressing against my thigh. My brain sends out a warning signal, but I'm just too lost to listen to it. His lips let go of mine, then slid down to my jaw to the side of my neck. My breathing starts to feel ragged and heavy. Lust has blurred all of my logical reasoning.

My fingers dig into his back, giving him encouragement to continue what he is doing. I know that this will end badly for both of us, but I can't bring myself to care. I don't care about the responsibility waiting for me outside this room. I just want to feel more of him.

That's when a loud knock on the door interrupts us. We both look at the door in unison. Atticus seems irritated, but I, on the other hand, feel as if someone has thrown a cold bucket of water on me. Panic starts to rise in my chest.

What the heck am I thinking?!

"Who the fuck is that?" my beloved hisses with frustration clouding his eyes.

I can't help but smile seeing how we share the same emotion at the moment. But I know that the knock is more of a wake-up call for me. I push him lightly to create a space between us. I need to leave this bed before I end up losing my sanity again and make love with him.

"You open the door. I'll take a bath first. See you in the dining room for lunch, my King," I quickly say and give him a quick peck on the lips.

I rise from the bed and make my way towards the bathroom, sensing Atticus's eyes tracing my movements, though I opt to ignore it. As soon as I step inside, I swiftly close the door, shutting out the outside world and giving myself a moment to catch my breath. I lean against the door and fall to the floor as I hug my knees close to my chest.

I facepalm in frustration. What the heck is happening to me? Did I just wish to replace Lady Naya for real? I was not that unreasonable. This is not me anymore.

I gaze up at the mirror positioned beside the hot tub, my own reflection capturing the unshed tears welling up in the corners of my eyes. My heart tightens with anguish, a blend of guilt and an overwhelming sense of emptiness washing over me as the realization settles in that I cannot remain by Atticus's side forever. The thought of us going on separate roads is enough to fracture me into countless shards.

I bite down on my lower lip, attempting to stifle the tears, but they continue to fall one after another. I bury my face in my palms, pouring out all the pain and disappointment I feel. My mind and heart descend into sheer turmoil. I feel lost...

After several minutes of letting my emotions run their course, I finally managed to stop sobbing. I wipe my tears away and take a few deep breaths to calm myself. I can't focus on my own feelings right now. Whatever I feel for Atticus, I need to put it aside and concentrate on solving this case. With another steadying breath, I collect myself.

I walk towards the hot tub and prepare it before taking off my clothes one by one to step inside it. The warm water envelops my whole body, and I take a few deep breaths, allowing myself to relax as I stare blankly at the ceiling. I can't keep worrying about what's going to happen tomorrow. From now on, I need to focus on what's in front of me. If this is meant to shatter me, then so be it. I will confront it with every ounce of courage I possess when the time demands it.

***

The King was nowhere to be found in the room upon finishing my bath. I'm guessing that whoever knocked a while ago has a piece of very urgent news for the King.

Taking a moment to ensure my appearance is presentable, I dress myself in a yellow silk gown before setting off towards the dining hall. I haven't seen Idris today, but I have a feeling that he will be joining us today for lunch. As much as I don't want to see him as it will only ruin my appetite, I know that it would be unwise to miss a meal when the King was in residence.

Also, I need to know more about Idris. I need to figure out where his weakest point is. I need to find a way to catch him and reveal his atrocities to the King.

I am on my way to the dining hall when someone pulls me towards one of the palace rooms. I am caught off guard and unable to fight back. The next thing I hear is the sound of the door slamming behind me.

In an instant, I am forcibly thrust into the centre of the room, finding myself face-to-face with the last person I wish to encounter today. Instinctively, I survey my surroundings.

My eyes fall upon the towering four-poster bed draped in silk curtains of deep royal purple. The room is filled with ornate furnishings made of rich, dark wood, and magnificent paintings hang on the walls. The windows are tall and grand, with thick drapes made of the finest silk, and the scent of fresh flowers and burning candles fills the air. If I am not mistaken, this is one of the guestrooms reserved for esteemed nobles.

"Hello, my Queen. It's been a while, hasn't it? Did you long for my presence?" Idris taunts, a smug smirk playing on his lips as he appraises me with malicious intent.

I meet his gaze once again, my expression devoid of any emotion. This man should be thankful that I am not a murderer because I want to kill him in ten different ways right now.

"Why would I yearn for the company of someone who subjects me to sexual abuse?" I reply, my tone dripping with sarcasm.

I cross my arms firmly over my chest, asserting my position. If I were truly Lady Naya, I might be trembling in fear at this moment. However, the thing is, I am not Lady Naya. I am a detective who loves to play childlike games with criminals.

If I want to, I can use this situation to my advantage, but it is not yet time. I need him to talk. He is one of my keys to solving the mystery behind Naya's death. Once I manage to obtain the information that I need from him, that's when I'll send him to prison.

He lets out an empty chuckle and closes our distance. His massive height is towering over me. Despite the pretentious grin on his lips, I can see the fire of anger in his eyes as he approaches me. I make sure to stay alert for any unexpected attacks. My right hand unconsciously reaches down to the side of my waist, where my dagger is securely tucked. I don't know him that well, but I can recognize that demonic glint in his eyes.

"I must admit, I admire how much stronger you've become, but you know what? I miss the old you. I yearn for our games and relish hearing your screams. Did you know that you look even more exquisite when you're helpless and in tears? That's why I derive such pleasure from witnessing your visage drenched in sorrow as I..."

He doesn't have the opportunity to conclude his sentence. In a mere heartbeat, I am already before him, the tip of my silver blade poised at his throat.

This man is a demon. I'm going to make sure that he pays a high price for the sin he has committed. My grip tightens on the handle of the dagger. I'm so close to losing myself right now, but I know better than to take justice into my own hands.

"The innocent and helpless Naya is gone. Don't forget that I am your Queen now," I say, looking up at him and meeting his eyes. I can see a little bit of surprise in them. He probably didn't expect the fire in my eyes. "Remember this, Idris, this week will not end without you bowing your head to me. Mark my words. I will strip your title and throw you in the dungeon where your kind belongs!"

I can feel my insides shaking with a combination of hatred and disgust. I am so close to losing my temper, but I do my best to pull myself together and move the dagger away from his neck.

At that moment, the door swings open, and both of us pivot towards the sudden intrusion. Samuel stands in the doorway, his eyes brimming with loathing as he regards the man before me. I can feel his fury and urge to murder the man, but we've already talked about this. Idris is going to prison after I retrieve the information that I need from him.

Samuel clenches his teeth, his gaze shifting to meet mine. "My Queen, the King awaits your presence in the dining hall for lunch," he informs me.

I nod in acknowledgement and carefully return the silver dagger to its sheath.

This is just the beginning. I'm going to make sure that Lady Naya's mother pays for her greediness as well. I will not miss any of them. They will all pay dearly for the lives they have destroyed. I turn to look at Idris, who's looking at me with confusion and anger.

"See you in the dining room, Idris," I retort, my back now turned towards him as I stride towards the awaiting door.

"I can't believe you actually had the courage to threaten a Duke face to face like that," Samuel remarks with a smile of approval on his lips after closing the door.

I smirk at his comment. "Trust me, you haven't seen the best of me yet."

CHAPTER 13

Naya

The remainder of the day proceeds uneventfully. I resolve to dedicate the entire afternoon to the library, immersing myself in the pursuit of knowledge. My goal is to delve deeper into their language and understand the intricacies of the kingdom's power structure.

Samuel has been so patient in explaining each and every minor detail about Puer Lunae, including its history. Gradually, I begin to grasp the fundamentals of reading in their language and unravel the layers of their society. This kingdom has so much knowledge to offer.

"I want to train," I mutter out of nowhere, catching Samuel off guard as he raises his gaze to meet mine. He promptly closes the book he was engrossed in and returns it to its designated spot on the shelf.

"Where did that come from?" He queries, his eyebrow arching in curiosity.

"I feel like I need to be prepared. I had my training back in the human world, but my enemies back then lacked supernatural strength and fangs. Despite my agility and tactical prowess, I fear that my comparative lack of physical strength is going to be my downfall," I explain, conveying my concerns to my butler.

I am honestly worried about the fact that I don't know who my enemy is. The best way to win is to know the strengths and weaknesses of your enemy. That is precisely why the saying 'Keep your friends close but your enemies closer' holds significance. Gaining insight into the strengths and weaknesses of your foe can provide a strategic advantage. However, in my case, I have no idea who is behind this. All I have are assumptions. I don't have solid evidence. This is the reason why I need to be prepared for all possibilities.

"I can train you, but we need to keep it a secret," he offers and takes the chair in front of me. "You've only been a queen for two days, and I must say, you have already made quite a number of enemies. It would be wise for you to maintain a low profile for a while."

I let out a groan of frustration at his words. He is right. I'm surprised that none of my subjects is questioning me about my 'suspicious' changes yet. I'm either so good at acting, or some people really believe that being mated to the King and bearing the crown can make a drastic change in someone.

"What do you suggest, then?" I close the book I'm reading and turn my gaze to Samuel. "I'm worried, Samuel. We don't know what the next move of Lady Naya's murderer will be, but I want to be prepared when it happens."

Samuel looks at my face as if he is trying to weigh our best options. He knows that I got a valid point. Idris is our main suspect, but if I'm going to base it on our conversation this morning, it's not him. He didn't mention anything related to Naya's death. Harriet is much more suspicious to me. The way she talks to me makes me feel like she has something to do with Lady Naya's murder.

"My suggestion?" He crosses his arms over his chest and locks eyes with me. "Stay inside the castle. We have numerous warriors around who can protect you. Enemies will think twice before striking."

I roll my eyes at his suggestion and scoff. The confidence in his tone contradicts his words. I had hoped for a bolder idea. I'm disappointed.

"That's an act of cowardice," I point out and rise from my chair. "I can't stay here and wait for the King to discover my true identity. We need to act fast, or else we'll both die without uncovering the truth behind Naya's death. You have no idea how anxious I feel every time the night falls."

I don't know if I can survive the third night without the King insisting on his claim on me. I'm going to look suspicious to him if I continue to avoid the consummation of our union. We need to think fast, or else the King's claim on me will be our downfall. If that happens, all the things that I've gone through will come to waste. I don't want that to happen.

Samuel lets out a tired sigh as he rises from his seat and walks toward the library's open window. He turns his gaze to the breathtaking blue sky outside, his hands balling into tight fists. A moment of silence descends upon us, and the chirping of birds from outside becomes more pronounced, filling the library's silence.

"I hate how you and Lady Naya look exactly the same but different at the same time. You are very sure of yourself, fearless, and know exactly what the next step is despite being at a disadvantage. You take over with confidence, and you sure know how to talk back and manipulate people," he suddenly blurts out, his eyes still fixed on the clear sky outside the window.

I frown. Okay... That speech came out of nowhere and is definitely off-topic.

"Do you miss her?" I ask softly.

Samuel keeps his silence, choosing not to answer my question. He doesn't need to say a single word; the way his knuckles clutch hard on the metal window rails is enough for me to understand how he feels.

"Naya is gone, as dreary as it sounds, but you need to let her go. You need to accept that she's no longer coming back," I point out, trying to knock some sense into him. Naya is a great person, but I have my own identity, which I don't want to lose because I'm her double. "I am not her. Of all the people in this kingdom, you are the one who knows that. Just because I pretend to be her to solve this case doesn't mean that I want to be her mirror. I have my own identity."

"Yeah, I know," he responds, his voice heavy with the burden of yearning and remorse. "It's just that sometimes I can't help but wish I didn't know she died."

I let out a heavy sigh. Losing someone is painful, and to have another person constantly reminding you of that loss only intensifies the suffering. It is no wonder some individuals prefer to live in a lie than face the truth.

"I don't think Lady Naya wants her death to be unknown to you. You have mentioned that she often tells my story to you, right? If there's one perfect person here who can assist me, it would be you."

I have this feeling that Lady Naya wants Samuel and me to partner in solving the mystery of her death.

My brows furrow as I come to this conclusion. Now that I think about it, I've been so occupied in the past two days that I didn't have a chance to ask Samuel how Naya became aware of my existence. I believe the letter she sent was intended to capture my attention, to lure me into this world.

"How did she come to know about me?" I question, brimming with curiosity.

Samuel turns to face me, a frown forming on his forehead. "What do you mean?"

"Lady Naya," I reply, "the first time we met, I recall you saying, 'You're the detective she's blabbering about,' right? How did she come to know about me?"

I am genuinely curious about how a vampire from an ancient medieval kingdom became aware of my existence. We are literally worlds apart. Where could she have obtained information about me?

Samuel's smile emerges the flicker of sadness that adorned his eyes earlier starts to dissipate.

"I thought you'd never ask, but I've been pondering it, and I believe there's a connection between your soul and Lady Naya's soul," he says, his eyes gleaming with intrigue, causing me to furrow my brows.

"I'm sorry?"

"She dreamed of you almost every night. You know what those vivid dreams are like? I remember her saying that it's like seeing herself and experiencing the thrill of being a detective. She thought it was just a normal dream, but then her dream of you was too clear and too detailed to be ignored. Then she met Zizina."

"Zizina?" I repeat.

Samuel takes a step closer to me, his hands finding their way into the pockets of his suit as he leans against the chair he was sitting in moments ago.

"Zizina is a vampire witch. She's the daughter of the kingdom's sorceress, Nemue. Basically, the heir to her mother's position. A little bit hardheaded and loves to break the kingdom's rules to venture into the human world. She's a dear friend of Lady Naya, and one day she brought a newspaper with news about you solving a suicide murder case."

I am left speechless by his revelation. So basically, someone from this world can freely cross over to the human world? That sounds dangerous.

"Suicide murder case? When is that?" I ask curiously. I have solved many murder cases during my five years of service, and it is impossible for me to remember each one.

Samuel furrows his eyebrows, racking his brain to recall the answer to my question. "Approximately three years ago," he replies, sounding somewhat uncertain.

Three years ago? Now that I think about it, there was one suicide murder case that left an unforgettable mark on my memory. It wasn't because of the case itself, but because of the young girl I chose to be my partner.

"If I remember correctly, that is Lynn's case. Her stepfather is the murderer." I narrate as I recall the specific case.

It was a special case that I handled where I partnered with a 17-year-old pharmaceutical heiress to solve it. I wonder how Amber is doing now. That kid looks normal, but for some reason, she gives me the creeps. She's kind and beautiful, but I feel like there's more to her than meets the eye. She's a mystery that I want to solve too, but I decided against that idea. Despite her secretive nature, she is genuinely a good person. In the end, I concluded that some things are best left in the dark.

"The details of that case amaze her, and the fact that you two had the same name and the same face thrilled her. I wasn't aware that she sent out a letter to communicate with you. I'm pretty sure Zizina is the one who made the delivery," Samuel explains.

His words freeze me in my spot. "That's it, our missing puzzle piece," I exclaim, my voice filled with excitement. I shoot Samuel an accusing glare. "Why didn't you inform me about her earlier?

"You never inquired about it until now," he explains, attempting to justify his actions.

I can't help but shake my head in frustration at his response. There are moments when I adore this man, but there are also moments when I want to strangle him. Seriously?

"I can't believe you," I retort sharply, hastily gathering the scattered books strewn across the table. "Summon that witch to the castle. We need to speak with her."

I stride toward the bookshelf from where I took the books, and I put them back one by one. This medieval library is literally my version of paradise. I love books; they are a compilation of human knowledge.

"I don't think that's a good idea," Samuel interjects.

I pause in my task of returning the books to the shelf, pivoting to face him with a perplexed expression, my eyebrows furrowed in confusion.

"What do you mean it's not a good idea? She's the one who relayed the letter to me. She's our key to solving this case," I assert, my voice growing more impassioned as I try to make my point.

Samuel responds with an eye roll, his expression dismissive. "She's wild, eccentric, hardheaded, loud, and obnoxious."

I cringe at his unflattering description of her. "Okay, you don't personally like her. I understand that, but I'll be the one to deal with her, not you. So, get your ass out of my face and tell her that the Queen wants to talk to her in private," I dismissively gesture him away.

He rolls his eyes but eventually relents as he straightens and walks towards the door. I watch as Samuel begrudgingly leaves the library, muttering something under his breath.

I can't help but smile when he is already out of sight. It's only my second day, and I'm already making progress. Just a little more time, Lady Naya. I've got this. I'll uncover the mysteries surrounding your death.

Chapter 14

Naya

A smile spread across my face as I stand in awe in front of the wide and expansive garden of the palace. I inhale deeply and revel at the autumnal scent that fills the air while marvelling at the sight of the Asters and Chrysanthemums in full bloom. The vibrant colours of the trees and leaves surrounding this part of the castle are a sight to behold. The leaves had taken on a life of their own, bursting forth in an array of oranges, yellows, and reds, giving the trees a fiery appearance.

A faint thud resonates through the air with each step I take on the stepping stones that serve as the pathway winding through the garden, blending harmoniously with the gentle rustling of leaves stirred by the passing breeze and the pleasant melodies sung by the birds.

Samuel hasn't returned yet. I got bored in the library, so I decided to take a little stroll around the castle and familiarize myself with the place. I found myself in this beautiful garden filled with flowers of all kinds.

"This place is so beautiful, don't you think?"

I stiffen upon hearing that familiar voice behind me. My palms close into fists in irritation. This man surely knows how to ruin the mood. I roll my eyes in annoyance, contemplating leaving the place. This location is another paradise in my eyes, and I refuse to let a rapist tarnish my view of it simply because he decides to accompany me on my afternoon walk.

I am about to turn in the direction of the castle when I feel his hand catch my wrist to stop me from walking away.

"Leaving already, my Queen? Afraid of me?" He taunts.

I let out an impatient sigh and forced myself to look at him. This man is blessed with good looks. He has a perfect exterior. I guess it's normal for vampires. I haven't encountered anyone from this kingdom who lacks attractiveness. Most fiction books portray them as handsome and exquisite beings. I suppose even those of their kind who are criminally minded need to live up to the expectation.

I cannot stomach how he abused Lady Naya, and yet he can approach me without hesitation or guilt. It's as if he is confident that Lady Naya won't tell the King about what he has done.

"Leave me alone, Idris. I want to spend my afternoon peacefully. I've had enough encounters with you in one day," I hiss at him and pull my wrist from his grip.

But instead of letting me go, his hold only tightens on my wrist. That's when I notice the bracelet he's wearing. It has a blue opal stone on it, and the design is relatively similar to the ring I have.

"Too bad because I rather fancy spending the remainder of the day in your company," he sneers, his smirk twisting his lips, making me raise my gaze and meet his. "You know, just like the old days?"

A sinister glimmer gleams in his eyes, hinting at a malevolence lurking beneath his facade. If I were the real Naya, I'm pretty sure I would be shaking in fear by now. I can't believe this man is a Duke. How I wish I could just command the castle guards to behead him. I hate murder, but this demon makes me want to be a murderer.

"If you wish to keep your hand intact and attached to your wrist, I suggest you release your grip," I assert, my voice laced with a hint of warning. I make another attempt to pull my hand from his hold, slightly wincing when his hold only tightens to the point of pain. Despite my growing impatience, I refrain from losing my composure in his presence, recognizing that it would likely yield no good outcome.

"Scary," he mocks, his voice dripping with a malicious tone. "I've been wondering whether your fiery demeanour is genuine or merely a facade. Since your loyal dog is not around, it seems the perfect opportunity for me to uncover the truth."

An intense pounding echoes in my chest, a telltale sign of impending danger. Panic washes over me, realizing that I am not in a good position at the moment.

I scan the garden, desperately searching for anyone who can help me out of the situation, but for some unexpected reason, there is no single warrior in sight at the moment.

He drags me to an isolated part of the garden. I give all of my strength to struggle, but he is a vampire. He is much stronger than I am. I pull the dagger from my hips, but to my frustration, Idris is quick to take it away from my hand and throw it in the distance. I let out a series of curses.

"Fuck it, let go of me!" I scream, desperately attempting to pry his hand from my wrist.

But it's as if he doesn't hear my pleas. He pushes me onto a grassy patch of ground. The skin on my arms scrapes against the sharp pebbles from the harsh landing. Tall, fully bloomed flowers cover the place where he has brought me. Damn it, I need to do something, or else this will end up so bad for me.

"I thought being mated to the King would make you physically stronger. Why do you feel so much weaker now than you used to be?" A demonic grin spreads across his lips, and the glint of hunger and lust gleams in his eyes, sending a wave of revulsion through me, threatening to make me retch.

"I'm going to enjoy this. Just like how I used to enjoy using you." His grin widens as he closes the distance between us, sending chills down my spine.

I am afraid, but I am not going to give him the satisfaction of seeing that fear in my eyes. There's no way that my pride will allow me to act helpless and vulnerable in front of a demon like him. I refuse to cower in front of a soulless criminal.

His hand grabs the front of my gown and forcefully rends it in half, exposing my red lacy bra underneath. Fear immediately creeps through every fibre of my being as his gaze feast on my nakedness. I cross my hands over my chest to cover myself from his prying eyes.

Idris seizes both of my hands and firmly pins them at my sides. His eyes turn into a crimson hue, a signal that his beast is now awake. I struggle with all the strength I have, but deep down, I know it is useless.

"I can't say I hate the new you; the old you did nothing but cry. It's irritating. I think I prefer the feisty you much more," he remarks, his lips trailing towards my neck.

At that moment, the harsh reality of the situation crashes down upon me. I am about to be violated...

"No!" I thrash beneath him, but my efforts prove futile, a mere display of resistance.

I squeeze my eyes shut, determined to withhold my tears. I refuse to cry. Where is Samuel when I need him the most? I won't allow myself to become his victim!

Idris forcefully places both of my hands above my head, using one hand to hold them in place. Fear has fully consumed my whole system, and my mind can't even process the self-defence training I have learned in the police academy. I am scared shitless.

Tears well up at the corners of my eyes as I feel one of his hands reaching for the clasp of my brassiere.

Just when I thought everything was hopeless for me, I felt him being forcefully torn away from me. The events unfold in a blur, leaving me struggling to comprehend what just happened. I witness Idris sprawled on the ground while Atticus looms over him, delivering hard punches to his face.

I curl into myself, seeking solace in a corner, attempting to make myself as small as possible. My eyes remain fixed on the chaotic scene before me. A surge of both anger and relief courses through my veins, mingling with my overwhelming emotions. Tears cascade down my cheeks, but I try to stifle my sobs. I may be a fake, but the fear Idris has inflicted on me is beyond real.

"Atticus..." I call out, my voice trembling with a mixture of fear and desperation.

Tears persistently cascade down my cheeks, an unyielding stream. I have faced the most ruthless criminals that the human world could offer, yet none have instilled in me the same level of terror as Idris.

Atticus comes to a halt, his panting audible and heavy. His eyes, once a familiar hue, now blaze with intense, blood-red colour. This is the first time I've seen that kind of bloodlust in his eyes.

Unconsciously, I retreat further into the bushes, trying to make myself even smaller. Suddenly, the fear I felt from Idris vanishes and is replaced with fear towards the King. His appearance didn't change. The only thing that changed in him was those warm hazel eyes that I always adored. They now radiate an ominous, deep crimson hue.

He must have noticed that I am trembling in fear. His eyes soften while looking at me.

"My King, what a surprise," Idris interjects, a malevolent grin adorning his lips, capturing our attention. "I thought you were preoccupied with Harriet, so I took the liberty of entertaining the Queen in your absence—"

Before Idris can finish his sentence, Atticus unleashes a swift and powerful punch directly into his face. A palpable aura of darkness and menace envelops the King, his simmering anger radiating in waves that instinctively makes me want to flee, even though I know it is not directed towards me.

"Speak another word, and that will be your last," The King warns, gripping Idris tightly by the collar.

Yet, instead of shrinking in terror, Idris defiantly wipes the blood from his mouth and unleashes a chilling laughter that reverberates through the air. After a long moment, his laughter subsides, and his gaze locks with Atticus.

"Why are you so angry, Atticus? I'm quite certain you sensed it on your very first night together. She is not as innocent as you believe. I cannot fathom how a King would stoop so low as to choose a defective wench as his consort. She is a defective good, and no amount of mending could restore her worth." Idris sneers, his words dripping with venomous contempt.

Atticus chooses not to utter a single word in response. Instead, he raises his hand, allowing me a glimpse of the menacing silhouette formed by his razor-sharp claws before he drives them mercilessly into Idris's chest.

My hands instinctively clasp together, pressing against my mouth in a desperate attempt to stifle the combined screams of terror and disbelief. With trembling intensity, I tightly shut my eyes, unable to witness the brutal scene unfolding before me. I hear the cacophony of flesh being crushed and a choking sound similar to those of a dying person.

"The only defective good here is you. You know I am not the kind to threaten people, Idris," I hear Atticus say.

I cautiously open my eyes and find the King steadily advancing towards me. Atticus's eyes have returned to their usual hue, yet the copious amount of blood that coats and drips from his hand is enough to make me instinctively cower in fear.

My gaze shifts to the lifeless form of Idris sprawled on the ground. A profound wound marks his chest, where his heart once resided. An ample amount of blood is flowing continuously from his dead body, and to my horror, I can't seem to remove my eyes from him.

"He can no longer harm you," the King reassures me, now standing directly in front of me.

He removes his outer coat and gently drapes it around me, fastening it at my chest with a pin adorned with his distinctive crest.

"You... you killed him," I squeak.

My strength is depreciating too quickly, and for the first time in my life, I feel too weak to stand up. I am not Naya, but Idris's words are enough to carve a deep wound in my heart. Tears flood my eyes once again. I never thought that there were insults that would make me feel vulnerable and weak. I'm not defective, nor is the real Naya. But I don't want Atticus to think less of me.

"Death serves as the most fitting punishment for his insolence," the King remarks, his tone devoid of emotion, his words delivered with chilling finality.

I remain silent, unsure of how to respond. Atticus skillfully slides his left arm beneath my thigh and the other around my back, effortlessly lifting me from the ground as if my weight holds no significance. With resolute steps, he carries me back towards the castle, leaving behind the lifeless body of Idris. Compelled by a morbid curiosity, I can't help but turn my head to observe his blood-soaked corpse. Similar to what happened with Lady Naya, Idris's body succumbs to a transformative fate, dissolving into a pile of ashes. The bracelet he wore rests motionless atop on one of the stepping stones.

Idris is dead.

Conflicting emotions swirl within me, torn between relief and apprehension. I divert my gaze from his remains and nestle against the King's chest, fearing how this unexpected death will affect my investigation and the kingdom.

CHAPTER 15

Naya

Atticus gently places me on the bed, and I continue to sob quietly, my body still trembling with the aftermath of the harrowing experience. I clench my palm tightly into a fist, a swirling mix of disappointment and anger surging through me, directed inwardly at my own lack of caution.

Glancing down at my wrist, I'm confronted by the vivid red marks and bruises left behind by Idris when he forcefully dragged me earlier. They serve as a painful reminder of the overwhelming helplessness I experienced at that moment.

Noticing my distress, Atticus speaks softly. "I'll prepare a warm bath for you. Stay here, alright?" His gentle touch caresses the side of my cheek, offering solace and comfort in its tender warmth.

I nod in response, too depleted to muster a coherent reply to his question. It feels as though every ounce of strength has been drained from me, leaving me emotionally, mentally, and physically spent.

The King lets out a sigh of defeat upon seeing my reaction. I can tell that what he sees right now is the opposite of the confident and capable woman he met just two days ago. Without a word, he walks towards the bathroom, leaving me to grapple with my thoughts in solitude.

I hug myself tightly, burying my face in my knees. The memories of what just happened flood my mind, and I can't help but wonder what would have happened if Atticus hadn't arrived on time. I can still feel my whole body trembling with fear. That son of a bitch almost got me, and I hate that I'm too weak to fight back.

I take a few deep breaths, allowing myself a moment to gather both my composure and my thoughts. Despite feeling a slight tremor within, I recognize the importance of maintaining control over my own emotions.

After a few minutes of wallowing in the corner, my racing heart gradually begins to steady its pace. I wipe away the remnants of tears from my cheeks, steeling myself for the task at hand. I am Naya, the fearless detective. I didn't earn the title 'Sherlock Holmes of the 21st century' for nothing. I am not a broken woman. I am here to solve the mystery behind Lady Naya's death, not to become the next victim in the clutches of those who have harmed her.

I make my way toward the bathroom and give two firm knocks on the door, patiently awaiting the King's response. The door swings open, and my glassy blue eyes meet with his warm hazel ones.

I can see so much compassion in his eyes as he looks at me with sadness in them. My attention is drawn to his hand, but the traces of blood that once stained it have vanished. Atticus must have noticed my reaction that he glanced at the hand that he used to kill Idris.

"I'm sorry you have to see that. But even if I don't do it, he will still face public execution," he explains in a soothing tone, emphasizing the inevitability of justice.

His calm demeanour makes me realize that the incident is nothing out of the ordinary in this world. It is a realm where vampires adhere to medieval laws, and public executions are an accepted part of life. Although Idris deserves to pay for his sins, I can't shake off the guilt I feel for his death. The violence is barbaric, but it seems to be the norm here.

"I understand. It's okay. I'm still in a state of shock, but I'll be okay. I want to clean myself," I respond and avert my gaze from him.

Atticus nods in understanding and steps aside to give me space to walk inside the bathroom. As I step inside, a gentle, sweet floral fragrance envelops my senses, coaxing my tense nerves into a state of serenity. Gradually, a sense of tranquillity washes over me. I find solace in the knowledge that my beloved genuinely cares for my well-being.

"If you need anything, just call me, alright?" he instructs before closing the bathroom door, granting me the privacy I need.

I gently remove the gown, allowing it to gracefully cascade onto the bathroom floor. Then, with a renewed sense of purpose, I approach the bath brimming with an array of aromatic flowers. Despite the recent turmoil, I find myself unable to suppress a smile upon witnessing the King's meticulous preparation. Atticus's care and concern for Lady Naya are evident. Despite having just discovered the extent of the abuse she suffered, there is no trace of pity or disgust in his eyes.

I step inside the tub and let the warm water cleanse all the dirt and bloodstains from my skin. If only this water could also wash away the memories. I settle inside the tub and let the warm water envelop my whole body.

Everything around me gradually fades into a hazy blur, not only due to the wisps of steam emanating from the warm bath but also because exhaustion begins to weigh heavily upon me. My entire body throbs with fatigue, and my mind yearns for rest, even if only for a fleeting moment. Unbeknownst to me, the tranquil embrace of sleep envelops my consciousness, plunging me into a calming abyss.

With a jolt, my eyes snap open, abruptly awakened by a resounding bang that echoes from beyond the confines of the bathroom. My forehead creases in confusion. I stand up from the bathtub and look around me. A sigh of relief escapes my lips as I realize I am alone in the bathroom. However, that fleeting sense of solace quickly transforms into concern when a cacophony of crashing sounds reverberates from outside, as though something has been shattered.

Without hesitation, I swiftly exit the water, reaching for the nearby rack where a white robe awaits. From the sound of it, it looks like there is a small commotion in our room.

Once I secure the ribbon of the robe, my footsteps carry me towards the door. I twist the doorknob and swing the door open, only for my heart to leap into my throat at the sight that greets me. Atticus stands in the middle of the room, his grip firm around Samuel's neck, a deep crimson hue engulfing his eyes, emanating a murderous aura across the room.

Samuel looks down to show his submission to the King, but I can see the blood dripping from the side of his lips. His left cheek is also visibly swollen. Both men turn their eyes on me as I step out of the bathroom.

"Atticus, let go of him," I command firmly, my voice carrying a tone of authority.

The King's grip on Samuel tightens for a moment before he lets out a deep breath, trying to control his anger. But despite his efforts, it is clear that he is seething with rage.

Finally relenting, Atticus abruptly releases his hold on Samuel, flinging him to the far side of the room. Samuel swiftly regains his composure, but his gaze remains fixed upon the floor, avoiding direct eye contact with me. I can't help but raise my eyebrows at his actions. What is their issue now?

"Forgive me, my Queen. I should not have left you unguarded and unprotected," he speaks with a tinge of guilt and regrets lacing his tone.

"No, it is not your fault. I'm the one who asked you to fetch someone for me," I respond and walk towards the walk-in closet to get something to wear.

"Well, since my beloved seems too merciful to administer your punishment, perhaps I should be the one to decide your fate instead," Atticus retorts, causing me to pause in my tracks and turn towards him.

"What do you mean?" I frown.

Atticus remains silent, his gaze fixed upon Samuel, who can't even raise his head to meet his King's eyes.

"You have demonstrated your incompetence and proven yourself unworthy of your position. For that, I am relieving you as the Queen's butler. Leave!" The King's voice booms across the, eliciting a startled expression from me as my eyes widen in surprise.

"No!" I exclaim, panic gripping my voice, causing both men to pivot their heads in my direction. I march towards Atticus in a purposeful stride. I can't allow him to remove Samuel from his post. I can't have any other butler other than him. We are in this together. He is the only person who can help me solve Lady Naya's case.

"He left you alone, unguarded, and open to any attacks. If I didn't arrive on time—."

I raise my left hand in the air to make him stop. The bath and the nap I have in the bathroom seem enough to make me forget about the incident back in the garden a while ago. I am calmer and more composed now. I don't want anyone to keep reminding me of it.

I shift my gaze towards Samuel's direction and offer an apologetic smile.

"Samuel, could you please give us some privacy for a moment? I need to have a private conversation with my husband," I request, the tone of my voice gentle yet firm.

Samuel nods in compliance, his eyes remaining glued on the floor as if he is hesitant to meet my gaze. What happened today will surely remind him of what happened to Lady Naya, the woman he failed to protect. The weight of his guilt is palpable in the air, making me regret the words I said to him yesterday after learning the extent of the abuse Lady Naya had suffered.

Once the door closes, I pivot to face my beloved and let out a deep sigh to ease the overflowing tension inside the room. My gaze falls upon the shattered remnants of a vase, a silent testament to the turbulence that has unfolded.

Damn, my beloved certainly has a penchant for unleashing violence.

"Samuel has been my butler since I was a child. He is not merely a servant but also my closest confidant and guardian," I begin, emphasizing the inherent truth of Lady Naya's connection to her butler.

"Guardian? Idris has committed an unforgivable act against you, yet that man whom you refer to as a guardian didn't even dare to wield a sword to protect you. He has demonstrated his incompetence in this role, and as such, I am relieving him of his duties!" His voice remains steady, devoid of raised tones, yet the unwavering resolve in his words resonates with finality.

I let out a harsh exhale and locked my gaze on my husband. "Samuel gave his best to protect me. I am a noble, yet I am not able to do anything to save myself. How could I expect a butler to single-handedly rescue me from the clutches of a Duke? Samuel protected me in the best way he knew how..." My words trail off as a familiar warmth well up at the corners of my eyes. Though I did not endure the abuse firsthand, I can empathize with the overwhelming helplessness Lady Naya must have experienced. It makes me think of the possibility that she committed suicide to escape all of this. "You cannot dismiss him. I know that what he did was not enough to save me, but he did everything within his capabilities. At that time, that was the help that I needed the most to survive."

Tears cascade down my cheeks, one after another. I avert my gaze from Atticus, not wanting to let him see me in my weakest moment. Sensing my distress, my beloved emits a sigh and draws me closer, enfolding me in the shelter of his embrace.

"I'm so sorry, Naya. I didn't mean to shout at you. I regret not being there to protect you when you needed me most," he offers solace, his words laced with remorse.

I wipe away my tears and lift my eyes to meet his gaze.

"No, please don't blame yourself for what transpired.

Cruel things happened, but it's all over now. I have been shattered into countless fragments, and it falls upon me to gather those fragments and piece myself back together. I refuse to remain broken indefinitely, Atticus." I declare with unwavering determination lacing my voice.

Atticus offers me a compassionate smile and tenderly runs his fingers through my hair.

"It seems that, by chance, I have chosen the strongest woman in the entire kingdom to be my queen," he remarks, eliciting a smile from me. "I've always been aware of the fiery spirit that resides within you despite your shy and timid personality."

"And should I perceive that as a flaw?" I retort, arching my eyebrow playfully.

Atticus chuckles softly in response to my question.

"No, it's one of the aspects I adore most about you," he responds as he captures my lips.

I swiftly reciprocate, savouring the mingling of our tongues. I close my eyes and encircle my arms around his neck to pull him closer to me.

The effect of his kiss on me never changes. In fact, if Atticus wishes for us to take this to bed, I doubt I would possess the willpower to resist. His kiss resembles a forbidden wine— It's sweet and toxic, yet I find myself unable to satiate my craving for it. However, just as I am on the verge of surrendering to the heat of passion between us, he withdraws, breaking our connection.

I emit a disappointed groan and reluctantly open my eyes to meet his deep, bloody ones. There's a contented smile on his lips, but his gaze is sending me a clear message. He wants this as much as I do.

However, he quickly dispels any notion of getting intimate, and a thoughtful expression replaces his smile.

"I don't want us to go further because I know you're not ready for it yet. I've been meaning to talk to you about this after our first night together, but I never really got the chance. I don't want you to think that I'm suspicious of your actions. I want you to feel that I have trust in you, not only because you are the Queen of my kingdom, but because you are my other half."

My eyebrows knit together in confusion, and my mind races with possibilities of what Atticus could be implying. Suddenly, my body tenses and my heart races at an accelerated pace. Despite my efforts to remain calm, my voice shakes slightly as I ask, "What is that supposed to mean?"

Atticus' eyes narrow into slits, and his gaze intensifies, making me feel uneasy. Our gazes lock, and he speaks, each word feeling like a hammer blow to my already-racing heart. "Our first night together, nothing really happened between us that time, right?" he speculates.

I swallow hard. My throat suddenly feels dry and constricted. I'm dead. I'm so, so dead.

CHAPTER 16

Naya

I take a step back as fear and confusion start to consume me from within while Atticus' eyes remain on me. My mind goes blank, leaving me at a loss for words.

I run my fingers through my hair unconsciously as I try to ease the tension that envelops me. Atticus is a king in a powerful kingdom full of vampires; I should have known better than to think I could easily deceive him.

"I- it's just that... it's just that..." I can't help but stammer, and I feel like a child caught in the act.

"I'm sorry..." I finally manage to say and avert my gaze. That apology probably means nothing to the King, and this could be the end of this pretend game I am playing.

"It's okay, Naya. You don't have to be afraid of me," He reassures me upon seeing the panic in my eyes.

Atticus reaches out a hand, but I flinch away, unable to control my reaction. I retreat a step, my heart racing in anxiety despite his attempt to appear comforting. I can't shake the fear that grips me. He knew that we had poisoned him. Oh, God, I'm busted.

Sensing my distress, Atticus speaks once more, "Idris has hurt you in ways that I cannot even fathom. I understand if you are not prepared to consummate our marriage on our wedding night."

"What?" I ask as I blink in confusion, not understanding what he means by those words.

Atticus's kind eyes meet mine, and he repeats softly, "You don't have to be afraid of me, Naya. And you don't have to do anything you're not ready for. We can take things at your pace. If you don't want to consummate the wedding yet, I'm willing to wait."

I stare at the King as I try to process his words, and then it sinks into me. Relief washes over my face when I finally realize what Atticus is trying to point out. "I mean... I mean, yes! Yes, of course," I let out a sigh and smiled weakly. "Thank you for being so patient with me."

I bite my inner lip at my own lie. I feel terrible for using Lady Naya's agony to get out of this, but Atticus is the one who came to that conclusion. It's my only way out without giving away my disguise.

The King nods in understanding despite my strange reaction. Somehow, I feel guilty for lying to my beloved, but I have no choice. It's a good thing that reading minds is not a natural ability for vampires. If the rules in fiction books are valid, I'm definitely dead.

"What kind of husband would I be if I were to remind you of those dreadful memories?" He closes our distance and reaches for my chin, pushing it a bit to lock my gaze with his. "I know that life has been particularly unfair to you before I entered the picture, my Queen. Rest assured that I am not going to force you into anything that you're not ready for."

I stare into his eyes and feel myself starting to fall deeper and deeper into the ravine I created, a trap that I have no idea if I can still get out of.

"Forgive me, Atticus," I murmur, then look down. "Trust me, I don't want to lie to you either. However, things aren't as easy as they seem. Thank you for understanding me." I lean into his chest, pressing myself against him, feeling his body close to mine.

I feel his hand brushing my back to ease me. I love that even though he can see through my wall, he chooses to ignore it and comfort me instead.

"You're forgiven, my beautiful Queen. Although next time, I'd prefer you to tell me that you're not ready for 'it' rather than serving me a poisoned wine," he says, causing me to chuckle a bit.

I distance myself from him and wipe my tears to dry my cheeks.

"I promise to keep that in mind, my King," I vow.

A charming smile forms on his lips, making me want to tiptoe and capture his lips. To be honest, I am starting to feel alarmed about what I am feeling for him, but I am choosing to ignore the red sign. It is a dangerous game I am playing here, but I have no choice anyway. I need to finish this, or else all of my previous efforts will come to waste.

"Great," he says, his voice firm but gentle. "So, from now on, let's have no more lies between us. I want you to be completely open with me, to tell me everything that's on your mind, whether it's fears, worries, or happiness. Be vocal. If it's a no, it's a no, and if it's a yes, it's a yes." His hopeful smile and unwavering gaze convey his sincerity.

For a moment, I'm rooted to the spot, struck by the weight of his words. No more lies? I can't help but feel a pang of guilt and apprehension. This entire relationship is built on lies and deception. How can I possibly comply with such a demand? Why do I have this nagging sense that every time I open my mouth, I'm only digging my grave deeper and deeper?

I force a smile and nod at him.

"No more lies, I promise," I agree and tiptoe to seal it with a kiss.

My hands close into fists as he returns my kisses wholeheartedly. I can't help but hate myself more as I enjoy the heat and passion of the kiss we're sharing.

Once all of this is over, every memory I have with the King will be the one to destroy me. The moment I solve this case, I will be broken beyond repair.

Am I stupid?

Why do I need to give my all just to solve the mystery behind her death? Why am I investing my life, heart, and soul in a woman who isn't even my friend? I'm aware that I'm being foolish, but there's no way I can back out now.

***

"I shouldn't have left you," Samuel sighs while pacing in front of me.

I'm sitting in front of the vanity mirror, watching my butler go back and forth in the room like a nervous duck. Atticus had left us in the royal chamber to attend something important a moment ago. However, before he walked out of the door, he gave a strict instruction to Samuel not to let me out of his sight. Atticus had told me that since he had killed the Duke of Caceres, he needed to call a meeting to address the issue.

The Kingdom of Puer Lunae is divided into three major towns, which are Caceres, Vago, and Teles. Each town has a duke, equivalent to a town mayor in the human world. Atticus said that he needed to inform the Ministers and the two other Dukes about what happened. He also needs to appoint a new duke to Caceres. Hopefully, the next duke is not related to Idris.

"I asked you to summon someone for me. Stop acting like a constipated parrot and sit your ass down," I snap at him. Seriously, this man is making me dizzy. "Where is Zizina anyway?"

"You almost died, Naya. If Idris manages to know that you are a fraud, he could have framed you as the one who killed Lady Naya," Samuel insists, skipping my question.

"You need to stop overthinking. You are way too paranoid, Samuel. Idris is dead. We lost a possible suspect, but it's not that bad. Idris's death bought me more time," I inform him.

That gets his attention. He stops pacing and looks at me with a curious expression on his face. "What do you mean?"

I let out a knowing grin. I had initially thought that what happened was a disadvantage for us, but it turned out to be in our favour. It gave us more time, time that I really needed to solve this case.

"Well, the thing is, the King knows about the poisoned wine we pulled off on our wedding night. But he thinks that I did it because of what Idris had done to me. He promises not to force me to do something that I am not ready for," I say, a victory smirk painted on my lips.

I expected Samuel to be happy with my news, but he winced. I honestly understand his reaction. I'm not that familiar with all the laws in this kingdom yet, but I am pretty sure that poisoning the King is punishable by death. I guess I'm pretty lucky that the King is deeply in love with Naya, or else it wouldn't end well for us.

"He knew that the wine was poisoned, but he still drank it for you?" Sam shakes his head in disbelief. "Crazy things we do for love."

I roll my eyes in irritation at his comment.

"Yeah, he's really in love with Lady Naya." Not with the fraud Naya.

A bitter smile forms on my lips at my own statement. A painful ache tightens around my heart, almost as if a dagger is piercing through it. I take a deep breath to collect myself. I need to stop feeling this way towards the King. Whatever it is that I feel for him, I need to kill it, or else it will be the one to destroy me in the end.

"Well, come to think of it. If he is really in love with Lady Naya, why can't he differentiate you two? I mean, you both have the same face, but even I can tell that you are way different from each other. The way you talk with confidence and authority. You are the exact opposite of each other, but the King can't tell who is who."

A heavy sigh escapes my chest at his statement, and I stare fresco at the ceiling of the room. I know that Atticus can sense that there is something odd about me. I can feel his suspicion, but he keeps disregarding it. A sad smile forms on my lips. The King doesn't need to say anything for me to understand why he is not confronting me about it.

"It's not that he can't differentiate me from the real Naya. You said it yourself, Samuel; you wish you didn't know that Lady Naya is dead. It's just that sometimes we choose to be comforted with a lie rather than face the dreadful truth." My eyes turn to the open window not far from my seat, where I can see the sun now starting to set on the horizon, giving the sky a slightly golden-orange hue. "Sometimes our unconscious knows that the answer to our question will destroy us. That's why instead of confrontation, we accept what someone is offering to us. It's easier that way, less painful."

Samuel lets out a harsh exhale and nods gently. He stands up from his seat and makes his way toward the open window. If anyone here can understand Atticus's situation, it is him.

Can I really blame Atticus for allowing himself to be blinded by a lie? He lost his true love, the woman he loved the most. Accepting that she is now gone is not going to be easy.

Once the King learns about Naya's death, he will be devastated, and that devastation will turn into anger. The worst part is I know he'll hate me. His anger will be solely directed at me, and just thinking about it is more than enough to break my heart into smaller pieces.

CHAPTER 17

Naya

"I'm pretty sure that Idris' family will demand justice and an explanation for his death," Celestine says while sitting beside me.

I let out a sigh while staring at the blade in my hand.

What had happened yesterday had sparked a lot of chaos throughout the Kingdom. Celestine had offered to teach me a little bit of self-defence. I had trained for five years in the police academy and more than five years in the field, yet all of it was not enough to prepare me for this world.

We had been training for hours until I decided to raise the white flag due to exhaustion. Now we are resting at the root of an old willow tree right in the backyard of the palace. I can see the forest in the distance as the soft wind caresses my sweaty skin.

"Is the King in trouble?" I ask while putting the blade back in the sheath.

I know that the Kingdom is in chaos even though Atticus is not really giving me any information about it. Lady Naya mentioned it in the letter I got from the manor. The Kingdom is meant to fall. She summoned me here not only to solve the mystery of her death but also to help Atticus.

The problem is Idris is now dead. I'm not sure how close he was to Caceres' people, but what I'm sure of is that even the worst government leader has loyal followers who believe them. The last thing that I want to happen is for Idris's death to spark a rebellion.

Remembering the events from yesterday, I realize that Idris didn't say anything that linked him to Naya's death, so I can be at least eighty percent sure that he had nothing to do with it. He was not the killer.

"He is the King. He might need to explain why he acted on his anger; however, no one can really blame him. You are his beloved. It is his duty to protect you. He did what he needed to do to keep you safe," Celestine replies as she drinks the ale from her leather flask. "This is just between us, but I actually hate that guy. My instinct tells me that he is the kind of guy who won't do anything good, but nobody seems to notice that."

I can't help but smile at her observation.

"Idris always has this gentle smile that can easily fool everyone. My blood boils every time I remember what he has done to me. I'm honestly relieved that he is dead now," I agree.

Celestine turns her eyes to me and nods. I think Celestine is the type of person who can see behind other people's masks. She's observant.

My smile slowly fades at the thought of it. Does this mean there's a chance she will be able to see beyond the mask that I am wearing too? I wince internally at my own thought. I hope not. The last person I want to be added to my long list of enemies is her. I genuinely like her.

"That is true. Well, at least he's gone now." Celestine shrugs and then sighs. "He is supposed to accompany you and the King to Kaedal tomorrow morning, but Niall will take his place now that he is dead."

My forehead creases as I turn to look at her. Kaedal? Now that doesn't sound familiar. Is that another town?

"Kaedal? For what reason?" I ask with a questioning look on my face, but careful not to hint that I don't have a single idea where the place she is talking about is.

"Yes. Instead of Idris, the Minister of Peace and Treaty will be accompanying you on your journey. Now that you are the Queen, it is important for you to meet the leaders of neighbouring Kingdoms," she explains.

I look at Celestine with disbelief. What the heck? I've been so busy solving Naya's murder case that I have completely forgotten about my responsibilities to the Kingdom. Of course, I am the Queen now. I have royal duties.

"Are you okay?" Celestine asks in a concerned tone when she notices that I am spacing out.

"I'm fine, just a bit terrified, I guess," I admit as I take a breath to let go of the tension that suddenly encloses me.

Celestine lets out a soft laugh upon seeing my agony.

This is scary. What am I supposed to expect for tomorrow? I need to prepare for it. I stand up from the root of the tree and face her. "Forgive me, but I am leaving. I need to talk to Samuel about this," I say, ready to depart. "Thank you for informing me about it."

Celestine nods at me and offers me an understanding smile.

I turn my back on her to make my way back to the palace. I need to ask Samuel about this.

I am about to enter the front door of the palace when I cross paths with the King, who seems to be on his way out. I give him a sweet smile, and he smiles back at me with admiration in his eyes. I love how it makes me feel like I am the most beautiful woman he has ever met despite the fact that I probably look more like a warrior right now than a Queen with my all-black fitted suit.

"Hello, my Queen," he greets me. "How was your training? I hope Celestine was not too hard on you."

I cross the small distance between us to plant a kiss on the side of his cheek. I could get used to these sweet gestures. In fact, there are times when I wish we could be like this forever, acting so in love with each other.

"Celestine is a great mentor," I answer while surveying the two men he is with.

One of them is an old man, and the other looks the same age as me. I make sure to keep my smile intact while looking at them, not wanting to appear suspicious, just in case they know Lady Naya personally.

"Good morning," I greet the two men who give me nothing but a stoic look, making me want to cock my eyebrow if I hadn't caught myself in time.

"Oh, of course," Atticus chimes in. "Where are my manners? Anyway, I want you to meet the two other ministers of our Kingdom. This is Remus, the Minister of Trade and Finance," Atticus says and motions to the much older man.

The old man bows to show his respect. His face is stoic and formal. He doesn't even bother to smile back at me. It gives me the impression that he is the kind of person you cannot joke around with. It is going to be hard for me to identify if he is an enemy or an ally.

"And this is Niall, the Minister of Peace and Treaty," the King says, referring to the younger one.

The man presses his right hand on his abdomen to give his courtesy. I cannot help but frown while observing him. This was the first time I saw him, but for some reason, my intuition was giving me a red flag.

That is when my eyes landed on the ring he was wearing, and for some reason, other than the gem, the design of it was fairly similar to the ring Lady Naya gave to me. I frown.

"That ring looks beautiful," I say as I offer him a friendly and innocent smile.

Niall raises his eyes to meet my gaze. A knowing smile forms on his lips as he straightens, but I didn't miss how his eyes squint a bit at my question.

"A dear friend of mine gave it to me," he replies, and that piques my interest.

"Really? May I know the name of the friend you are talking about?" I ask again while eyeing him with curiosity. I highly doubt that he will give me a name, but I try anyway to play a little bit of a mind game with him.

Niall's smile remains on his lips, but the irritation in his eyes is unmistakable. It seems to me that the man doesn't like to be questioned. My smile widens while looking at him. The ring he is wearing simply means that Lady Naya's death has something to do with politics. This is because two people in high positions are likely to be involved in it.

"You seem so interested in that ring, Naya," Atticus's voice makes me turn my attention back to him.

"Oh," I smile sweetly to prevent myself from wincing. I become too occupied with my discovery that I almost forget that I'm still with my husband. "Nothing, Atticus." I shrug. "I'm just curious, that's all."

The King frowns a bit, probably sensing the oddness in my act. I decide to change the subject and shift our conversation away from me and my questionable actions.

"Anyway, I heard from Celestine that we're going to pay a visit to our neighbouring Kingdom. I'm rushing back to the royal chamber to prepare for it. You should have informed me about it sooner." I whine, hoping to sway the conversation in a different direction.

If we were to visit another kingdom, he should have notified me about it. I'm not so fond of surprises, especially if that surprise includes a task that has something to do with the Kingdom's welfare. I need to come prepared, or else I might end up accidentally spilling my secrets.

The curiosity in the King's eyes is suddenly replaced with an apologetic look. The guilt written on his face tells me that he didn't really plan to hide it from me.

"Yeah, about that. My morning became so busy that I forgot to inform you about it," He explains.

I nod in understanding.

After what happened yesterday, I'm pretty sure Atticus has many things to settle before the end of this day. I guess dealing with the sudden death of his duke was not in his plan for today. Now he needs to find a replacement for Idris. I don't know who he's going to assign to Caceres, but I hope it is someone trustworthy.

"I understand, Atticus. It looks to me like you have something important to attend. I won't take up too much of your time," I say, bowing my head to show my respect and stepping aside.

"Yeah, we are actually on our way to a meeting to attend today," he responds.

With a tender expression, Atticus leans down towards me and places a soft kiss on my forehead. The warmth of his lips lingers on my skin, and I feel a surge of affection for him. He nods to me before turning on his heel and striding purposefully towards the direction of the armoury with the two men following him from behind.

I lift my gaze and watch as they exit the castle grounds, their figures growing smaller and smaller in the distance. My eyes are drawn to the man with the platinum ring with emerald stone in it. I smirk. I think I am starting to see the pattern now.

I turn away from them and make my way towards the royal chamber. The marble floors gleam under my feet, the sound of my footsteps echoing through the empty halls. I'm pretty sure Samuel will be very interested in the new information I just obtained.

"My Queen, I've been searching for you around the castle,"

My eyes automatically shift towards Minna, who seems to have appeared out of nowhere. My forehead creases in confusion upon noticing the worry painted on her face.

"Is there a problem?" I ask.

Minna looks at me with hesitation written in her eyes.

"Your mother wants to talk to you privately before she leaves the castle today," she murmurs and looks down at the floor, avoiding my gaze.

My body stiffens. My mother? We haven't had a chance to talk since my short encounter with her in the dining hall. Today was the day she was set to leave the castle to go back to the mansion. She doesn't really care much about her daughter. She didn't even bother paying me a visit after the news of Idris attempting to rape me erupted.

"Yeah, sure, not a problem. Where is she?" I question.

"Follow me, My Queen." Minna turns on her heel, her long skirts rustling as she leads the way towards one of the guest rooms. With a flick of her wrist, she opens the door and gestures for me to enter, her face full of worry.

I step inside the room and take a deep breath, trying to steady my nerves. The air is thick with the scent of lavender, and the curtains flutter softly in the breeze. In the centre of the room, my mother sits in front of a small table, a crystal goblet of ruby wine in her hand. Her eyes are fixed on the view outside the window with a distant expression on her face.

"Minna said you wanted to talk to me," I say to get her attention.

Elizabeth turns in my direction. This is the first time I get a chance to observe her more closely. There's no denying that she is indeed Lady Naya's mother. Looking at her makes me think that she's me, just older. She aged well. Her beauty didn't even depreciate with time. I guess it has something to do with the fact that she is a vampire.

"Minna?" I can hear the mockery in her tone of voice as she speaks. "First, you allowed Idris to be killed by the King, and now you are addressing a lowly servant by her name."

She lets out a mocking laugh while shaking her head in disbelief. My eyes narrow in disgust. The fact that she cares more about Idris makes my blood boil in complete anger. No wonder even Samuel can't do anything to save Lady Naya. What kind of mother would simply ignore the fact that her daughter is being taken advantage of by someone?

"Idris tried to rape me!" I hiss in controlled anger.

"He is your ex-fiancé. You are his betrothed. I can understand his action because the woman he thought would be his was taken unexpectedly by the King," she says without any emotion written on her face as she puts the glass she's holding on the table. "We lost one of our allies, but it seems to me that you have the King in your hand."

She walks towards me and caresses my cheek. I, on the other hand, am lost for words. She understands Idris's action? This woman sure is something.

"Do your thing as a Queen for now. When the time comes that I will need your influence as a Queen, I will be sending you a message. Don't fail me, my dearest daughter. The success of our family lies in your hands." She says as she lets go of me and takes a step backwards.

She walks towards the door and instructs the waiting servant to bring her things outside. I am left inside that room unmoving. Both of my palms close into tight fists as I try my best not to lose my calm.

CHAPTER 18

Naya

The following day came faster than I expected. Yesterday, as I packed the things I needed to bring to Kaedal, Samuel and I talked about how the ring Lady Naya left me is connected to her death. The bracelet Idris is wearing and the ring that Niall has are very similar to the ring I possess. A part of me is telling me that it's not just a coincidence.

We came to the conclusion that the ring is a symbol of an alliance, probably a brotherhood or something. Now my question is, if it is really a brotherhood, what is their group's relation to Naya's death? If Idris is a part of it, then there's a big chance that Naya was exposed to that brotherhood.

My brows furrow as I stare at the open window of the carriage we are in. I initially thought that I was only hunting a single murderer. However, if that ring is a symbol of being part of a group, then there is a big chance that the person behind the murder is not just one person but a group of people.

The final letter Lady Naya sent to me says something about the Kingdom's downfall. If you think about it, it takes more than one person to make a kingdom fall.

I let out a sigh to release the tension in my chest. As time goes by, this case is getting more and more complicated. If my conclusion is correct, that means I am waging war here, which is not part of my job description as a detective.

"You seem so silent, my Queen. Is there something that's bothering you?" Atticus asks, making me turn to look at him.

I shake my head, then lean on his chest and listen to the soft beating of his heart. Weirdly, I can hear his heart beating steadily. I thought vampires were dead creatures. They weren't supposed to have a heartbeat.

Those vampire fiction books I read back in the human world were all wrong. They contained too much unnecessary information. However, that's probably the reason why they are called 'fiction'.

"I'm just thinking about what kind of person the king of Kaedal is," I reply, and I feel like I am really starting to get used to lying to my husband.

Atticus reaches for my chin, pushing it upward for our eyes to meet. His beautiful hazel eyes linger on my face as if he wants to read what I am thinking. We have been doing this husband and wife roleplay for less than a week now, yet I am still not immune to this man's charms. He never fails to give me those mini goosebumps whenever he looks at me like that.

He gives me an assuring smile and leans down to plant a soft kiss on my open shoulder. His fangs graze my skin, but he doesn't break it. For a vampire, he's been so patient and gentle with me. And I can't help but feel guilty for denying him. However, the thought of being bitten fills me with fear. I can't have him bite me. That would lead to my life ending in blood.

"I planned on informing you about this trip two days ago. I asked one of the castle guards where you were, and they told me that you were in the garden. I was so enthusiastic while looking for you because I wanted to surprise you. But you know exactly how it ended." He explains.

His expression immediately darkens as his palm closes into a fist upon remembering the incident that occurred two days ago. I reach out to hold his hand to calm him down. I should be thankful for this trip, then. If it were not for this journey, my husband wouldn't have looked for me, and only heaven knows what could have happened.

He pulls me close to him and buries his face in my neck. We are the only passengers in the carriage. That's why it isn't awkward to be sweet to him. Our entourage consists of five royal carriages and six horsemen who are guarding us from the outside. One of the carriages contains our belongings. The other has four servants to accompany us, including Samuel. A carriage for the Minister, and the last one includes gifts for the royalty of Kaedal.

"It's fine, Atticus. I'm glad that you looked for me that day, and thank you for accepting me despite how—." I swallow hard. I can't even say the word for it. "How broken I am." I finish.

I can't help feeling jealous of the real Naya even though she's already dead. Atticus is willing to drink poisoned wine for her, kill for her, and accept her wholeheartedly. I hate to admit it, but I can't help but wish to heaven that I were her. I want to be able to fall in love with the King so deeply without feeling guilty or afraid. I want to fall in love with him without all of these what-ifs and buts.

Is that even possible for us? Or is it too much for me to ask?

"You're not broken. You're the strongest woman I've ever met, Naya. You're not a victim. You're my survivor, my little warrior," he whispers near my ear.

I can't help but smile as I look up at him. I see nothing but pure admiration in his eyes. Back in the human world, I'm not so fond of being in a relationship. I've been in a few relationships before, but none of my past relationships can equate to how Atticus makes me feel.

Because of my dangerous job, I tend to take charge of my relationships. I'm a woman, but I'm so used to acting independently every time. However, with Atticus, I can be strong and weak at the same time, and that's completely okay because he doesn't mind it when I rely so much on him or act all independently. He balances me out, and I think it's rare to find a man who allows you to fly when you want to and protect you when you need him to.

"You are so perfect, do you know that?" I can't help but compliment him.

His lips form a lopsided grin at my comment, and there goes my heart again, fangirling at him as if he is the most handsome man to have ever existed.

"Is that supposed to be a bad thing?" he asks.

I roll my eyes at him. This man sure knows how to use his charms on me. Now that I think about it, if Lady Naya is Idris's fiancé, I wonder how she met the King. Did she fall in love with him the way I am slowly falling for Atticus right now? Why didn't she ask for Atticus's help if she knew there was danger waiting for her? Why didn't she fight for him?

I decided to ignore all those questions running in my head for now. I meet my husband's gaze and place a soft kiss on the side of his lips.

"Nope, definitely not a bad thing," I reply with a loving smile on my lips.

As I settle into my seat, the gentle rocking of the carriage lulls me into a sense of calm. But suddenly, the horses outside let out a loud noise, causing the carriage to shake violently before coming to a sudden stop. My heart starts to race as I realize something is amiss.

Atticus turns to me, his eyes locking with mine before it slowly turns into a bloody crimson colour. Without a word, he pulls me close to him, and I instinctively reach for the dagger on my thigh.

Atticus opens the small window connected to where the coachman is, shielding me with his body to ensure my safety. The thumping of my heart becomes apparent due to the mixture of fear and anticipation for whatever is happening outside. I can hear the sound of metal swords clashing with one another.

Are we under attack?

"What's happening?" Atticus asks the coachman, his tone full of authority.

"Rogues, my King. Three of them," the coachman replies.

My forehead creases at his answer. Rogues?

"What the heck are the warriors doing then? Do I need to get off this carriage and settle it myself?" I can hear the irritation in my beloved's voice as he speaks, making me flinch a little.

I haven't really seen him act or talk rudely to anyone before. But then again, we haven't been together for very long, and we're currently under attack. I'm pretty sure he's just as worried as I am.

"There's no need, my King. Give us a few minutes, and we can continue our journey," someone answers from outside.

Atticus closes the window but remains alert and vigilant. His eyes stay a bloody red colour, making me aware that he's still on edge.

"Is it dangerous? Do you think we should help?" I can't help but ask.

Atticus turns his eyes to me and gives me an assuring smile. He pulls me closer to him. I know that he can feel my fear. My fear is not really for myself but for those warriors who are fighting outside. Will they be okay?

"It's okay, my Queen. Our warriors are the best in the Kingdom. Three vampire rogues are nothing compared to them," he replies.

"Why are they attacking us, then?"

Atticus leans back and allows me to settle on his chest. I love how our closeness can calm the raging storm of fear in me. Seriously, who needs a therapist when you have this man as your lover?

"Rogues are vagabonds. They settled outside the Kingdom's territory. It's not their habit to attack travellers, and they mostly avoid royal entourages like this. I think someone hired them to attack us," he explains.

For a moment, I become frozen at his explanation. Hired to attack us? Does it have something to do with Naya's murder? Or is it related to Idris's death?

Moments pass, and the carriage door opens, revealing one of our warriors. He bows his head before us, giving me a chance to observe him. There are traces of deep, almost black blood on his cheeks and his suit. Other than that, I don't see any kind of injury on his body, so I assume he's okay.

"My king, I think you need to see this," the warrior says.

The King's eyes darken as he stands up. He's almost at the door when I reach out for his hand. I look at him with pleading eyes.

"Can I go with you, please?" I ask.

Atticus turns towards the warrior as if he's communicating with him through his eyes. The warrior shakes his head in disapproval, answering my question. Whatever it is that the King needs to see seems not allowed to be seen by their Queen. Suddenly, I'm curious why that is.

"I'm sorry, my queen, but you're much safer in here," the King explains.

I'm left with no choice but to nod in agreement. He leans towards me and puts a kiss on the side of my lips before leaving me inside the carriage. The King doesn't really hide that much information from me, but sometimes I need to understand that there are limits on things and information he can give to me. If I'm going to base it on the warrior's expression, it's probably too grotesque for me to see.

I remain seated on the soft chair, waiting in anticipation. I clasp my palms together to stop myself from opening the window and taking a little peek outside. I can barely hear whatever Atticus and the warrior are talking about as they're purposely using a low tone. I'm hoping that Samuel is outside right now and gossiping on my behalf.

After a few minutes of waiting, the King enters the carriage again but with a stoic expression on his face. I'm going to guess that whatever the warrior showed him is not good news.

"What happened?" I question with a concerned expression on my face.

Atticus lets out a deep sigh as he meets my questioning gaze. His expression tells me that the rogues are something I need to look up to once we are back in our Kingdom.

"Those rogues weren't sent by anyone," he replies as he takes the seat beside me again.

My forehead creases. "What is it then? A random attack?"

Atticus shakes his head.

"No, it's not. Those rogues are not just simple rogues. Their blood is almost black in colour. They're bewitched." He briefly explains.

The carriage starts moving again, but my frown remains painted on my face. What exactly does he mean by bewitched?

CHAPTER 19

Naya

I can't help but fall in love with the beautiful architecture around us as we enter the capital of Kaedal. The Kingdom is located in the middle of the scorching desert. Despite the harsh and unforgiving environment, it seems to thrive really well. It is almost the same size as our Kingdom, but its geographical location sets it apart.

What I notice is that they seem to be much stricter in their security, probably due to their location. There are a lot of patrols in uniform walking around the town, guarding the people against any potential threats from the surrounding desert. Other than that, I think this Kingdom is relatively peaceful and progressive on its own. I take the smiles on the people's faces despite countless patrols around as a good sign.

"What do you think about this Kingdom, my Queen?" Atticus questions, making me turn in his direction.

"The roads are in good condition, the architecture is breathtaking, and the citizens look happy, but it's still too early to judge," I reply with a smile.

Atticus nods in agreement with my observation. He turns his eyes outside the carriage and looks at the people who are busy doing their daily routine. A few people stop what they are doing and look at us with curiosity; some turn their eyes to the top part of the carriage where our flag is located. I'm pretty sure they are familiar with the flag of our Kingdom.

"The King of Kaedal is much stricter than other leaders I'm acquainted with. However, his Kingdom holds a lot of power. Being their ally will strengthen our defence, but I want to make sure first that King Silvan will be a trustworthy ally," Atticus states.

My hand reaches out to my husband's hand. I squeeze it a bit, causing him to look at me again. I guess little by little, I am starting to understand the basics of being a Queen.

"Leave it to me. Give me two days. I'll give you the necessary information you need to help you decide," I reply with confidence.

Building an alliance with neighbouring kingdoms will help our own growth, but we need to build partnerships with the right Kingdom. I understand that now. My observant nature as a detective is something that I can use to help my husband make decisions in this situation.

I turn my attention to the open window of the carriage and watch the people outside doing different kinds of handiwork and textiles. This Kingdom looks really peaceful, and if I were to stumble upon this place as a human, it would make me think that this is just an ordinary town that was frozen in time. The buildings and houses are somewhat similar to the ones you can see in the human world, made of adobe and rammed earth. Nobody would think that the people who reside here are all vampires.

One of the kids stops what she's doing and waves at me. I smile at her and wave back. However, my smile immediately vanishes upon feeling a sudden chill out of nowhere— my forehead creases. I gently put down my hand and scan the area. It feels as if someone is observing me from a safe distance.

I am a queen, and although it is normal for some people to look at me, this creepy feeling of being observed is alarming. I look around, searching for anyone or anything suspicious, but to my disappointment, I can't seem to figure out the direction it's coming from. I frown in confusion.

"Is there any problem?" My husband asks upon noticing the sudden change in my behaviour. A soft smile is on his lips as he reaches to caress the side of my cheeks, lessening the stiff atmosphere inside the carriage.

"Nothing," I shake my head and smile at him, closing the window to remove the chills that creep down my spine.

"You have nothing to fear, my Queen. I promise to protect you with my life. I won't let anyone harm you," he assures me as if sensing that I am not being honest.

I look up at him and meet his eyes. "Who do I need protection from?" I ask, wanting to pry a bit if our Kingdom has enemies like Lady Naya mentioned that Atticus is hiding from me.

I feel him stiffen at my question, and the uncomfortable silence between us grows thicker. The look on his face makes me think that he is not ready to tell me anything about it, and that realization only adds to my growing anxiety. I let out a deep sigh, turning my eyes away from him and focusing on the intricate tapestry on the empty chair in front of us.

The silence inside the carriage becomes unbearable, and the only thing I can hear is the rhythmic sound of the horses' hooves and the creaking of the wheels as it trots towards the castle. The King is hiding something from me.

"If you're not ready to talk about it, that's totally fine," I murmur without looking at him, hoping to convey my understanding of his predicament. "But please remember that I'm not your enemy, Atticus. I am your wife, your life partner. I have your back, and you have mine. That's how our relationship is supposed to be."

The King reaches out for my chin and gently tugs it, coaxing me to meet his eyes. A charming smile graces his lips, dissolving the unsettling atmosphere that previously filled the small room. He leans down towards me and plants a soft kiss on the tip of my nose. My eyes involuntarily close in response to his sweet gestures, and when I open them again, I see a glint of admiration in his gaze as he caresses the side of my cheek.

"I know that, but as your King, I am also meant to protect you," he explains. "You've already been through so much pain dealing with your manipulative mother and Idris. This is not a problem you should have to deal with."

"If it has something to do with our Kingdom and you, then it is also my problem to deal with. Give me a chance to help you, Atticus. Don't push me out just because you think I cannot handle it. Try me," I argue.

He smiles and raises his hands in the air as a sign of surrender.

"Okay, you win. But let's discuss it once we're back in Puer Lunae. For now, I want you to focus on why we came here. Silvan is hosting a ball on our second night here. I want you to enjoy it without overthinking so much about the current problem we are facing." I can sense the finality in his tone, so I choose not to argue anymore.

That is when I feel the carriage stop moving. I move away from leaning on Atticus's chest and wait for the door to open. Slowly, the door opens from the outside, revealing the grand entrance of a black medieval castle before us. I can't help but hold my breath as I take in the exterior of the castle. It is breathtaking in a darker way. It looks cursed with its black colour scheme and pointed roof design, but it is mesmerizing at the same time.

The horseman offers his hand to assist me as I descend from the carriage. I gladly accept it, but my eyes never really leave the castle in front of us. Its dark beauty contrasts with the cream-coloured sand of the desert where it was built.

"You look impressed, my Queen. I am jealous. You never look at me like that before," Atticus says when we finally get down from the carriage.

I turn my eyes at him and chuckle.

"If our castle were a beautiful golden stallion, this would be a magnificent pitch-black stallion. It looks amazing. It made me think of those cursed castles in fiction books that you can only find during a full moon and that vanish on the horizon before dusk."

Atticus raises his left eyebrow at what I said. I know that the way I define it sounds dramatic, but it is how it feels. It's dark, it's cursed, but it is beautiful. It intrigues me to think about what kind of person lives in this black castle. It gives me an idea of what kind of leader King Silvan is. I need to be careful, though. I have a feeling that the King of Kaedal is not someone I should mess with. I need him on my side. I don't want him to be one of my enemies.

"Greetings, Your Highnesses. King Silvan has been expecting your arrival," an old man wearing loose-fitting tunic and trousers says. He has a scarf wrapped around his head, probably to protect his face from the sun and sand. I notice that this seems to be the common clothing in this Kingdom.

He steps aside to make way for us and gestures towards the massive castle door. He bows his head to show his respect towards us. I know that bowing is customary to show respect to royals, but sometimes I find myself feeling uncomfortable with it. I shrug and put my hand on Atticus's arm as we walk towards the massive black door made of some kind of metal.

The hallway of the castle is filled with different kinds of trinkets, like luxurious paintings and battle gear. It is as if the King is showing off his wealth and power. Now I am even more intrigued about what kind of man is waiting for us at the end of this hallway. I really hope he is not bad news.

They open the door for us once we reach the end. I let out a friendly smile at the old man before entering the castle's receiving area. I hear the door close behind us, and that is when I get a chance to look around the grandiose room we are in.

Unlike what I expected, the room was decorated with gold and red furniture. I kind of expected it to be in a black-and-white theme. This room feels warmer compared to the outside. This is probably the reason why it's the receiving area for guests. The exterior of the castle looks magnificent but intimidating. This room feels welcoming.

"Greetings, King Atticus and Queen Naya. I'm glad that you have accepted my invitation," A deep and powerful voice interrupts my thoughts, his words echoing throughout the grand chamber.

I turn to the unlit fireplace where a man is standing. He has dark, amber-coloured eyes and a charming smile that I know many women would easily fall for. He is wearing traditional attire, a flowing white robe with intricate golden embroidery, and a matching headdress that covers his hair.

"King Silvan, it is an honour to be your guest. Who am I to decline your invitation to an alliance?" my husband replies from beside me.

King Silvan turns his gaze towards me, and his smile slowly turns into a knowing smirk. I stiffen, and the perfect smile on my lips fades.

"Trust me, Atticus, the pleasure is mine," he says without taking his eyes off me.

The way he looks at me makes me feel like I'm some kind of specimen he wants to study. This man is giving me a different type of creep that I cannot name. It feels like he's threatening me by just looking at me without saying a single word, and to be honest, I feel threatened. I put on a coy smile on my lips to hide the sudden fear that engulfs me.

I don't like this man in front of us, not at all.

CHAPTER 20

Naya

The room is bathed in the beautiful golden rays of sunset streaming in through the glass window. As the day starts to fade, the sky outside transforms into an enchanting pink-orange hue. A noise from the castle courtyard catches my attention, and I turn to see a coachman receiving instructions from someone within the castle walls. The serene beauty of the afternoon is soon to give way to a night of revelry as everyone in the Kingdom prepares to host royal guests and nobles.

I'm currently in the guest room King Silvan assigned to us when we arrived here yesterday. The room was spacious and opulent. The first thing that caught my attention was the wide glass windows that stretched from floor to ceiling, offering a breathtaking view of the castle's courtyard.

The sunlight streaming in through the windows illuminates the plush green carpet that covers the floor, giving the room a warm and inviting feel. A magnificent king-sized bed is the centrepiece of the room in a rich crimson colour that contrasts beautifully with the white pillows and sheets.

The walls of the room were adorned with intricate tapestries that depicted scenes from the Kingdom's rich history. There was also a small writing desk by the window, complete with a feather quill and ink, for those who wanted to indulge in some writing or journaling.

I pick up the cup of tea from the small table beside me and take a small sip. The sweet scent of chamomile fills my nose, calming my nerves. I put the small cup back on the table and looked at Samuel.

"What do you think Atticus would feel once he learned about Naya's death?" The question escapes my lips without warning. My curiosity tends to get me every time.

"Devastated for sure. You saw firsthand how much he loves Lady Naya. He adores her." He answers with all honesty. "He will be broken once he learns that she's long dead."

"How did they meet?" I ask. Atticus is already at the party downstairs, but I remain in the room with Samuel to make sure I look my best before walking out of this room. This is my very first royal party aside from my wedding, and it is making me a bit jittery.

Samuel takes the seat in front of me and smiles as he reminisces about something from his past. "A party was held in the palace, and Idris decided to take Lady Naya along with him. Idris spent his time flirting with other girls, so she decided to spend the rest of the night on the balcony, away from the crowd. That's where she met the King," he narrates.

I let out a smile upon remembering the party on the night of our wedding. Atticus did mention something about me reminiscing about our first meeting. So that is how it all starts. It sounds like a Cinderella story to me, minus the two stepsisters, but with the wicked mother.

"I see the opportunity to save Lady Naya from Idris. I went to her mother and informed her about what happened. She saw that as an opportunity as well, and she immediately breaks Idris' engagement with her daughter."

"So, it is her greed that puts her daughter in peril, but it is also her greed that saved her," I conclude.

Samuel nods in response. "You can put it that way. This is a kingdom that revolves around power and position. She's just being wise,"

The side of my lips lifts into a lopsided smile as I shake my head. Being wise? I don't think so. She's being selfish.

"She sold her daughter to the point that Lady Naya was taken advantage of and abused by someone. She just wanted her daughter to be the Queen because she thought she could be her puppet." I scoff.

I'm guessing she expects me to be her little marionette, but too bad for her. I dislike being controlled. I haven't had a chance to visit Lady Naya's family house or meet other members of her family yet, but I know I'm bound to meet them soon. I need to be prepared.

I stand up from my seat and walk towards the mirror to fix my makeup. Now that I'm feeling calmer, I'm ready to go down and join the party.

The night is just starting, and I know Atticus is waiting for me. I hope no other royals or nobles are flirting with him right now because I don't want to start any trouble. I left the room with Samuel beside me, leading me towards the lavish hall where the ball was happening. I hear the distant sound of music growing louder with each step.

As we approach the ballroom, the scent of roses fills my nostrils, intermingled with the heavy perfume of the wealthy ladies in their extravagant gowns. I take a deep breath, trying to calm my nerves as I see a swarm of people dressed in the most expensive fabrics. The walls are draped in red velvet, and the chandeliers are adorned with glittering crystals that cast a warm glow across the room.

As soon as I step into the party, I notice a few pairs of eyes turning in my direction. Normally, I wouldn't feel intimidated by the number of people, but some of the scrutinizing looks are making my stomach churn. I can feel their eyes on me, analyzing my every move. I adjust my dress, suddenly self-conscious under their gaze. The urge to go back to my room suddenly hits me, but I decide to shrug off the curious glances and focus on finding Atticus.

"Looking for someone, Queen Naya?"

A dark baritone voice makes me turn my gaze to the side.

"King Silvan," I greet and bow slightly to show my respect. "I'm looking for my husband. Do you happen to see him?" I ask.

King Silvan gives me a knowing smile and points to something with the hand holding a glass of champagne.

I roll my eyes at him and look towards the direction that he points out. My eyes squint in irritation and jealousy upon seeing Atticus on one of the verandas, talking to the woman who makes my blood boil faster than any fire can. What is she doing here?

I compose myself and walk towards them, trying my best not to look like a harpy about to lose her cool. My heels echo as I walk in their direction. Some people around give me curious glances. They can probably feel the murderous aura that surrounds me right now.

Atticus turns towards my direction the moment he feels my presence. I display the sweetest smile I can muster even though all I want right now is to slap that smile off Harriet's lips. I hate her. She's irritating. The idea of her being the next Queen once

I leave this world makes me want to banish her from Puer Lunae. I mean, that's not a bad idea, right?

I'm probably acting overdramatic, but I can't help it. She's really close to Atticus, and she's the granddaughter of the current minister of trade and finance. Her family has a powerful influence in the Kingdom. That's probably the reason why I feel so threatened.

"My Queen, are you feeling better now?" Atticus asks with a smile.

He opens his arms to welcome me, and I walk towards him, feeling the warmth of his embrace as I stand by his side. Without answering his question, I tiptoe a bit and boldly capture his lips. Atticus stands still for a second, taken aback by the kiss. However, after a few moments, I feel him smile between our kisses before responding with the same passion. We are both panting for air when we let go of each other's lips. A naughty smile plays on my beloved's lips as his eyes linger on my swollen lips.

"My queen," Harriet speaks from beside the King, making us turn to her. "The King told me that you're not feeling well, so I decided to keep him company for a while. I hope you don't mind," A friendly smile was on her lips, but I didn't miss the annoyance in her eyes at our display of affection.

I plaster a sarcastic smile on my lips as our gaze meets. She looks stunning in her royal blue gown, and I can't help but feel irritated by her presence. Vampires are blessed with incomparable beauty and authority, and Harriet is no exception.

"I don't mind, but I'm here now. Clearly, your presence is not needed," I respond in a sardonic tone, unable to hide my annoyance.

I know I'm being unreasonable, but Harriet has a way of getting under my skin. Every time we cross paths, she seems to go out of her way to insult and irritate me.

"Naya, is everything okay?" Atticus asks upon noticing the sharpness in my voice.

I take a deep breath and turn to face him. The serious look on his face tells me that he doesn't appreciate my tone. His eyebrows furrow, but he seems unaware of the silent war between Harriet and me.

I open my mouth to reply, but the words get caught in my throat as I realize this isn't the right time to express my frustration.

"I think I need some fresh air," I say while giving my husband an apologetic look, struggling to explain my rudeness towards Harriet. "Don't follow me."

I push him away slightly, creating some distance between us, and head towards the exit of that lavish ballroom. I need to breathe and clear my head before my jealousy consumes me. There are so many nobles and royals around, and this isn't the time or place for me to create a scene. I have to remember that I'm representing Puer Lunae and Atticus with my actions.

The chilling wind greets me as I step outside the castle. After leaving the grandiose celebration, I find myself making my way towards the back of the castle. I just need to be alone without anyone disturbing me.

I only stop walking when I can no longer hear any kind of chatter or noise from the palace. I take a deep breath, letting the fresh air fill my lungs and stare at the endless river of stars in the sky. I'm starting to hate myself for my unreasonable behaviour. This isn't who I am. My growing feelings for the King are messing with my emotions. I need to stay calm and focused on why I'm here, not on my feelings for Atticus. How many times do I need to remind myself that I'm not Lady Naya? Atticus doesn't love me. He loves Naya, the real Naya. I have no right to feel this way.

My gaze shifts to the ground, and I kick the innocent red stone that lies flat on the sand. The stone rolls over multiple times and stops when it hits something a few meters away from me. I look up to see what the stone has hit, only to take a step back upon seeing two men standing a few meters away from me.

My breathing hitches as I survey the two strangers in front of me. My eyes widen in horror. They both look hideous, with their pale white skin and black veins crawling on them. I feel my stomach churn while looking at them. Their appearance is gruesome, but what makes me scared is the horrifying smirk on their lips while looking at me.

One of the men lets out a clamouring cry. His scream echoes throughout the empty desert. He closes our distance at an unbelievable speed that I barely even get a chance to dodge his attack. My feet turned frozen solid in my spot. His claws are only inches away from my face when a sharp blade strikes his left arm, slicing it in half.

I take a step back as droplets of blood splatter on my cheek and gown. My eyes turn towards my unexpected saviour who is holding a sword while shielding me from my two attackers. King Silvan grins at me as he wipes some of the traces of blood from his jaw.

"Do you know that this is a dangerous place to stray on during the night, Queen Naya?" He says and steps forward to cover me from the man who's now holding his cut arm.

"What are those?" I ask in terror, my voice barely above a whisper.

"They are rogues based on their smell, but they are bewitched. This is the first time I see one of them this close to the castle."

My forehead creases with my eyes on the two creatures right in front of us. These are the bewitched?

CHAPTER 21

Naya

My gaze lands on King Silvan. He is badly wounded, with a few scratches on the side of his cheeks and a deep wound on his chest. The rogues have taken a toll on him, and I am standing beside him while remaining alert. I am holding the silver dagger tightly between my palms, but I'm not really much of help. The rogues are too fast for me to fight. They are machine-like, emotionless, and seem to feel no physical pain.

Are these the same rogues we encountered on our way to this kingdom? Is this what Atticus was hiding from me? If it's so vital and dangerous, I don't understand why he would keep it from me. Does he really think I'm that weak and vulnerable?

"We need to get out of here, or this will be our grave," Silvan speaks from beside me, pulling me from my thoughts.

His breathing is shallow, and the sword he is holding is covered in almost-black blood. The moonlight serves as a small lamp for us. After the two rogues, he defeated two rogues a moment ago, another two more showed up out of nowhere. I have no idea how many vampire rogues are scattered throughout this desert, waiting for the right time to attack us.

Frustration starts to grow within me. I should have stayed inside the palace. I shouldn't have acted irrationally. My jealousy got the best of me, and I didn't even think before running outside of the castle. I am stupid. This is a world of vampires; of course, I should have expected this kind of danger to lurk around the corner.

For the first time in my life, I finally got a chance to know the real meaning of fear. I am usually not the kind of person who is afraid of darkness and monsters, but tonight is different. The chilling night wind caresses my exposed shoulder, making me shiver in a combination of cold and fear. It is as if someone from a distance is looking at us, surveying us.

"You are not healing," I point out upon noticing that the wounds on his chest have barely healed yet.

"I know. Their claws have silver in them. It's preventing me from healing. Whoever sent them is serious about wanting to get you killed," he states before shoving the sword he's holding onto the ground to use it as a cane to stand up and balance himself.

I immediately rush to help him stand, and he grunts in pain. If one more rogue shows up, we're both dead. I'm sure of it. We need to return inside the safety of his castle, or else this will be our last night.

"Do you think there are still more of them around?" I ask while cautiously looking around the area.

I'm hoping that, since he is a vampire, he can somehow sniff them out.

"I don't know. Their scent has been overpowered by the rancid scent of this blood," he replies, referring to the sword he's holding. "I can't say exactly how many are left."

He balances himself using his sword while putting some of his weight on me to stand up. We slowly walk in the direction of the front entrance of the castle, only to halt when my sharp senses pick up something dark not far from where we are. I immediately turn toward the direction where I can feel the presence.

"We're dead," I mutter while looking at the shadows not far from where we are.

"Not yet. I think I can still handle a few."

I let out a sigh of defeat, feeling hopeless about our situation.

"Said the man who can barely stand up on his own," I retort. "You are gravely wounded, Silvan. I don't think you can still survive fighting one of those. You have seen how fast and fearless they are. They are a perfect killing machine."

My eyes remain at the distance where I can feel some eerie presence, making sure that we will not be caught off guard by any unexpected attacks. My grip tightens on the dagger. I know I don't have enough strength to fight them, but I can at least try.

A few moments later, I see two more rogues walking towards us. My breath hitches as I take in their gruesome appearance. They are as hideous as the first one we have encountered. Both men are as pale as snow, and the black veins inside their thin skin are clearly visible. Their eyes are all white with red veins in them, and their claws are extended and sharp enough to tear human flesh into pieces.

"Fuck." Silvan hisses under his breath.

"What's our plan?" I turn to look at him, not knowing how to react with the overwhelming fear filling my heart.

"Can you run?" Silvan asks, making me frown in confusion.

"I can run, but I can't outrun them," I reply sarcastically. Of course, I can run, but these creatures are almost ten times faster than me. They can literally outrun me even if I have a hundred-meter head start.

"Then we are basically both dead then," he remarks as matter-of-factly.

He steps in front of me, but I place my hand on his arm to get his attention. He might be a king, but this is a hopeless fight. In his current condition, there's no way he will be able to take on two of them.

"Let's just run. If you try to fight them in your current condition, you might end up dead. You invited us here to build an alliance, and if you die, there will be a war between our kingdoms. We might have a bit of a chance if we try to run," I negotiate with him.

Silvan gives one glance at the rogues, who are now looking at us with hunger. Realizing that fighting them head-on is not a smart idea, he puts his sword back in its sheath and scoops me from the ground. He turns towards the direction of the castle and starts to run.

It's a chasing game now.

The two rogues let out a loud scream. I cover my ears and hiss. Damn it! That scream is strong enough to break my eardrums.

I can't see them in this position, but I can hear the loud stomping of their feet on the ground and their heavy panting, a clear sign that they are tailing us. The chilly wind slices through my skin, but it is the least of my priorities right now. What's important is for us to be able to get back to the castle alive.

King Silvan's face is void of any emotion. He is gravely wounded, but his authority and charm haven't faltered a bit. It's funny because, despite our hopeless situation, he still looks like a handsome, aristocratic knight. I have a feeling that if I met him before Atticus, I might have fallen for him instead. He is a dark, strict, and authoritative person. However, those qualities only add to his charm.

"Why would someone want a Queen dead?" King Silvan asks as he sprints towards the castle's entrance.

"Trust me, I have the same question as well. What I don't understand is how they can command these mindless bewitched to come after me." I look away from him and wince. I have a feeling that I have the responsibility to explain everything to him once we manage to get out of this alive.

Silvan clenches his jaw. I'm pretty sure that he is already starting to feel suspicious of me. These rogues that are after me are not normal ones. They are stronger, faster, uncontrollable, and wild. It makes me question if it has something to do with Lady Naya's death. Because if it is, then I am dead. I am a human, for heaven's sake. This is a kind of battle I cannot win.

We are halfway towards the entrance of the castle when King Silvan halts. He puts me down on the ground and looks straight in front of us— my forehead creases at his actions. Just when I am about to ask him a question when I feel a horrifying aura not far from where we are. I turn my gaze towards the direction where he's looking at. Only to take a bit of a step back upon seeing a silhouette of a man holding a massive sword.

"What is that?" I ask in terror.

It's different from what we encountered a while ago. It's so much bigger than the ones that are chasing us, and it has a weapon.

Yep, we're dead.

"You need to leave and try to get some help. I'll handle them," Silvan says, making me look at him.

"No!" I contest, full of conviction. "There's no way I'm leaving you behind in this condition to face three killing machines at the same time. I'll stay. We will get through this. Why aren't you healing anyway? Aren't vampires supposed to heal fast?"

"The silver in their claws is poison to any kind of vampire, and it is in my blood right now," he answers and then looks at me straight in my eyes. "I am losing my strength faster than I expected. Stop being a hardheaded Naya and run back towards the castle. It will be hard for me to protect you and fight them at the same time!"

My palm closes into a fist knowing that he is right. I take a deep breath and think of my current options. He has a point, but I can't leave him either. He said it himself. He is losing strength faster than he expected. If I choose to leave him behind, he might die. There is no way I am not going to allow anyone to die on me. I am not the kind to leave a comrade behind.

"What can I do to help you then?" I ask him.

His brows connect into one line. "What the heck are you talking about? I need you to leave!" he hisses, completely annoyed with my stubborn attitude.

The two rogues that were chasing us earlier are now catching up with us. I can already hear their agonizing screams not far from where we are. The one in front of us remains standing while observing us carefully as if waiting for us to make the first move.

There's a part of me that wants to just follow King Silvan's instructions. But I'd rather die here with him than abandon a comrade. At this point, there's only one way for us to survive this. I position the silver dagger I am holding in front of my palm and cut my skin without hesitation— the sweet metallic scent of my blood envelops the place, and I can't help but wince a bit in pain.

King Silvan's eyes snap in my direction in surprise. His irises change colour into a deep blood red.

A wicked smile curves on my lips. I saw Atticus' beast once when he killed Idris. However, I haven't seen Silvan in that form yet. If the books I've read from the library speak the truth, human blood and anger can wake up their beast, and the taste of it can make them stronger and help them heal quicker.

"I've read that human blood can help. Bite me," I offer without hesitation. What I am doing is a gamble, but it is the only way I know to escape this situation alive. I don't know if King Silvan is an enemy or a friend. I'll take care of the consequences later. I'm doing this to save both of us.

I didn't need to tell him twice. The next thing I know, he is already in front of me, towering over me with his height. His left arm encircles my waist, and before I can even comprehend what he is about to do, I feel his fangs dig into the crook of my neck.

For a moment, I am frozen in my spot as I feel him suck my blood. I feel my knees buckle against his hold. Suddenly, I feel so weak and limp. His velvety lips against the sensitive skin of my neck are giving me a hazy and groggy feeling. I close my eyes and lean to the side to give him more access.

However, as I am about to fall into the void of darkness, I feel him withdraw his fangs from my neck. I open my eyes slightly, only to close them again as the sudden dizziness engulfs me. I feel my body being lifted into the air, and then I am put in a sitting position leaning against the castle wall.

"Rest for now. We will discuss this after I take care of the problem," I hear him say, but I am too weak to reply.

My breathing becomes heavy and ragged. Despite it, I force myself to open my eyes to see what's happening around me. I can see King Silvan crossing swords with a rogue almost twice his body size.

I remain still in my seat, trying to regain the strength I lost. I watch in amazement as King Silvan thrusts his sword with full strength at the last rogue he's fighting. A weak smile escapes my lips as I watch him walk in my direction. It seems that the knowledge I acquired from reading books in the library helped us survive tonight. I let out a sigh of relief. We're safe. I'm glad tonight is not my last night in this world.

I force myself to rise from the sand with a smile on my lips to congratulate him. However, that smile vanishes when he points his bloody sword at my neck, threatening to cut my throat with one wrong move. His deep red eyes meet mine. His expression is all serious, so I know he is not kidding around. I swallow the lump in my throat and take a step back.

"You are not the real Queen of Puer Lunae. How did a human manage to enter our world? Who are you?"

That question from him is enough to stop the world from moving around us. This time, I know that no amount of explanation can save me.

CHAPTER 22

Naya

A pale grin forms on my lips as I look at the bloodied sword that is currently pointing at my throat. I let go of the silver blade I'm holding, allowing it to fall to the ground. This is a hopeless situation. Fighting this man is suicide. He just killed seven rogues on his own. Even if I am holding a gun filled with silver bullets right now, I am not going to win, so why bother?

"Where is the real Queen Naya?" he demands once more, his sharp gaze and stern expression revealing nothing of his thoughts.

I let out a sigh in defeat. Sadly, the only option I can think of right now to escape this is to admit everything to him. Then it will be his decision if tomorrow is my funeral or another day that I need to survive.

If I am going to be honest with myself, I am tired of everything— the feelings I have for my beloved, the thought of being a million miles away from him after all of this, the fear of being discovered, the bewitched we barely manage to escape, the lies, the greed of this world, and the murder case I need to solve. It's just too much. If this is the end of it, so be it. I'm tired and drained, both physically and emotionally.

"Lady Naya was murdered on the day of her wedding. I am a detective she summoned from the human world to find her killer," I finally admitted.

I take a series of deep breaths to release the tension I am holding in my chest. King Silvan's eyes squint at me as if he is trying to see if I am telling the truth or playing with him. At this point, I don't really care if he decides to believe me or kill me. I think both will be in my favour. If I die right now, then this whole confusing murder case is not my problem anymore.

"And what evidence can you give me to prove your claim?" he questions. The tip of his sword remains on my neck, reminding me that in his eyes, I am an enemy. One wrong move and he will not hesitate to slit my fragile throat in two.

I shrug. "Nothing," I respond honestly. "I have no proof on me. It's all safely hidden in Puer Lunae. I'm not going to force you to believe me, and if you think I'm the bad person here, go ahead and kill me."

Silence falls into us for a moment, and the only thing that I can hear is our heavy breathing. Until finally, a wicked grin forms on Silvan's lips. He puts down his sword. I watch in wonder as his grin slowly turns into an amused laugh, echoing throughout the silence of the night.

The crease on my forehead deepens. I'm glad he finds the situation amusing because, to be honest, I don't.

"I like you. You know exactly when to push through and when to give up," he says and puts his sword back in its sheath.

I give him a questioning look, arching my left eyebrow. So, does that mean I'm safe now? His eyes turn to me with a spark of amusement in them.

"Let's make a deal, my Queen," he says as he starts to close our distance.

I sigh. Of course, there's always a catch.

"What happened tonight will remain between us, and my Kingdom will be a faithful ally of Puer Lunae." He halts his step right in front of me, towering over me with his height.

I cross my hands in front of my chest and look up to meet his gaze. "And what do you want in return?"

The smile on his lips turns wicked. His eyes are now slowly turning back to their usual colour, but I am still not letting my guard down in front of him. Why do I feel that I am not going to like the condition he will ask me in exchange for keeping my secret?

"I want your firstborn," he declares, making me still for a few seconds as I try to make sense of his condition. "I will keep your secret safe, and I will become your Kingdom's ally, but in exchange, I want you to promise me your firstborn." He continues.

I open my mouth to say something witty, but my mind suddenly goes blank for some reason. Silence envelopes us as I try to make sure that I understand his words accurately. I clamp my mouth shut while looking at him in disbelief.

"Are you kidding me?" I exclaim when I finally manage to gather back all my wits.

Seriously? He's not even sure if I'm going to have a firstborn. Once Atticus learns about my treason, I'll be dead, and that's it. What firstborn is he freaking talking about?

"Nope, I'm serious. Let me remind you, my dearest Queen. Your Kingdom is in peril because of you. Those rogues I killed are not after me. They're clearly after you. How many of those things do you think are waiting for the perfect timing to attack? That means your Kingdom needs this alliance more than mine," he explains with a tone full of confidence and certainty.

My palms clench into tight fists. He has a point. I have a feeling that those creatures have something to do with Lady Naya's murder.

"I think I am seeing the pattern now," I murmur out of nowhere, suddenly understanding why Lady Naya mentioned in her letter something about the downfall of the Kingdom.

"What pattern exactly?" King Silvan questions as he looks at me with curiosity.

I pull my attention back to the present. Yeah, I almost forgot that I have a problem at hand right now, which is this vampire king who wants my firstborn. I reach out to my forehead to massage it. Why is this world so complicated?

"What makes you think that I will agree to your condition? Why would I promise my firstborn to you? Are you crazy?" I argue instead of giving in to his demand.

He is giving me a severe headache. I don't even know if I can manage to stay alive until I get pregnant. That idea is just too stupid.

"Take it or leave it, my Queen," he replies with a playful smile plastered on his lips. "Once we're back in the castle, either I'll keep your secret and be your ally, or I'm going to confess your conspiracy to the King. Trust me when I tell you that the lowest punishment you'll receive for that is a public execution."

My eyes squint at his warning. I know that what he's saying isn't just a threat. That's the rule of this world. Either I trust my firstborn to him, which isn't even a hundred percent sure that I'll have a firstborn given the situation, or I'll be killed by the man I am now starting to have feelings with.

I sigh in defeat and say, "Okay, fine. I promise you my firstborn, but you have to keep your word." I pick up the blade that I had thrown on the ground a while ago and turn my back against him.

As I start to make my way back to the palace, I hear his footsteps trailing behind me. A sense of foreboding washes over me, and I can already anticipate the remorse that will accompany my decision today. However, I am left with no alternative, no other recourse. I'm trapped, and there's nothing I can do to get out of this.

I'm almost at the entrance of the castle when King Silvan manages to catch up to me. He catches my wrist to get my attention and makes me face him. Utterly annoyed by his actions, I turn to look at him and hiss, "What now?"

King Silvan turns my wrist around, showing me my palm with blood still oozing from it. I let out a deep breath upon remembering that I had wounded myself a while ago. I bite my inner lip in irritation. How could I forget that I couldn't heal instantly because I am a human?

"You're not planning to enter the party full of vampires with this open wound, are you?" The side of his lips lifts into a smirk.

"What should I do then? Wait for three days before entering the castle?" My tone is full of sarcasm. I've had enough of this day.

"Yeah, you can do that, or if you want, I can turn you into one of us," he offers.

I feel the atmosphere between us stiffen. I stand frozen right in front of him, trying to process his words. He can turn me into one of them? Is that possible? Why haven't I read anything about that before? Why didn't Samuel tell me about it?

"That's possible?" I ask in confusion. Not that I want to be turned. I just want to make sure that I heard it right.

"Oh, it is. I came from the lineage of royalties. Say yes, and I will be able to turn you into one of us. Think about it. If you're turned, Atticus is unlikely to find out that you're a fraud. Also, you'll be able to fight off rogues and other threats because you'll have the strength and the speed of vampires."

I swallow hard. King Silvan's offer sounds really tempting, and he is right. Being a turned vampire will give me so much advantage, however...

I pull my hand out of his hold and give him a stern look.

"I've already lost a lot by accepting Lady Naya's case. I'm not going to lose the only thing that connects me to the world where I came from," I reply in a voice that is full of conviction.

I refuse to lose my humanity. It's never been easy, but I've made it this far without dying. I don't want to lose something that sets me apart from everyone in this world. My goal is to solve the murder case, confess to the King, and go back to the human world. That's it, no more, no less. If I agree to his offer, everything is going to be more complicated for me. I can't have that. I'm so close to solving this case. I'm not going to give up my humanity for this.

King Silvan nods at me in understanding.

"I have a feeling that you would say that. But if in case you change your mind, you are always welcome to visit me in my Kingdom," he states with a smile. "Now, let me tend to your wound before we enter the castle."

I extend my wounded palm to him, knowing that their saliva can heal minor wounds instantly. He takes a lick on my palm, and I turn my eyes away, feeling nothing but irritation. It's odd, given that a handsome man licking your palm is usually supposed to be sexual, but I can't feel any attraction towards him.

"It's because you are King Atticus's beloved," he speaks as he lets go of my hand.

"What?" My forehead scrunches at his statement, and I take a closer look at my palm to inspect it. It's good as new again. No one will suspect that I had a deep wound in it a few seconds ago.

"You are not attracted to me because your soul is already connected to Atticus's soul," he explains and proceeds to walk towards the castle's entrance. "That also means that you won't be able to leave this world unless you break your bond with him."

"You're kidding me," I roll my eyes at his statement as I follow him inside the castle. That's not possible, right?

"Unfortunately, I am not. You can leave if you want. You can go back to the human world at your will. But trust me when I tell you that it will kill your soul to be separated from your beloved."

I can't help but feel scared at his explanation. Samuel keeps telling me the same thing as well. It's just that I won't listen.

"I'll cross the bridge once I get there. I am not the kind of person to worry about things that are far off. I can't allow myself to be afraid of unforeseen things, so shut up and do your thing. I'll do mine," I seethe under my breath.

The truth is, I am worried. I can feel how powerful my connection with Atticus is. I saw firsthand how irrational I was when he talked with Harriet. I need to stop acting like this, but I just can't control it when it comes to him. Do I need to build a wall between me and my beloved to avoid getting hurt in the end? Is that the only way I can save myself from the quicksand I stumbled on?

As we enter the black metallic door of the castle, a few of the guests turn their eyes in our direction. I hate the attention, but I can't really blame them. My dress is torn, and a few droplets of blood decorate it. Some of them probably notice the smell of blood from King Silvan's sword as well.

Atticus walks towards me with concern lacing his eyes. He crosses our distance and pulls me into his arms, enclosing me in a protective hug.

"What happened? You've been gone for so long. I've already asked Samuel to look for you," he questions with so much worry and concern.

He buries his nose in the crook of my neck, taking a sniff and feeling my soft body against his. My whole body relaxes, and suddenly the fear that occupied my heart a while ago vanishes. With my beloved holding me like this, I know I'm safe. No one can harm me.

I turn my eyes towards King Silvan. He is looking at me with a knowing smile on his lips. Even if I don't admit it verbally, I know he can feel that I am slowly falling for my husband. The side of my eyes starts to heat up. Suddenly, I am torn between the life I left behind in the human world and the life that this world can offer.

King Silvan is expecting me to surrender to the bond sooner or later. He knows that it's just a matter of time before I completely give up the only thing that's left of me for Atticus.

CHAPTER 23

Naya

"Rogues attacked you? Why the heck did you run away in the first place? Don't you understand how dangerous it is for you to be alone? Yet, you strayed outside without any warriors to protect you! We are in unfamiliar territory. Damn it!"

I can't help but grimace upon hearing Atticus curse. I bite my lower lip as he walks back and forth in front of me. I keep my gaze down, looking at the patterned floor as if it were the most interesting thing in the room. He is completely pissed off, and I can definitely understand why. Heck! I am pissed off with my actions. It turns out that being in love with the King is not really ideal for me. My feelings are clouding my judgment. I almost died, and now King Silvan knows my real identity. I messed up so badly.

We are currently in our room which he pulled me into after King Silvan told him about what happened. I can see the fear in my beloved's eyes after learning about our encounters with the rogues. I can't really blame him for being angry. If King Silvan hadn't followed me outside, I would probably be dead by now. There's no way I can survive those rogues on my own. I am ten times weaker and slower than they are.

"What the hell were you thinking running away like that, Naya?" He stops pacing and looks at me.

I can't find the courage to meet his gaze or answer his question. How am I supposed to admit that I am jealous of Harriet?

"So?" he asks when he notices that I don't have any plans to respond.

"I just..." I take a deep breath, not knowing what to say. "I feel suffocated, and I just want to breathe some fresh air. I thought it would help if I got out for a little while. I didn't expect that there would be rogues waiting for me." I explain, hoping that it will be enough to justify my actions.

On our way to Kaedal, he explained a bit about those rogues. However, how am I supposed to know that they will be following us all the way to King Silvan's castle? I know that my actions are unreasonable, but how would I know that those creatures were waiting outside to kill me?

"Those rogues. Are they the same ones who attacked us on our way here?" I ask and look up to meet my beloved's hazel-coloured eyes.

Atticus frowns, and his eyes darken as he looks at me as if he is trying to weigh something inside his head. In the end, he lets out a sigh of defeat and takes the seat beside me.

"Yes, they are the same ones," he confirms. "That's the reason why we don't want you to see them. Those are bewitched rogues. They are way different from normal rogues."

My forehead furrows at his confirmation. The bewitched rogues, the unexpected murder of the future Queen, and the fan mail Lady Naya sent me. Are they all connected?

"So, they are much more dangerous and much stronger?"

He nods in answer to my question. I want to ask him more about rogues, but I'm afraid that might spark suspicion towards me. Right now, I need to avoid making people suspicious of me. It's enough already that King Silvan knows about my real identity.

"I want to know more about them, Atticus. It seems to me that an army of them can destroy a whole kingdom." I say as fear and worry start to creep under my skin.

I highly doubt that Atticus will give me the exact information I need, but I still need to try. If our Kingdom has problems with rogues, as a queen, I should be aware of that. I need to be informed about it. That way, I can see if there's something that I can do to help and if it has a connection to Lady Naya's death.

"That's impossible. Bewitched rogues are rare, and I don't think their numbers can go up high enough to destroy a kingdom. They are uncontrollable, and they can only stay alive for a few hours after drinking the potion," he explains, making me suddenly more curious.

"I'm sorry, they can only be alive for a few hours? And what potion?" The frown on my forehead deepens. This is starting to get more interesting. Why would someone drink a potion that could make them like a monster for a few hours and die afterwards? That's suicide and very stupid.

"There's a kind of potion that was invented by a coven of witches centuries ago. It was experimental. They tried using it on vampire warriors, turning them into killing machines. Luckily, bewitched vampires can only stay alive for a few hours. After that, their bodies will explode into pieces due to pressure," he explains further.

"That's cool and gruesome at the same time," I can't help but wince as I mentally picture what he said. "What happened to those witches who invented those potions then?"

"Kingdoms built an alliance to destroy the coven, and it was a successful mission. All of the potions were destroyed. However, every now and then, one or two bewitched vampires show up. It doesn't alarm us that much because most of the victims are rogues, and the numbers aren't really going up."

My eyebrows furrow. It is clear to me that those kingdoms involved in the investigation showed poor judgment about the situation. Bewitched vampires showed up every now and then, yet none of them bothered to look further and check where those potions were coming from.

"I can't believe you would disregard this issue. That sounds really disturbing. Have you ever seen those creatures?" I stand up from the bed and start to pace in front of him. Why on earth am I just learning about this now? If I hadn't left the palace, I would never have known about this issue. Why on earth none of the kingdoms are taking this seriously? It definitely sounds like a severe problem to me.

Atticus closes the distance between us. He pulls me to his chest in an attempt to comfort me. "Calm down, my Queen. We are not taking this as a serious threat because only one or two bewitched vampires show up every once in a while. Kingdoms tried to figure out where the potions were coming from, but we could not trace them. We decided that it would be much better to deal with those bewitched instead. The coven has been destroyed, and the witches who invented it have been killed. We cannot get any leads on who's behind it," he clarifies.

I feel his arms protectively encircle my waist. I look up at him and meet his eyes. I'm sure he can feel how scared I am right now. I can deal with assassins. But enemies are sending bewitched vampires to kill me instead. Those creatures are killing machines, and they will be unstoppable in large numbers. That's what I'm so afraid of.

"That is so stupid, Atticus. I have encountered seven of them just tonight. You are a King; you understand that you need to prioritize the safety of your subjects, right?" I can't help but sound irritated. I push his hand away from me and walk towards the side table where a bottle of wine and two glasses are placed.

I need a drink to calm down. What I encountered tonight terrified me, not to mention that I also agreed with King Silvan's condition for him to have my firstborn. I screwed up so badly tonight.

"We didn't anticipate that it would be this dangerous. We are trying our best to locate the source of the potion, but we have had no success," Atticus defends himself.

I let out a harsh exhale in annoyance. I take a sip from the glass, relishing the sweet and tangy taste as it hits my tongue.

I need a whole bottle of this to forget the trauma I have incurred tonight. I want to laugh at his explanation. They hadn't anticipated this to happen? Seriously? I am new to this world, but I can already picture the worst that can happen.

"You need to call a meeting, and I must be included in it. We will address this together once we are back in Puer Lunae. I want to create a search party for the source of the potion," I demand and throw a threatening glare at him.

However, my husband's response only infuriates me further. He wears a smug grin on his lips as if he finds my frustration very amusing.

"I never thought that you would look so hot when you are angry," he comments, his tone playful and suggestive.

I can feel my eyes narrow in annoyance as I look at him with disbelief. I slam the glass down on the side table, the liquid spilling a bit on the wooden table. How can he act like a horny, sex-deprived dog when I am pouring out my fears and concerns?

"Atticus, I am serious," I say, making sure to put intensity in each word to ensure he understands that I am dead serious. But that only makes his grin widen. I let out a sigh of frustration as I combed my rustled hair with my palm. This man is not taking me seriously.

"You're not funny, Atticus!" I hiss and turn my back to him to make my way towards the open balcony of the room. The north wind greets me quickly, gently caressing my skin and soothing my frayed nerves. The moon looks beautiful on this cloudless night, providing me with a clear view of the Milky Way.

I hear Atticus' footsteps following me from behind. To my surprise, he snakes his arm around my tiny waist, forcing me to look at him. My eyes narrow into slits as I meet his hazel-coloured gaze.

"You are so irritating! Quit acting like that," I seethe.

"Quit acting what?"

"Quit acting like you don't care about my opinion. Especially in this kind of matter!"

Atticus rolls his eyes as if finding my reaction childish. "I'm not trying to disregard your opinion about this matter. I simply do not want you to stress yourself too much. I'll take care of it once we get home, alright?" He assures me and plants a soft kiss on my temple.

I slap his arm that's enclosing my waist to get away from his hold. Why can't he understand it from my point of view? I want to be part of this. I don't want him to see me as someone who constantly needs protection.

"Why can't we both deal with it? I am your Queen, Atticus. Why on earth do I feel like you don't want me to be part of it?" I can't help but raise my voice at him. I thought he looked at me as his equal, but he wanted me to hide inside the castle at the first sign of danger while he dealt with it ineffectively.

"Because I don't want you to run straight towards the fire." He reasons out with seriousness lacing his voice, his gaze locks on mine. His expression softens as he cups my cheeks with both his hands. "Those rogues are dangerous. A single one can kill a fully trained warrior. Let's discuss this more once we are back home. For now, take a rest. I need to discuss something important with King Silvan."

He leans down and puts a quick kiss on the side of my lips. A gentle smile is on his lips as he finally lets go of me. He turns his back on me and walks out of the room. I am left alone on the balcony, staring at the door closing behind him. I let out a bitter smile.

He left.

That's it.

He didn't want to argue with me and talk things out to solve the problem, so he decided to retreat and leave me hanging. I suck on my inner cheeks as irritation fills my chest. Well, that turned out great.

"Don't hate him. He's just thinking about your safety," Samuel says as he enters the room without warning.

I roll my eyes at him and divert my attention towards the vast territory of Kaedal. This Kingdom is almost as big as Puer Lunae. The houses in the far distance look so aesthetically beautiful from where I am standing. I take a deep breath to release the tension inside my chest.

"Those bewitched vampires are dangerous, Samuel. And I think I just realized something tonight." My hold on the railing tightens.

"What is it?" Samuel questions from behind me with a keen interest in his voice.

"What if Lady Naya is a whistleblower, and they killed her because they want to make her shut up?" I turn to face him and make my way to the bed to take a seat on it. I really hope that my conclusion is wrong. However, for some reason, I cannot shrug off the idea that Lady Naya knows something about the bewitched who attacked me tonight.

"If that's true, then why did she keep silent about it? She could have told Atticus or me. She could have asked for our help, but she didn't. Instead, she dragged you into all this chaos and allowed herself to get killed." He remarks with frustration in his tone.

I take a deep breath and nod in understanding. My shoulders slump in defeat upon realizing that Samuel has a point. He's right. Lady Naya had so much time to confess to Atticus, but she didn't do it. She knew they would kill her. That's the main reason why she sent those letters to me. What puzzles me the most is the fact that she accepted her death willingly. She's the future Queen, yet she let herself get killed. My question is, what made her think that she must die to save the Kingdom?

I don't get it. What am I missing?

CHAPTER 24

Naya

The morning has come, and it is also our last day in Kaedal. We are set to head back to Puer Lunae before dark. Atticus still keeps dodging my questions about the bewitched vampires. Clearly, it is a problem he doesn't want me to be included in. I don't know if he is doing that to protect me, but if he is, he is not doing an excellent job. I will run straight into the fire with or without his permission. He can either fight beside me, or I will wage war with our enemies without him.

"A penny for your thoughts,"

That voice captures my attention, breaking the serene silence surrounding me. I am currently in the courtyard of the castle, staring at the man-made fountain that flows towards a pool in the middle. The sound of the stream is calming my insides, and it helps me relax despite my current situation.

"What are you doing here? Where's my husband?" I ask without bothering to hide the irritation in my voice. After all that I've been through in these past few days, I need this silent moment on my own. I need to have a little time to be at peace with my thoughts.

"Atticus is with Harriet. I guess they are having a small talk," he replies, completely ruining my mood.

"Their conversation cannot wait until we are back in the Kingdom?" I huff, my eyes squinting in annoyance. Harriet can be included in the issue of bewitched vampires, but I can't?

King Silvan lets out a smile at my reaction. He closes our distance and stands in the empty space beside me.

"You're jealous," he says, pointing out the obvious.

I turn my gaze away from him and look at the clear pool in front of us. Yes, I am jealous, but so what? I am his wife.

"I am his wife." My palms ball into a fist. Pain envelops my chest at the thought that Harriet and Atticus are together at the moment. "I may be fake, but our bond is real. I am his beloved, and he is mine."

"Of course, but that's exactly why you shouldn't get jealous of Harriet. Atticus is yours, and there's nothing Harriet can do to change that. You need to trust your beloved."

A sad smile forms on my lips at his futile attempt to console me. That's the problem. Atticus is not mine. His heart belongs to Lady Naya, not to Detective Naya. We are two different people.

"I'm pretty sure I don't need to voice my greatest fear, King Silvan. Harriet likes Atticus, and once Atticus learns about my conspiracy, that's the end of our pretend relationship." I feel the side of my eyes starts to heat up. I swallow hard to stop myself from crying. "Once he learns that I am a fraud, I will be gone, and I'm pretty sure that Harriet will be the one to take my place in his life."

"You are being too pessimistic, Queen Naya," he says, "If you are scared that Atticus might find out your secret, then accept my offer."

I can't help but let out a mocking laugh as I shake my head. I wish it was that easy. Even if I were to accept his offer and allow myself to be turned into a vampire, that wouldn't guarantee that Atticus wouldn't find out about my secret. As a detective, it is my job to uncover hidden truths, no matter how deeply buried they may be. There are no secrets in the universe that can remain concealed forever. It's only a matter of time before Atticus finds out about my secret.

"I will have your firstborn, so rest assured that if things don't go according to plan, I have your back," he assures me.

His words make me take a deep breath. That's one of the things that's been weighing on my mind. I turn to look at him with questioning eyes, wanting to know what his plan really is.

"Why do you want to have my firstborn? What are you planning to do with it? Hide it in a high tower with no doors?" I can't help but add a hint of sarcasm to my tone as I speak. I am curious and so confused as well. Why would the King of a powerful kingdom take an interest in a child that has never been born yet? A child that is highly unlikely to be conceived in the first place.

King Silvan meets my eyes with a playful smile on his lips, and a spark of amusement dances in his eyes, making me feel as if he is toying with me. I want to demand an explanation, but I know I am powerless over him.

"I don't know. Maybe I just want to own a walking blood bag. After all, human blood is of the finest quality." He shrugs.

My eyes squint in anger at his answer. "Try to do that to my child, and trust me, I don't care if you are a King. I'm going to have your head!" The intensity in my voice makes my chest vibrate. There's no way

I am going to allow him to hurt my child in any way.

King Silvan lets out a soft laugh of amusement at my threat. He probably thinks that I can't do that and that it is nothing but an empty threat. However, what he fails to remember is that even a deer can pose a threat when backed into a corner by a lion.

"Relax, I'm just kidding. Your firstborn is likely to be Atticus's child too. Each firstborn is important to every royalty. They are the future bearer of the crown. Atticus will resent me once he learns about our agreement, but there's nothing he can do to change it. Our contract has been sealed."

My forehead creases in confusion. What contract? I don't remember signing any contract. I feel my chest starts to race in worry for my child and for my Kingdom. Why do I feel like this man in front of me took advantage of my weakness and ignorance?

"Contract?" I parrot, my eyebrows connecting into one line in bewilderment. I give him a puzzled look. What exactly does it mean to be promised in this world to a certain person? And why even a king like Atticus can't do anything about it?

"Yeah, a contract. You sealed it the moment you verbally promised your firstborn to me," he briefly explains, but that does nothing to clear up the questions in my head.

"And what does that mean?"

To my dismay, King Silvan simply replies with a knowing smirk and a shrug. I shake my head in disbelief while looking at him. Knowing that he won't answer my question, I turn my back on him and walk away. Talking to him about it won't help me clarify things about the situation. I need to speak with Samuel about this. If King Silvan refuses to give me the information I need, I better check it on my own. I just hope I didn't mess up as badly as I think I did.

***

"You did what?!" Samuel's voice echoes through the room after I confess to him about the contract I have with King Silvan.

I can't help but grimace at his reaction. Judging by how loud his roar is, I conclude that being promised a vampire is not a good thing.

"I have no choice, Samuel. King Silvan learned that I am not the real Naya. What do you want me to do?" I explain to defend myself.

"Do you know what you just did? Your firstborn is the next King or Queen of Puer Lunae, and you promised it to the King of Kaedal. Do you understand what this means for the future of Puer Lunae?" He reaches out to his forehead and massages it. I can tell from his expression that he is not amused by our situation.

I let out a heave and shrug. "I mean, we are not even sure if I will have a firstborn. Once Atticus learns about our secret, I am basically dead, so I didn't really think about that. Also, even if I survive, I don't think Atticus would want a human to bear his child." For some reason, I can't help but feel sad at my own words.

I hate to admit it, but that is precisely the main reason why I am confident in promising my firstborn to King Silvan. I am expecting to either die or go back to the human world after solving this case.

"You don't understand, Naya. If you promise someone to anyone in this world, especially to a King, you are already forging that child's destiny. You will have your firstborn, and yeah, we are not sure if it will be King Atticus's firstborn, but still. There's a big chance that it is going to be," he explains as he paces in front of me.

"I get it, but what could be the worst that can happen? If it is Atticus's child, then I'm sure he will do something to protect our child,"

Samuel stops pacing and turns to look at me as if I've grown a second head or something.

"If you are promised to someone, that means no man alive can separate you from the person who owns you. You just chose your child's destiny, and that is to be King Silvan's puppet all its life. The future King or Queen of Puer Lunae can't be someone else's puppet, or else our Kingdom is set to fall into his hands," he explains, making me freeze in my spot.

"I'm sorry?" I stand up from the bed and look at him in disbelief, wanting to make sure that I understand his words correctly.

"Yes, you just sold our Kingdom to King Silvan," he confirms.

I stand frozen in front of him, unmoving. My hand reaches for my head as I feel a headache coming. I still can't believe that King Silvan did that to me.

"That fucking manipulative son of a bitch!" I hiss in anger upon realizing the mistake I have committed. I rub my palms on my face out of frustration. I messed up so bad, really bad.

CHAPTER 25

Naya

"Do you still worry about those rogues, Naya? You seem tense," Atticus questions upon noticing my uneasiness.

We are on the carriage, currently on our way back to Puer Lunae. The alliance has been successfully signed between Kaedal and our Kingdom, and King Silvan has vowed to be on Puer Lunae's side as long as he remains the King of Kaedal. Unfortunately, I haven't had a chance to confront him before we left. Now, I am stuck with the fact that I just sold Puer Lunae to that cunning pig. I still can't believe that I fell for his trap. I want to kick him in the gut for swindling me, but given the situation, it's not as if I have any other choices.

King Silvan proves himself to be a worthy enemy and ally. He is the kind of person who loves to keep a low profile but is dangerous. The problem is, I can't even confront him with Atticus around because that would raise suspicion. Another issue is that if I try to confess what I have done to my husband, it will resort to a total chaos. So now, I am stuck with no idea how to fix the mess I have created.

With a heavy heart, I release a tired sigh before mustering a smile on my lips as I meet the gaze of my beloved. Drawing closer to him, I lean my head on his chest, wishing I could divulge all the struggles weighing me down. I long to weep in his arms and pour out my woes, but it's impossible.

"It's nothing... I don't want to talk about it right now. Let's address it once we're home," I rasp.

He places his arm on my shoulder and begins to rub it gently, a sweet gesture that brings a genuine smile to my lips. I know that when I leave this world, his presence will be one of the things I'll miss most. I close my eyes and shut off my thoughts. Though I'll never admit it, his name is already etched deeply in my heart, and my feelings for him are only growing stronger as it goes by.

"I'm wondering, what do you think of having a child, my Queen?" my beloved asks out of nowhere, forcing me to open my eyes.

For a few good seconds, I am at a loss for words. I don't have any idea how to respond to that.

"Of course, I would love to have your child, Atticus. I'm pretty sure the whole Kingdom is expecting an announcement about an incoming heir anytime soon," I manage to say despite suddenly feeling lightheaded from the topic. I look up at him and reach out a bit to put a soft kiss on the side of his lips.

I hate how easy it is for me to get lost in the waves of love and lust between us. Samuel says that my body will respond according to my beloved's needs. I wonder if what I am feeling right now has something to do with what he is feeling.

"Tonight will mark our ninth night since our wedding." He says, his grip tightening on my shoulder. His head dips down as he captures my lips in a deep, breathtaking kiss.

I close my eyes and allow him to lead the kiss, letting myself get lost in that sweet sensation only his touch can give. I know what I am doing is dangerous. Atticus could bite me suddenly without asking for permission. It is pretty common for vampires to crave blood once they have been entirely overtaken by lust.

"I know I promised to give you time, but we need to complete the mating tonight," he whispers after letting go of my lips.

My eyes flutter open and meet his bloody red ones. I give him a curious look, confused about what he means by the ninth night.

"Do we really?" I ask, plastering a teasing smile on my lips to cover my sudden confusion.

Atticus' expression softens while looking at me. His eyes remain in their beautiful, deep, bloody red colour, a telltale sign that his beast is just beneath the surface. My beloved never really pushes himself on me. He's always calm and composed. Those are the qualities that made me fall for him. He is respectful, and he is not the kind of man to demand his needs from a woman even though he has all the right to insist on it.

He reaches out for my chin and has his thumb play a little bit on my cheek, caressing it softly as if he is tracing it.

"I will try my best to control my beast, but I do not promise anything. The last thing I want to happen is for me to be all possessive and accidentally hurt you," he explains, making me more and more confused.

Okay? Now, this is starting to sound a bit disturbing. What exactly does the ninth night mean? It's funny because Samuel didn't even mention it to me. I distance myself from Atticus a bit and straighten in my seat. Samuel is so good at putting me in a not-so-pleasant situation without giving me a warning. I always find myself dealing with the mess right on the spot because my excellent sidekick lacks the sense of responsibility to explain the unwritten rules of this world to me.

"Who in their right mind would reject the King's mark?" I reply, trying my best to cover my confusion with an enigmatic smile.

I am going to pray to heaven that the ninth night does not mean death for me. I want to clarify with Atticus what he is referring to. However, I have a feeling that the ninth night is common knowledge for vampires, so it would be stupid to ask him about it. I keep my mouth shut about the topic and try to divert his attention to other things.

We spent the rest of the travel time flirting and cuddling with each other. We talked a bit about the future of the Kingdom and his plans for it. We also discussed the alliance with King Silvan.

When we arrived in Puer Lunae, I excused myself and told Atticus that I wanted to rest. Samuel immediately followed me to the royal chamber. Once we are back in the room, I turn to him with questioning eyes. I need to ask him about what I should expect for tonight. I need to be prepared for it.

"Are you kidding me, Samuel? Why the heck didn't you inform me about it sooner?" I yell in a combination of shock and terror.

He explains that the ninth night will trigger the heat in a woman. Basically, it's a night when male vampires can lose control of their beast. It's not really a big deal because it only happens to pairs without a mark. The heat does not affect marked couples. The problem is I am Atticus's beloved, and he hasn't marked me yet.

I'm basically dead.

I run my fingers through my hair in frustration. If I had known this would happen, I would have accepted King Silvan's offer. I think I would have a better chance of survival if I were a vampire.

"It didn't cross my mind. The heat is not something that most vampires deal with because, usually, they consummate the marriage and complete the marking on the nuptial night. It didn't really cross my mind until you mentioned it today. Besides, you're human, not a vampire," he reasons.

I roll my eyes at his explanation. In the corner of my eye, I can see the sun starting to set on the horizon through the glass window of the room. It's just a matter of time before I experience the heat. Apparently, heat is nature's way of ensuring that those who have spoken their vow will consummate the wedding and ensure a child is on the way.

I reach out to my forehead to massage it. Why does it feel like all the rules in this world are created to be against me? I figure out a way to dodge an incoming danger, but then the unspoken or unwritten rules they have fuck me up again. This is frustrating and tiring. I hate it.

"What am I going to do now, then?" I ask him. "This is bad. If we don't do anything tonight, it's basically over for both of us."

Suddenly, the gruesome scene when Atticus lost his control over his beast and killed Idris crosses my mind, making me slightly shake in fear. I know that my beloved won't hurt me physically, but if that is the beast that I am set to encounter tonight, no, thank you.

I can't stop myself from fidgeting due to mixed emotions. I have a feeling that tonight is going to be a total nightmare for me.

"Well, you are in luck then because you have me by your side," A velvety voice interrupts us, drawing our attention towards the open balcony of the room. A woman with a stunning appearance captures our gaze, possessing purple-coloured eyes and blonde hair.

My forehead creases in confusion while staring at the newcomer.

"And who are you?" I cross my arms in front of my chest, feeling a bit uneasy about someone overhearing my conversation with Samuel.

"My Queen, it was you who summoned me here," the mysterious woman replies in a calm and measured tone as she gracefully walks towards an empty seat and settles into it.

"Zizina, I'm glad you received my message," Samuel interrupts, making me arch my left eyebrow while still looking at the woman.

So, is this the messenger we have been searching for?

The woman turns to look at Samuel. I cannot help but notice the spark of interest in her eyes as she gazes at my butler. Her purple-coloured eyes are incredibly expressive, enabling me to read her emotions with ease.

"I did. I'm in the coven for my training and just got home this afternoon. My mother told me that Lady Naya summoned me to the castle, which is quite surprising because I figured that she would be dead by now," she replies.

"So, you knew about her death?" I question, making her turn in my direction.

She lets out a sigh and shrugs. "Of course, Ms. Cirillo. I am the one who delivered the fan mail to you, aren't I?" she confirms.

A spark of hope starts to fill my heart at her answer— finally, the big missing part of the puzzle. Does this mean this case is getting closer to the end now?

This feels so anticlimactic, in my opinion.

"Well, that's cool. Let's stop the chase here. Just tell us who killed Lady Naya," I demand. I can feel the rays of the sunset on my cheeks passing through the window, reminding me that we are getting closer and closer to nighttime.

This world of vampires, covenants, and murder is just too much for me. The fear of what's about to happen tonight makes me want to rush back to the safety of the human world. After solving this murder case, I'll probably go on a long vacation or something. This experience has given me more than enough scares I can handle in one lifetime.

Zizina lets out a sigh as she slowly shakes her head. "You've been summoned here by Lady Naya for a reason. Her murderers are out there, waiting for the right time to attack the Kingdom. This Kingdom needs you." she explains.

I stand frozen in front of her. My throat starts to feel dry. That little spark of hope that I have started to die slowly until there's nothing left of it, not even a tiny ember. I have a feeling she would say that, but I still chose to hope, only for that hope to be shattered in the end. Both of my hands close into tight fists.

"I am a detective. My job is to investigate a certain crime and find the real murderer. After that, I am out. I have nothing to do with your Kingdom. This is not why I came here!" I seethe in anger while looking at them with resentment.

"You are the Queen," Zizina stands up from her chair and meets my heated gaze. "You have an obligation to protect the kingdom, your Kingdom!"

"Your real queen is dead." I contest. "Now I'm begging you, tell me who is the person behind her death, please?" My tone is almost close to begging, and I can feel the sides of my eyes starting to water, my heart shrinking for every second that passes.

Zizina releases a tired sigh while looking at my hopeless expression. She takes a step back and averts her gaze away from me.

"That's the problem. I know Idris has involvement in this, but I know nothing more than that."

I look at her with disbelief. Frustration starts to creep into my chest. "Do you expect me to believe that?"

"I hope I am lying," she swallows hard and turns to lock eyes with me. "Lady Naya didn't tell me anything because if someone finds out that I know something, I might suffer a fate similar to hers. You probably knew more information now than I do."

I take a step back and allow myself to slump down into the nearby chair. "Damn it!" I hiss under my breath and reach out to my forehead to massage it.

I take a few deep breaths to calm my racing heartbeat. I don't want to be selfish, but this is starting to feel overwhelming. I want to help the Kingdom. I want to help Atticus. However, staying in this place puts not only my life in danger but also my heart. This mission is asking so much of me. It is asking not only for my life but also for my heart and soul.

How did I end up in this situation again?

CHAPTER 26

Naya

"Okay, fine then. I don't know what information you have, but what I know so far is that the ring Lady Naya sent to me has a connection to her murder. Niall wears the same ring, and Idris has a bracelet that has a very similar design to it." I begin the moment I start to feel calm and collected. "I have a hunch that her death has a connection to the bewitched we've encountered on our way to Kaedal, but I don't have any proof yet for that."

"The stone in the ring is what connects their group. At least, that's what I know. It's like a symbol of brotherhood." Zizina adds as she folds her arms in front of her chest.

My eyes squint while looking at her. I got that now, but that still doesn't really answer my main question.

"What is this group for?" I question. "I understand that Lady Naya wants me to solve the mystery behind her death, but why exactly do I need to do that. Clearly, this is not about justice, this is something deeper than that." I arch my eyebrow at Zizina, waiting for her to explain or at least give me more information.

"They are building a resistance," she reveals. "Those bewitched you have encountered, someone or rather some people from the kingdom are trying to weaponize them as a means to destroy the Kingdom. I'm still trying to look for the source of the potions, but I'm having a hard time tracing where they are coming from."

"I don't think that's possible," Samuel chimes in. "Most people in the Kingdom are loyal to the King. I don't think they can recruit enough numbers to overthrow Atticus."

Zizina turns to Samuel and lets out a heavy sigh. I can see how bothered she is with the current situation we are dealing with. "Rogues are easy to recruit, Samuel. However, that's the other issue. I tried to check with the rogues that settled on the Kingdom's border, but I'm not seeing any threat coming from them. I don't think they are even aware of the issue with bewitched vampires."

I open my lips to say something, however, the sudden loud thumping in my chest stops me. My eyes turn to the window, only to see that the sun has completely descended on the horizon. My hand flies to my chest, making them turn to look at me with worry written in their eyes.

"Damn it! We're out of time. We need to act quickly, or it'll all be over tonight." Samuel grunts upon noticing that darkness has fully blanketed the whole Kingdom. His eyes turn to the witch. "Zizina, do you have any potion that can lessen the effect of heat?"

Zizina raises her left eyebrow at Samuel's question. "You can't avoid it, idiot. If they don't consummate the wedding tonight, what do you think the people in the castle will think of that? She needs to be claimed by the King."

I can feel my throat starting to feel dry. Is she serious? How am I supposed to do that without revealing my real identity to the King? Atticus will murder me once he learns that I am not Lady Naya.

"If the King claims me, it will be the end of this mini-roleplay we are playing. I can't let Atticus do that," I argue. I turn to look at Samuel with panic written in my eyes. I feel so helpless.

"You need to consummate the marriage, my Queen," Zizina insists. "If this night passes without you bearing the King's mark, that will bring so much suspicion towards you. Trust me, lots of people in this castle would love to know why the King hasn't marked and completed the mating with the Queen yet."

I run my fingers through my hair in frustration and take a few deep breaths to steady my heartbeat. Of course, she's right. People will question why we haven't consummated the wedding yet.

"What do you want me to do then?" I whine in a helpless tone. "I can't let the King bite me or even mate with me. That will be a disaster," I make my way towards the nearest chair and slump on it. I rub my palm on my face out of helplessness. Even if there's a way for me to be claimed by the King without being noticed, I still can't do it. If I let something happen between Atticus and me, then there'll be nothing left of me.

"Why do I need to give my all for this?" I can't help but complain. "I want to help, but you guys are asking too much of me, and I can't afford to give my all in this," I whimper as tears start to well up on the side of my eyes.

Zizina looks at me with a pained expression. She's a woman too. I know she can understand what I am feeling right now.

"He's your husband. You are the Queen. In your eyes, you're probably just pretending. However, in our perspective and Atticus's eyes, you are the Queen. His wife. There's no turning back now, Naya. When you chose to accept the vow, you had already chosen your destiny," she explains.

Looking up at her, a wave of helplessness and vulnerability engulfs me, rendering me acutely aware of my powerlessness. She closes the gap between us, extending her hand and presenting me with something she fetched from her small bag. I stare at the small red bottle she has given me. The liquid within it emits a radiant glow as if it is purposefully designed to enchant and mesmerize me.

"This is also one of the things that I've been working on while I was at the coven. That bottle contains an essence that will change the taste and scent of your blood into that of a vampire," she says and offers me an understanding smile. "In the end, the decision is still yours, my Queen. I know that what we are asking of you is too much, but it will cost us our own Kingdom if we don't. I hope that you can reconsider..."

My eyes remain fixed on the red bottle in my hand. Tonight, Atticus's beast will take over, and if I refuse to drink this, our game will be over. Who knows what will happen after that? He could kill me, throw me in the dungeon, or even banish me back to the human world.

A blank smile spreads across my lips, and a lone tear falls from the corner of my eye. The truth is, no matter how many times I tell myself that I am doing this to help Lady Naya, there is no denying that my feelings for Atticus have something to do with it as well.

The big question is, am I ready to give up my growing love for the King? Can I bear to end our pretend arrangement?

I hear the door opening and closing, followed by footsteps as they exit the room, giving me time to think. I let out a tired sigh while staring at the enchanting bottle. A hollow smile forms on my lips.

My grip on the bottle tightens. I wish it was that easy. I wish I could simply turn my back on this world. I wish I could drink this and complete the mating with my beloved without complicating things in the future.

If I choose to confess to Atticus, all the things that I've done and the progress I've made will go to waste. However, if I drink this bottle in my hand, I might end up in a sandpit with no hope of getting out in the future. Either I go back to my normal life as a human or lose everything that I have right now— including Atticus.

I let out a heave and twist the lid of the bottle open. Smoke rises from it, making me feel a bit scared of what I am about to do. I take a deep breath and bring the bottle up to my nose to take a sniff. A sweet floral scent fills my senses, making me smile a little. The smell brings back some kind of nostalgia.

I drink the contents of the bottle in one gulp, not giving myself a chance to back down. My eyes automatically close upon tasting the mixture of bitter and spicy liquid in my throat. My face contorts as I open my eyes and stare at the empty bottle. The scent of this liquid had tricked me into thinking it would taste sweet.

I can't help but grimace upon feeling the aftertaste on my tongue and throat. I throw the bottle into the nearest bin and stand up from my seat. I make my way towards the table where there is a pitcher of water. I need water to wash the bitter taste from my tongue.

"What the heck was that made of?" I grumble under my breath as I place the empty glass of water back on the table.

I am about to walk towards the door to look for my husband when my vision suddenly turns red. I halt and lean on the nearest piece of furniture I can reach. I take a few deep breaths and clutch my chest to steady my heartbeat. Everything around me suddenly becomes vivid. The sound of the insects outside, my heartbeat, and even my breathing— everything seems so loud. I can hear it all clearly. It feels as if I have suddenly become fully aware of my surroundings.

"What the heck is happening to me?" I groan as I push myself to walk towards one of the chairs to sit on it.

That's when my eyes catch my own reflection in the vanity mirror not far from me. My forehead creases as I stare at my image. My skin doesn't look fairer, but for some reason, it seems to be glowing or something. My lips are a deep red colour, but what shocks me is my eyes. Similar to my lips, they are now a bloody red colour, far from the deep blue colour they used to be.

I unconsciously reach out to my cheeks while looking at the mirror. So, this is how I look in vampire form? My gaze shifts to the bin where I threw the empty bottle a while ago. I thought that the potion was only set to change the taste of my blood, but no, it changed me entirely to the point of giving me a vampire look, and probably some of their abilities.

I take a few deep breaths to collect myself. I walk towards the veranda and feel the gentle caress of the wind against my skin. Looking at my vast and mighty kingdom, I can't help but reminisce my life back in the human world. My hand reaches for my chest as I feel a void starting to build up inside my heart.

After tonight, I'm pretty sure that my feelings towards my husband are just going to deepen. I don't know exactly what is waiting for me ahead, and thinking about the future is quite overwhelming. I am starting to feel scared of it. However, I can't turn my back on this now, even if I want to. I can't do it, not when I know I am willing to give my life just for a short moment with my husband.

I take a deep breath and force a smile on my lips. I can't help but wonder what my life would be like right now if I hadn't followed the clues sent by Lady Naya. Maybe I would still be at home, or perhaps I would be currently following traces of another murderer.

I am lost in thought when I hear the door opening and closing from behind me.

Suddenly, I feel my body firing up as if someone has ignited some kind of flame inside me. I don't need to turn around to see who it is. I can feel my husband's waves of authority filling up our room.

"Is there something bothering you, my Queen? The night is still young, but I can sense your uneasiness even though I am on the other side of the castle. What happened?" he asks with concern in his tone.

He can feel my worries? Interesting...

I turn around to meet his gaze with a sweet smile on my lips. Tonight, I have decided. I am going to give my all to him. I don't care if this will break me in the end to the point of no repair. I am done being afraid of the uncertainties of tomorrow. Atticus is my beloved, my husband, and my King. I want to own him fully. And this time...without fear or restrictions.

CHAPTER 27

Naya

I close the distance between us with short, but sure strides, feeling butterflies fluttering in my stomach from anticipation. With a swift movement, I pull out the pins securing my hair and toss them carelessly at a nearby chair, allowing my thick, fiery red hair to cascade down my shoulders, framing my face.

I stand right in front of my husband with my eyes not leaving his.

"Atticus," I murmur as my fingers start to trace the golden embroidery of his buttons. "You're always so patient with me, and I really appreciate it." My palm grasps his collar, pulling him closer to me.

"I'm ready," I continue, my voice low and husky as I tiptoe and start to land short, feathery kisses on his lips, savouring the feel of his warmth against mine.

Atticus' arms snake around my waist, pulling me close to him and dominating our kiss. I feel his fangs brush against my inner lips, making me dizzy as strange sensations flood my senses. My eyes shut automatically as if it is the most righteous thing to do at the moment. I have nothing to fear now. I'll be his fully after this. I should be afraid of it, but for some strange reason, I find myself enthralled by the idea. I want to feel his fangs sinking into my flesh. I want to know how it feels to become his Queen.

I feel myself float into thin air as my husband lifts me in his arms and makes his way towards the waiting bed. He pulls away from me for a bit as he places me right in the centre of the soft bed. His eyes fixate on mine as he gathers a few pieces of my bangs that are scattered on my face and pin them to the side of my ear.

"You're not going to trick me again with poisoned wine, right? It won't work on me tonight," he asks with a playful smile carved onto his lips.

I can't help but chuckle upon remembering our first night together.

"Nope, no poisoned wine tonight," I reply. "Just poisoned kisses, I guess."

His smile widens at my response.

"Your kisses are to die for anyway, so it's fine," he mutters, and once again, our lips brush against each other.

He captures my lips in an intimate manner, without rushing, sandwiching my body between his strong muscular one and the soft mattress of the bed. My arms snake around his neck to pull him closer to me. Tonight is something that I will surely cherish until the day I die, and as much as possible, I want it to be memorable for both of us.

My fingers reach out to his buttons without breaking our kiss. I want to feel his body without any barrier against mine. I want to taste every inch of his skin and shower his chest with small little kisses, something that I've been wanting to do since our wedding night. I am his wife anyway. I own him as much as he owns me. He helps me remove the suit he is wearing. Then I feel his hands on my back where the zipper of my gown is located as he drags it down to my waistline. I push him a bit to help him remove the flimsy fabric from my body.

My whole being is burning with desire as his lips land on my jaw, trailing their way down to my chest area. His lips and tongue start to play with my left breast while his hand cups and gently massages the other one. I let out an audible moan. His touch and kisses are like wine. It is easy for me to get drunk in sensation with every touch and kiss. His rough palm caresses my body, leaving no parts of me untouched.

"Atticus..." I call out his name, grinding my body against him sensually. My core is aching so bad and I feel like I am about to lose my mind anytime soon.

His lips move up to my neck, feeling the sharpness of his fangs on my sensitive flesh. The fear that used to occupy me whenever I thought of him feeding on me is nowhere to be found now. Instead, the exhilarating desire of being his completely excites me. I close my eyes as my fingers dig into his broad shoulder. I tilt my head a bit, giving him access to the most vulnerable part of my body, showing my submission to him.

His pointy fangs graze that sensitive spot on my neck as he starts to lick my skin, numbing it in the process. I stifle a moan of pain as I feel a sharp sensation followed by immense pleasure. A lone tear falls on the side of my eye. I know that from this moment on, Atticus owns every inch of me. I am his, completely.

***

My eyes flutter open, still feeling a bit drowsy. I let out a soft yawn and look around the room. Then my eyes turn to the man who is peacefully sleeping beside me. Happiness fills my heart upon seeing that small, contented smile on his lips despite being in deep sleep. I scoot close to him, wanting to feel his warmth against mine. Morning cuddles are undoubtedly one of those small moments that are so underrated. Atticus must have sensed my small frame squeezing into his body that he slips his arm around my waist, pulling me close to him. Our naked bodies mould perfectly with each other as if we are meant to be together from the very beginning.

I take a deep inhale as I bury my face in the crook of his neck, taking in his fresh pine scent that can easily bring me to cloud nine. I want to spend the rest of the day inside our room with us cuddling like this. I never really got a chance to spend a day with my husband since we got married. He's always busy with his royal duties, while I, on the other hand, am always busy chasing shadows.

"Atticus..." I murmur. I can feel that he is already in his half-awake phase.

When he doesn't respond to my call, I look up at him and reach out to plant small little kisses on the side of his lips, on his cheeks, lips, his closed eyes, and the tip of his nose.

His eyes flutter open, meeting my bluish ones.

"Hey, good morning, my Queen," he greets me with a smile and lets out a yawn.

"Good morning," I respond and put one last peck on his left cheek, only to let out a muffled scream when he flips us over, and he is suddenly on top of me. A playful smile never leaves his lips as his eyes survey my face.

"We haven't got a chance to eat dinner last night. How about breakfast in bed?" He teases with a suggestive smile playing on his lips.

I nod at him in response and smile. Based on the smirk on his lips, I know he is talking about another 'kind' of breakfast in bed. But literally speaking, we actually both completely forgot to eat dinner last night. Surprisingly, I don't feel a bit hungry at all. I wonder if it has something to do with me drinking his blood. I need to talk to Zizina about it once the effect of the potion subsides, but for now, I want to focus on us.

Atticus's lips trail down to my neck, and he starts planting light butterfly kisses on my skin. I close my eyes and let out soft mewls. His lips leave a trail of currents on my skin, enough to wake up the sleeping desire inside of me.

However, as much as I enjoy what he is doing, there's something important that I want to ask him. The past few days have been tough on both of us, and we haven't really had a chance to spend time together, so maybe today can be that day.

"Atticus, would you mind taking the day off today?" I ask in a very small voice.

My question makes him halt. He distances himself a bit from me, locking our eyes with each other. His forehead creases a bit, but the captivating smile remains on his lips.

"A day off?" he parrots.

I divert my gaze away from his warm amber eyes down to his broad chest, tracing the lines on it with my forefinger. I know what I am asking is probably a little childish, but I really want to spend a little bit of time with him away from our responsibilities. Just him and me on an average day, like a date or something.

"Yeah... a day with no royal duties and responsibilities, just the two of us spending time with each other," I murmur without looking at him. It might be a selfish request, but I really want to take a little bit of a step back today. I want us to spend time together. I want us to enjoy each other's company without worrying about rogues and our royal responsibilities.

"So you want me to spend the whole day with you?" he asks. His eyes are sparkling with amusement upon noticing my discomfort.

I lift my gaze to look at him as I gently nod in response. I'm not the kind of person to beg for someone's time or attention. I love Atticus, but to be honest, I hate how I am becoming dependent on him. I hate how messed up and confused I feel whenever I am with him.

"But if it's not okay, it's fine. I know you're busy with all the things that need fixing and the threat of the bewitched, so yeah... Just— just forget it." I immediately take back what I just said and push him away from me to sit on the bed.

I turn my eyes away from him to avoid his gaze and grab the blanket to cover my nakedness. If he was not in front of me, I would have slapped myself. What was I thinking anyway? Why would I think that going on a date with Atticus is more essential than our royal duties? That was stupid. My husband is a busy person, and I don't think it's fair for me to ask for this given our current situation. I hate how I am becoming unreasonable when it comes to my mate.

Atticus doesn't respond to my request for a long moment. He just looks at me with that knowing smile on his lips as I gather the silk comforter to cover my body. That makes me even more embarrassed than I already am. When I can't bear it anymore, I turn to look at him with annoyance.

"What?" I hiss at him in irritation.

His smile widens until it turns into a smug smirk. He shakes his head in amusement. Before I even know what he's going to do, he grabs the comforter from my hand and pushes me back onto the bed.

My eyes widen in surprise. "Hey, Atticus, stop it! Let me go!"

I push him away from me with all my might, but he is so much stronger than I am. I give all of my strength to create a bit of space between us, but it's a hopeless struggle. Atticus's strength is scary sometimes. He's a King, and I've seen him kill Idris without breaking a sweat. I wonder how strong a King of vampires really is. Realizing that I'm fighting a losing battle, I decided to stay put and look up to meet his eyes.

Those beautiful hazel orbs are now a bloody red colour, indicating that his beast is starting to take over. He blinks twice, and then his eyes slowly turn back to their original warm amber colour. This man is so handsome. How did I end up with him again?

"I'm sorry, it's just that you look so painfully beautiful when you're acting so unsure of yourself like that," he whispers and leans down to playfully bite the side of my neck. "You don't have to be shy to ask me for anything, my Queen. I may be a King, but I'm also your husband. Yes, I have an obligation to protect our Kingdom, but I also have an obligation to you as my beloved."

I keep my mouth shut without tearing my gaze away from him, not bothering to respond. He dips his head and places a soft kiss on the side of my neck, up to my jaw until his lips reach my waiting lips. I close my eyes and allow him to lead me to the ocean of pleasure where we both drowned last night. Giving myself a chance to get drunk on some kind of ecstasy that only my beloved can offer.

I pant for air the moment he lets go of my lips.

"I'm all yours today then. What's your plan for today, my Queen?" He asks me with a sweet smile plastered on his lips.

"Well, how about you take me on a date?" I ask him, trying hard to contain the happiness and excitement that fill my heart at the moment.

"A date it is." He hums and leans down a bit to put small kisses on my exposed chest. "But for now, I want my breakfast in bed..." He continues as I feel his fangs graze the skin on my neck.

I lean sideways to give him more access. My eyes automatically shut as his fangs pierce through my veins, enjoying that heavenly pleasure that envelops my body as he directly feeds on me. It is addicting, the pleasure increasing immensely for every moment that passes.

My grip on his shoulder tightens upon feeling his tongue playfully lick that sensitive part of my neck to close the wound on it. I let out a groan of satisfaction as I meet his deep bloody-red eyes. The heat building in my stomach starts to feel unbearable, silently asking for release.

This is probably one of the best things about being the Queen of Puer Lunae— being the King's lover...

CHAPTER 28

Naya

My gaze lands on the man holding my hand protectively. Just what the King had promised me this morning, he took the day off today, and now we are walking on the streets of Puer Lunae like an average couple on a date.

This is my first time exploring the Kingdom on foot, and all I can say is that Puer Lunae proves to be bountiful in all directions. The people are respectful and hospitable. Children play carelessly around the town without fear. I can see genuine happiness in our subjects' eyes, which only reflects how well our Kingdom is doing.

"Where do you want to have lunch?" Atticus asks.

I shrug as I look up to meet his gaze with a smile. "I have no idea, to be honest. Do you have one?"

I honestly don't have a single idea what is the best place to dine within our Kingdom. I kind of want a date in a secluded spot where we can spend time together in silence. I wonder if there's a restaurant here that could offer such kind of accommodation.

"I know a few, but since this is your day, I want you to decide," he answers with a warm and encouraging smile on his lips.

I tear my gaze off him and think for a bit. I want to be in a place near nature where I can relax, and of course, a place far away from the crowd.

"How about a picnic?" I blurt out as that's the first thing that comes to my mind. The suggestion is uncalled for, but I really miss being close to nature. I tried to reconnect once to the earth during my stay in the Kaedal Kingdom, but I encountered bewitched vampires.

Hopefully, this time will be a little bit different from that night. I really want to spend this day without having to deal with any of those shits right now. I want it to be as perfect and peaceful as possible— a romantic day with my beloved.

"Picnic it is," Atticus agrees without a second thought.

The next thing I know, he is already pulling me to one of the stalls that sell baskets and blankets. We end up getting two medium-sized baskets and one blanket. After that, we check out the nearby stalls and shops for food to eat.

After filling up our baskets with a variety of food and a bottle of wine, Atticus leads me to a place that I never expected him to bring me to, catching me completely off guard. He places the blanket on the ground under the shade of the willow tree while I remain frozen in my spot.

"Why here?" I ask, suddenly feeling uncomfortable about the place he has chosen.

He places both of the baskets on top of the blanket and motions for me to walk towards him. A hesitant smile curves on my lips as I close the space between us. I can't help but give a short glance at the tree where I know the remains of Lady Naya are buried. Of all places, why does he need to bring me here?

"Because I remember you telling me before that this is your favourite place in the Kingdom. I thought you would love it here," he replies.

My smile turns genuine. Sometimes it's nice for someone to remember small details about you. It warms my heart to know that my beloved always thinks of my welfare. This could be the most romantic date I could have in this lifetime if I were the real Naya.

"I'm glad that you remember that. This place is beautiful during sunsets," I mutter as I take a seat on the blanket.

Perhaps, no matter what I do, I can never erase her from Atticus's life. She's dead, but to be honest, she played a vital role in protecting this Kingdom even after her death. Maybe she was a pushover, and this world must have broken her multiple times, but she possessed a strong heart fitted for a Queen. She was a selfless leader. She never thought of herself or her feelings. She put the Kingdom's welfare first. On the other hand, I came here for personal interest.

Jealousy and self-hate started to fill my chest. I could never replace Lady Naya, not as the Queen of this Kingdom or even in Atticus's heart. I could never be her, and to be honest, I don't know if I should hate that or not.

I open one of the baskets to take out the food and arrange it on top of the blanket. I remain silent and keep my mouth shut while I busy myself arranging the food. I'm afraid that my voice will give away what I really feel once I say something.

"Do we have any problem?" Atticus asks, noticing the odd silence between us.

I raise my gaze from the food to meet his. I let out a feeble smile before shaking my head gently to respond. It seems that my beloved can easily feel whatever emotion that's dominating me. I wonder if it has something to do with his bond and us completing the process of mating.

"Nothing really. I just realize how lucky I am to be loved by you in this lifetime." I confess before taking a deep breath. I turn my eyes away from him to avoid losing courage. A smile escapes my lips as I stare at the horizon. "You are the perfect husband every woman can ask for in this Kingdom, Atticus. To be honest, I'm scared. What if one day you fall out of love? What if you wake up one day and you realize that I am not the woman you loved? I can't think of a future without you in it..." I whispered the last part, but I know he still heard them.

From the corner of my eye, I see the glint of joy in my beloved's eyes slowly falter until it is completely replaced with worry. In just a snap, he is already beside me, enclosing me in a protective hug. My eyes turn towards the food on the blanket, refusing to meet his gaze. I feel him bury his face in the crook of my neck, planting a soft kiss on it.

"Stop thinking like that, my Queen. Have you already forgotten how strong the bond between two people in love can be? I love you, and I always will until death do us part." His voice is full of conviction as he continues to comfort me by caressing my back with his palm.

Beloved's bond? I wonder how strong it is compared to the lies, deception, mistakes, and betrayals I am committing. Even the strongest relationship in the whole universe would shatter like glass against those sins. I am committing grave treason, not only to Atticus but also to his Kingdom. This is not just about Atticus and me anymore. I owe this Kingdom their true Queen.

I look up at him, finally meeting his gaze. "When the time comes that you realize I am not the woman you fell in love with, can you promise me one thing?" I ask in a soft tone.

A long silence fills the place for a few moments. Atticus must have noticed the sincerity and sadness in my voice because he lets out a sigh and nods after a few seconds.

"That will never happen, but if it will make you feel more secure, then sure, what is it?" He inquires.

I force myself to smile, a gentle one. "Remember that I love you. I always have. Millions of lies might have been said and done in this world, but that won't change what I feel for you. If there's one thing that's real about me, it is my love for you." I finally confess as my voice starts to crack in the end, my eyes welling up with unshed tears.

Atticus frowns while staring at me, completely clueless about the meaning behind my words. Of course, he has no clue what I am talking about, but I know that the time will come when he will understand everything. I hope that once that day comes, he will remember me not as the woman who tricked him but as the woman who fell in love with him, the woman who gave her all to be deemed worthy of his love.

Atticus's eyes soften. He raises his hand and caresses the side of my cheek.

"You love me. That's all I need to hear from you, my Queen. That's the most important thing that needs to be real. I'm blurring everything else," he replies as he pulls me closer to him to capture my lips for a kiss.

I close my eyes and savour the taste of his velvet lips against mine. My hands are on his chest while his arms are securing my waist. The kiss is short, but it is enough to remove my mind from my fear. My heart thumps so loudly as I open my eyes to meet his. The love on his mirrors mine, and I can't help but smile upon realizing how lucky I am to be his woman.

"I'm hungry..." I mutter out of the blue, making him chuckle, breaking the heavy atmosphere between us.

He shakes his head in amusement and helps me take the food out of the basket. We stay under that tree, enjoying each other's company. Then, when the sunset comes, I lean on his chest as we admire the breathtaking view of our Kingdom.

I can't help but close my eyes and feel the warmth of the sun caressing my skin. I finally understand why Lady Naya loves this place so much. It's not just the sunset; this place can clear your mind and give you so much realization in life. It helps you think clearly and make rational decisions. Perhaps it's time for me to make a rational and fair decision as well, not just for myself but also for my husband and our Kingdom.

CHAPTER 29

Naya

After enjoying the view of the sunset, the King and I decided to stay for a little while to count the stars before heading back to the palace. That day turned out to be the break I needed from all the chaos in our life. For the first time since I arrived in this Kingdom, I finally got a chance to feel at peace. Suddenly, I felt so hopeful for what tomorrow could bring us. What I didn't know at that time was that there was dreadful news around the corner waiting for us to discover.

Samuel was the first one to greet us the moment we arrived at the palace. Everything about that day turned out to be great, including the heartfelt dinner I shared with my husband. After finishing our food, I decided that the night was still young for me to retire and call it a day. I ended up asking Samuel to accompany me to the palace library to look for a book I could binge on, preferably one that could give me a bit of information about bewitched vampires.

"So, how was your date with the King?" The taunting in Samuel's voice was evident as we made our way towards the castle library.

"It's awesome," I tell him with a dreamy smile on my lips.

Samuel lets out a smile of amusement upon hearing the enthusiasm in my voice. I can't help it, though; my husband is the sweetest person I got to meet in this lifetime. I enjoyed every moment I spent with him, and today is one of the hundreds of memories that I will cherish forever. This relationship might come to an unexpected end, but at least I have some memories to look back on, if ever.

"It's good to hear that you're enjoying his company. Zizina left more of the potion for you; she says that the effect of it will only last for more or less than a day, so you might need more."

I nod. Now that we have fully consummated the wedding, I know that Atticus will continue to feed on me, and as his wife, I would love nothing more than to comply with his needs.

"I've read somewhere that once beloved tastes each other's blood, they will continue to feel the thirst for each other from time to time," I respond. Atticus has fed on me multiple times today. I guess it's going to be a habit for him now that we have completed the mating. I need to keep up with my husband's appetite. I can't risk him discovering that I am human when he randomly takes blood from me.

"She left a bottle of potion for you today. It's in the closet, inside your backpack," My butler says as we finally approach the door of the library.

Samuel opens the door of the library for me, allowing me to enter first before following me from behind. The smell of books fills my nose, creating that homey feeling that never fails to relax me. I can't help but smile upon noticing how the library and the garden are my favourite parts of any castle. Who can blame me, though? Flowers beautify the world, while books give me knowledge. And I think having those two things near you is very crucial for a happy and fulfilling life.

I am just about to walk towards one of the shelves when my eyes catch something dreadful on a table near the open window. My breathing hitches as I feel the thick air get stuck in my throat. My eyes widen in fear and shock while staring at the lifeless body of an old man sitting on one of the chairs. Blood is oozing from his chest with a silver dagger deeply buried in it.

Samuel's forehead creases upon seeing the sudden change in my demeanour. His eyes quickly turn to the direction where my eyes seem to be stuck. I hear his loud gasp filling the library upon recognizing the identity of the man lying dead a few meters away from us.

"Shit!" he curses under his breath before pulling me behind him to shield me from the gruesome scene.

However, it's already too late for that. The grim look on the minister's face, with blood flowing out of his chest, is forever imprinted in my mind like a nightmare. My eyes turn to the creamy white wall near the open window where I can see a short message written in blood saying— 'You're next, my Queen.'

My palms close into fists as I swallow hard in fear. This is the first death threat I have received from the enemy. My gaze turns back towards the dead body, which is slowly turning into ashes before us. The message written in blood on the wall slowly vanishes as it turns into ashes as well. Vampires are supposed to die almost immediately after being fatally stabbed with a silver weapon. Once dead, their body is set to turn into ashes. If that is the case, it means that the minister was killed only a few minutes ago.

I take a step back with my palm instinctively covering my mouth. Seeing a dead body is not new to me anymore. It is something I have grown accustomed to in the human world. Yet, the weight of this particular case strikes me with an intensity that I have not experienced before. The impact reverberates through my being, causing a tremor in my knees that threatens to buckle beneath me.

Samuel regains his composure quickly, and he speaks with a calm and steady voice. "Let's go, my Queen. I know you're tired. I'll accompany you to your room. I'll let the warriors handle this."

I take a few deep breaths to calm myself and shake my head in resolute disapproval. I can't afford to run anymore. This is where I'm at my best, and I refuse to lose my edge.

"I'm not running anymore, Samuel," I reply and turn to look at him, my voice filled with determination. "I'm done running. It's time for me to chase them."

I walk past him and head towards the victim. It's a good thing that the potion I drank last night hasn't lost its effect yet, as I still have a strong sense of a vampire. I take a long exhale to check if there's any scent that I can pick up. Unfortunately, the only thing that is evident to me is the smell of old books in this library. It's weird because I can't even catch the scent of blood in the air, as if it's been purified or something. I can't help but frown at my own discovery. How is it possible that there's no scent of blood in the air at a murder scene where blood is all over the place?

"My Queen, I'll need to call a warrior to report what happened. You need to leave this place," Samuel insists from behind me.

Instead of listening to him, I make my way towards the wall where the message was written a moment ago. Weirdly enough, there's also no trace of the smell of blood on it. This is probably one of the big disadvantages of being a vampire. They turn into ashes as soon as they lose their life. How can I investigate the body further if it's gone now?

I take a step towards the open window to survey the area and take a deep breath to see if I can sense anything unusual. However, just like inside the library, there is nothing, only the fresh night air.

"Samuel, call out the warriors. Send a few of them to search the entire Kingdom. The person who killed the minister is still around the castle, and they have covered their scent to avoid being caught. Capture anyone who looks suspicious," I command in a firm and steady voice, determined to catch the culprit.

Samuel's forehead contorts in disagreement as he shakes his head in defiance. "I can't leave you alone in here, Naya. What if the murderer suddenly comes back and kills you? The King will have my head if something happens to you," he protests.

I turn to look at him and let out a sigh. It's highly unlikely to happen. "No, whoever did this won't come back for me anymore. They won't risk being caught," I reply to him.

Samuel lets out a defeated sigh, bows his head, and takes a step backwards before turning his back on me to call the guards. I look around the room as he leaves the library. I walk towards where the minister is sitting, and my eyes land on the silver knife on the floor. It's almost identical to the silver knife that was used to kill Lady Naya— a weapon with a silver blade and silver handle.

There's a big possibility that the murderer used a pair of gloves to wield this kind of weapon because silver is known to be fatal to vampires. But why silver, though? Why not use a blade made of a different metal? I wonder if they're using silver blades with silver handles to keep the mystery in the murder case or if there's a logical or practical reason behind it.

I pick up the silver knife from the floor and take a closer look at it. This blade seems to be crafted intricately. Maybe I can start my investigation by looking for a possible shop that sells this kind of blade or a blacksmith who uses this kind of material?

I probably need to ask Celestine if she knows anyone who can craft a blade with a silver handle. After all, she seems to have a lot of knowledge about weapons. My eyes turn towards the open door of the library when I hear footsteps approaching it. I immediately put down the knife back on the floor. I don't want anyone to accidentally see me holding a silver blade and become suspicious of me.

Samuel enters the door together with Atticus and a few other guards behind them. The last person to enter the library is Harriet. My eyes never left her face as I crossed the distance between me and my husband.

Harriet's eyes immediately turn glossy upon seeing the ashes scattered on the table, chair, and floor. Her body shakes in anger as tears start to fall down from her beautiful green eyes to her cheeks. She slowly walks towards the ashes with disbelief written in her eyes. I saw firsthand how close Harriet is to her grandfather. I never had a chance to meet my grandparents, but I certainly know how hard it is to lose someone you love so much.

Personally, I may not harbour any fondness for her, but an undeniable ache tightens within my chest at the sight of this heart-wrenching scene. She stands before the remnants of ashes, her hand pressed against her mouth in anguish, tears cascading down her cheeks. Since her grandfather was killed using the same method that was used to kill Lady Naya, I guess I can already take her clan off my list of suspects. The reason being none of her family members would dare to orchestrate the murder of their own clan's leader, fully aware that such an act would only result in the transfer of the ministerial position to a leader from another vampire clan.

I take a deep breath to clear my lungs and look up at my husband. His eyes are solely focused on the ashes of his dead minister. His face is void of any emotion, making it so hard to read whatever he is thinking. The unexpected death of the Minister of Finance is a big blow to the Kingdom. We have lost an ally.

The main question remains unanswered; who are the people behind this? And, most of all, how can I help my husband with all of this? I lean on Atticus's chest to silently ask for support. I guess it's time for me to be more involved in the Kingdom's politics. People are being killed right under our noses, and we cannot even pinpoint who the enemy is.

"You!"

That shaky voice makes me raise my eyes back to Harriet. Her hands are curled in tight fists, while her eyes are all red with a combination of tears and hatred written on them. She takes long strides to close our distance. A bitter smile curves on her lips while she looks at me with a fire burning behind those two green orbs.

"Congratulations, I heard how much your father wants to replace my grandfather in his position," she says in a calm yet accusing tone. The grief is clearly evident in her voice. "What a coincidence for you to be the one to discover my grandfather's death."

I blink twice, shocked at her sudden accusation. I know how painful this is for her. She's hurt. I open my mouth to defend my family, only to close it again upon realizing that her words actually make sense. I am fully aware that their family's loss is an opportunity for my family.

I swallow hard to find my voice to respond to her. "I'm deeply sorry for your loss, Harriet." I meet her gaze as I reach out to her shoulder. Somehow, I want to show her that I am her ally in this situation. "Whoever did this will pay dearly with their life..."

Tears start to stream down from her eyes again as she takes my hand off her shoulder in a harsh manner.

"You and your family will pay for this!" she hisses at me before stomping towards the open door of the library.

Defeat weighs heavily on my shoulders as I gaze upon the remnants of the fallen minister, his ashes scattered before me. This is no ordinary death; it signifies a significant loss for the Kingdom, stripping away one of its most formidable allies. The disquieting thought lingers, casting a shadow of apprehension— there exists a strong likelihood that the individual to assume the vacant position harbours ill intentions towards the Kingdom. Regrettably, the most probable candidate is none other than my own father— Lady Naya's father.

CHAPTER 30

Naya

"Fuck it!" I hiss in anger and impatience as I stare at the notes and evidence I've collected so far on the table in front of me. I know Niall is involved in this rebellion. After the death of the Prime Minister of Finance, I am certain that Lady Naya's family is most likely a part of it. However, I need evidence to prove my conclusion because gut feeling is never enough in any courtroom.

I reach out my temples to massage it, and that is when a cup of tea is placed on the small table in front of me. My eyes turn towards Samuel who's holding a metal tray.

"You've been brainstorming since this morning. You can use a bit of rest," he tells me.

I take a deep breath to clear both my lungs and my mind. I have never left the royal chamber since this morning. I need to find substantial evidence that can link Lady Naya's father and Niall to the murder. They both have motives to commit the murder. I just need a piece of evidence. But where can I find it?

I place my elbow on top of the table and rest my chin on my palms. Atticus didn't retire to our room last night. I know he's currently being hammered with the murder that happened. I want to help him, but the murder is so clean that I can't seem to find a hole in it. It was so well planned.

"Where's the King?" I look up at my butler with a tired expression on my face.

"He's arranging the funeral for the late Minister. He made a trip to the house of Malvagio with Harriet to give his condolences to the family," he answers.

My brows furrow, and my face contorts in displeasure. I take a deep breath as I try to get a hold of my emotions and keep calm. "Why on earth didn't he even notify me about it?" I scowl.

Samuel smirks upon seeing the sudden jealousy in my eyes. If he knew how irrational women act and think when they are jealous, I'm pretty sure he wouldn't be amused by it. My gaze turns to the cup of tea in front of me, and I pick it up. I'm feeling so stressed out at the moment that I think I need a whole kettle of chamomile tea to contain my emotions.

"The reason why the King decided not to bring you along with him is that your presence might spark chaos in the house of Malvagio. Malvagio and Nardelli have been in a silent feud for a long time now. Trust me, they won't appreciate your condolences," Samuel explains.

I roll my eyes in irritation. Right, how could I forget the family feud issue? Not to mention that I'm pretty sure most of them are thinking that I am one of the people behind the Minister's death.

"But it's important for me to be there. There's a big chance that the person who killed the Minister is in that place. I can't be left out here," I reason. I stand up from the chair and walk towards the window to open it, allowing the afternoon wind to enter the room. I walk back to the table and pick up the dagger that was used to kill Lady Naya.

"Do you have any idea where we can find this kind of weapon?" I turn to my butler to show him the blade.

"I don't know. We have a lot of shops here that sell different kinds of silver weapons across the Kingdom, but none of them will craft something with a silver handle," Samuel replies as he glances at the small notebook on top of the table where I note down the names of possible suspects.

I let out a deep sigh, suddenly feeling hopeless about my situation. I guess if I want an answer, I need to look for it myself. However, for me to do that, I need to leave the safety of the palace. But after what happened in the Kaedal Kingdom, I highly doubt that Atticus will allow me to leave the premises of the castle without warriors to follow me around.

"How about Zizina? Do you think she has information that can help us find the blacksmith who forged this blade?" I ask again.

Samuel turns to look at me with a frown and thinks for a bit. "She might. Zizina went back to the coven to be our eyes in there. She's trying her best to get information about the potion that can be used to bewitch a vampire. She thinks that if she can get a hold of it, she might be able to create an antidote to remove its effect."

I nod at him with a smile. Having a witch at our side makes everything so much easier. "That's great. We need more information about that potion. I need to know where they are brewing it and where they are getting vampires to drink it."

I'm honestly concerned about where they are recruiting those vampires. I mean, why on earth are we still not receiving any reports about missing people? We have already killed a handful of bewitched, and that number might be low, but we are talking about real people here, people who had families and lives before becoming bewitched.

"Rogue vampires are scattered inside and outside the Kingdom. The problem is no one will really report missing rogues. They are a threat to the Kingdom, and no Kingdom will help them," Samuel explains.

I can't help but arch my left eyebrow at his explanation. "So, because they are acting like rebels, Kingdoms have no compassion towards them? Like they don't matter? That's stupid," I express with disbelief on my face.

A rebellion is starting, and there's a possibility that enemies are using what the Kingdom has overlooked for so many years to their advantage. Why is this world like this? So if you don't belong to a particular group or government, your life doesn't matter anymore? That's just unfair. Kingdoms need to show some consideration to those kinds of people.

"My Queen, rogues are uncontrolled. They are the kind who betray leadership. That's why they are called rogues," he explains as if he is talking to a 5-year-old child.

"That's not a reason for us to turn our backs on them and refuse to lend some help. If they do not want to be under any leadership, I guess it's fine as long as they are not creating havoc," I reason while shaking my head in disagreement. I need to find a way to get out of this castle without being noticed. If I can't use whatever I have right now to connect my suspects to the murder, maybe I can look outside the castle for evidence.

I start to gather all of the notes and evidence I have on the table and put them back in my backpack. After that, I pull out my old clothes from the bag and lay them on the bed. I can't help but smile upon seeing the black turtleneck long sleeve, denim pants, denim jacket, and my black leather boots.

Samuel follows me with a questioning gaze, probably wanting to know what I am up to.

"What are you going to do with those?" He asks with a keen interest in his tone.

I look up at him with a smirk and say, "I can't leave the castle as Queen Naya. But I am pretty sure that I can leave this place as Inspector Detective Naya Cirillo." I walk towards the bathroom while carrying my clothes.

After closing the bathroom door, I start stripping off the expensive silk gown from my body and toss it aside. I pull the turtleneck long-sleeve shirt over my head and put on my pants. I then put my denim jacket over the long-sleeve I'm wearing.

I can't help but smile while staring at my own reflection. It's been too long since I last saw the real Naya. The woman standing in front of the mirror feels so strange, yet at the same time, she's very familiar. I raise my hand and touch my reflection.

"I miss you..." I murmur while staring at the mirror.

I had almost forgotten the real me, the strong, smart, and independent woman who refuses to back down in any kind of danger— the woman who won't even blink despite a gun on her forehead. I take a deep breath and smile while looking at her. It's time for me to solve this puzzle and expose the monsters hidden behind the curtain. I'm ready.

I walk out of the bathroom with a confident smile on my lips.

Samuel scans me from head to toe, and then his frown turns into an approving smile. I'll take his reaction as a sign that he approves of my outfit.

"I almost forgot how beautiful you look in this kind of clothing," he compliments.

I look down at my outfit and nod in agreement.

"Yeah, I almost forget how it feels like when I'm not being treated like royalty. When I am not wearing the crown," I reply and stride towards the vanity mirror.

The golden tiara on my head is the symbol of my status in this Kingdom, a title given to me after I accepted Naya's case. I lost myself after wearing this crown. And I am acutely aware that if I fail to solve this case swiftly, I will continue to lose fragments of myself in the process. Even though I'm so in love with my husband, I can't deny that I'm scared of losing myself completely. I'm afraid to lose the woman who has been hailed as the Sherlock Holmes of the 21st century.

I reach for the crown and slowly remove it from my head. I'm not taking this off because I want to give up this position. I'm taking it off because I need to prove to myself that I deserve to be the bearer of this crown. I gently place the crown on the table and turn towards Samuel.

"I'm ready. Let's venture out in the castle as commoners and see what we can find out," I say to him.

Samuel folds his arms in front of his chest and raises his left eyebrow at me. "And care to tell me where you plan to look for evidence?"

I shrug, not having a single idea where to start my investigation.

"I don't know, to be honest," I reply with all honesty, making my butler frown. "But I need you to take me to a place where I can purchase illegal items or places that is popular for rogues to hang out. I'm pretty sure we can find something starting from there."

I straighten my jacket and walk back to my backpack. I take out the dagger that Celestine gave me and put it in the little pocket of my boots. I also pull out my handgun and a few pieces of silver bullets I stole from the armoury. The thing is, I'm pretty sure there's a big chance for me to meet the murderer while investigating, so I better be prepared.

"What if the King catches us?"

My eyes turn towards Samuel. I can't help but grimace at his question.

"I don't know," I shrug as I meet his gaze. "But I don't want to live on what-ifs anymore. Fear keeps me alive, but it's preventing me from living. I'm tired of that. If Atticus finds out and decides to convict me, then so be it. It's the end of my story," I reply and walk towards the veranda while carrying the gun. My eyes scan the vastness of Puer Lunae territory. "But if I manage to succeed in gathering the evidence. If I succeed in identifying the man behind the killing of a high-ranking official and the future Queen of Puer Lunae, then cheers to me... I may be the fraud Naya, but I am the real Queen of this Kingdom. It is my duty to protect my subjects no matter what the cost is.

I can hear Samuel's footsteps from behind me as he closes the short distance between us. I feel the warmth of his palm on my shoulder, making me turn to look up at him. A gentle and proud smile is painted on his lips while looking at me.

"Lady Naya chose you not only because you two have the same face but also because she believes that you are the right person to be hailed as the Queen of Puer Lunae," Samuel states. To my surprise, he puts his fist on his left chest and bows his head towards me. "With or without the crown, you are my Queen, Naya."

I feel my heart stop beating for a few seconds. That is a very simple statement coming from him, but it is enough to make my heart swell with pride and happiness.

I smile and nod at him with tears brimming from the side of my eyes. It's good to know that there's one person in this Kingdom who believes in me even if I am full of hesitation myself. My gaze turns to the gun on my waist. It's time for me to prove that I am the rightful bearer of that crown I left behind on the table.

CHAPTER 31

Naya

The scent of freshly baked bread to old rusty metals fills my senses, giving me a feeling of nostalgia, subtly reminding me of the flea market I used to go to back in the human world. The chatter of the people haggling with merchants is enough to make me smile as I check each stall with keen interest.

Samuel is following me from a distance as I navigate my way through the thick crowd. I am currently at one famous street in the Kingdom known as Raven's Row, a go-to place for anyone when looking for illicit goods and contraband. Some of the things they sell here are everyday items like food, household goods, books, and paintings. However, some stalls sell items that are considered illegal without a license from the palace. And that includes weapons, shields, bows, silver arrows, potions, and other items used to brew magic potions.

This world seems to have a little bit of everything a fantasy book can have, and I find that rather amusing. I will not be surprised if I end up meeting a werewolf or a dragon shifter soon. They have vampires, witches, and warlocks here, so expecting the unexpected is a must.

One peculiar sword catches my attention while looking around one of the stalls. The sword is not that long, probably just a foot and a half, but it is intricately crafted, easily capturing anyone's attention. It's beautiful.

"How much is that?" I can't help but ask the merchant.

The man raises his eyes at me and turns his gaze to the sword that I am pointing at.

"That one costs only two gold coins. It's not useful, but it will make a great decoration," he replies, then turns back to talking to another person who is also asking for the price of a different item.

I look at the man with confusion.

"But why? I mean, it looks like a well-forged weapon to me," I question with a puzzled look on my face.

The man looks at me again before picking up the small sword from the display. I can't help but notice how he picks it up through the sheath, not touching the grip of the blade.

"This sword is made of pure silver, including its handle. Wielding it on a battlefield will be a disadvantage," he explains.

That makes me grin. Interesting... It appears that acquiring the necessary clues for my investigation is proving to be far simpler than anticipated. Who could have imagined that all I had to do was venture beyond the protective walls of the castle without wearing a crown to get the information I needed?

"I'll take it," I tell him. "But I'll pay you 10 gold coins if you can give me any information on where you obtained that piece of art."

The man's lips form a smirk. My offer piques his interest, and his eyes scan me with obvious curiosity.

"Twenty gold coins. The item is cheap, but the information is quite expensive in this part of the Kingdom," he negotiates.

My forehead scrunches at his words. It's not that 20 gold coins are expensive for me, but I don't want to give him the impression that the information I'm looking for is overly important. Instead of negotiating, I turn my back to him, about to walk towards the next stall when he speaks up.

"Okay, then. You win. Ten gold coins it is," he finally agrees.

My smile almost reaches my ears as I turn to look at him. He shakes his head in disbelief at the victory smile on my lips. He takes out a piece of brown paper and writes something on it before using it to pack the sword. He lets out a gentle smile as he hands me the wrapped sword.

I take out my small pouch containing a few pieces of gold that I stole from my own Kingdom. I give him the ten gold coins I owe, closing our deal. I knew beforehand that I might need to bribe a few people to get the information I wanted. Money can be a useful tool to make people talk sometimes.

My insides churn with excitement as I look at the sword in my hand. I know I'm still far from solving this case, but it feels like I'm taking a step closer to the end of it. I feel like celebrating at the moment.

This has probably been said multiple times before, but I'm going to say it anyway; it's not the destination that makes our life memorable, but the journey towards it.

It doesn't matter whether our story ends happily or tragically. What truly makes it unforgettable is not the conclusion but rather the journey we undertake to reach it. The choices we make, both wise and foolish, the courage we exhibit, the mistakes we commit, the sacrifices we must bear, and above all, the lessons we learned while struggling to navigate life's winding path. It's why I always try to celebrate even the smallest successes in life.

Of course, major triumphs have their own merits. They can bring us immense joy and satisfaction. Yet, it's important not to overlook the significance of minor accomplishments. After all, great achievements are often composed of many small victories. So, let us cherish each and every one of them with a grateful heart. Who knows? They may one day elevate us to the spotlight when we least expect it.

"Excuse me, but I can't help but notice you're a new face around here. Are you visiting from a neighbouring kingdom?" The man inquires out of nowhere, causing me to glance up at him.

I nod. "Yes, I just moved in here from Kaedal." I lie. "Thank you for this. Also, do you happen to know any place around that sells a unique kind of potion?"

"Yeah, why?" he asks in return.

I try my hardest not to roll my eyes in irritation at his obvious nosiness. "I'm looking for a shop that sells a love potion. I have a friend who wants to make a certain woman fall in love with him," I reply.

Sometimes, I want to applaud myself for being a good liar. I can speak lies while looking straight into other people's eyes without blinking. Even the most observant detective would have a problem identifying whether I am lying or speaking the truth.

The man nods at me with amusement written in his eyes, buying my pathetic reason. He points to the end of the alley. "At the end of this road, a small shop sells the most exotic potions in this Kingdom. Her prices are a bit expensive, but I can assure you that she sells only the best quality."

I offer him a grateful smile and turn my gaze in the direction he points. His sales pitch for the potion shop was so effective that it piqued my interest. I wonder if they have any necromancer potions or spells here. That would be incredibly helpful for me in solving this case.

After bidding him goodbye, I turn on my heels and head towards the end of the alley. I can feel the man's curious gaze on my back, but I decide to ignore it.

I'm not scared of my enemies finding out that I am gathering information by roaming around town. I know that this will threaten them and may even prompt them to send someone after me. If they do, it will work in my favour. Sometimes, the best way to catch a predator is to become its prey.

My forehead creases upon arriving at the end of the alley and not seeing a stall that sells potions. That is when my eyes catch sight of a small door. It was barely noticeable because the material used to build it was similar to the wall.

I walk to the door with long strides, knock twice on it, and then open it. A foul stench greets me as I take my first step inside, making me scrunch up my nose. My eyes immediately scan the room. The air is thick with the scent of strange herbs, and the dim lighting casts eerie shadows on the shelves lining the walls. But my eyes are drawn to the two shelves in the middle of the room, each one full of potions of different colours. Some glow softly, while others seem to swirl with a life of their own.

I walk towards one of the shelves and pick up one of the potions on display. I open the bottle and bring it towards my nose, curious about its scent, only to grimace upon smelling a rancid odour. I immediately closed the bottle and put it back where I got it. I don't need to ask the owner of this shop what kind of potion this is. I'm pretty sure it's poison. Goodness, that's disgusting.

"Who are you?"

That sweet and warm voice coming from the left side of the shop makes me turn my head in its direction. I let out a friendly smile upon seeing a beautiful young woman standing, seemingly hidden by the shadows, not far from a wooden table. I kind of expected to see an old, ugly, and creepy woman in this shop, but I guess I'd forgotten the fact that they were vampires. Vampires are not ugly, but one thing is for sure—they are creepy.

"Hi, I'm a customer," I introduce myself. There's no way I'm going to give her my name. From her face, my eyes dart to the book she's holding, wondering if it is a book about spells and potions.

The woman frowns as she scans me. She walks towards the table and puts the book down on top of it before turning to look at me. "How can I help you then?" she asks.

I let out a friendly smile as my eyes scan the shelves full of potions. "I'm looking for a potion or spell that can bring a dead person back to life," I reply, wondering if such kind of magic exists in this world.

Silence fills the atmosphere between us for a few seconds. Then her amused laughter echoes inside the small shop. I turn my eyes back to her, giving her a deadpan look. She stops laughing and looks at me with a glint of amusement in her eyes.

"Wait, you're serious?" she questions when she realizes that I am not joking.

I nod in response. If I can summon Lady Naya from the other side, it will be so much easier for me to solve this case. If only dead people could talk.

The woman shakes her head with a smile. She walks to the other side of the table and occupies the odd-looking chair in front of it.

"Too bad, I am a witch, not a goddess. Unfortunately, I can't bring dead people back to life. That's against the natural cycle of life," she explains.

I can't help but feel a bit disappointed. Well, that's dumb. I expected more from this world, but I guess expectations are always associated with disappointment. I walk towards the table and take the visitor chair in front of her.

"Well, that's unfortunate," I grumble. "I'm also looking for a very rare potion that is said to be able to bewitch a vampire and turn them into a killing machine."

My eyes never leave her face as I speak, wanting to see her reaction to my question. The woman's lips form into an upward smirk. Suddenly, her warm aura and the atmosphere inside the shop slowly change, making me feel cold and alert to my surroundings. I notice her eyes briefly dart towards the door behind me, and they narrow as she looks back at me.

"Those potions are not allowed to be sold in the Kingdom," she replies in a controlled tone.

A taunting smile forms on my lips as I open the book she had placed on the table a moment ago, turning it to the fifth page, where the table of contents is mostly located. Usually, the table of contents gives you a little idea of what kind of book it is.

"Well, that is why I decided to come to this alley. I hear that this is the best place to buy something illegal," I respond.

I raise my eyes to meet her gaze. The smirk on her lips gives me a warning sign inside my head. I notice how the iris of her eyes shifts behind me for a quick second. The scent of potions around the room is overpowering. However, with my enhanced senses and observant personality, it is easy for me to identify if there's a threat around the corner.

I am quick to pull out the gun from my waist and point it at her. That catches her off guard, and it's my time to smirk.

"Take one step closer towards me, and she's dead," I say to whoever is behind me.

I stand up from my seat and slightly take a step to my side to see who the newcomer is. I gasped upon seeing a man standing two meters away from me. His black obsidian eyes stare at me with rage. Purple-coloured veins are almost visible on his snow-pale white skin, and because of my enhanced hearing, I can clearly hear his irregular heartbeat.

A smile curves on my lips while surveying the newcomer. Bingo!

CHAPTER 32

Naya

I observe the bewitched vampire in front of me, and my grip on my handgun tightens. I never expected to discover anything so soon. Now the main question is, how is this woman related to the bewitched and Lady Naya's death? Is she the one who brews the potions?

"What the heck are you really thinking? Do you believe that wearing odd clothing will help hide your identity?" the woman asks, making me turn and look at her.

She recognized me? I smirk. She did well in pretending not to know who I was a while ago. I'm not wearing any kind of mask or anything, but I highly doubt that a commoner can identify me as their Queen.

I puff out some air through my mouth, disappointed that my disguise isn't so effective. "I thought it would work as a great disguise," I say with a shrug while retaining my alertness.

"I admit I didn't recognize you until you closed the distance between us," she tells me, her gaze fixed on my face. "I never thought that wearing the crown could give someone so much confidence."

My smirk widens at her remark.

"I guess being mated to the King comes with a lot of perks," I reply.

The woman stands up from her seat and looks at me from head to toe with a sarcastic smirk on her lips.

"You should have died," she says, making me frown. "It would have been better that way. Do you think that just because you're helping the Kingdom, Atticus will easily forgive you?"

Her words catch me completely off guard. My forehead scrunches in confusion. My eyes squint into a thin line as I meet her gaze. This is becoming so much more interesting now. Lady Naya committed treason against the Kingdom? How so? What is the relation of it to her death?

I take a deep breath and bring my attention back to the present. I'm not in the ideal situation to brainstorm right now. One wrong move, and it could be the end for me.

Despite the multiple questions running through my head, I know it's time for me to leave. I take a step back, but I don't remove the gun from the woman's head. I can still hear the heavy breathing of the bewitched vampire a few meters away from me. I need to get out of this place quickly.

"You know what, that's my problem to deal with, not yours," I say, giving her my sweetest smile. "Unfortunately, I didn't come here for life advice but rather for a piece of information that I know you can provide. Where are you getting the supplies for the potions, sweetheart?"

The woman gives me a surprised look. She's the first person I've met who is related to Lady Naya's death, aside from Idris and Niall. I can use her to put Niall in the spotlight, but I need to find a way to make her talk.

"You don't think I'll give you the information that easily, do you?" she lets out an empty chuckle.

I notice her hand moving down under the table, and that is my cue to leave. I can't stay here any longer, or it won't end well for me. I pull the trigger of the gun, targeting her knees. A deafening scream echoes through the tiny shop as blood rolls down from her wounded knee.

The bullet is made of silver, enough to slow her down. The only problem left is the bewitched vampire in the room. I turn my eyes towards him as he lets out a loud screech strong enough to break my eardrums. He closed our distance faster than I expected. His claws are only inches away from my face when I manage to pull out the sword I bought from the vendor earlier.

The man halts and takes a step back upon seeing the silver sword in my hand. He hisses at me with raging anger in his eyes.

My eyes squint in anger as I realize one thing; the bewitched vampires, which we initially thought were mindless killing machines, are not mindless after all. They can think, and they can be controlled.

I point my gun towards the shelves and give the woman one last glance before deciding on my escape. "I guess it's time for me to leave now. Let's meet again in the future. When that happens, it will be your death, not mine." I let out a smug grin at her before pulling the trigger, targeting each bottle I could see on the shelves.

I don't know anything about potion-making, but I know that mixing up potions is dangerous and can create a deadly reaction. Five elixirs explode, and, to my luck, they produce a thick, pure neon-coloured smoke inside the four-cornered room.

The overwhelming toxic scent of the potions makes my eyes water, but I know that it is to my advantage.

A vampire's strong sense of smell will be their weakness in times like this. I walk in the direction of the door as silently as I can and push it open to get out. The thick smoke follows me from behind.

I step outside and immediately close the door behind me. A few people in the alley give me curious looks. I let out an awkward smile towards them, not wanting to attract any unnecessary attention.

"I accidentally broke one of the potions, but I promise I paid for it," I tell them, though no one is asking.

As I am about to take a step forward to leave the alley, a sensation of familiarity tickles the back of my head. Suddenly, my body is lifted off the ground before I can even turn around to face the source of the disturbance. Before I know it, I find myself standing on a rooftop, with a sturdy stone chimney concealing me from the view of the curious onlookers below.

"What the heck are you thinking? Entering a dangerous place with no one that can help you if something goes wrong?" Samuel hisses at me, looking so pissed off at the moment.

I give him a sharp look. Though his presence is familiar, I can't deny the fact that his sudden appearance makes my heart stop for a second. I thought an enemy got me.

Realizing that I am far from danger, my heartbeat starts to steady.

"I'm alive. I don't have a scratch, so it's fine," I glare at him and sit on the roof. I sigh and turn my gaze to the horizon that marks the boundary of the Kingdom.

This day looks so peaceful, and the Kingdom looks breathtaking from this place. After what I learned inside that potion shop, I finally understood Samuel when he said that not because the Kingdom looks prosperous from the outside doesn't mean it isn't bound to fall into mishap anytime soon.

Is Atticus aware of all this? If he is, why is he turning a blind eye to it? I rub my palms on my face in frustration.

"Is there something wrong? What happens down there?" Samuel questions when he notices the fear lacing my face.

"A lot," I manage to say as I try to get a hold of my emotions, my eyes focus on the distance. I need to be calm and composed right now. "The letter Lady Naya has sent to me doesn't pertain to anything related to my father's death. She used it to get my attention, and, at the same time, she used it to relay the person we didn't expect to be part of this bullshit." I reply in a weak tone and finally raise my gaze to meet Samuel's eyes.

Samuel's face scrunches up in confusion. I know that my revelation is going to shock him, but I also know that Samuel is the only one I can trust right now. I have an obligation to tell him each piece of information I manage to acquire through my investigation, even if that information sets to break his trust in the woman he adores so much.

"What do you mean?"

"She's part of it. She's part of the resistance." I look down and stare at the ring that symbolizes my union with Atticus. "Lady Naya is part of this uprising rebellion. That's the reason why she wrote in the 2nd letter that she's far from being saved. Somebody sent someone to kill her, and she allowed herself to be killed because she couldn't be crowned as a Queen. Her downfall will be the Kingdom's downfall to the resistance, and she used me to save her Kingdom."

A bitter smile forms on my lips. That woman is smart. I will give her that. She's weak, she's broken, and everything, but she planned it all carefully. I can't believe I have fallen into a trap a dead woman has created. It all makes sense to me now, her letters and her actions. The message that she wants to relay to me is all clear to me now.

"That's just an assumption, right?" Samuel clarifies, completely taken aback by my revelation.

"I wish it were nothing but an assumption," I say, shaking my head as a faint smile form on my lips. All of the evidence I have, and the woman's word back in the potion shop, says it all. I stand up from the stone roof and turn my eyes back to the horizon. "Do you know what this means? It means Harriet is right. My family, or rather Lady Naya's family, is the one behind her grandfather's death."

Samuel shakes his head in disbelief. "That can't be true. Lady Naya is a kind-hearted person. You never met her. I did. She would not allow herself to be part of it," he contest in a firm voice, not wanting to acknowledge my accusations.

I can understand his reaction. He's been a loyal servant of Lady Naya before I came into the picture.

"I have a feeling that Lady Naya's whole clan is part of the resistance. You said it yourself. She's a kind-hearted person. There's a big chance that she's part of it not by will, and the only way I can prove that is by paying a visit to her family's lair as soon as possible." I state. "Come to think of it, if she became the Queen, the resistance would have a major advantage having the Queen as their puppet."

"If that is true, if she is really a part of the resistance, then what is the main reason why she changed her mind in the end and turned against the group and her own family?" Samuel questions with scepticism in his tone. "Why did she summon you here as her replacement to fight on her behalf?"

I take a deep breath to clear the blockage in my lung before meeting my butler's gaze. This is just a conclusion, but I have a feeling that the reason behind her deeds is similar to why I am doing all of this.

"She fell in love with the King..." I whisper in a low tone, with a weak smile on my lips. "She fell in love with Atticus, and she wants to protect him and his Kingdom, even if that means not standing beside him and a sure death for her."

'Death is an unavoidable destiny that awaits all of us.'

It doesn't matter how long we have lived in this world; nobody can get out of this life alive. We are all set to die in the end. Unfortunately, some people die without purpose. Lady Naya is different. She used her death to protect the man she loved. She used her death to lure me into this world because she knew that my curiosity would make me do things that would attach me so much to this Kingdom to the point of no return.

She used that unavoidable destiny to protect the man and the Kingdom she had learned to love.

CHAPTER 33

Naya

"Hey, is everything okay?" I can't help but ask upon seeing the forlorn expression of my husband, making him look in my direction.

A weak smile curves on his lips as he lets out a deep sigh. I can feel the weight of our current situation on his shoulders. I walk towards him to close our distance and grab the glass of some kind of hard tonic in his hand to drink it myself.

Atticus's smile widens at what I did. He snakes his arm around my waist and pulls me towards him for a brief kiss. My blue eyes meet his captivating hazel ones. The sadness that was written on them a while ago vanishes and is replaced with warmth.

When I came back to the royal chamber from my investigation, I immediately changed into my normal clothing. When I got out of the bathroom, I found my husband in our room drinking on his own, standing in front of the window and staring blankly at the outside world.

"Yup, I feel better now," he replies with his eyes never leaving mine. His hand reaches out to my cheek and caresses it with gentleness.

I can't help but smile at his sweet gesture. Atticus shows nothing but kindness and love to me. I lean on his chest and feel the heat of our bodies against each other, allowing it to calm my senses. If you think about it deeply, Atticus and I are galaxies apart from each other, yet the universe decided to play with our destiny, and now we are here.

To be honest, I don't care anymore if our destiny is set to separate us at the end of our journey. A dangerous storm is soon to arrive in our life. The thing is, no matter how much I try to hold on to him, this storm is bound to break both of us. At this moment, I guess I finally understand why Lady Naya allows herself to be killed to save Atticus and his Kingdom. She may be selfish for pulling me into this mess, but I am the best choice she has during that time. Most people have backup plans when everything in life starts to fall apart. I guess Lady Naya didn't have that. She just reacted depending on her situation, and the only way out she saw was me.

"I hate to see you bearing such a heavy burden, Atticus. Is there anything I can do to help?" I inquire as I meet his gaze with a concerned expression.

He takes a deep breath and looks at me with a serious expression on his face. I can see the hesitation cross his eyes for a few seconds, but then it vanishes after a while and is replaced with a blank look. He leads me to sit on the chair in front of the coffee table. After that, he takes the seat in front of me, and our hands intertwine with each other.

"I don't want to tell you anything about it because I don't want you to worry. It's nothing that big anyway, nothing that our Kingdom cannot handle. However, I guess I have underestimated my enemies," he starts.

Furrowing my brows, I press further, "What do you mean? Underestimated how?"

I have a hunch that Atticus knows something about the resistance, but he keeps it to himself. I need to know any information he has because he could be the key to identifying the other people involved in the rebellion.

Atticus averts his gaze from mine, so I reach out and squeeze his hand, letting him know that I want to help him. Even though I may not be as physically strong as him, I am capable of contributing. If he only gives me a chance, I can prove that I am not someone who needs constant protection.

"Atticus, please look at me," I urge him. He turns back to me and offers a weak smile. "You're not alone in this. You have me, and you have our Kingdom standing behind you. Please let me fight alongside you." I need him to trust that I am capable of handling this.

He lets out a sigh of defeat and nods. "Before Remus's death, he informed me about a rebellion," Atticus says, his eyes now fixed on the circular wooden table between us. "I dismissed his concerns and told him that I would have someone investigate it thoroughly."

"Did you send someone to investigate?" I inquire.

Atticus nods, his expression grave. "Yes, and he returned with information that I wish I hadn't heard." His fingers draw small circles on the back of my palm, creating a jolt of electricity across my arm, momentarily diverting my attention from our conversation. "He mentioned that your family is involved."

I look at him with my lips hanging open. I already expected it, but still, hearing it from him hits differently. The room falls silent as my husband's revelation starts to sink in. He clearly knows more than he's letting on, but he's reluctant to involve me. I wrench my hand from his grip and rise from my seat without tearing my gaze away from him.

"Is that why you don't want me to get involved? Because you don't think I'd go against my own family?" I demand, my brow furrowed with suspicion. "Or are you suggesting that I'm somehow involved in this mess?"

I can't really blame him for coming to that conclusion. However, I have been trying to convince him to delve deeper into the bewitched issue in the past few days. I want to help him solve this; it's the main reason why I am in this mess anyway. Lady Naya wants me to aid Atticus and his Kingdom, to aid in saving his people.

"Nothing has been proven yet, my Queen. But if it is true, the people will lose their trust in you. That's why I don't want you to get involved. I don't want the other ministers to think that I am being biased in my judgment because you are my beloved," he explains.

I let out a deep breath to calm myself. I can't blame them. If my family is responsible for this, it will lead to a great deal of distrust, not just towards me but also towards the King.

"I am aware of that," I begin. "But if my family is behind this, trust me, I am the last person who will tolerate it. I won't force you to involve me in the investigation. I don't care if people lose their trust in me. What's important is for them to continue to trust their King. If there is indeed a rebellion, you need your people to stand by you. I won't stand in your way."

Atticus looks at me with relief in his eyes. He stands up from his seat and crosses the distance between us, leaning down to gently kiss my forehead.

"You are my Queen and my beloved. I will die to protect this Kingdom, but I won't allow anyone to disrespect you," he says, reaching out to gently squeeze my hand.

I can't help but smile at his promise. It feels comforting to know that my husband genuinely cares about my well-being. I want to spend more time with him, to enjoy a few more days with my beloved, but I know it would be selfish. The Kingdom needs its Queen and King right now. I won't let my personal feelings interfere with my duties.

"I appreciate that, my love," I say as I distance myself from him and walk towards the open veranda. "I've decided to pay a visit to my family's manor tomorrow, and I'll have Samuel accompany me."

I can feel Atticus's eyes on me as the atmosphere between us shifts.

"You're not going anywhere, Naya," he says in a firm tone with finality in his voice.

I turn to face him and meet his beautiful hazel-coloured eyes. Somehow, I knew he would say that.

"Do you trust me, my King?" I question.

"I do," he replies without hesitation. "I don't just trust you. I love you. That's why I won't let you run straight into danger."

A smug grin forms on my lips as I shake my head. If only he knew that I'd been running straight towards the danger ever since I said 'I do' on our wedding day. All this time, I've been trying to avoid death itself.

"Listen, my King. I am much more useful to you right now as a member of the House of Nardelli than as your Queen. If my family is part of the rebellion, this is the only way I can get information from them," I explain.

Protest becomes evident in Atticus's eyes. "I understand, but what if they try to harm you? What if they try to use you against me?" he reasons.

"But all we have right now is a conclusion. Nothing has yet been proven. We need this. Our Kingdom's safety must come first,"

I really hope he will give me his permission because if he decides not to, I will be forced to leave the safety of the castle grounds without his consent. I need more information to know how strong our enemy is, and I am the most capable person to retrieve it.

To my dismay, Atticus shakes his head in disapproval without tearing his eyes from me. He walks towards me and pulls me close to him. His arms slip around my waist as he buries his face in my neck. "Forgive me, my Queen, but I can't give you what you want. I will have Celestine prepare the warriors to strengthen our defence. Trust me on this. I will send someone to investigate your family," he promises and starts to place small kisses on my exposed skin.

I understand his fear, but I am not doing this because I don't trust him. I am doing this because I want this to end as soon as possible.

I let out a tired sigh. As much as I want to stay in the safety of my beloved's arms, I can't. I need to go back to the house of Nardelli, for it might be the only way to identify the other people involved in this rebellion and help our Kingdom.

CHAPTER 34

Naya

"If the King learns about this, he'll kill me," Samuel states as he helps me down from the carriage.

I know Atticus will surely hate me after this, but what choice do I have? I have decided to fulfil my duty to protect the Kingdom. No matter how much I try to keep my secret, I know that the truth cannot be hidden forever.

"I can't let my husband resolve this all on his own. I have to help him; that's the reason why I am here," I reply as I stand tall in front of a huge mansion that is very familiar to me.

This place brings back a lot of memories. It is the house where Lady Naya was murdered and the house that leads me to this world. Remembering the past, I can't help but wonder what would happen if I ignored the letter and turned my back on Lady Naya. I wonder if things would be different if I knew that solving the mystery behind the fan mail would lead me to this day.

"This house is beautiful," I say as I take a step towards the front door. "I didn't get a chance to admire its beauty the first time I was here because you were rushing me to the church to marry a stranger."

Samuel let out an amused chuckle upon remembering the first day we met. He looks up at the house and sighs.

"That was a chaotic, heartbreaking, and heart-stopping event. I lost one of the most important women in my life that day," he agrees and walks right beside me. "However, that day also led me to you. That was the day when I met you."

A smile escapes my lips, and I stop walking to look at him. "Well, at least there's one person who appreciates my existence in this world," I grin and step inside the mansion.

He is right. That chaotic day led us to this. Who would have thought that the fan mail I received had this kind of backstory? Multiple murders and, most of all, an uprising rebellion. It is intimidating, to be honest, but after all the shit that I've been through, I'm not that scared and overwhelmed by it anymore.

My eyes turn towards the grand staircase as an unfamiliar man walks down it. My eyes squint as I look at him. I don't know who he is, but I can sense strong authority coming from him. For some reason, I suddenly feel intimidated.

To my surprise, the man lets out a welcoming smile upon seeing me.

"My Queen, this is unexpected. You should have sent a messenger to inform us that you were going to pay a visit. I should have prepared a banquet to welcome my beautiful daughter," the man exclaims in a cheerful tone as he crosses the distance between us with long strides.

Suddenly, I am engulfed in a warm and protective hug. I stand frozen in my spot while giving Samuel a questioning look. So this man is Lady Naya's father? Why on earth I didn't see him at my wedding? It was my wedding day, and it was his daughter's wedding day too. Why is Samuel the one who walked me to the altar and not him? And now he is acting like a loving father? Am I missing something?

I distance myself from him and fake a warm smile. I can't help but notice the ring he is wearing besides his wedding ring. It is oddly similar to the ring I owned. That confirms Lady Naya's father's involvement in this.

"This is a surprise visit, Father. That's why I didn't send any messenger," I answer and walk past him.

I can hear my father's footsteps following me from behind as I make my way towards the receiving area of the house. The room is grand and opulent, with high ceilings and intricate mouldings adorning the walls. A crystal chandelier hangs from the centre of the ceiling, casting a warm and inviting glow across the space. The room is furnished with elegant Victorian-style pieces, such as a plush velvet sofa with tufted buttons and ornate wooden chairs with embroidered cushions. I take a seat on the glamorous sofa and look around the room as my father takes the chair opposite me.

"I heard about the unexpected death of Remus. Does that have something to do with your surprise visit?" my father questions, taking my full attention.

I turn my gaze back to him with a grave expression on my face.

"Have you already paid a visit to give your condolences to the house of Malvagio?" I ask instead of answering his question.

My father smiles and shrugs. "I would love to do that, my Queen. However, I'm afraid that my visit will only lead to commotion. Since I am a candidate to replace Remus from his position, the House of Malvagio thinks that I am the man behind his murder," he tells me.

I lean on the sofa and look at Samuel for a moment. He stands a meter away behind my father. My eyes shift back to my father. He picks up a bottle of tonic from the table in front of us and pours himself a drink.

"Yeah, about that," I start. "Do you have something to do with Remus' death?"

My question makes my father stop pouring the whiskey into his glass. I can see a smile forming on his lips at my bold question. He shakes his head as he resumes pouring the liquid into the half-empty glass. After that, he closes the bottle and puts it back on the table.

"Before I answer that question, let me ask you one thing, Naya," he says as he picks up his glass of whiskey and takes a sip from it.

"Sure, what is it?"

His eyes darken as he looks at me. His eyes seem to pierce through my soul. "Who are you right now? Are you my daughter or the Queen of this Kingdom?"

His question catches me off-guard, but only for a few seconds. An amused smile forms on my lips. Of course, he will question my loyalty towards the House of Nardelli. The problem is I am not his daughter. The real Lady Naya has been long dead. I am the Queen of this Kingdom, the detective that his daughter lured into this world to solve a murder case. We all know what my answer to that question would be.

I meet his gaze still with an amused smile on my lips.

"I am your daughter. I will always be, regardless of who I have become," I reply.

A long silence fills the room after that. My eyes never leave my father's gaze. I want to know what he is thinking. If his expression gives me a red flag, then I need to plan an escape as soon as possible. Luckily, his face remains calm. I don't see any sign of worry or hesitation in it, so I guess I am safe.

"I'm glad to hear that," he finally says after the moments of silence. He lets out a sigh of relief, releasing the tension from his chest. "About Remus, that old man sent someone to investigate us. Unfortunately, his man managed to relay the information to him before our people could kill him. We need to do some damage control."

I nod, now starting to feel a bit uncomfortable. "Remus informed the King about the resistance. The Kingdom is preparing its warriors for the war we are waging," I reveal, giving out a little information to make my act believable.

My eyes didn't miss it when his knuckles clenched into tight fists. It seems to me that he didn't know the information about the King's preparation for the uprising rebellion yet. This makes me wonder. Does that mean my husband is also discreet with the information he has? Maybe I am underestimating my husband's capability to identify our enemies.

"Remus is bad news to us. Now that he is dead, you need to convince the King to assign me to a Ministerial position," he says, his expression starting to calm as he speaks. He takes a long sip of his whiskey and sets the glass down on the table with a sharp clink. His fingers tap against the armrest of his chair in agitation.

"Niall hasn't relayed any information to me about the King's action in response to Remus' death." he continues, his voice strained, his eyes boring into mine.

I grin internally. If Niall hasn't relayed that information to my father, then he is either a traitor to the resistance, or Atticus didn't give him any information. I'm guessing it is the latter one. I think I did underestimate my husband when it came to gathering information. Also, I'm glad that we both do not trust Niall. That man gives me the creeps for some reason.

"So, does this mean you are really the one who sent the assassin that killed Remus?" I questioned. I doubt that he is the one who sent the assassin. Whoever killed Remus is the same one who killed Lady Naya. I'm pretty sure this man in front of me has no idea that his daughter is long dead.

"He didn't. I did." A familiar voice from behind me catches my attention.

Both of our eyes turn towards the newcomer. My eyes narrow in slits while looking at Niall striding into the receiving area of the house, stopping only a few meters away from where I am sitting. Of course, it is him. Why would I think it could be another person? This man gives off the vibe of a murderer.

I sit still, frozen in my spot, my heart pounding heavily in my chest. I feel Samuel's aura growing stronger and stronger. The hairs on the back of my neck stand on end, and a cold sweat breaks out on my forehead. Suddenly, the atmosphere in the receiving area turns deadly, the air thick with tension and malice.

Despite the danger, a dangerous smile slowly spreads across my lips as the person we have been hunting since the very beginning of this chaos finally reveals himself.

"Well, this is way too anticlimactic than I expected it to be," I state as I stand up from the sofa to face him.

The smug grin on Niall's lips tells me that I am currently in grave danger.

"Well, probably the reason for that is because we are far from the ending yet," Niall responds.

I can feel Samuel's presence from behind me becoming more sinister. He is trying to hold back his anger, which is good, but I don't think he can suppress it much longer. We need to escape.

"Why are you so interested in that information anyway, Queen Naya? So that you can relay it to the King?" Niall accuses me with disdain lacing his voice.

"Are you accusing my daughter of treason, Niall?" My father's voice thunders across the room as he stands up from his own seat, making all of us turn our eyes on him.

I let out a sarcastic smile. Lady Naya's father is unaware that Niall sent someone to kill his daughter on the wedding day. That's a good thing for me. That means Niall will either shut up or confess the crime he committed. That will create a huge ruckus and division in their group.

"I am," Niall says without hesitation. "But are you sure she's really your daughter, Stellian?" He questions in a tone filled with mockery while pointing in my direction.

The tension inside starts to become more and more suffocating, making it hard to breathe. Samuel must have felt it as well, as his aura immediately shifts from murderous to more protective. He knows we need to make an exit as soon as possible, or the odds will not be in our favour.

"What do you mean by that?" Lady Naya's father frowns in confusion.

Niall, on the other hand, appears completely unfazed. "I refrained from discussing this earlier as I wasn't entirely certain," he admits. "I had believed that the assassin I dispatched to eliminate your daughter on her wedding day had failed in their mission. Yet, as it turns out, he did succeed in assassinating the future Queen." His gaze shifts towards me, his face contorted with unmistakable rage.

He pulls something out of his pocket and throws it in front of us. The empty bottle shatters on the floor, filling the room with its sweet floral scent.

I stare at the broken pieces of the bottle. I bite my inner lip in annoyance upon realizing my mistake. I thought I had been discreet with my identity, but apparently, throwing an empty bottle of potion that can change the taste and scent of my blood in the trash bin was not a good idea.

Well, I guess that's it. I'm as good as dead.

CHAPTER 35

Naya

"You sent an assassin to kill my daughter?!" Stellian's voice thunders across the room with a mixture of fury and surprise lacing his tone.

I turn to look at him, his face all red and his knuckles clenched in tight fists. The side of my lips lifts into a confident smirk as I shift my eyes back to the man who's now giving me a murderous look.

Niall turns his attention back to Stellian, suddenly looking more alert now. He had sent someone to kill Lady Naya without informing the other people involved in the resistance. Lady Naya was aware that someone was set to send an assassin to kill her, and for some sick reason, she saw it as an opportunity to save the Kingdom. She knew Niall was going to kill her. Now my question is, what is Niall's reason for killing Lady Naya?

"Your daughter is going to be the King's beloved. If I didn't kill her, she would have given information to the King. You are underestimating the bond of a beloved. Do you think that slut wouldn't sell us to the King after the wedding?" Niall respond. "None of you have the balls to stop her! I had to do damage control myself, or else all our hard work will come to waste!"

In just a blink of an eye, Stellian is already in front of Niall. His hands are on Niall's neck, threatening to break it in two in just a second.

My eyes darken while looking at them. Niall is stupid. Despite his reasons, he shouldn't have killed Lady Naya. His actions created huge distrust and division within their group. He set aside the fact that Lady Naya is not just a member of the resistance but also the daughter of one of its powerful members.

Somehow, I'm glad that Stellian seems to care a lot about the welfare of her daughter more than anyone else I've met in her family.

"We need to leave now, my Queen," Samuel whispers silently, making my head turn towards him.

I didn't even notice that he was already able to close the short distance between us. I nod at him in agreement. I know how dangerous it is for us to stay in this place, especially now that Niall already knows my secret.

"And you think the best way to resolve it is to kill my daughter? My own flesh and blood?" Lady Naya's father seethes in controlled anger. "You're lucky my daughter didn't die that day, or else I would be the one to slit your throat with a silver dagger!"

"Your daughter is dead!" Niall snaps back, pointing in my direction. "That woman is not your daughter. She's an impostor!"

His eyes burn with rage. I cross my arms over my chest and smirk at him in return. Now that I know who the murderer is and the motives behind Lady Naya's murder, I can finally reveal my identity to my beloved. I just need to find solid evidence against them.

"First, you sent an assassin to kill her, and now you are accusing my daughter of being an impostor and traitor to the resistance?" Stellian's eyes narrow to slits.

I cock one of my eyebrows towards Niall. Does he really think that a father would simply accept the news that his beloved daughter is dead? He's stupid. He has completely forgotten that most people would rather be comforted and blinded by lies than suffer from the truth. Lady Naya's father will eventually accept her death, but it will take a lot of time. Niall's unexpected news will result in denial.

My father turns to look at me for a second. That must be the interruption that Niall is waiting for. He uses my father's sudden distraction and strikes him with a dagger, thrusting it into my father's shoulder.

Niall's unexpected move leaves me and Samuel stunned for a few seconds. The scent of blood fills the whole room, and I know it will attract the attention of the other vampires nearby. My father falls unconscious onto the carpeted floor.

I let out a gasp of surprise and turned my eyes back to Niall. He is now looking at me with a smug grin on his lips. The dagger he is holding is clearly not made of silver. However, since my father lost consciousness after being stabbed, it probably contained some kind of poison. I'm guessing that it is not his intention to kill Stellian. He just wants to make him unconscious so that he can focus his attention on us.

"For a Minister of Peace and Treaty, you sure do invoke so much chaos," I comment while looking at the dagger in his hand. Droplets of blood pour from it down to the floor.

This man is dangerous. He is more than willing to kill his comrades just to ensure that his plan succeeds. He sent an assassin to Lady Naya and Remus. He is the kind of person who won't give a second thought to killing anyone, but at the same time, he doesn't give off that kind of murderous aura that most criminals have. He has a peaceful presence that can make you think that he is someone you can trust.

In just a snap, Samuel is already in front of me, ready to protect me from any sudden attack. Niall's smirk widens. He lets go of the dagger he's holding. It falls on the floor just inches away from my father.

"Who are you?" Niall questions, his eyes on mine.

"She's your Queen," Samuel answers on my behalf.

Niall shifts his gaze at Samuel. "Of course, the useless butler is also involved in this," he says in a voice that is laced with pure venom. He starts to close the distance between us, step by step, each one deliberate and menacing.

My hand automatically reaches out for my silver dagger. It would be so much easier to kill him right now, but I know that it will not benefit the Kingdom. I need to prove that Niall is guilty of murder, and then Atticus will be the one to judge the necessary punishment for him. Also, we need them alive to gain more information about the ongoing rebellion.

Niall's anger is unmistakable, his eyes burning with fury as he glares at us. "I wonder, was it all planned? A human who looks exactly like Lady Naya showed up out of nowhere and replaced her on the day of her wedding. Isn't that a very funny and unexpected coincidence? Who's behind all of this shit? How the fuck did I miss it?" His every word is laced with bitterness and frustration, and his tone is filled with a dangerous edge that sends shivers down my spine.

He pulls out the silver sword tucked in his waist, making me turn to look at Samuel with worry filling my chest. I know he can fight, but fighting Niall while protecting me is suicide. We need to leave because Niall is going crazy, and I don't like it.

But how can we escape?

I look around the room to find an exit. The first thing that catches my eye is the glass-stained window not far from the sofa where I was sitting a moment ago.

I grin. That would be perfect. Now I just need to create a distraction or injure Niall to escape and avoid being cornered.

I hold onto my silver dagger tightly, and without any hesitation, I throw it in Niall's direction. As expected, he vanishes like smoke right in front of us. What I didn't expect was to feel his presence behind me.

My eyes widen in a combination of fear and surprise. I am literally inches away from death as I feel him sway his sword towards my neck. I stand frozen in my spot for a moment, unable to make any move to save myself. I held my breath, waiting for his sword to cut through my flesh, but that didn't happen. Samuel's sword cuts Niall's attack as he pushes me aside to the couch not far from us.

Their swords cross against each other, anger and hatred both filling their eyes.

"You little rat, I should have instructed Idris to kill you long ago," Niall rages.

He's right on that. The main reason I managed to stay alive this long is because of Samuel. The butler played a big part in solving this murder case successfully. Though I can't really consider it a success yet, not until I manage to put Niall behind bars and stop the incoming war.

"I'm glad you didn't," Samuel replies with a grin, one I recognized that is full of hatred. "That gives me a chance to take revenge for the innocent life you have taken. You shouldn't have killed her. She has nothing to do with all of this shit!" His eyes darken with fury as he pushes Niall with all his force.

"Are you sure about that?" Niall sneers, his tone drips with mockery as he speaks. "She's part of the resistance. She's an enemy of the monarchy. No amount of innocence can change that,"

He gives a vicious kick to Samuel, landing his foot on his stomach. Samuel has been thrown several meters away to the floor, colliding with an antique vase that shatters into a thousand pieces with the impact.

My attention immediately snaps back to Niall as he fixes his bloody red eyes on me, his lips curled into a sinister smile. I can feel the weight of his gaze, a heavy and suffocating pressure that seems to bear down on me. With a deep breath, I steel myself for any potential attack from this madman, my muscles tense and ready to spring into action.

"The resistance, what is it for? What is its purpose?" I ask. Despite my life being on the verge of certain death, I can't stop my detective side from taking over. I need to understand why these people would build resistance against the Kingdom.

My question makes Niall halt for a second. His eyes darken in hatred before they entirely turn blank and emotionless. I let out a deep breath and prepared myself. This man is not up for small talk.

In just a snap, he is already in front of me. Luckily, I am fully prepared this time. I pull out another dagger from my waist and thrust it deeply into his stomach just as he appears in front of me.

I take a step back and watch as his knees give in, causing him to fall to the floor while holding his stomach. I let out a cocky grin. He may be stronger than I am, but as always, stirring emotions in people can mess up their focus.

"You'll pay for that," he snarls with his eyes on mine and starts to steady himself. Niall lunges towards me with a sword in his hand, his eyes blazing with a newfound fury. But before he can reach me, Samuel suddenly appears behind him, wielding a sword that glints against the light.

With a swift and merciless motion, Samuel plunges the sword through Niall's back, puncturing his heart with a sickening squelch.

Niall lets out a strangled gasp, his eyes widening in shock as he stares down at the hilt of the sword protruding from his chest, blood spilling out in a gruesome fountain.

For a moment, there is a deafening silence as everything in that room stands frozen, watching in horror as Niall slowly collapses to the ground, his body going limp. The only sound is the soft thud as his lifeless form hits the floor, his eyes now vacant and devoid of life.

My heart races as I gaze upon the macabre scene, with my breaths coming in ragged gasps. I turn to my butler, who stands amidst the carnage with fierce determination in his eyes. He tightly clutches the bloodied sword in his trembling hands, his knuckles turning white from the intensity of his grip.

He had been Lady Naya's most devoted servant, and her brutal murder had shattered his heart into a million pieces. But now, he had finally brought the man responsible for her death to justice. I couldn't help but notice the grim satisfaction etched on his face, with the droplets of blood adding to his sinister appearance.

That is when the door of the receiving area bursts open, causing me to shift my attention to the newcomers. I swallow hard as I come face to face with the woman whom I didn't expect to meet in this place today.

Celestine lets out a slow clap as she crosses our distance with amusement in her eyes. She has a small grin on her lips as her gaze turns towards the two men lying bloodied on the floor, then on Samuel, and back to me.

"I must say that I am impressed with the information I have gathered today," she says in a cool, composed voice.

A few warriors walk into the room from behind her, and before I know it, swords are pointed at my neck. I freeze, knowing full well what's coming next. Even Samuel doesn't put up a fight as two warriors approach him, disarm him, and take his sword away.

"Queen Naya, or whatever your name is, in the name of King Atticus of Puer Lunae, you are under arrest for conspiring against the Kingdom. Niall, you are under arrest for multiple murders and treason," she declares with authority. Her gaze then shifts towards my unconscious father. "Stellian, head of the House of Nardelli, you are under arrest for plotting against the Kingdom and treason."

The room falls silent for a few moments after her speech, the only sound being the heavy breathing of those present. A humourless smile forms on my lips. Finally, the game I've been playing has come to an end.

It's time to face the consequences of my actions.

CHAPTER 36

Naya

I remain silent as we make our way back to the castle, my mind full of questions and my heart occupied with overwhelming fear about what will happen to me now that I have solved the murder case. Stellian was captured alive while Niall's body disintegrated into ashes.

I reach out to my forehead and gently massage it while staring at the wooden ceiling of the carriage. Samuel had killed a powerful member of the resistance, but I don't remember Celestine informing him about his arrest, which means somehow Celestine recognized that Niall being dead was much more favourable for the monarch. It makes me question if Celestine purposely waited until Niall was killed.

It's all over now, but I can't seem to feel any fulfilment for some reason. I thought I was entirely prepared for this day, but the fact that I cannot approach Atticus the same way anymore makes me want to cry and throw a fit.

"I admire your bravery," Celestine breaks the silence, making me turn my gaze towards her. Her eyes are fixed on my face, studying me with a quiet intensity. She leans back against the carriage's seat, appearing relaxed, but there's an underlying tension in her posture that belies her apparent ease.

I let out a sad sigh and shook my head in frustration. They say that there is a thin line between bravery and stupidity, and I guess I cross that line.

"Same," I agree in a weak tone, my eyes flickering to the window to catch a glimpse of the passing scenery. The carriage's interior is dimly lit, and the only sounds are the steady clatter of the wheels on the dirt road and the soft rustle of my dress as I shift in my seat. "To be honest, I don't even know how I managed to get this far without being caught or killed.

Celestine nods in understanding as she looks at me with a gloomy expression on her face. I really like her, but sadly, we are now in two different boats. Despite what had happened, I am glad to know that her loyalty lies with the Kingdom. I am honestly afraid she might be one of the enemies, but I am relieved to see that she will stand by my husband's side once the rebellion erupts.

"I've seen Lady Naya once, and she's charming and stunning," she remarks. "From the first moment I saw her, I knew she'd be the perfect Queen for the Kingdom. She's an excellent match for the King."

A bitter smile curves on my lips. "She's the perfect Queen that this Kingdom never had the chance to have. She sacrificed her life to save Puer Lunae and protect Atticus and his Kingdom. She knew she would never get the credit she deserved, but she still did it without hesitation and paid for it with her life."

I look down at the floor as tears threaten to fall from my eyes. Lady Naya's life is a tragic story— she died, leaving the man she loved for another woman. In the end, she became a sacrificial lamb for the greater good, and I can't help but admire her for her selflessness. How many of us are willing to die for the sake of others without getting credit for it? It's sad, but it is true that greed and selfishness are deeply embedded in the human soul.

"I don't know the whole story yet, but I do know that you're not on the enemy's side. I'll do my best to convince the council, the ministry, and the dukes to give you the benefit of the doubt. That's the only help

I can offer," Celestine says with a soft smile on her lips as if to reassure me that there is still hope. However, deep down, I know that I am far from saving.

I force a nod and offer a grateful smile in return. A benefit of the doubt sounds promising, but only if the Kingdom is willing to listen to my side of the story. I have all the evidence to prove my innocence, but I fear that they will not allow me to explain my actions. My punishment is not what frightens me the most; it is my husband's reaction that terrifies me. He loves Lady Naya, and I'm a hundred percent certain that he will hate me after this. I betrayed him and lied to him, and I hate to admit it, but the thought of my husband hating me is enough to shatter me into pieces.

After a few minutes, we finally arrived at the castle. My heart pounds with anticipation, and fear gnaws at my insides. As I expected, Atticus is waiting for us on the castle grounds. Celestine had already dispatched a warrior to inform the King of what they had discovered a moment ago.

Zizina is standing beside Atticus, and I can see the worry filling her eyes upon seeing two of our warriors escorting me back to the castle. Then my gaze turns towards Harriet standing on the other side of my husband.

I bite my lower lip to stop the tears from falling from my eyes. My chest clenches in pain as I look at her hand holding onto my husband's arm. My downfall will be Harriet's reign, and I accepted that long ago. I know it's time for me to back down. I have no reason left to fight. If Lady Naya could sacrifice her life for this Kingdom, then I guess it's time for me to sacrifice my heart as well. Letting go won't kill me, at least not literally. This decision will destroy my soul, but it's fine. I need to be okay with it.

Celestine bows her head to show her respect to the King. "King Atticus, just as you instructed, we followed Queen Naya to the house of Nardelli and gathered every piece of evidence we could get. Stellian and Niall are part of the resistance, as is Lady Naya," Celestine reports, diverting her eyes back to me. "However, based on what I've understood from their conversation, Lady Naya is long dead. She died the day of the wedding and was replaced by a human."

Atticus remains silent, his eyes blank and void of any emotion as he looks at me. Gone is the loving and caring look that he always had whenever our eyes met. My hand closes into a tight fist as the sides of my eyes start to heat up.

I know I am a fraud. I am not the one he loves. But I learned to love him. I fell in love with him, and that was never part of my plan. My plan was to solve the murder case, gather evidence, and leave this world. No strings attached or anything, no heavy heart. Just return to the human world and continue my journey as a detective. Easy, right? But I fucked up. Everything became complicated the moment I fell in love with the King. The very moment I developed feelings for him, I fucked up.

"Bring Stellian to the interrogation room. I have a lot of questions to ask him," Atticus says without even bothering to look at me. "Bring her and her butler to the dungeon. I'll let the council decide what would be her punishment."

The coldness in his voice sends chills down my spine. I look down at the ground as tears start to roll down my cheeks. I'm a strong person, not just physically but also mentally and emotionally. But that blank tone coming from my husband is enough to break me into tiny pieces. I can't believe that the day I've feared the most has finally come.

I willingly walk towards the dungeon without saying a single word. I did my part and gave my all to solve this case. This is what Lady Naya wanted me to do when she sent the letter to me. Wherever she is right now, I hope that she can finally rest in peace. All of her plans worked out perfectly. They worked out perfectly for the Kingdom and for Atticus but not for me, never for me.

I remain silent even after arriving in the dungeon. Samuel also doesn't dare to say a word. He follows the warrior's command without complaint. This is the end of our battle. I don't know what he plans to do now that her already killed the man behind the murder of Lady Naya. Whatever it is, I am entirely out of it.

Breaking the heavy silence, Samuel murmurs, "I'm sorry..." causing me to glance his way.

We are in separate prison cells, but it is facing each other, allowing us to communicate without a problem. I turn my back on Samuel and settle on the cold stone floor, my back resting against the metal bars. Above, the ceiling looms dark and empty.

"No, it's not your fault, Samuel," I say in a monotone voice, tears cascading down my cheeks. "You did what you had to do, and I did what I had to do. I have no regrets,"

"You don't deserve any of this! After all you've been through, the King has no right to put you in this situation," he seethes in a voice that is full of anger.

"I know that", I reply, my voice hoarse as I force a sad smile. "But Atticus has a duty to protect his kingdom, and right now, he sees me as a threat to Puer Lunae."

It's ironic that I'm in such a vulnerable position, yet I'm still defending my husband's actions. This is what I hate so much about myself. I can understand the reasons behind other people's actions by putting myself in their shoes.

I wish I could hate Atticus, but I know he's hurting too. Today he learned the woman he loved had died weeks ago, and he's been duped into marrying a weak, fragile impostor.

Despite that, I can't help but wonder what he's thinking of me right now. Will it ever occur to him that I did everything I did to help him? That my actions were born out of love... I hope he can see that. I know it's too much to ask, but I still hope he can see things from my perspective.

Eventually, after shedding countless tears, my soul starts to grow weary, allowing me to drift off into the endless void of darkness. The sleep gives me a sense of comfort, even if it is brief. But the peace within my cell is short-lived, shattered by the sound of the iron door opening.

I rise, feeling a little bit dazed and confused as I survey the cell. A soft smile forms on my lips when I spot Minna entering. She walks straight to me and sets down a tray before enveloping me in a warm embrace.

"My Queen, I heard what happened from one of the warriors and came here as soon as I could," she tells me.

The corners of my eyes begin to water, and I bury my face in Minna's shoulder, finding solace in her embrace. It's comforting to have someone who genuinely cares for me at my lowest point.

"The King is busy preparing the Kingdom for the impending war with the rebellion. He wouldn't be able to handle your case, and it could result in a death sentence if we don't act quickly. We need to get you out of here." She whispers in a very small voice as if she's afraid that someone will hear her.

Minna's words catch me off guard. I pull back from her slightly to meet her gaze. "A death sentence?"

A hollow smile creeps across my face. After all the shits I've been through, this is the fate that awaits me? Tears start to stream down my cheeks once again. Why am I even surprised? I've been expecting this outcome from the very beginning.

"That's not totally surprising," Samuel says from the other side of the cell, making me turn to look at him. "Most of the council members are part of the House of Malvagio. If they want Harriet to be the next Queen, they need to eliminate you."

Minna nods in agreement, and my hands close into fists. My husband knew this, and yet he allowed the council to handle my case? I run my fingers through my hair in frustration. I never thought that my husband would be heartless enough to push me directly into the fire.

I take a few deep breaths to get a hold of my emotions. I know that Zizina won't leave me to die. Surely, she will lend a hand when the worst comes to worst. However, I don't think I can ever handle the thought of my husband fully abandoning me.

"Minna, I need you to look for the backpack in our closet. It's safely hidden behind the dresses. Look for it and hand it directly to the King," I instruct with a grave expression on my face. It is my last hope. I'll pray that my husband will reconsider after seeing all of the evidence I've collected while I'm here. I hope that is enough to prove my innocence to him.

Minna nods and gives me an assuring smile. "Will do, My Queen."

CHAPTER 37

Naya

Two days had passed quickly in that dungeon, and Minna gave us a visit every now and then to serve us food. She assured me that she had managed to hand the backpack to the King. What bothers me is that Atticus still hasn't paid me a visit even after receiving the evidence. I am starting to lose hope that my husband will ever forgive me.

He's hurt, and I understand that. But can't he at least reconsider the fact that I am his beloved? If only he would give me a chance to explain myself.

I don't really care if he decides to banish me back to the human world. I am willing to accept his decision as long as he listens to me first. However, it seems that what he is planning to do is ignore me and pretend that I never existed.

I don't want to lose hope, so I keep telling myself that I can still get out of this prison. However, on the third day, I know I shouldn't keep my hopes too high. That same night, a warrior opens our cell and informs me that it's the night of my trial. This is the evening when my fate will be decided.

I can't help but let out a bitter smile as I walk out of the cell. The warrior puts handcuffs on me as if I could escape with the three of them guarding me so securely. Now I finally understand how most criminals feel when they're being escorted to the courtroom. The irony of life is really funny sometimes...

My mind wanders back to the last letter I received from Lady Naya and the message it contains.

'As the future Queen, it is my duty to protect my kingdom to my last breath.'

Well, not to brag or anything, but it looks like I will face the same fate as her tonight.

When we arrive at the courtroom, my eyes automatically look for my loving husband, only to frown upon seeing him seated right beside Harriet. I cock my left eyebrow while looking at him. I love him to the point that I almost gave up everything just to help him. And yet, he is looking at me right now as if I am some kind of criminal he's never known before.

Hatred starts to fill my heart as my palms ball into a fist. If he is expecting me to cry tonight and beg for forgiveness for them to spare my life, he's going to be disappointed. If this is the end of my journey, then so be it. I've lived a pretty adventurous and chaotic life. I have no regrets. I'll be tossing and drinking wine with the grim reaper once he fetches my soul. Yup! That sounds like an excellent plan to me.

"Naya, is that even your real name?" the man in front of me asks.

I tear my eyes away from my husband and look at the man in front of me. I recognize him as the priest who wedded my husband and me a few weeks ago, Cassius.

I let out a grin at the priest. Well, it seems that my husband didn't even bother opening my backpack. Because if he did, my identification would be in there.

"Does it really matter?" I retort with a sigh. "Why would I even bother answering your question when I know firsthand that I'll be judged and condemned tonight without a proper and fair trial?"

Cassius's eyes darken at my insolent remark. I snort at him. I work as a member of the local authority back in the human world. Does he really think I don't have a fucking idea where this is going?

"Why don't you just speak your final judgment instead of interrogating me? I'm ready to face your baseless judgment and accusations. My job here is over, and my presence in this Kingdom is now useless." My words are as sharp as daggers, and so is my tone. I walk towards the table and lean on it.

"Baseless accusations? You manipulated the King into marrying you, pretended that you are his beloved, and—."

"I am his beloved," I cut him off. "Lady Naya manipulated me into marrying the King to save this Kingdom," I correct him.

I got caught up in a web of lies and became entangled in it with no way out. If the council were to do a formal investigation, this would be easy. But no! None of the people in this courtroom even bother to give me a chance. They brought me here to convict me. I don't even have a lawyer to defend me, and they have the audacity to call this a trial?

Cassius's eyes narrow into slits as he glares at me. "Save the Kingdom? You are human. What makes you think that—."

"I didn't come here for you to insult my humanity," I cut him off again before turning my attention to the King. A smug grin forms on my lips upon seeing how dark his expressions are while looking at me. "I have nothing to do with all of this, yet here I am, being convicted for a crime that the woman you love has committed." I bite my inner lip to stop myself from weeping. I'm done crying.

I turn my eyes back on the priest who looks like he is about to explode right in front of me. I can't help but wonder if Cassius has a personal vendetta against me. He's always mad at me. Why can't he just say that I am guilty and I will be scheduled for a guillotine first thing tomorrow?

"Why don't we end this here?" Defending myself is basically useless now. And to be honest, after everything that has happened, I'm simply glad that it is over. "Let's not waste each other's time. I'm tired already."

Cassius's palm forms into a fist at my blatant disrespect. I roll my eyes at him. What the heck is wrong with him? Is it because I am not following the script they expected me to speak? If they think that I will blabber here and defend myself, they can all go to hell. I'm not the kind of person to beg. I'd rather face my death than beg.

If this were a typical courtroom in the human world, I could prove myself innocent after presenting all of the evidence I have collected. The problem is this is not a courtroom. This is a judgment room. This isn't a trial. The decision had been made before I even entered the door. Why beg? It won't change anything.

Cassius shakes his head in disbelief before turning his eyes to the book in his hand. I smirk while looking at him. What can I say? I have a talent for calling out the bullshit, even in my most vulnerable situation.

"Queen Naya, you have committed treason towards the Kingdom by stealing someone's identity and tricking the King into marriage. The council has decided to give you the highest punishment. You are scheduled for public execution tomorrow to set an example for other citizens who might end up following in your footsteps—."

"No!"

Cassius's speech is interrupted by a powerful voice coming from the entrance of the courtroom. All eyes turn towards the man who has the audacity to disturb the trial with his dramatic entrance. I feel like I am seeing my guardian angel in vampire form as King Silvan strides towards us with his own warriors and Zizina standing right beside him.

"King Silvan, this is truly unexpected," Cassius says in an unamused tone as he bows his head towards the newcomer.

"What are you doing here? I don't remember inviting you to enter my territory," Atticus's voice echoes throughout the courtroom, making us turn in his direction. For the first time since I entered this place, I finally heard him speak.

"I came here as soon as I could after hearing from Zizina that a trial is being held for the Queen," King Silvan speaks, sparing a glance in my direction.

"And what right do you have to interfere with the internal affairs of the Kingdom?" Harriet retorts with irritation lacing her voice.

"A lot," King Silvan answers without even bothering to look at Harriet. A confident smile formed on his lips as our gaze met. "She's a human. She's not one of us. Therefore, she is not required to comply with the rules of this Kingdom. I've seen the evidence that King Atticus didn't even bother to look at. Lady Naya was the one who manipulated the situation. Detective Naya Cirillo simply acted on the situation she had been pulled through to survive."

Atticus's face darkens as he looks at me. I can't help but shake my head at his reaction. He hates me for pretending to be Lady Naya, but he can't even stand the fact that Lady Naya is the one who started all of this. He knew that Lady Naya was part of the resistance.

A bitter taste fills my mouth as the green monster starts to consume me from the inside. I finally understand the reason why my husband wants the council to condemn me. It's all because he wants to protect the memory of the woman he used to love before I entered the picture.

I shift my eyes away from him, hating myself for falling for him even though I know firsthand that I am nothing but a rebound. Hating that part of me that wants to beg for his forgiveness.

An empty chuckle escapes from Harriet's lips. "What now? Are we playing the victim game here?" she comments as she folds her arms right in front of her chest. "What are you doing in Puer Lunae? I don't think you have the right to interfere with the Kingdom's internal affairs."

"Just like I said, she's a human. As a member of the oldest royal blood family in the entire land, I have all the right to interfere. This is not your Kingdom's internal affair anymore. Unfortunately, since she is also the Queen of this Kingdom, it needs to be forwarded to the higher council," King Silvan replies with confidence.

"No!" Cassius yells from in front of me, catching me off-guard as I sense the anger in his voice. "That woman has committed a crime against our Kingdom. Therefore, the council of Puer Lunae will be the one to decide the necessary punishment for her," he insists.

"I'm pretty sure that the council of Puer Lunae will give the fairest judgment, but I'm afraid it is a protocol that all the Kingdoms need to comply with," King Silvan explains as if it is some kind of general knowledge everyone should be aware of. He diverts his gaze towards his own warriors. "Take Queen Naya and her butler. She will be staying in Kaedal for the time being. The trial will be held three days from now. Both the prosecution and defence can present their evidence in front of the higher court. If proven guilty, Queen Naya will pay with her life. If proven innocent, she will be given a chance to decide for her freedom. You have three days to prepare."

King Silvan's warriors walk towards me and lead me towards the exit. I follow them without another word.

As we make our way out of the courtroom, I can't help but give my husband one last look. Hatred and pain are written in his eyes while looking at me. For some reason, I feel my heart being squeezed tightly upon seeing the anger in his eyes.

He hates me... That is the most painful punishment he could ever give me.

CHAPTER 38

Naya

"Sad, aren't we?" King Silvan breaks the silence inside the carriage.

I raise my head to meet his eyes and then gently shake my head in response to his question.

"I don't feel sad. I feel empty," I say in a very small voice. "I feel so hollow. And... I don't know if that's a good thing or not."

King Silvan nods in understanding. His eyes bore into my face. He extends his hand to reach for mine, a simple gesture in an attempt to comfort me.

"You are a strong person, Naya. Numbing yourself emotionally is the first response I expected. However, trust me when I tell you that there will be an aftermath associated with it. You will feel all the pain like a flood after a few days," he explains.

I sigh. I wish King Silvan were wrong. I'm okay with feeling numb. I don't want to feel the pain of losing my husband. I shift my gaze to the open window of the carriage and marvel at the breathtaking view outside. The Kingdom of Puer Lunae sprawls out before me. Its grandeur is unmistakable even from a distance. The palace, with its towering spires and ornate carvings, is a sight to behold. The moon casts a pale glow over the Kingdom, highlighting the intricate details of the palace's façade.

"I expected the worst to come when I entered the palace. So I guess I already prepared myself emotionally before the storm landed." I force a smile as I turn my eyes to King Silvan. "Anyway, now that the resistance has been revealed, and one of its powerful members has been captured while the other one has been killed, what do you think Atticus will do?"

Silvan lets out a soft laugh, seemingly amused by my question. "I am impressed. Puer Lunae is a step closer to killing you, and you still think of its welfare?" he comments while shaking his head. "For once, try to be selfish and focus on yourself."

I let out a heavy sigh as I pull my hand out of his hold. I wish I could be that selfish. However, a strong sense of justice runs deep in my blood. It's the main reason why I became a detective— to help bring closure to those whose souls have been damaged. You don't follow your passion for glory. You follow it to satisfy your soul.

I bite my lower lip and turn my gaze back to the carriage window. We are almost at the border of Puer Lunae and Kaedal. For some reason, it feels like I'm leaving a piece of myself in the Kingdom of Puer Lunae. The emptiness inside me intensifies, and I can't help but feel as if I'm suffocating.

I take a few deep breaths to clear the tension inside my chest. King Silvan is right. Maybe I'm numbing myself emotionally, using it as a coping mechanism to protect my heart from the pain. Or perhaps, I'm unconsciously doing it because I have more things to accomplish than having a mental breakdown.

The side of my eyes starts to well up upon remembering the time when Atticus told me that I don't need to force myself to be strong in front of him. That I can always lean on him when everything gets too tough and overwhelming for me.

My heart clenches in pain inside my chest. I feel so weak right now, and everything feels so overwhelming. I need someone to be strong for me, but he's nowhere near to comfort me. At the end of the day, the vows and promises we made fall apart in front of me, and there's nothing I can do to save it.

"I love your dedication. It's such a shame that you met Atticus first. That idiot is lucky to have you as his Queen. This Kingdom is blessed to have you as their Queen," King Silvan states with a gentle smile on his lips. "You don't have to worry about the trial. I'll be the one to defend you in the higher court. Focus on solving the case of the bewitched vampires. You have three days to fully find out where the potions are coming from. Zizina and Samuel will help—."

"Why are you helping me?" I cut him off.

My question hangs in the air as the deafening silence envelopes us. The only sound that echoes in the carriage is the rhythmic clatter of the horse's hooves against the cobblestone road. I can feel the weight of King Silvan's gaze on me. And then, he lets out a lopsided smile.

"You will bear someone who belongs to me. I'm doing what I need to do to protect it," he replies, his voice laced with an air of finality.

A sarcastic smile forms on my lips, but inside, fear starts to prickle at my skin. King Silvan is not someone to be trifled with, and his words make it clear that he will stop at nothing to protect what he believes is his. As the ruler of a powerful kingdom, he has already proven that he is capable of anything to ensure that his objectives are met.

If he is willing to enter the Kingdom of Puer Lunae without permission and assert his authority in front of Atticus and the whole council to release me, then I should be even more apprehensive about what he is capable of doing for my unborn child.

"Tell me, King Silvan, why do you want my child? I mean, your name isn't Rumpelstiltskin, right?" I try to put humour in my voice, but my trembling tone betrays my inner turmoil. "There's a big chance that I'm not going to bear Atticus's child."

King Silvan's smirk widens, and he gives me a dismissive shrug. "I think you've got it all wrong, my dearest Queen. I don't want Atticus' child. I need your child," he corrects me with a sly grin. "It doesn't matter who the father is."

That catches me off guard, my forehead scrunching in confusion. His words sound like a riddle that I can't seem to solve. If what he's telling me is true, then that means his intention isn't to take over the Puer Lunae Kingdom like we initially thought.

"What do you mean by that?" I ask, my voice laced with scepticism.

"I'm afraid that is not something that I can discuss with you right now, Queen Naya. Rest assured that I will not allow any harm to come to your child. Right now, your safety is my priority," he answers and leans back in his chair.

I cock him my eyebrow. Having an alliance with King Silvan is really useful, especially in my current situation. What I'm afraid of is the fact that I don't know if he is an enemy or a friend. I have a feeling that he is someone I can trust, but I'm also worried about what he's planning to do with my child. Why would the King of a powerful vampire kingdom need my child?

When we arrive at the castle, King Silvan instructs one of the warriors to bring me to a room where I can rest. Tomorrow, I can start my investigation promptly.

His warrior leads me to the room that Atticus and I occupied when we first visited this Kingdom. I step into the room, and to my surprise, my eyes immediately catch sight of my backpack resting on top of the bed. Apparently, Zizina decided to take the backpack to King Silvan and ask him to rescue me from the council of Puer Lunae.

I settle into the room and start looking at all the evidence I have collected. Now that I know the rebellion started in the house of Nardelli, it will be easier for us to identify the other people involved in it. The only questions that still need an answer are what the motive behind the resistance is and where they are getting the potions they are using to bewitch those vampires.

"Why are you still awake? You should rest. We still have a lot of investigation to do tomorrow." My eyes turn towards the door, only to see my loyal butler leaning against it.

I cock my left eyebrow while looking at him. "I can't sleep, so I decided to check the evidence we have. We have three days left to figure out where the potion is coming from," I reply.

Samuel closes the distance between us and takes a seat on the bed right beside me.

"I'm glad that even after everything we went through in that dungeon for three days, you still care about the investigation," he sighs before leaning against the headrest of the bed.

I can't help but smile as I turn my gaze towards the evidence spread out in front of us. After all the hardships we've faced, Samuel is the only person who has remained by my side from the beginning until the end— the loyal butler who is willing to give his own life to save his Queen. He is one of the good things that has happened to me in this world.

"Lady Naya gave her life for this. I can't fail her. Puer Lunae is our home, and I don't think she wants to see it destroyed. Besides, we've come this far already. Why back down now?" I retort.

Samuel picks up one of the letters from the bed and begins to read it.

A smile forms on my lips while looking at Samuel as he examines the first letter I receive. "It seems to me that Lady Naya intends for us to be partners in this case. None of this would be possible without your help, Samuel," I remark.

From the letter, he raises his gaze to meet mine. "No, I should be the one to say that my Queen. We are halfway to saving the Kingdom because of you. And let's be honest here, I am the one who dragged you into marrying the King. It's kind of my fault that you are heartbroken right now." he replies with a slight wince on his face.

I let out a soft chuckle upon seeing the guilt etched on his face. It was indeed his idea that I pose as Lady Naya and wed the King. This is the craziest case I've handled in my lifetime, but I must admit that this is the best so far as well. Until now, I still can't imagine how I ended up being the Queen of vampires. It's both daunting and terrifying.

"Ah, that's true, isn't it?" I quip, giving him a playful smirk. However, as a random thought occurs to me, the smile on my lips vanishes, and I look at my butler with curiosity. "Back in the house of Nardelli, I asked Niall about the goal of the resistance, but I didn't get the answer I wanted. You've been with Lady Naya since she was a child. Why do you think a powerful family, a minister, and a duke would plot a rebellion against the Kingdom?"

Samuel looks at me with keen interest beaming in his eyes. My question hangs in the air, causing the room to fall silent. I recall his previous mention of Lady Naya's family's opposition to Atticus's leadership. Is there a history behind that? If there is, then maybe the answer to that question will lead us to other people who might also be involved in this rebellion.

CHAPTER 39

Naya

"The Nardellis and the monarchs of Puer Lunae are not exactly on good terms for as long as I can remember. It's one of the reasons why many people were shocked when the King announced his intention to wed Lady Naya," Samuel starts. "I thought the wedding would be the start of something good for both parties. However, Lady Naya was killed, and we discovered the resistance."

Now that the case is coming to an end, everything finally makes sense to me. At first, I thought I was only looking for a single murderer. But now that I have more puzzle pieces in my hand, it makes me wonder why I didn't realize earlier that Lady Naya had summoned me here for a much bigger purpose.

"Why, though?" I question with a frown on my forehead without tearing my gaze from Samuel's eyes.

He responds with a shrug and says, "They're loyal to the late monarch of Puer Lunae. You see, the old monarchy committed a grave crime not only against our people but also against the nearby Kingdoms. It caused a lot of chaos, and the two other kingdoms even threatened to wage war against us. Atticus's father led the rebellion against the monarchy and successfully ended the threat of the uprising war with the nearby kingdoms by publicly executing the previous monarch and sending their loyalists to Viria for life imprisonment."

I furrow my eyebrows in confusion. Well, that revelation was completely unexpected. "So there was a rebellion that happened before pretty similar to this?" The frown on my forehead deepens. "Why didn't you tell me about it sooner?"

"I wasn't even born when that happened," Samuel explains, defending himself. "Atticus was born on the throne, so he doesn't know much about it either. The elders are the ones who knew the details about that rebellion. However, they rarely talk about it because it's considered to be a shameful part of our history. It's not written in our history books for a reason."

I release a sigh as I process the new information I have. Why would they decide not to include that important information from history books? Does none of them ever hear the saying that those who refuse to learn from the past are doomed to repeat it?

My butler stands up from the bed and gazes at the open window of my room. I follow his gaze and take the time to admire the view outside. The sky seems oddly beautiful tonight, with millions of stars forming like a river flowing in endless darkness.

"Monarchies come and go, and that's just how it is. So, it's not really surprising if you ask me." Samuel remarks and turns his eyes back to me.

Instead of answering, I pick up the 2nd letter I received from Lady Naya and read it again silently. I think I finally understand why Lady Naya needed to allow herself to get killed. It's because if she ever gets married to the King, there is a big chance that the resistance will succeed in killing Atticus. If that happens, her family will have control over the Kingdom because she's the Queen. If my conclusion is correct, then that means this rebellion is an action to overthrow the current leadership, a resistance to take the throne from Atticus.

"My husband has every right to hate me, not only because I am a fraud but also because if we had not uncovered the rebellion on time, he would have been so close to losing his Kingdom," I murmur without taking my gaze from the letter in my hand.

"I don't think he hates you. You are his beloved, my Queen. I have a feeling that it is the Ministers and the Dukes who have convinced him that you need to die. You are still the Queen of Puer Lunae. If something happens to the King, you have every right to take over. They are afraid of that power," Samuel explains, making me turn my eyes to him.

His words spark a bit of hope in my chest, silently hoping that it is really the case. I'm pretty sure Atticus doesn't have much time to investigate everything. It breaks my heart to think that I am an enemy in my husband's eyes.

After all the shit I've been through to solve this case, I find it so unfair for them to treat me like an enemy. For my husband to treat me as if I were a criminal.

I start to pick up the items on top of my bed to put them back inside my bag for safekeeping. I can feel my chest clench in pain. My husband's betrayal of our vow is now starting to take a toll on me.

"I hate him..." The words escape my lips in a raw, almost broken voice. "I gave everything for him. He didn't even give me a chance to defend myself, to explain. He condemned me, his own wife, without a second thought. He left me to suffer alone." My voice grows louder with each word, my anger and pain fueling my words. My gaze narrows into slits as the pain inside my chest intensifies. "Fuck him! He can have Harriet as his Queen for all I care. Once all of this is over, I'm leaving this place. I'm going back to the human world where he can't hurt me anymore!"

My attention turns to my left arm when I feel something wet drop on it. That is when I realize that tears are already falling down from my eyes. My fists clench at my sides, my heart heavy with the weight of my husband's betrayal.

I understand his pain and his hatred, but can't he see that I'm in pain too? This world is cruel, and I'm just a human caught in the middle of powerful vampires, trying to solve a case that has nothing to do with me in the first place. For god's sake! I'm not even getting paid for this!

Samuel reaches out and pulls me into his chest, a silent comfort that I desperately need. We both know that there's nothing he can say to make me feel better.

And to make matters worse, the bond that connects me to Atticus makes me question my own feelings. Do I really love my husband, or is this just the bond clouding my judgment? The pain in my heart is unbearable, and I don't know if it's because I truly love him or if it's because he betrayed the very bond that brought us together.

I don't know...

All I know is that I have to help him. I must help him save the Kingdom because it's the right thing to do, even if it means pushing aside the pain I feel. I'll get up tomorrow and continue my investigation, not because I'm confident in my ability but because it's my duty.

I weep in silence, grateful for Samuel's comforting arms. Lady Naya is asking for too much, but I can't refuse. The fate of my warriors and subjects hangs in the balance. If I don't find all the powerful people behind the resistance soon, lives will be lost. As their Queen, it's my responsibility to protect my people, and I can't let them down.

"Forgive me, my Queen... Forgive me for dragging you into this situation. On behalf of the Kingdom, I apologize for all the pain we've caused you..." My butler murmurs gently as he caresses the back of my head, comforting me.

After a few minutes of crying silently in his arms, I distance myself from him and wipe my tears away from my cheeks.

Three more days and this will all be over. It will either be my death, my freedom, or my continued reign as the Queen of Puer Lunae. I take a deep breath to fill my lungs with air, trying my best to calm my raging emotions.

"Let's stop this. I need to focus," I shake my head gently and turn my attention back to the things on top of the bed to continue putting them back in my bag. Once all of this is over, I can cry my eyes out and curse heaven for putting me in this situation. But for now, I need to focus on what's more important.

Samuel helps me put the stuff back into the bag until he picks up the ring that Lady Naya sent to me. He takes a closer look at it for a moment before putting it inside my bag and closing it.

"Do you know what amazes me the most about us?" he asks out of a sudden as he hands me the bag.

"What is it?" I raise my gaze to him as I take the bag from his hand.

"It's the fact that after being in the dark for weeks, we are now seeing the light at the end of the tunnel," he remarks with a tinge of amazement in his voice, the side of his lips tugging into a proud little smile for us. "It's not easy, but we have made it this far already."

I let out a warm smile upon seeing the genuine excitement sparkling in his eyes. That is honestly my favourite part of being a detective— having many sleepless nights and squeezing my mind to find the connections in each piece of evidence to figure out who the criminal is.

"It's satisfying," I agree. "This is why I love my job. At first, everything feels so blurry because you are starting from scratch with only a few bits and pieces of evidence in your hand. Then you begin your investigation, you start questioning people, and you start to see the pattern. You slowly uncover the truth that was hidden beneath thousands of lies. Having the ability to give a happy ending to those people who lost their lives cruelly, unexpectedly is amazing, even though only a few can see and appreciate that."

Samuel meets my gaze as he nods, still with that proud look in his eyes. "We both deserve a pat on the back for this,"

I let out a soft laugh and nod. Yup, we both deserve that. Even though we know we are still far from solving this murder case, I can't help but be proud of how far we've come. It's amazing. We messed up so badly in some parts, but no one can deny that we have already achieved great success. In fact, I think we are only a few steps away from fully closing this case.

CHAPTER 40

Naya

That night passed so quickly than I expected. Although tired, I didn't get a chance to sleep for too long. There was just too much going on inside my head for me to get proper rest. King Silvan informed me that I am allowed to roam outside the palace, granted that I have Samuel and two other warriors to guard me.

I decided to wear my casual detective outfit this time. Gone are the times when I needed to wear fancy gowns and dresses fit for royalty. It's not really a big deal for me, though. Denim on denim is much more comfortable, and it gives me the ability to move flawlessly when needed. It hides weapons too.

"Where are we going?" Samuel turns to me with a questioning look. "This road will lead us outside the territory of Kaedal."

I shift my gaze to him and nod. "The map given to me by the man who sold the silver sword leads to the border of Kaedal and Puer Lunae. We might need to enter Puer Lunae territory," I answer. I need to know if the person who forged this sword has a direct relation to the resistance.

Samuel's forehead creases, clearly not amused at the prospect of going back to Puer Lunae. "I don't think it's safe for us to enter Puer Lunae. There's a big chance that some of the people in the Kingdom might harm you, especially those loyal to the house of Malvagio."

I shrug and give a quick glance at the two warriors that are accompanying us. I didn't want to involve them, but King Silvan insisted that it was for my own safety. I let out an impatient sigh.

"We don't have much time left, Samuel. I need to take a gamble." I reason as I turn my gaze back to the road. We only have three days left, and I need to take bold action.

"I get that, but do you think the person who forged this sword will cooperate?" Samuel asks.

I can't help but smirk as I meet his gaze. I say proudly. "I'm a police officer back in the human world, Samuel. Trust me, I have my ways of making people talk."

After a few minutes, we ride into a small village. Strangely enough, this little town is situated right between Kaedal and Puer Lunae. The locals look at us with curiosity, probably wondering what we are doing here with two warriors from the Kaedal Kingdom.

I dismount from my horse and take a quick survey of our surroundings. I need to find someone I can trust— someone who can potentially help me in my quest. And then, my gaze lands on an elderly woman with a stoic expression on her face as she watches me intently.

"Hello," I greet her with a warm smile. "I apologize for the abrupt intrusion. But I'm in search of the person who crafted this sword."

I untie the rope that keeps the sword secured to my waist and show it to the woman. For a moment, she didn't respond or even glance at the sword I held out to her. Instead, she simply stares at me with sheer curiosity. But then, after a minute or so, her eyes finally land on the silver blade in my hand before it goes back to my face.

"You're the Queen of Puer Lunae, aren't you?" she asks with her voice filled with intrigue.

I give her a friendly smile and nod. There is no point in denying my true identity. If I want her honesty, I know I need to commit to it first and show her that I am trustworthy.

The woman smiles at my answer and bows a bit to show her respect. That makes me confused. If she's showing me respect, then I guess the news of me being a fraud hasn't reached this town yet.

Her eyes then return to the sword that I am holding. "That sword was forged by the old blacksmith of this town. Just follow this stone path." She points out a mossy cobblestone path on the side that seems to lead towards the depth of the forest.

I follow the trail she points with my gaze and sigh. "Whoever this blacksmith is, he seems a bit of a loner," I remark upon seeing where the stone is leading.

The old woman nods at me in agreement. "He lost his wife and their only daughter to a bewitched a few years ago. After that incident, he decided to leave the town and live on the outskirts of the forest," she explains further.

Her words catch my attention, and I frown in confusion. If that is true, why would the blacksmith sell silver weapons to a man who seems to have a connection with the bewitched vampires? That doesn't make sense at all.

I turn my attention back to the old woman and give her a thankful smile before bidding farewell. I make my way back to my horse, and with a graceful swing, I mount my horse and lead my group towards the direction of the forest, the sound of hoofbeats echoing through the tranquil village.

"Do you think this man has a connection to Niall?" Samuel breaks the silence between us as soon as we are out of the village's earshot.

"He has to be. It's uncommon for a blacksmith to craft a weapon that is made with full silver."

"And when you find him, what exactly is the information that you need from him?" one of the warriors questions.

Samuel and I turn to look at him. I can't help but grin as our eyes meet. Warriors are often silent when accompanying royals. It seems that it is in their work code not to communicate with royals unless we initiate it first.

"During my first visit to Kaedal, King Silvan fought a few bewitched vampires to save me. He mentioned something about their claws being covered with silver," I reply. "Silver and potions, those are the two crucial things I've noticed during my investigation. Let's look for the source of the silver today. Then, after that, we can go ahead and look for the source of the potions."

"Will you be able to accomplish all of that in the next three days?" The warrior interjects with his voice laced with concern.

I let out a sigh, and I turn my eyes back at the shabby cobblestone path ahead of us. I don't think our enemies will wait for the next three days before attacking. One of their most powerful members has been captured and is probably being questioned by now. Niall has been killed. If they have eyes inside the palace, I'm pretty sure that they are now aware that the Queen has been exiled.

I feel that most of the people in the Kingdom have lost their trust in the monarch, especially after knowing the involvement of the Queen's family in the resistance. The palace is in its vulnerable state right now. If I were in the enemy's shoes, I would definitely use that to my advantage.

I am not worried about what will happen after three days. I am much more concerned about what will happen within those three days.

"I don't know." I shrug. "I have a feeling that we don't need to wait for three days to get the information we are looking for," I add, voicing out my thoughts.

The warrior beside me falls silent, and a long awkward pause follows as we approach an old cottage where I suspect the old blacksmith resides. I halt my horse and dismount from it to look around, frowning in confusion upon noticing that the place seems too empty and has been long abandoned. Despite that, I walk towards the door and knock twice on it. When I didn't get any response, I knocked a little louder, but still to no avail.

"Wait, Queen Naya. Allow me to do it," the warrior beside me offers.

I nod at him and step back to give him room to work his magic. He wastes no time, barging into the house without bothering to knock. His powerful kick sends the door flying as it smashes to the dirty floor with a cracking thud. Though I prefer more polite methods when entering unknown territory, I can't help but smirk in amusement at the sheer force of his entry. I guess that could work as well.

The warrior enters first, and I follow him inside. The spark of amusement in my eyes starts to fade, and my smile vanishes, replaced by a look of terror as I take in the scene inside the small cottage— a lifeless body of a man sprawled on the ground and if my hunch is correct, this man the blacksmith that we are a looking for.

I can feel my heart sink down to my stomach, despair washing over me like a tidal wave. We're too late. The enemies have already anticipated our arrival. What now?

"Fuck!" Samuel curses vehemently from behind me. The frustration is clear in his voice.

I raise a hand to my temple and start to massage it, trying to quell the rising panic. "We're late," I say quietly, my voice heavy with defeat.

I look around the house and notice three large crates in the corner. I walk towards them and open them one by one, but just as I had expected, they are all empty. I let out a tired sigh. If this man was the blacksmith who forged those silver weapons, I could conclude that these crates were once used as storage for silver weapons.

"I don't understand..." I whisper to myself, feeling confused out of a sudden.

"What is it?" the warrior asks me, making me turn towards him.

"If this man's family was killed by bewitched vampires, why did he forge these weapons? It doesn't make sense to me," I reply.

The warrior nods at me in understanding. He walks towards me and looks at the empty crates in front of us. If all of these crates contained silver weapons, then I can say that Puer Lunae is in grave danger.

"If the Kingdom had looked into this sooner, we might have had a chance to win. The amount of weapons these crates could accommodate is more than enough to supply an army. The thing is, we're not talking about a normal vampire army here. We're talking about bewitched vampires that are much stronger and faster than normal vampires, not to mention they also have immunity to silver." The warrior says as his hand balls into a fist, his expression dark while staring at crates.

I take a deep breath to ease the tension in my chest. I need a clear head right now. We hit another dead end, but I can't let that dishearten me. "Where are they getting their army, though?" I question even though I already know that none of us have an answer to that. "I mean, let's say they have weapons. Where are they getting the manpower for the war?"

There are so many questions left unanswered. Besides that, I also can't help but wonder how they can create bewitched vampires with immunity to silver. Is that even possible? I mean, they are still vampires, right? How are they not dying with silver in their claws and skin?

"My Queen, we need to leave!" That panicky voice of my butler catches my attention.

The warrior and I turn to look at Samuel. My forehead furrows in confusion upon seeing the horror etched on his face. I follow his gaze, only to freeze on my spot when I realize what it is that makes him panicky. A cold shiver runs down my spine, and my heart starts racing upon seeing the dead man on the ground starting to stand up. The air around us turns icy as a chill settles in. I can smell the stench of death and decay as the corpse slowly rises from the floor, making my stomach churn a little.

All of us stand there frozen in shock, watching in disbelief as the once-dead man comes back to life. The hairs on my arms stand on end as I feel his eyes lock onto us, his gaze cold and lifeless. The silence is deafening, broken only by the sound of his bones creaking as he moves.

The blacksmith's skin is now as white as snow, a striking contrast to his earlier appearance. Black and violet veins are visible, crawling across his flesh. My heart thunders inside my chest like a drum as I watch the dead vampire transform into a bewitched creature before our very eyes. We should have noticed that a vampire's body is supposed to disintegrate into ashes upon death, yet the blacksmith's body remains intact. This oversight should have alerted us that something was amiss with his corpse.

"We need to leave," I mutter under my breath, speaking quietly enough for the soldier beside me to hear.

However, my voice seemed to have attracted the attention of the bewitched in front of us. His eyes lock onto mine, and his deafening scream fills the air. Before I can react, he charges toward me, his sharp claws aimed at my chest.

"Queen Naya!"

"My Queen!"

"Fuck!"

Those are the last words I hear before I stand frozen in front of the monstrous creature. Its claws rend my chest, tearing apart my flesh and plunging toward my heart.

CHAPTER 41

Naya

Everything happened so fast that none of us four could make a move to stop what was about to come. My gaze focused on the eyes of the bewitched before me, and I could almost imagine the horror written on my face upon seeing his hand covered with my blood as he pulled it out of my chest.

"Naya!" I hear Samuel scream my name in panic.

I turn to look at him, a faint smile making its way to my lips as I start to cough up a considerable amount of blood. I don't want it to end this way, but I guess none of us has control over that. Only destiny gets to decide.

I summon all of my remaining strength, hoping that I can still make it. However, upon looking down at my chest and seeing the blood that is continuously flowing from my open wound, I know that the bewitched has managed to pierce through my heart."

A lone tear escapes from my eyes. Ironically, I can't feel a bit of pain coming from the fatal wound in my chest. I guess after all that I've been through, my body just decided that I had enough and numbed all of my senses, removing my ability to feel anything, including physical pain.

The warrior beside me is the first one to recover from the shock. He is quick to pull the silver sword from my waist. In just a snap, he was already behind the man who attacked me, thrusting the sword into its lungs and chest. The bewitched turns into ashes almost instantly, vanishing like a speck of dust in the wind before us. The sword falls to the ground with a silent thump. The warrior's hand burnt down to flesh from the silver, but his gaze remains on me, not caring one bit about his own injury.

My knees give out, and I collapse onto the floor, my body weight resting heavily on my bent knees. But before I even hit the ground, a hand catches my waist, preventing me from falling to the floor. I look up to see Samuel holding me tightly with a worried yet hopeless expression on his face.

"My Queen, hold on, please... I beg you, just for a few minutes... Help is coming. I promise you that just hold on for a few more minutes..." His tone is pleading, almost as if it is meant to break at any moment.

My hands cup his cheeks as I try to get his attention. I want to hold on, but I know I don't have much strength left for that. No matter how strong we are, we are destined to fall one day. I guess for me that one day is today.

I force myself to smile. Samuel is the only person who has never left my side after everything that has happened. Somehow, I am thankful that I am destined to leave this world while in his arms. It is comforting to know that I am not meant to die alone, and instead of feeling the cold hard ground, I am inside his warm and caring embrace.

My breathing starts to become shallow, and everything around me feels like it's spinning. I try to take a deep breath, only to cough up more blood as it fills my lungs. Samuel's hold tightens on me. Clearly, he is not ready to let me go.

I open my lips to say a simple thank you to him for staying by my side all this time, but unfortunately, I can't find the strength to voice those words. I see panic cross his eyes as my hand falls to the ground. I'm no expert in the medical field, but as darkness slowly fills my vision, I know that the grim reaper is coming to fetch my soul.

I close my eyes and finally allow the darkness of the void to take over. If this is my end, I am accepting it wholeheartedly. I gave my best to help the weak and those who relied on me. I've done my part. There are no regrets, only memories to cherish...

***

What lies beyond death? Have you ever asked yourself what's waiting for us in the afterlife? Is heaven real, or is hell real? I often asked myself that question when I was a child. I thought this was the day I was set to know what lies beyond death, but I was wrong.

I feel the air filling my lungs once again. All of my senses start to become active, more vivid. I have no idea what is happening, but I can feel a sudden surge of energy filling my whole body, forcing me to open my eyes. My palm closes into a fist. I hear the slow beating of my heart until it gradually becomes stable.

"You can't die, not on my watch. Open your eyes and rise once again, Queen Naya of Puer Lunae..." A familiar voice whispers near my ear. For some reason, his command seems enough to force me to open my eyes.

I sit up on the bed in a panic, panting so hard as if I am trying to catch my breath. I look around me with a confused expression. My gaze lands on my butler, who is standing on the side of the bed. Then it turns towards the man who owns the voice that called me out from the void of darkness.

"What have you done?" My hands clutch the silk comforter of the bed; anger is slowly filling my chest.

I didn't need him to answer my question. It was pretty obvious to me what he needed to do in order to save me from sure death. Before I even realized what I was doing, I was already in front of him, holding his neck tightly with one hand as I pushed him to the wall not far from where he was standing a while ago.

Realizing my unexpected actions, I immediately let go of him and stared at my hand in confusion. Seeing how swiftly I can move with my newfound strength is both surprising and terrifying. This is not me anymore. I am far from being human anymore. My eyes snap towards King Silvan who's now looking at me with a proud smile on his lips.

"What have you done!" I repeat my question, this time with more intensity in my voice.

"I did what I needed to do," he answers and gives me a nonchalant shrug. "Welcome back to the living world, Queen Naya."

My palm closes into a tight fist. I want to cry, I want to slap him, and I want to scream at him. But I know that hitting a king can lead to war, so instead, I run my fingers through my soft, amber-coloured hair in frustration.

"For once, can't I have a chance to decide for myself?" I seethe with a dark expression on my face. "Isn't it enough? I'm done! I'm not even allowed to have a fucking rest in peace!"

"You are being selfish, Naya," King Silvan remarks without tearing his gaze away from me.

"Selfish?" I parrot his words in a mocking tone. King Silvan's accusation left me dumbfounded. "Wow. Now, I'm the selfish one? After everything I've done for this world?" I felt a surge of frustration burst within me. I had solved a murder mystery that had nothing to do with me, gave myself entirely to a stranger who didn't lift a finger to save me when I needed him the most and died trying to save a kingdom that wanted me dead. And yet, I was being called selfish.

"What about me?" I rant as I point to my chest, my voice filled with anguish. "I lost everything trying to save everyone— my life, my humanity. And now, you have the audacity to call me selfish?"

I can't help but feel a sense of betrayal. It seems like no matter how much I give, it's never enough.

"Your death will be Puer Lunae's downfall," King Silvan says as he straightens his back, his eyes never leaving mine.

"Puer Lunae wants me dead. Not all of them, but I'm pretty sure most of them." I shake my head as I walk back to the bed and slump on it. I bury my face in my palms. I want to cry. My death was so sudden, but I accepted it. Don't get me wrong, I don't hate my life, but the pressure of what's waiting for me in this world makes me think that death is a much better option.

"Have you ever thought about what Atticus is feeling right now?" King Silvan asks after a moment of silence, making me raise my gaze to meet his.

"Is he even thinking about what I am feeling right now? Does he even consider how hopeless I feel right now?" I retort in a weak voice.

The King keeps his lips sealed. He stands not far from where I am, leaning on the wall while looking at me. I let out a bitter smile. Tears start to fall from my eyes in a combination of frustration and agony. I had lost my humanity completely... I lost that part of me that connects me to the world where I belong.

"The death of a beloved is more than enough to make a King fall on his knees. You can't die, Naya. Not while your Kingdom is on the verge of collapse," Silvan explains.

That makes me confused for a second. I wipe my tears harshly and take a sharp inhale to calm the raging storm in my heart and mind.

"You think I'm going to believe that? If you didn't arrive during the trial, the council could have killed me in front of him. Atticus didn't even give a damn about—."

"King Atticus instructed me to do it," he cuts me off.

My palms ball into fists, my expression filled with disbelief. What is this? Another lie? Another mind game? I'm tired, and I'm done with the people of this world trying to control me using my emotions. A faint smile curves on my lips.

I shake my head and let out a humourless laugh. "Do you really think I'm going to believe that?" This world is just as ridiculous as the people who reside in it.

"Your husband can't protect you. That will create a division within the Kingdom. That's the last thing Atticus wants to happen, especially since the Kingdom is facing a crisis." King Silvan explains further. "You are his beloved. He is bound to you, and a beloved's death is critical for vampires."

"He abandoned me!" I seethe with controlled anger, not wanting to believe any of his explanations.

"He didn't," he insists. "If he had chosen you, the house of Malvagio would have turned against the

Kingdom. That's the last thing Puer Lunae needs right now. There is an uprising rebellion, and Atticus needs all the help he can get to protect his subjects. Try to see it from his perspective, Naya," The King finishes before walking towards the door, leaving me feeling even more confused as he walks out of the room.

I stare at the empty space where he was standing just moments ago. Is that really what happened? My husband didn't abandon me all this time? Was it all part of his plan?

My eyes turn towards Samuel who's standing not far from me. I give him a questioning look.

He shrugs in response. "I know nothing about it. Trust me, I'm just as shocked as you are right now."

I let out a harsh exhale and stared blankly at the floor. We've both been imprisoned in the dungeon for three days and if anyone knows anything about what's going on, it's either Minna or Zizina.

"King Silvan's explanation does make sense. If King Atticus did something to save you, the house of Malvagio would be an enemy, and that's dangerous. That would significantly reduce the Kingdom's power. Remember that the house of Malvagio controls the trade and finance, and there are many powerful families in the Kingdom on their side," Samuel explains to back up King Silvan's claims.

I nod in understanding and try to pull myself together. I think the best thing I can do right now is to stay neutral and wait for Atticus to explain it himself.

"I'm not going to ask how I'm alive. It's clear to me that King Silvan decided to turn me into one of you without asking for permission," I say after regaining my composure. "How long have I been asleep?"

"You didn't sleep," Samuel murmurs as he closes the short distance between us. Without a word, he pulls me close to his chest for a hug. I stay still inside his arms, unable to find the strength to push him away from me. "We lost you... You died in my arms, and I didn't know what to do. I feel so useless..." I can hear a tinge of pain and distress in his voice as he speaks.

I let out a weak smile and buried my face in his shoulder. Maybe King Silvan was right. I'm selfish for choosing death.

CHAPTER 42

Naya

"Any news?" I ask Zizina as she strides into the room.

We are currently situated in the east wing of the palace, poring over the map of the two Kingdoms that is laid on top of a wooden table. Kaedal had pledged allegiance to Puer Lunae, and King Silvan had promised to dispatch his army as reinforcement in case of the worst possible outcome.

Right now, we do not know what to expect. I am still lacking any solid information regarding the potion used to create the bewitched. It is probable that the witch I encountered at Raven's Row is the one responsible for their production. However, her identity remains unknown to me.

"I came here as soon as I heard the news about your death. What happened?" Zizina questions in a concerned tone as she closes the distance between us.

"We tried to track down the blacksmith who forged the silver swords," I recount, cringing at the memory of what occurred next after that encounter. "Unfortunately, it goes out of hand, and unexpected things happen," I explain in a concise, less detailed manner.

"You are a vampire now," she states, noting the evident change in my appearance and aura.

I nod to confirm and shift my attention back to the colossal map before us. It displays both the Kaedal and Puer Luna, both of which are stunning. It is undoubtedly a utopia for those who relish living in the Medieval Gothic era.

"King Silvan had no other option but to turn me into one. Sadly, I am of no use to the Kingdom as a lifeless body," I comment with a weary sigh at the end.

I am exhausted, and I want to mourn the life and humanity I just lost. However, I can't do that, at least not right now.

"How do you feel about it?" The witch asks, her eyes remain fixed on me.

I turn my gaze to meet hers and frown. "What do you mean?"

She shrugs. "I mean, are you okay with it? Don't you want to go back to the human world once all of this is over?"

A forced smile forms on my lips at the concern that is lacing her voice. It's nice to know that someone from this world thinks that I have a say in how I should run my life.

"Nothing changes about my decision. But I'll deal with it once I am already in that situation," I answer. "I don't have that much choice anyway. Besides, we are not even sure if I will survive until that day. I still have a trial to attend. That could be my death. Nobody knows."

Zizina shakes her head, but her gaze remains locked on mine. "I don't think it would. You're a remarkable Queen, Naya. It'll be heartbreaking to see you leave and return to the human world, but I'll be more than willing to open the gateway for you if that's what it takes to make you happy. It's the least I can do."

A warm feeling envelops my heart upon sensing the sincerity in her voice. I have a love-and-hate relationship with this world. This world has taken away everything from me until there's nothing left but an empty shell. However, I cannot deny how this world has forged me into a much stronger version of myself. I have learned to set aside my emotions, work under immense pressure, and pull myself together even when I'm on the verge of breaking down. It has helped me come up with an idea right on the spot just to survive for another day.

This world has shown me how weak I am, what it's like to be at the bottom of the food chain, but still rise the next day with my pretend courage.

"You and Samuel are the people on whom I know I can lean on. This world is unforgiving, but I have managed to stay alive to this day because of you two. Thank you," I say with the utmost sincerity I can muster.

Zizina's gaze softens, and I feel a pang of sadness knowing that I am bound to lose her and Samuel when I return to the human world.

"Hey, before we end up crying here. I think I have news for you," she says to sway the conversation from being emotional. She reaches into her small body bag. The crinkling sound of paper fills the room as she retrieves a torn newspaper clipping from her bag.

I furrow my brow in confusion, unsure of what to make of the torn scrap in her hand.

"You visited the human world?" I ask and take the piece of paper she's handing me to read the headline on it. "Missing inmates?" I didn't bother hiding the confusion in my voice, wondering what the relation of this news to our current situation.

"Yes," She confirms. "They didn't make any upgrades to the potion. Instead, the resistance looked for a species of vampire that could withstand the effect of the potion. It turns out that turned vampires have much more immunity than naturally born ones," she explains, leaving me frozen for a few seconds as I try to process the information she provided.

I raise my eyes to meet hers with bewilderment on my face. Turned vampires? Now it is starting to make sense. I look at the silver sword on my waist and pull it from its sheath. As expected, I can hold the blade with its silver handle without any problem. A vampire that has immunity to the effect of the potion and silver?

My eyes widen in realization. Anger starts to fill my chest, and suddenly I want to tear the newspaper in my hand into smaller pieces. No wonder there are no reports of missing vampires or rogues. There are no missing vampires in the first place. Instead, they are using turned humans.

I run my fingers through my hair in frustration as my palms start to shake in anxiety. "Call King Silvan. We need to know who are the other vampires in this world have the ability to turn humans into your kind," I command.

The witch nods at me and turns to face the door to follow my orders. I am left inside the room feeling hollow about the situation. This seems to have been ongoing for a very long time now. Why on earth this news about missing inmates didn't get any of my attention back when I was still in the human world?

My fingers reach out to massage my forehead. Tomorrow will be my trial, and I don't know if I still have enough time to investigate further and look deeper into this.

The door of the room opens. King Silvan enters the room with Samuel and a few other warriors accompanying him from behind. Zizina is the last one to enter. The tension slowly rises inside the room, and I can see from the grim look on King Silvan's face that he also has a terrible news to share.

"What happened?" I ask with concern lacing my voice, bracing myself for the worst.

Zizina's discovery about the turned vampire immediately fades from my mind as I wait for King Silvan's response. His face remains stoic, and seeing his dark expression makes me think that something terrible is happening right now.

"Puer Lunae is under attack. King Atticus has sent one of his warriors to inform us to stand by," He declares, his tone grave and sombre.

My muscles tense up, and I find myself unable to move as I process the news. The lump in my throat feels like a boulder, making it hard to breathe. I knew the war was coming, but the reality of it hit differently.

"I have to return to the kingdom," I say, not fully considering the weight of my words. All eyes turn to me, but I push the attention aside. This war isn't just about Puer Lunae; it's about the innocent humans caught in the middle.

King Silvan's disapproving headshake sends a shiver down my spine. "King Atticus instructed me to keep you inside the castle. Naya, I promise you that Puer Lunae will not fall. My warriors are on standby, ready for your Kingdom's signal."

I look at him with disbelief etched on my face. I can sense the finality in his voice as he speaks, but there's no way I'm accepting it.

"They're using humans as their soldiers. I'm sorry, King Silvan, but I can't stay here. There's much more at risk now than just Puer Lunae's safety," I reply in a stern voice, not leaving any room for argument.

The King's forehead creases as he looks at me, a puzzled expression on his face. "Humans?" he parrots.

I nod at him to confirm. "Yes, humans. That's why we can't track where they're getting the manpower for this rebellion. They're using humans as their army. Humans turned into vampires. This isn't just about the Kingdom anymore. If the resistance wins, the monarch of Puer Lunae will fall, but if we win, you'll be slaughtering hundreds of innocent humans."

My voice starts to shake as I feel the tension slowly building up inside my chest. We're too late. We've gathered the information too late. There's no way I can stop this now.

King Silvan's eyes slowly turn blank as he looks at me. In just a snap, his expression becomes emotionless. My palm closes into a fist as I stare at him. I know that look, and I can feel myself slowly shrinking.

"You can't kill them. They're innocent. They have nothing to do with this world or the war between kingdoms," I plead. My voice is almost shaking, threatening to break at any moment.

King Silvan slowly shakes his head in disapproval. "Forgive me, Naya. We can't save them," he replies without any emotion in his voice.

Teardrops start to fall one after another from the side of my eyes. I look at him with anger and hopelessness filling my chest. "So that's it? They are just going to be pawns in this? They are like me, Silvan. I am one of them," I point at myself with my eyes not leaving his, pleading, trying to make him understand that they are not enemies. They are victims.

"The war takes no prisoners. The moment you enter the battlefield, it's either you survive and be remembered or turn into ashes and be forgotten. I want to help them, I want to help your kind, but we need to prioritize your Kingdom's safety," he explains in a grave and grim tone. "I need to choose the one that I know will lead to a lesser casualty. Forgive me, Naya."

His words silence me. A bitter smile forms on my lips. A lesser casualty? That's it? Everything that I've worked for leads to this? I take a seat on the nearest chair as I feel my own strength starting to leave my body.

In the end, I can't even save anyone...

CHAPTER 43

Naya

My grip tightens on the silver sword between my palm as my gaze fixes on the endless desert right in front of me. A battle rages within me as I weigh my decision of whether to obey King Silvan's instructions to stay behind or take action and escape.

I let out an impatient sigh and turned my attention to the part of the desert where I first encountered five bewitched vampires. King Silvan acted swiftly, eliminating them without hesitation. They were once our enemies, but the tables have turned. We have come to discover that they are humans, just like me, who were thrown into an alien world with no way of returning.

"Are you worried about what is happening in the Kingdom right now?" Zizina asks, making me look over my shoulder to meet her gaze.

She leans casually against the stony castle wall, her expression unreadable, leaving me clueless about her thoughts. I inhale deeply and nod.

"I feel so useless right now, Zizina. I feel like I am abandoning my people at a time when they need me the most. I want to fight alongside my subjects and save those innocents who should not be a part of this," I fume.

A bitter smile escapes my lips. What kind of queen am I if I end up abandoning my people amidst a war? Besides, I don't really have anything left to lose. I've already lost my life and my humanity. If I choose not to take action right now, there's a possibility that the news I'll receive tomorrow will be even more excruciating than death itself.

"It's okay, that's normal. You're a leader. You have a deep connection to our Kingdom. Even though you're far away, you can feel its pain and agony," she consoles me.

I turn my gaze from her to the thick forest in a far distance, seemingly covered with thick and dark mist. That forest also serves as the border between Kaedal and Puer Lunae.

"I can't stay here... I need to go," I murmur in a low voice as I stare at the sword in my hand.

The sole reason I have been summoned to this world is because of this war. I am not supposed to sit in front of the fireplace and enjoy the serenity of the castle while my warriors fight for their lives. This is not the reason why I am here. This is not why Lady Naya entrusted me with her crown.

"I'm leaving," I finally state with conviction.

My grip on the sword tightens. I don't care if death awaits me in my Kingdom. I am not going to abandon my subjects. I am much stronger now than when I was a human. I am a skilled detective. I trained for more than four years in the police academy and worked in the field for more than five years. I am fearless when it comes to catching criminals. How am I to use my newfound strength if I'm going to be a coward tonight?

"I'm literally waiting for you to say that!" Zizina exclaims from behind me, making me turn to her with a questioning look on my face.

A proud smile plays on her lips as she looks at me with excitement gleaming in her eyes. Without hesitation, she straightens her back and reaches into her bag. She pulls out a small bottle of potion from it and then hands it to me.

"What's that?" I ask with a frown before accepting it to take a closer inspection.

"This will hide your scent," she explains. "It will help us escape the Kaedal Kingdom without being noticed." She pulls out another tiny bottle from her bag and drinks its contents in one gulp.

The side of my lips tugs into a smirk as I remove the cap of the bottle she gave me and empty its contents. I grimace at the bitter taste of the potion the moment it touches my tongue. I need to keep reminding myself that potions are not the sweetest wine you can ever have. It tasted like tequila combined with some bitter mint. I hate it.

I throw the empty bottle in the bin nearby and walk inside the room King Silvan assigned to me. I need to make a few preparations before leaving. Opening my backpack, I take my gun from it and a few pieces of small blades. This is probably my last day in this world. I might as well cherish every moment I have left.

It's a good thing that I am not wearing my lavish gowns anymore. Since we left Puer Lunae, I've been so used to wearing a turtleneck long-sleeve with a denim jacket on top of it and denim pants, my usual detective outfit. The only thing that I kept on wearing was my crown. This is my symbol as the Queen of Puer Lunae.

I gently lift the crown off my head with a sad smile on my lips. This crown is such a beauty, a golden tiara that matches my fiery spirit, a beauty worthy enough to be owned by a Queen. I caress the red stone that serves as its ornament. This crown has taught me a lot about life, and it's just sad that I am meant to lose it after tonight.

I place the crown on top of the bed, wishing I could take it back to the human world, but I know it won't be possible now. I have no idea what awaits me once I arrive in Puer Lunae. Besides, if I survive and face the trial tomorrow, I don't think I still have a chance to go back to Kaedal and retrieve this crown.

I let out a smile and turn to look at Zizina who's patiently waiting for me at the door that connects my room to the balcony.

"I'm ready. Let's end this tonight." I say and walk towards her.

The night air caresses me with a chill the moment I'm out of the room. I can't help but wonder. If I had turned my back at the last minute before entering this world, what would have happened?

I gently shake my head to dismiss the thought. If I had the chance to turn back time, I know that I would still choose to do the same thing over and over again. I'm a detective, and it is in my blood to be consumed with a sense of justice and curiosity, a deadly combination that can lead me to hundreds of uncompromising situations.

Zizina interrupts my thoughts with a question. "Let's go?"

I look at her and nod, determined to see this through. "Let's go," I reply and clamber onto the railings to survey the ground twenty meters below.

I feel a surge of confidence filling my heart as I prepare to jump down. Closing my eyes, I allow myself to fall towards the ground. I feel the wind whipping harshly against my skin as I get closer to the earth. When I feel that I am only a few meters away from the ground, I open my eyes and balance myself, landing gracefully on my feet. I'm pretty sure my eyes have turned bloody red by now, a sign that my senses have sharpened and become more vivid.

With newfound strength and enhanced senses, I search for the safest exit from the castle and run towards the direction where I can't smell or feel any warriors roaming around. After over an hour, we're already on the outskirts of the Kingdom. We stand firmly at the border of Puer Lunae and Kaedal, our hearts pounding with adrenaline from running and jumping through the seemingly endless desert and thick trees of the forest.

I am not sensing any presence behind us, indicating that none of King Silvan's warriors has discovered our escape.

"Where to now?" Zizina's voice cuts through the silence, breaking me out of my thoughts.

"I'm heading to the castle. If the resistance wants to take down the monarchy, Atticus will be their primary target." I reply, and without hesitation, I sprint towards the nearest house and vault onto its roof, my muscles working in perfect harmony to execute the move flawlessly. I have always found it easier to travel above ground than on the dusty earth.

I can hear the faint sounds of battle in the distance, and my heart starts to race.

"Do you have a plan?" Zizina asks as she follows me closely, her footsteps light and nimble from behind me.

I allow a small smile to grace my lips. Do I need a plan?

"Just don't die, I guess..." I reply uncertainly.

"That works for me. I'll cover you from behind. Go, help your husband save the Kingdom and your people."

I nod in agreement and focus my attention on what's in front of me. From a distance, I see a man pull his hand out of another person's chest. My smile vanishes, and my expression turns blank as I recognize the victim as Puer Lunae's warrior and the perpetrator as a bewitched vampire with a bloody hand. The method used to kill the warrior is similar to the one used on me.

I draw my sword and prepare myself for what's to come. The screams of anguish echo throughout the place, but I refuse to let them affect me. Compassion is a liability on the battlefield, and right now, I need to focus on survival.

The bewitched notices my presence and snaps his head in my direction. Despite the darkness enveloping us and his grotesque appearance, I still managed to recognize him.

A pale smile curls on my lips as I halt and stand a few meters away from him.

"Who would have thought our paths were meant to cross again," I say while staring into his lifeless eyes.

The man's eyes do not even show any spark of recognition. He was a monster when he was human, having killed his girlfriend and innocent people for a bag of money when he robbed the local bank. Does he deserve this fate? Perhaps, but even for him, this is unfair. Being used as a marionette puppet is something I personally detest.

"I didn't expect to meet you here, but I guess it's destiny's way of telling me that this war has something to do with me as a detective. Life didn't drag me into this situation for nothing," I tell him, even though I know he won't understand me.

I tighten my grip on the sword. The man lets out an ear-deafening cry as he closes the distance between us, ready to strike a fatal blow. However, the same tactics that killed me before won't work on me again. I easily dodge his bloody hand, and in just a split second, I am already behind him, thrusting my sword with all my strength through his chest from behind.

"Forgive me. Right now, this is the only way I know I can save you," I murmur in a blank tone as I pull my sword out of his body.

His body falls flat on the roof of the house and quickly turns to ashes. My eyes land on the blade of my sword as the ink-like blood drips from it onto the stone roof.

So, this is how it feels to be a murderer?

"Do you know him personally?" Zizina questions from behind me.

"Yeah," I nod, a heavy sigh escaping my lips. "Nothing close, though. Just an old acquaintance." My gaze shifts towards the distant castle of our Kingdom, a magnificent Victorian structure that stands proudly amidst the darkness of the night and the countless deaths that surrounds it. Bathed in the ethereal glow of the full moon, its ornate architecture emanates an air of grandeur and mystery.

A sense of anticipation lingers in the air. In this nocturnal realm, it is as if the fabric of time pauses, promising a fateful culmination, signalling the beginning of the end that I can keenly perceive.

CHAPTER 44

Naya

I look up to the sky when I feel droplets of rain trickle on my skin. The atmosphere around us feels a bit eerie and sinister. I take a deep breath and survey my surroundings. As the night deepens, the endless war continues. I can hear the sound of metal swords crossing against each other and the deafening screams of the battlefield, yet I can't seem to feel fear or terror. The warzone is cold and unforgiving, and all of us are now far from saving. The only choice left is either to survive or to die.

My grip tightens on the silver sword in my hand. Blood oozes down from it onto the metal roof where I am standing. There are a few scratches on my skin, but I can't feel the pain from them.

A bitter smile appears on my lips. It seems like everything that happened to me has made me emotionally and physically numb.

"My Queen, the eastern part of the town looks less dangerous and more open than other locations," Zizina speaks from behind me.

I nod at her and tuck my sword back into its sheath.

"Let's head in that direction then," I reply as I draw the gun from my waist. "I'm starting to feel tired already. I managed to kill a few, but their numbers seem endless."

This handgun has 17 rounds in it. Hopefully, it will be enough for me to gain access to the castle. I expect the surrounding area to be heavily guarded. If the chance is given, I want to talk to Lady Naya's father. I want to know the main reason behind this rebellion— why and how it started.

I turn east and begin to run in that direction, gracefully jumping from one roof to another. The rancid stench of burning human flesh makes me want to retch, but I force myself to ignore it. Now is not the time to have a sensitive and weak stomach. I remove the safety lock from my gun and take aim at the first bewitched vampire that crosses my path.

A loud bang echoes throughout the area, but it's drowned out by the shouts and the sounds of metal swords clashing against each other. My bullet hits the target in the chest, and it falls lifelessly on the ground before turning into ashes.

As I approach the castle grounds, a piercing screech from a young girl catches my attention. I come to a halt and swiftly turn towards the source of the scream.

"Is there a problem, my Queen?" Zizina inquires, causing me to momentarily divert my gaze towards her.

"I hear something," I reply and change my direction towards the house where the scream came from.

Through a clear glass window, I see a child on the floor with her palms covering her mouth, fear in her eyes as a man slowly advances towards her. Without a second thought, I leap towards the window, shattering it in the process. I land on the floor amidst the shattered glass.

Both the bewitched vampire and the child turn their gaze towards me. I don't give the enemy a chance to make a move. I aim my gun at his chest and pull the trigger. The child lets out another terrified scream as the man turns to ashes before our very eyes.

I stand up from the shattered glass and debris on the floor and slowly walk towards the frightened child. I lean down and cradle her in my arms. My heart clenches in pain at the sight of her distressed appearance.

The child didn't say anything. She buries her face in my shoulder and whimpers inside my arms while shaking in fear.

"What happened to your parents?" I ask, hoping to comfort her in some small way.

The child raises her tear-streaked face towards me and points to the side of the house. My eyes follow where she's pointing and settle on a pile of ashes scattered across the floor. I swallow hard and pull the young girl close to my chest.

"I'm sorry, little one," I whisper, my throat hurting from trying so hard to contain my tears. I turn my eyes to Zizina and hand her the child. As much as I want to stay here and help the warriors fight, I need to be in the castle. If I want to end this, I need to target the roots. I hope I can do it fast enough to save the lives of the commoners in the Kingdom.

"Isn't there supposed to be an evacuation? Why are there so many civilians here?" I ask in confusion.

"It's because the war broke out unexpectedly." A familiar voice makes me turn to the door. "We tried to evacuate as many as we could. However, a lot of them have been trapped in the middle of the siege."

"Celestine," I acknowledge her presence, eyeing her warily. "Why are you here? Aren't you supposed to be in the castle with the King?"

Celestine bows respectfully before her gaze flickers towards the child in Zizina's arms. The young girl bears bruises and wounds on her cheek and arms, but nothing that seems life-threatening.

"Atticus is with some of our strongest warriors. I am the general of the Kingdom's first line of defence. I'd rather die on the battlefield than stay in the safety of the castle," she replies, her tone unwavering. "One of the warriors informed me that they saw the Queen headed towards the palace, so I rushed in this direction to confirm."

I tighten my grip on my gun, preparing myself for a fight if she intends to stop me from entering the castle. Enemy or not, I will not allow anyone to stand in my way.

"I am here to put an end to this rebellion. If you want to be on the battlefield to fight side by side with your warriors, I am here for my subjects. I will accept the higher council's conviction once this war is over. But for now, I am here to fulfil my duty as the Queen of my Kingdom," I respond. I am hoping for her to understand me. I don't know which side she is on, but I hope that she is not with the House of Malvagio.

"I am not here to stop you," she replies, making me feel relieved. "I am simply curious when the warrior told me that you managed to get this far without dying. Some of my warriors died, and a few are probably dying as we talk right now. They are all trained fighters. A human surviving amidst a vampire war is very uncanny."

Her eyes survey me, and then her lips lift into a grin. I'm pretty sure she has already noticed that I am no longer human. My humanity is gone. I want to hate this world for taking away something that connected me to the human world, but I guess it was necessary. This battlefield is not for humans. King Silvan said it himself, once you enter the battlefield, you either die or survive. I need to live.

"A lot of things happened while I was in Kaedal," I reply. Now is not the time for us to catch up. I need to go to the castle as fast as I can. I don't know what's waiting for me inside, but I know it will be the enemy's primary target. "As much as I'd love to sit down and chat with you, I'm afraid we have a kingdom to protect and save. I'll be taking my leave now."

Celestine nods at me and smiles.

"The King's life is in danger. There's a big chance that enemies have sent an assassin to kill him. Of course, I am confident that the King won't go down easily. However, at this point, nothing is guaranteed," she says. "I'm putting my trust in you, my Queen. Go on. Rest assured that I will protect our people with my life."

She bows her head to show her loyalty and bids goodbye. I smile and nod at her. I am thankful to heaven that Celestine is on the King's side. Having her as our ally is a huge advantage. I walk towards the broken door of the house and jump onto the nearest roof.

The scent of burning flesh still hangs heavily in the air, making me worried about our people. How many of them have died protecting the Kingdom? How many of them have become sacrifices in this battle for power?

I continue to make my way towards the castle, and as I get near the gate, I feel fear rising in my chest. I'm not worried that I might encounter a few enemies; my greatest fear is anticipating what Atticus's reaction will be once he sees me. I still hate him, but I am aware that I need to set aside my feelings for now. It's not the time for me to sulk or confront him about his actions.

A longing feeling envelops me as I stand right in front of the massive gate. This castle is breathtaking, but more than that, it's my home. It's a place where my heart and soul will always belong, no matter where I go.

Unlike what I expected, the castle ground is silent. It feels eerie and unsettling. I hold the gun tightly between my palms. The castle no longer feels safe anymore. My chest is pounding so fast as if it is trying to warn me that I am in danger. I look around and enter the front door as silently as I can. The outside isn't heavily guarded, and that's unusual given the situation. Either Atticus is complacent that the enemy won't make it to the castle, or the enemies have already managed to get through the gate and kill all the guards. I am praying that it will be the former. I walk through the path towards the throne room, hoping that my husband will be there.

As I get closer to the room, I can hear Atticus' faint voice as he gives instructions to his warriors. The chatter inside makes me realize that an important meeting is currently taking place. A faint smile forms on my lips. Despite everything, hearing my husband's voice still manages to stir a mix of pain and excitement in my heart. If we were not in this situation, I would probably be berating myself for feeling this way. How can I long for his presence after everything that has happened? That's just stupid.

With a deep breath, I push open the door to the throne room. I make sure to hold my head high as I come face to face with the man I both hate and love. Atticus stops talking as soon as his eyes meet mine. The entire room falls silent, and the only sound I can hear is the clanging of my heels against the marble floor of the castle.

"What are you doing here?" he asks with a perplexed expression as if he can't believe that I am standing right in front of him.

"I am your wife and the Queen of Puer Lunae," I reply, my tone full of authority as I close the distance between us. "As Queen of this Kingdom, I pledged to give my life to protect my subjects. I am here to fulfil my duty and stand beside my King, to stand beside you."

I make sure to hold his gaze as I speak, watching as his eyes narrow in irritation. Clearly, he does not appreciate my boldness, but I cannot bring myself to care anymore. I am not here to beg for his attention or forgiveness. I am here to save whoever I can save.

This will be the last night that I stand with him, the last night of my reign.

CHAPTER 45

Naya

"The audacity!"

Harriet's voice makes me turn towards her direction, and my smirk widens as our eyes meet. Of course, she has to be here too. Why do I keep forgetting about her?

"Have you forgotten already? Your family started this rebellion. The House of Nardelli is a traitor to the Monarch of Puer Lunae," she says in a firm tone, her eyes narrowing in anger as she glares at me. "What gives you the right to be here?"

"I am not part of the House of Nardelli. Lady Naya summoned me to be her replacement. And let me remind you that I am still the Queen of the Kingdom. Until you can prove that I am guilty of conspiring against the Kingdom in front of the higher council by tomorrow, I am still the bearer of the crown," I reply with a hint of mockery, raising my left eyebrow in challenge.

I turn my attention back to my husband and close the distance between us, halting just a meter away from him.

"The bewitched vampires you're fighting aren't vampires. They are humans turned into vampires," I begin, not wanting to give anyone a chance to stop me from relaying the information to my husband.

Atticus's forehead wrinkles. "Humans?" he questions.

I nod.

"Lady Naya knew her family was creating an army of turned vampires as their weapon in this rebellion.

She summoned me here to solve the mystery of her death. I never realized there was more to it than meets the eye. I know it was too late for me to do anything to save them, but at the same time, I can't allow your warriors to kill them."

My husband's eyes darken while looking at me. His hands close into fists as he takes a deep breath, clearly not liking the news I brought.

"Save them?" His voice raises in pitch, and his gaze narrows into slits. "And what about my warriors and my subjects? And how sure are we that you're not playing with us?"

I stop myself from rolling my eyes in annoyance. King Silvan said that my husband did what he did to protect me? Right now, that doesn't feel like it. Atticus clearly doesn't trust me.

Well, I guess it's a good thing that I, myself, was a turned vampire. I draw the sword from my waist and point it towards Atticus's neck. The sound of metal slashing through the air fills the room. The warriors around me are quick to move to protect their King, but my husband raises his hand in the air to stop them. His warriors halt, making me let out a cocky smile.

Gripping the hilt of my sword, I press its blade against my own flesh, carving a deep wound into my arm. The sharp scent of blood fills the room, and I can feel the warm, sticky liquid trickle down my skin. Despite the pain, I keep my gaze locked on Atticus.

"A human turned into a vampire possessed the strength of a vampire but without its weaknesses," I explain, my voice low and sombre. "Unlike your kind, we're not weak to silver unless it hits the heart. You've fought bewitched vampires before, Atticus, and you must have noticed how they're unaffected by silver weapons. These enemies you're trying to destroy aren't your true foes. They're merely victims of this world, chosen as sacrificial lambs by your kind because they're perceived as a weaker kind."

My hands curl into fists, and I can feel my anger simmering just beneath the surface. I feel the wound in my arms starts to close, leaving only traces of blood that drip down to the marble floor.

Though most of those human-turned-vampires are not innocent, they don't deserve to suffer this fate. I've killed a few tonight out of necessity, but I vow to do my best to save as many as I can from their tragic destiny.

Atticus takes a deep breath, his eyes on mine. I know he understands where I am coming from. Those people fighting outside have nothing to do with this; they're being used as pawns of war. My fate doesn't differ much from theirs. Lady Naya brought me here and trapped me in a marriage to become a weapon of war. The only thing that makes my situation better than theirs is that I can decide and fight for myself.

"Go on then. What is your suggestion?" My husband finally breaks the silence.

I inhale deeply as I try to release the tension that's built up in my chest. My husband's words give me hope despite our current situation.

"Allow me to talk to Lady Naya's father. I need to know the mind behind the resistance," I state and turn my gaze to Nemue, Zizina's mother, who is currently standing on the right side of the King. "I met a woman during my investigation. I have a feeling she's the one who is in charge of making the potions being used to turn vampires into bewitched.

She sells her potions in Raven's Row. Her shop is located at the end of the alley."

Zizina's mother frowns for a second, and then her eyes spark with recognition.

"I know her. She's the same age as Zizina but not close to my daughter," she replies.

"Do you know where she lives?"

The witch nods to answer my question. "I do. Vampires with witches' blood are quite rare. That's why it's important that we know each other's identity and location."

I let out a satisfied smile at her answer. Well, that was easy.

"Bring some of the warriors with you. Go to her house and take everything you think is valuable. If you ever see her, kill her," I order strictly and face my husband. "Let's go." I turn my back on him and make my way out of the throne room without another word.

I can feel the curious eyes of people around me following my every step, but I can't bring myself to care.

There's too much at stake at the moment for me to feel conscious of others. I hear Atticus's footsteps following me from behind, and as I am about to reach the door of the throne room when he catches up to me.

My husband turns left towards the east wing of the castle. I silently follow him. Suddenly, the atmosphere between us starts to feel awkward. Though we are not really on good terms right now, I can't deny the fact that I do miss him. I long for his caring ways, and a part of me yearns for a return to the way things were, but that seems nearly impossible now.

"You look hot when you take over," he comments out of the blue as soon as we are out of earshot from the people in that throne room.

I scrunch up my face in confusion, my brain struggling to process what he just said. It takes me a few moments to collect my thoughts and respond.

I look at him and smirk sardonically.

"Yeah, it turns out that being in a dungeon for three days, accused of conspiring against the Kingdom, and nearly dying can add so much to your sexual appeal," I retort in a sarcastic tone.

I know that I am acting like a bitch, but I can't help it. I know this is not solely the King's fault, but he contributed a lot to it. Remembering the time when I woke up as a vampire and hating Silvan for reviving me from the land of the dead made me realize how much I've become weak emotionally and mentally. During that time, I realized that I didn't want to live anymore, and I couldn't believe I had come to the point where hopelessness had overtaken my mind.

To my surprise, Atticus reaches out and takes my hand, stopping us both in our tracks.

"Look," he says, "when I learned that your family was behind this, I was aggravated. And then I found out from Celestine that you weren't Naya at all. The woman I love was long gone, and instead, I had married a human who seemed to have sprung up out of nowhere. How was I supposed to react? Did you expect me to welcome you with open arms?"

My face darkens, and my lips purse into a thin line. Right, I almost forget. What right do I have to demand anything? I am just a replacement for the woman he loves. Why do I keep forgetting that I am not Lady Naya? Why do I keep expecting him to treat me the same way he treated her? I take a deep breath and hide all the rage inside me behind a blank expression.

"Yeah, I apologize, my King," I say, surprised at how emotionless my voice sounds. "You're right. I am just a replacement for a dead woman. Why did I even expect you to come to my rescue?"

I turn my back on him and continue walking towards the east wing. Only to halt again when he grabs my wrist and pulls me towards him. In just a snap, I am already in his arms with his gaze locked on mine. His eyes are full of emotions that I am afraid to name.

"I want to help you. Trust me, the moment I saw all the evidence from Minna, I wanted to rescue you. But I couldn't do that. The house of Malvagio just lost the head of their family. If I made any move to help you, it would create a huge division in the Kingdom's power. That's why I asked King Silvan to lend me a hand to buy us some time," he explains as he buries his face in the crook of my neck. "I wanted to talk to you, but I didn't get a chance because Harriet is always with me."

A familiar pain envelops my chest at his words, and tears begin to well up in my eyes. Suddenly, all of the hatred in my heart melts away like a block of ice under the scorching heat of the summer sun. I don't want to hope. I need to remind myself that our story is not a fairy tale, and it will never end with a happy ever after.

"It felt like you abandoned me, Atticus. I did everything to help. But in the end, the Kingdom I wanted to save convicted me like a criminal," I whisper in a voice that is full of resentment. I hate

Lady Naya for putting me in this situation. She didn't even give me a chance to say no. She manipulated everything. I know she did it because she was helpless at that time, but she's so selfish for dragging me into this mess.

I feel my husband's hand caressing my back to comfort me.

"I know," he says in a soothing tone and plants a soft kiss on my forehead. "I admire your bravery, my Queen. Forgive me if I didn't have the strength to protect you at that time," He reaches for my hand and locks it with his. "Let's go. We have a rebellion to end."

As we traverse the hallway that leads to the cell, our hands remain entwined, and a smile tugs at the corners of my lips as I steal a glance at our locked fingers. It's as if our hands were made for each other, perfectly fitting together in a way that makes my heart skip a beat. And then my gaze drifts to the ring on his finger— our wedding ring. It's still there, a glimmering symbol of our commitment to each other, and somehow, it fills me with hope for our future.

Upon entering the prison room, I quickly disentangle my hand from Atticus's grasp and come face to face with two castle guards standing watch in front of the cell. My gaze was automatically drawn to the man sitting at the corner of the cell. Stellian raises his gaze at me. The shadow beneath his eyes makes the once powerful man looks so defeated.

Seeing him in his current state makes me understand why Lady Naya had chosen to summon me here instead of taking matters into her own hands. Despite not being Stellian's biological daughter, I can sense the love he holds for his daughter, having seen it firsthand when we first met. If I were in Lady Naya's position, I don't know if I could betray my family like this. A loving daughter like her will not be able to do that.

I make my way over to his cell, my footsteps echoing through the narrow corridor. The air around us feels damp and musty as if the walls have not seen sunlight in years. The sound of the iron bars clanking against each other fills my ears as Atticus signals for one of the warriors to open the cell for me to enter.

"What are you doing here?" Stellian asks in a lifeless and raspy voice.

I can feel the hopelessness in his voice. And that's more than enough to bring so much pain to my chest. He is not my father, but I can't help but feel some kind of compassion towards him. If my father is alive right now, there's no chance that I will allow anyone to put him in this situation.

"I am here because I need you to tell me the head of this rebellion as well as the other people involved in it," I ask directly, my voice sharp and commanding. I tried my best not to let any sympathy show in my tone. You can't empathize and interrogate a person at the same time. If you want to get information from them, you need to show your authority.

The dim light in the greyish ceiling above us flickers, casting eerie shadows across Stellian's face. The hopeless look on his face is like a sharp knife piercing through my chest.

An empty smile curved on his lips.

"So it is true, you are not my daughter. Because if you were, you would have known that information already," he murmurs, his tone heavy with grief. Regardless of whether one is a hero or a villain, losing one's child is a crushing blow.

"Lady Naya is long dead," I confirm without tearing my gaze away from him. "She sent a letter that brought me to this world. I am here because your daughter wants me to stop the rebellion on her behalf. She wants me to be the one to bring down her family and stop the war," I explain further and take a deep breath to collect and steal myself. "Let's not make this harder than it needs to be. I really don't have the patience to deal with this right now. After everything I've been through, torturing an old man who just found out his daughter died a few weeks ago isn't something I can handle emotionally."

I grab the blade from the side of my boots and look up at him for our eyes to meet. "But if you refuse to talk, trust me, you will beg for your own death the moment I'm done with you."

CHAPTER 46

Naya

Silence envelops the prison cell for what feels like an eternity. Stellian's gaze is fixed on me, his eyes full of disbelief.

As the words escaped my lips, I felt a surge of emotion, an overwhelming intensity that caught me off guard. My voice quivered with a hint of desperation, almost begging for understanding. I don't want to hurt him, and I don't want to do this, but I have people to save. If this is the only way to get the information I need, I will do so without hesitation.

To my surprise, Stellian breaks the eerie silence with an amused laugh. My gaze narrows into slits. I am glad that he finds amusement in the situation because I do not. Have you ever gotten to a point in your life where you just want the night or day to be over? That is what I am feeling right now.

"I always wonder why my daughter chose a human as her replacement. But now, I understand her reasoning. You have come this far to save the kingdom. It's admirable for a human," he says, his smile tinged with sadness. "I've heard from the warriors that you're a detective in the human world. Such an interesting job. And your choice of clothing is also fascinating."

I stare at him with a blank expression on my face, not knowing how to properly answer his remark. I take a deep breath to release the tension inside my chest and clear my throat before responding.

"Your daughter is a brave and smart woman. She faced death with her head held high and gave her life to protect the people of the kingdom. Although she didn't get a chance to wear the crown, she proved herself worthy of it," I tell him, hoping that it is enough to honour the memory of her daughter.

If there's one person I want to meet in this world, it's Lady Naya. I solved the mystery of her death, but she herself remains a mystery. She had the bravest heart of all the people I've met in this world. A woman who is capable of sacrificing her life, her love, and her family for the greater good. How many of us can truly claim to possess such gallantry?

"I failed her," Stellian utters in a bitter tone, his shoulders slumping as he gazes down at his palm. "I failed to protect my daughter. That is the greatest mistake of my life."

I let out a harsh exhale. I'm at a loss for words. What can I possibly say to ease his pain? After all, he did fail to protect his daughter.

After a moment, Stellian raises his gaze to meet mine. A small woeful smile was still on his lips. "I can see the exhaustion in your eyes, my Queen. This world has pushed you to the brink of losing your soul. I won't make things more complicated for you. In exchange for the information I'm about to give, could you give me a hug? The kind of hug you'd give to your real father?" He requests in a gentle tone.

I stare at him for a long moment, wanting to read what is in his mind. A hug? Is that all he wants? A daughter's embrace? For a moment, I'm unsure whether he's playing with me or not. But when I see the sincerity in his eyes, I know that it's not a trap.

I let my guard down and placed the silver dagger back in its sheath. Without saying a word, I close the distance between us and give him a warm hug. It's the kind of hug I'd give my father if he were still alive. The small gesture seems to trigger all the emotions I've been holding in my chest. Suddenly, all the anxiety and pain come crashing down on me, overwhelming my chest with so many emotions. Tears start to pour from my eyes as if it were the most natural thing to do at the moment. Stellian is a father who lost his daughter. I am a daughter who entered this world with the hopes of uncovering information about my father's death.

"This world is cruel, and so is this war. Forgive my daughter, child. I'm sure she doesn't mean for you to suffer like this," he pleads, his tone carrying a hint of anguish.

Tears stream down my face as I nod, seeking comfort in Stellian's embrace. Lady Naya couldn't have foreseen the devastation her actions would cause me. She held me in such high esteem, thinking I could weather any storm with ease. But life has a way of breaking even the strongest of us, tearing our very souls into tiny pieces.

I know all too well that life isn't all rainbows and unicorns. My line of work has exposed me to the harsh realities of the world. However, my journey to this world breaks me into pieces, shattering me to the point where I'm already begging heaven to take my life.

"I know," I say, my voice thick with torment and sorrow.

After a short moment of silence, I finally managed to calm myself. I take a deep breath to collect myself and draw back from Stellian, my hand moving to wipe away my tears. I move away from him, but before I can even take a step back, he does something I never expected.

The events unfold rapidly, leaving me with no time to react. With a forceful shove, Stellian propels me backwards, sending my body hurtling backwards through the air. Time slows to a crawl as I crash against the unforgiving floor, my senses momentarily stunned.

And then, in an act that defies reason and defies sanity, he raises the stolen sword high above his head, driving the blade deep into his own heart.

"Naya!" I hear Atticus from outside the cell calling for my name, his voice full of concern and urgency, but I am way too lost to respond.

Everything comes to a standstill as I stare in disbelief at the bloodied body of the man I had grown to care for. Tears fall unbidden down my face, and I struggle to process what has just happened.

"No!" I scream in anguish, my voice breaking as I finally snap out of my shock.

Rushing over to him, I cradle Stellian's dying body in my arms, desperately trying to stop the bleeding. "Stellian, no! Why did you have to do this?" I whisper in a very weak voice, my strength starting to leave my body at the unexpected death.

I run my fingers through my hair in desperation, my heart breaking at the sight of tears pooling in the side of his eyes.

"I believe..." he whispers in a raspy, dying breath. "The person you're looking for is... Cassius,"

For a few moments, the world seems to stop spinning as I struggle to process his last words. And before I even realize it, his body turns into ashes right inside my arms. The room falls eerily silent until my silver sword clatters onto the marble floor, jarring us out of our stunned trance.

I press my palm over my mouth, trying to stifle any sound of my agony. It feels as if my chest has been pierced multiple times, and I'm left gasping for breath as tears continue to stream down my face. The smell of ash and smoke fills my senses, a grim reminder of the death I just witnessed.

Atticus enters the cell, and I feel his arms encircling me from behind. I still. Not even bothering to break away from his comforting hold. I allow myself to remain in his arms, crying for yet another life that has been taken away right before my eyes.

"This is too much. I just want this to be over." I whisper in a very weak tone. My voice is hoarse, feeling drained both mentally and physically. Atticus remains silent as I pour my heart out inside his arms for what seems like an eternity.

But after long moments of misery, I eventually found the strength to compose myself. I distance myself from my husband and take a deep breath to steady myself. The night is almost over, and so is this war. I wipe away my tears and retrieve my sword from the floor. I turn to my husband, who is now looking at me with a concerned expression on his face.

"You need to rest for now, Naya. Now that I know the person behind this rebellion, I can take it from here," He speaks in a gentle voice as if he is trying to assure me.

I firmly shake my head at him in disapproval and defiance. This is my battle, one that I must win. I refuse to give up, especially since we're so close to the end.

"I can handle myself fine, Atticus. I know that you know where Cassius is," My face darkens in fury, my eyes narrowing upon remembering the face of the man behind this mess that I've been pulled into. "I'm confident that he's the one who can turn humans into your kind, pretty much like King Silvan with his old blood."

Atticus lets out an impatient sigh, his eyes fixed on mine. I know that he understands there's nothing he can do to change my mind. They dragged me into this mess, and it's now my turn to end it all.

"Cassius is the head of the council. You might remember him as the one who presided over your trial three days ago. He's a member of the house of Malvagio," my husband explains.

That makes me frown. "He's part of the house of Malvagio?"

"Yes," Atticus nods at me. "He is one of the candidates as the next head of Malvagio after the death of Remus. But after what we have learned today, I don't think the members of the house will be keen on voting for him."

My mind swirls with confusion. Cassius belongs to a prominent clan. The house of Malvagio seems to be loyal to both the Kingdom and Atticus. What makes Cassius the black sheep?

"Is he related to you?" I ask as I try to make sense of it.

My husband gently shakes his head. "No, not by blood."

"Then, is there something I need to know?" I press further, wanting to know more about my husband's connection with Cassius.

However, to my dismay, Atticus remains silent. I raise an eyebrow at him, wondering what he's hiding. Clearly, there's something I need to know, but it seems like my husband doesn't trust me enough to give me more information.

That is when the door of the cell opens, revealing Zizina looking a bit bruised with a few scratches on her arms and cheeks. Our gazes lock with each other, and she offers me an apologetic smile.

"Hey, sorry it took me a while to get here." She begins. "I had to ensure the child's safety and fought a few bewitched on my way here," Her curious eyes scan the room until they settle at the ashes of Lady Naya's father on the floor.

"It's okay," I say as I wipe away the remnant of tears from my cheeks. I rise from the floor and start walking towards Zizina. "We found the man behind the resistance. I'm on my way to confront Cassius. Is there any way for you to remove the effect of the potion from those bewitched vampires?" I ask her.

"We could try using the previous antidote that was used by kingdoms when they destroyed the old coven." She suggests, her voice sounding a little bit unsure. "Initially, I thought it wouldn't work because they seem to have changed the recipe for the potion. But upon realizing that they changed their test subjects and not the potion recipe, I think the old antidote will do. At least, that's what I hope,"

I nod in agreement. It's a long shot, but I guess it is so much better than having nothing at all. It's our only chance to save those humans who have been caught in this war without their knowledge.

"Then I will give you that mission. Brew as many as you can and give them to the warriors afterwards," I instruct, then I turn my attention back to my husband, who is now making his way towards us. "Where can we find him?" I ask, pertaining to Cassius.

In a brief moment, I notice the flicker of doubt in my husband's eyes. I can sense his reluctance to let me confront Cassius, but he should understand by now that nothing will deter me. Eventually, he succumbs to defeat. He lets out a heavy sigh before reluctantly revealing the information.

"He's at the church."

My brow knits together in a perplexed frown. The church? The very place where my wedding happened? Is that where Cassius chose to end this war? In the place where everything began?

CHAPTER 47

Naya

My breath hitches in anticipation as I stand before the grandeur of the Victorian Gothic church. Its spires stretch towards the heavens, reaching for the clouds. The intricate details carved into the stone facade tell stories of a bygone era, each one more fascinating than the last. The rose window, with its intricate stained-glass design, shimmers in the sunlight, casting a kaleidoscope of colours across the church's interior.

This is the place where I took my vow as the Queen of Puer Lunae, where I was bonded to my husband and this Kingdom. It holds a very special place in my heart, a symbol of my commitment to this Kingdom and to all who call it home.

"Who would have thought that the person who gave me his blessings to be the next Queen of Puer Lunae is also the same person that I need to destroy to free myself of this Kingdom," I say as I take a step towards the entrance of the church, my every step echoing against the daunting silence of the night. I find the irony of it very amusing.

"I didn't expect it either," Atticus replies as he walks right beside me. "When you entered the throne room a while ago and informed us that those bewitched are not rogues but humans turned into vampires, Cassius was the first person who came to my mind."

My forehead creases as I turn to my husband with a puzzled expression on my face. So he already has his suspicions even if we didn't get the information from Stellian?

"How can you say so?" I ask, my eyebrows furrowing in confusion.

Atticus turns to look at me, his expression dark and serious.

"Everyone in this Kingdom expected Cassius to be the next head of the House of Malvagio. He came from an old lineage of royalty, just like King Silvan. It's a bloodline that I do not possess. He's the only living vampire in this Kingdom who can turn humans into one of our kind," he explains. "However, despite his bloodline, Remus surpassed him in almost everything."

My face contorts in confusion.

"Cassius came from a bloodline of royalty?" It is not a question but more of a statement of realization. The conversation I had with Samuel started to come back to me. But I thought all members of the previous royalty had been executed publicly? I give my husband a curious look, wanting to know more about the history. "What happened then?"

"The potions... The neighbouring kingdoms learned that it was the previous royals of Puer Lunae who were funding the creation of those potions." He reveals.

I halt my step and turn to him with a frown. "I thought you said before that nobody knows why the witches of the coven brewed those potions." If he had only informed me about this sooner, it would have helped my investigation and made this case much easier to solve.

"It's because it is a can of worms that no one wants to open," he shrugs. "The higher council proved that the royals of Puer Lunae are guilty of funding and creating those potions. Most neighbouring kingdoms feel threatened. Imagine if Puer Lunae manages to perfect the recipe. Imagine how much power this Kingdom would hold. They would have an army of bewitched vampires, each with strength comparable to three or more warriors."

I swallow hard. Yep, that sounds terrifying. Our enemies right now are just a handful compared to the numbers of our warriors, but I can see how hard it is for us to win this war.

"What happened after that?"

"Neighboring kingdoms declared war against our Kingdom. The royals were captured and killed in a public execution. It was a brutal scene. Only one royal was left alive because he was still a child at that time."

"Cassius..." I utter.

Atticus nods to confirm my conclusion, then continue to speak. "My family, as one of the most powerful houses in the Kingdom due to my father being one of the five ministers, was hailed as the new monarchs of Puer Lunae. It was my father's decision to give Cassius to the House of Malvagio. That's how he became a part of it," he ends.

I let out a harsh exhale. Somehow, I am already starting to understand the complexity of the history of the Kingdom.

"Let's continue this conversation once the chaos is over. For now, let's focus on the most important thing." Atticus says as he shifts his attention back to the church in front of us.

I nod in agreement and follow his gaze, my eyes settling on the church's entrance. The sight of it sends a shiver down my spine. It all makes sense to me now— Cassius's motives for starting this rebellion were rooted in his desire to reclaim his family's position in the Kingdom. As a member of the royal family, he had a rightful claim to the throne.

However, he had resorted to using forbidden methods to achieve his goals.

I stride confidently into the church with a determined expression on my face. I feel for Cassius, having lost his family and his title, but I cannot condone the methods he employed to achieve his goal. Though his family was brutally murdered and he was adopted by strangers, becoming an orphan in the process, his actions cannot be excused. He recklessly dragged countless innocent people into this war.

Being a true leader is not about sitting on the throne while wearing a golden crown. A true leader is someone willing to sacrifice everything for the safety and well-being of their subjects. It is not about gaining power or riches but about the responsibility one takes on to protect and serve their citizens.

The sound of my heels echoes throughout the church as I walk purposefully down the aisle towards the altar. My gaze is fixed solely on the imposing chair at the end of the aisle where Cassius sits, waiting for us. I come to a stop a few meters away from him and draw my sword in a swift, fluid motion.

Atticus comes to a halt beside me and speaks with full authority, his voice echoing against the silence of the church. "Cassius, it doesn't have to come to this."

Cassius sneers as he rises from his seat, his gaze sharp towards my husband as he speaks. "It doesn't have to come to this, but here you are anyway. My plan is flawless. Years of preparation, gathering resources and allies, all wasted because your little harlot decided to send a human detective to ruin everything."

His hatred is palpable as he slowly turns his gaze towards me. And before I can even guess what his next move is, he is already in front of me. He draws his sword from his waist as he lunges at me at lightning speed, his blade aiming for my neck.

Our gaze locks and I feel frozen in my spot at the unexpected attack. Atticus is quick enough to shield me from Cassius' sword with his, but not quick enough as the tip of Cassius' blade grazes the side of my neck, drawing a trickle of blood.

I instinctively reach up to the small wound to stem the flow, the small droplets of blood drenching the tip of my fingers.

I hiss. Damn it! Cassius is faster than I anticipated.

"Leave her alone, Cassius. I am your enemy. I am the one you need to kill!" Atticus seethes as their swords cross against each other.

Cassius sneers in response, a cruel smirk twisting his lips as his gaze focuses on my husband.

This time, I know it's my time to retreat and watch. I take a step back and put my sword away, my eyes darting between the two men as they circle each other. I can only watch and wait, praying that Atticus will be the one to come out victorious.

"Let's make a deal," Atticus offers without tearing his gaze from Cassius. "I'm going to give you a chance to take back what you believe is rightfully yours. We'll fight to the death, and the victor will be the one to sit on the throne."

My eyes widen in surprise at my husband's words. Did he just wager our entire Kingdom?

"Are you fucking kidding me? You're giving him the opportunity to take the throne? What the fuck are you thinking?" I hiss at him incredulously. I have given everything to protect this Kingdom and its people, and now he plans to risk it all?

Wow. Talk about good leadership.

The side of my husband's lips tugs to a small smile at my sudden explosion, probably finding my unexpected outburst amusing. Though I can't really understand what is funny in our situation.

"My Queen, sometimes the only way to prove you deserve something is by pushing it to the edge," he states with his eyes fixed on his adversary. "When you're on the brink of losing something vital, that's when you hold tightly to it. And let's not forget that Cassius has every right to reclaim the Kingdom."

Cassius's laughter reverberates across the church, making me turn to him.

"Is that so?" Cassius's tone drips with amusement, but the anger simmering in his eyes betrays him. "Shouldn't it be the other way around? Prove to me that you're worthy of the throne your family stole from mine!"

Cassius relentlessly strikes Atticus' sword with his own, but my husband skillfully parries every blow, countering with a swift kick to Cassius' stomach. The impact forces them apart, creating a brief respite in their intense clash.

Cassius flies several meters away, crashing onto a wooden chair and breaking it into pieces. He rises from the debris, his grip on his sword tightening. Atticus's attack seems to have had little effect on him. With his royal blood, Cassius undoubtedly possesses immense strength.

"My family didn't steal anything from yours, Cassius!" Atticus retorts confidently as he straightens his stand.

"Your father sold us out to the other kingdoms!" Cassius roars in anger. "How do you think the higher council managed to connect the relation of the potion to my family? Your father betrayed the royals of Puer Lunae and took the throne! You really have the guts to call yourself a King?!"

His rage was evident in every word he spoke. Although I can understand that Atticus's father only did what was right, I can't help but feel Cassius's pain. Losing your whole family is hard, not to mention having to serve the people he believed had betrayed his family. He's in pain, and this rebellion is his last hope to reclaim the throne.

In the blink of an eye, Atticus materializes before Cassius, brandishing his sword with deadly intent. The steel glimmers in the light as it cuts through the air towards Cassius's heart. Cassius doesn't seem to expect it and barely has time to avoid my husband's attack. The blade slices through the side of his chest, creating a deep and bloody gash.

Cassius stumbles backwards, one hand reaching to cradle his wounded chest. His lips twist into a dangerous smirk as he looks back at Atticus.

"My father had to do it," my husband spits out in a controlled yet powerful voice. "The method your family wanted to use is heartless. The greed of your father is what pushed him and his family to their death!" Atticus clenches his fist, his knuckles turning white as he tightly grips the handle of his word.

To my surprise, Cassius lets out an amused laugh while still holding his wounded chest. That's when I feel a cold wind caress my nape, making me slightly shiver. I swallow the lump that's starting to form in my throat. I'm not keen on predicting my enemy's next move, but I consider myself a person with a powerful intuition. I reach for the blade in my boots and grip it tightly in my palm, silently waiting for the worst to come.

"This is hopeless," Cassius declares, his voice calm and collected despite his clear admission of his own defeat. "I know that tonight is set to be my end, but before that, I want to take something away from you, my king. Just like how your family took everything away from me."

My heart sinks down to my stomach upon realizing what he means by that. Before I can even react, I feel his imposing presence behind me.

"Damn it, Naya!" Atticus screams out my name in terror, his voice echoing against the solemn silence in that church.

I turn around just in the nick of time to see Cassius's sword plunge into my chest. The sensation of cold metal puncturing my flesh sends a jolt of pain through my body, but my reflexes kick in. With lightning-fast speed, I grab his wrist and pull him towards me, leveraging his own attack against him. My grip on the silver dagger tightens as I thrust it into his chest with all my strength, catching him off guard. I pivot and deliver a forceful kick, driving the blade even deeper into his heart.

Cassius staggers back several meters away from me with a look of shock and disbelief etched on his face. His hand reaches out to the silver blade protruding from his chest, but it's too late. Blood gushes out of his mouth, and my vision blurs as tears prick at the corners of my eyes.

I pull the sword from my chest with my eyes locked with Cassius's. A pang of sadness fills my heart while looking at him for the misguided choices that led him down this path. A defeated smile curves his lips as he falls to his knees. Then slowly, his body crumbles into ashes on the cold, hard marble floor of the church.

The pain from my wound starts to numb, and I don't know if I should be afraid or thankful for that. My gaze falls on the sword in my hand as it slips from my grasp and lands on the cold floor with a clanking sound that reverberates throughout the silent church.

Then, amidst the darkness that threatens to consume me, I hear the panicked voice of my husband calling out my name. In a split second, he is already holding me tightly in his arms, his eyes scanning my face and the wound in my chest. I lean into his chest, drawing comfort from his warmth as weariness envelops me.

My breaths come in short gasps, and black dots dance before my eyes.

I feel so tired...

And with that realization, I willingly succumb to my exhaustion, my eyes fluttering close as I allow the darkness to swallow my consciousness. In my final moments of awareness, I offer up a prayer to the heavens, pleading for the salvation of my beloved Kingdom as the war rages continuously outside the church.

CHAPTER 48

Naya

From the moment I stepped into this world, I had no clue where my adventure would lead me. My journey has been far from easy, filled with unexpected twists and turns that nearly brought me to my demise. Even now, as I reflect on my experiences, I can't help but shake my head in disbelief.

What am I saying? One turn of events ended up killing me, both in body and soul.

And now, with everything finally over, I'm unsure whether to celebrate or feel gloomy about it. Seeking justice was the fuel that kept me going, the force that drove me to survive in this world. Now that the end is here, for some reason, I feel empty and hollow. The ending has left a void in my soul that cannot be filled, a sense of emptiness that goes far beyond my comprehension.

Taking a deep breath, I rise from my bed and make my way towards the open balcony. After sleeping for two full days and nights, I feel slightly disoriented. Luckily, when Cassius thrust his sword into my chest, he missed my heart by a mere few centimetres. Though my body gave out from exhaustion, I escaped without any fatal injuries.

Whether Cassius purposely missed my heart or it was just sheer luck, no one can say for certain. What I do know is that I am still alive, and that is something to be thankful for.

I take a moment to survey the vast expanse of my kingdom before me. My time in this world is short, but it has created a drastic change in my life. I close my eyes as I feel the winter frost touch my skin. Despite the slight bite of the wind, I choose to savour the solemn silence that envelopes the surrounding. My eyes flutter open, and I gaze up to the sky just in time to see the first snowfall of the year.

I take a few deep breaths and smile, taking in the fresh scent of the first snow of winter. Winter has finally arrived, marking the end of one season and the beginning of another.

"The carriage is waiting for you, my Queen. It's time," Samuel's voice from behind me interrupts my thoughts.

I look over my shoulder and nod as I meet his gaze. I follow him without another word. The higher council has decided to move the trial date due to recent events. Even if they hadn't, I am confident in my ability to win the case. After surviving the war, uncovering the mystery of the bewitched vampires, and Cassius's death, I believe King Silvan will attest to my innocence.

As we make our way towards the waiting carriage, I turn to Samuel and ask, "What happened to Lady Naya's mother?"

Samuel gives me a quick glance before answering. "She was captured on the border of Puer Lunae together with some influential members of the House of Nardelli. However, they tried to fight the King's warriors, which ended up killing almost all of the members, including Elizabeth. Only a handful of them decided to give up and submit to the King. They will be exiled to Viria."

That makes me frown. "Viria?" I recall him mentioning it before, but I never got the chance to ask what kind of place it was.

"It is an isolated island in the far east. Most criminals are exiled to that place for committing heinous crimes." He briefly explains.

So, there is such a place in this world?

"Is that so? If I'm found guilty today, will I also be sent there for the rest of my life?" I ask, turning to my butler with a smile.

Samuel turns his gaze towards me and raises an eyebrow in my direction.

"Don't even dream about it. Believe me, the accommodation on that island is terrible. Zero out of ten stars," he remarks with a grin playing on his lips.

The smile on my lips widens. Well, I prefer exile to a public execution. I'm sure staying on an island full of criminals would be far better than dying.

"That bad, huh?" I grumble. "And what about the bewitched vampires? Where are they?"

I silently hope that my husband took pity on them and saved those he could save.

"Thankfully, the royal witch managed to make quick changes to the existing antidote. Many have been killed, but many have also been saved," he says as he offers his hand to assist me in climbing the stairs of the waiting carriage.

I breathe a sigh of relief. That's exactly what I needed to hear. That is when I remember the witch. Her name is Sybil, if my memory serves me right.

"And what about the witch who made the potion? Were they able to capture her?" I ask while settling into my seat. The warmth of the carriage envelops me, providing a much-needed respite from the chilly weather outside.

Once he's sure I'm comfortable, Samuel takes his seat in front of me. "Sybil managed to escape. They weren't able to capture her, but the King has vowed to stop at nothing to find her. Zizina has also promised to hunt her down."

I nod. I believe that's not going to be a problem. With Cassius dead, I highly doubt Sybil can still use the potion effectively.

The carriage begins to move, the sound of the horses' hooves filling the silence. They're taking me to Agaptus, another neighbouring kingdom of Puer Lunae, where the trial will be held. It seems that Agaptus is the last place I'll be visiting before I turn my back on this world completely.

Is this really the end of my stay in this kingdom? Is it the end of my misadventure in this world? I thought that solving the mystery behind Lady Naya's murder would set me free, but I guess I was wrong. An endless void fills my heart upon realizing that I won't be able to see my husband anymore after this day. Suddenly, my breathing becomes ragged and heavy, and I feel numb but at the same time in pain.

"Are you worried about the higher court's decision?" Samuel questions when he notices my silence.

I look at him and shake my head. I know I will win the case. What worries me is what will happen after the trial. I wonder what my husband's plan is after this. I haven't seen him since I woke up yesterday. Is he avoiding me purposely?

"I'm not scared of it. I have my full trust in King Silvan,"

"King Silvan is quite intimidating, but he is a good friend." Samuel smiles for a bit then his expression turns serious. "I just hope that him trying to get your child won't create any harm between the two kingdoms in the future."

I reach out to my forehead upon feeling a headache coming through. Once Atticus learns about my deal with King Silvan, I'm pretty sure that it will be a disaster. I hope that day won't come at all. Kaedal is the ally Puer Lunae needs the most.

I can't help but peer out the window as the carriage slowly makes its way through the rocky mountainous terrain, taking in the sights of Agaptus. The landscape was stunning, with the towering mountains providing a dramatic backdrop to the lush spruce forests that surrounded the kingdom.

Many of the homes we pass by are made from sturdy stones, probably quarried from the nearby mountains, while others were constructed using a mix of wood and stone. The thick stone walls of the houses looked strong and durable. The wooden components of the houses, such as the frames, walls, and roofs, were crafted from the surrounding spruce forests, giving the homes a rustic, natural look.

After a while, the carriage comes to a stop in front of a grand structure that seems to resemble a stadium in the human world with its dome-shaped roof towering above the surrounding trees. The white marble columns supporting the dome are intricately carved with elaborate designs. The exterior of the dome is a mix of red brick and stone, with ivy crawling up the walls in patches.

The entrance is flanked by two towering statues, each depicting a warrior wielding a sword and shield. Their stern expressions seem to watch over the entrance as if guarding against any potential threats.

Samuel offers me his hand as I step out of the carriage. As I look around, I can't help but notice the several carriages around the area. But what catches my attention is the royal carriage of Puer Lunae. I know that my husband is inside that carriage.

"My Queen, let's go," Samuel says, his voice cutting through the stillness that shrouds the courtyard.

Nodding in acknowledgement, I make my way towards the entrance of the dome where the trial is set to take place. The snow is beginning to cover the ground, casting a melancholic pall over the already sombre atmosphere. As we step inside, my senses are immediately bombarded by the grandeur of the interior. The high ceilings are adorned with breathtaking frescoes that depict the illustrious history of the kingdom, while the crystal chandeliers suspended from above radiate a bright, welcoming light. The walls are richly decorated with intricate tapestries and paintings of such exquisite beauty that I find myself stopping at each turn to appreciate them.

A stern-looking man approaches us and leads us to the front row, where we find five empty seats. The place is already teeming with people who are busy settling themselves into the hundreds of chairs encircling the stage at the centre. Amidst the crowd, a certain person catches my attention. He stands not far from us, his gaze fixed on me with keen interest.

Although I have never seen him before, the way he gazes at me makes me wonder if we have met previously. To my surprise, the man lets out a friendly smile on his face as he starts to close our distance. He stops right in front of me.

"Hi, I've heard a lot about you. I'm very fascinated with your case. I think you're amazing," he says with his eyes gleaming with admiration.

I grimace. When did I become this popular? I observe the man in front of me silently. He has deep brown eyes that make you crave dark chocolate, sharp jaws, prominent eyebrows, and lips that offer the friendliest smile in the kingdom. However, his boy-next-door appearance is not enough to hide the waves of authority emanating from him, which leads me to conclude that the man in front of me is also an influential person.

"Who are you?" I ask, my face twisted in a frown.

"Oh yeah, where are my manners?" He lets out an amused laugh before extending his hand towards me. "I am King Eilif of Agaptus, the head of the higher council."

My mouth forms an 'o' in surprise. This man in front of me is a King? The King of Agaptus is also the head of the higher council? Oh wow, that's a piece of information you cannot just read from books. I accept his hand, expecting a handshake, but the King dips his head and places a soft kiss on the back of my hand.

"So, the man who is judging me claims to be my biggest fan? Doesn't that seem a little unfair for the prosecution?" I remark as I gently pull my hand from his hold.

King Eilif lets out a grin and shrugs his shoulders.

"Rest assured that my judgment won't be based on my admiration of you but on the evidence presented by both parties. As the head of the higher council, I guarantee that the final verdict will be fair to both prosecution and defence," he assures me.

I nod at him and offer a small smile, satisfied with his answer. With that being said, I believe the result of this trial will be in my favour.

King Eilif bids his goodbye as soon as he notices that two other Kings walk inside the stadium. That would be my husband and King Silvan. Atticus greets him with a smile and taps him on the back, indicating that they know each other personally. King Silvan, on the other hand, simply gives an acknowledgement nod.

I focus my gaze on my beloved husband. For some unknown reason, a part of me is overwhelmed with joy for him. He did it. He saved the kingdom successfully, proving to everyone that he was deserving of his position and that he would stop at nothing to safeguard his people.

As if Atticus can feel my eyes on him from a distance, his piercing gaze shifts towards me, giving me a blank look. I swallow the painful lump in my throat as I feel a dagger painfully pierce through my heart at his nonchalant stare. I long for his presence. No matter how much his actions hurt me, I still crave his warmth. I miss him terribly. I miss his sweet and protective gestures. I miss us.

My hands curl into a tight fist, and I avert my eyes, intentionally avoiding his gaze. I can't bear to look at him for too long, or I may end up surrendering to my pathetic heart again.

The entire trial process is straightforward. The prosecution presents all of their accusations and evidence to the higher court, and then the defence provides every piece of evidence we have to prove my innocence, including the fan mail, the ring, and the key that led me to this world.

"Detective Inspector Naya Cirillo did commit conspiracy against the Kingdom of Puer Lunae. However, she did not do it with ill intentions but due to her passion and dedication to solve the mystery behind Lady Naya's death. She did it to save the kingdom from an uprising rebellion. There are hundreds of vampires, both nobles and commoners, in this stadium right now. However, how many of us here are willing to go beyond our capabilities to fulfil our duties? Detective Inspector Naya Cirillo went above and beyond, fulfilling her duties not only as a detective of the human world but also as a Queen of Puer Lunae." Those are King Silvan's last words before leaving the centre stage.

The whole stadium goes silent after that. Nobody dares to speak. Of course, who would dare to talk against a King? Their words alone are considered laws in this world.

After a minute, a woman wearing a cape stands in the middle of the stage. If I am not mistaken, she is the one who will announce the results of this trial. The woman looks up to the hundreds of audiences before her gaze settles on me.

My heart pounds in my chest as I wait with bated breath for the decision. The silence in the courtroom is deafening, broken only by the sound of my own heartbeat.

Finally, the woman in the flowing cape speaks. "After hearing both sides and taking into consideration all the evidence presented in the higher court," she starts, "I hereby proclaim Detective Naya Cirillo innocent of all accusations. However, she will be released from her royal duties as a queen of Puer Lunae." Her words are delivered with unwavering confidence and authority, earning a collective gasp from the audience.

"Whatever road she chooses to take after this day is solely in her hands," the woman continues before turning to look at me directly. "Naya, the higher council has decided to give you a chance to start over. You will have the freedom to choose whichever kingdom you prefer to reside in. You don't need to answer now—"

"I want to return to the human world," I interrupt.

Silence falls over the stadium as everyone processes my words. I take a deep breath and continue.

"If you're giving me a chance to start over, I want to do it in the world where I truly belong. With all due respect, I would like to go back to the human world."

Each word feels like a heavy weight on my chest, reminding me of the painful reality of my situation. I can't stay in this world anymore. It's time for me to move on. I glance down at the granite floor, clenching my fist tightly to the point that my nails start to cut into my palm just to stop myself from breaking down.

I don't need to look at my husband to know that he's staring at me right now. I can feel his heated gaze from a distance. The side of my eye starts to well up as I realize where this will take both of us. We're not husband and wife anymore. Instead, we are two strangers from two vastly different worlds. The universe played with us, entangling our threads of fate together only to tear us apart in the end. My mission in this world is over.

The murder mystery of Lady Naya is now officially closed.

CHAPTER 49

Naya

I clutch the thick jacket tightly to my chest to protect my skin from the cold weather. A pale smile curves on my lips as I walk towards the place where Lady Naya's remains are laid. The sun is nowhere to be found, and the snow has been falling endlessly all day. However, despite the bad weather, I still take the time to visit her grave and bid farewell.

I take a seat beside the tree where she lies and survey the kingdom of Puer Lunae in awe. The view from this place never fails to take my breath away, regardless of the season. During the autumn season, it is simply breathtaking and so homely, but in the winter, the view from this spot is different. It gives off a magical vibe of a gothic fairy tale. The snow blanketing the ground and the roofs of the houses in the kingdom create a grotesque ambience. It seems unreal, yet it stands so beautifully right in front of me.

"The peacefulness of this kingdom in exchange for your life," I say and reach for the necklace on my neck. "I agree with you. This kingdom is worth it. At least, it's worth the view."

A light chuckle escapes my lips at my messed-up sense of humour. I take off the golden necklace and place it on top of the snow covering the soil beside the tree. It is a gold necklace with an 'N' pendant. This is one of the gifts I received from her.

"Tonight, when the moon rises to the sky, I'm going back to the human world, and I think it's necessary for me to return this and bid you a formal farewell before I take my leave," I mutter. I'm pretty sure that if someone sees me right now, they will think I'm crazy for talking to the tree, but I can't help it. This is a long-overdue conversation that I need to have. "You're so selfish for trying to trap me in this world. You used your own death to lure me here. I must admit that's a smart move, but it's also selfish. You didn't give me a chance to say no. You dragged me here, and all of a sudden, I'm in the middle of a war that has nothing to do with me in the first place."

I lean on the tree and stare at the white sky. Despite the cold wind and endless pouring of snow, this feels peaceful. This place feels calm and serene.

"Regardless of what happened, I can't really hate you. You did what you had to do to save this kingdom. Who am I to hate you?" I take a deep breath before standing up from the ground and shaking off the snow that clings to my clothes. "I'm going now. I need to go back to the human world. I just came here to say goodbye and pray for your peaceful travel to the other side. Goodbye now, and please don't send me any more fan mail or gifts."

I let out a smile while looking at the gold necklace on top of the snow. This time, it is a genuine smile. Everything that has happened to me has never been easy, but in the end, I have learned so much from it. I have lost so much, but I must admit that I have also gained a lot in exchange.

I turn my back on the willow tree and walk towards the waiting carriage not far from where I am. Leaving this world is never easy, but I know that I need to return to the human world. One of the things I have learned from this world is that to attain something, you need to give up something in exchange. I guess that's a general rule in life. If you want to be successful, you need to give up your comfort zone. If you want to gain knowledge and be wise, you need to lose your innocence and ignorance.

Life has a habit of taking things away from us. Nothing we have stays permanent, and no matter how much we try to hold on to it, we are bound to lose something or even people who are important to us one way or another. It's a tough pill to swallow, but it's just the way the world works.

"You sure about this?" Zizina asks as I clamber into the carriage.

"I need to do this."

"You don't need to leave. You're one of us now. You're not a human anymore. There's nothing left for you in the human world to go back to," Samuel chimes in, making me turn to him.

A deep, tired sigh escapes me as I sense the desperation in his voice. This goodbye is going to be brutal, but I know deep down it's what I need to do. I can't stay here even though every fibre of my being wants to. I can't bear to watch my husband from afar. Sure, our marriage had been nulled and voided, but nothing could erase our bond or the feelings I have for him. It's the best for everyone if I go.

"I can't stay, Samuel," I say flatly. I don't want to explain to anyone why I need to go back to the human world.

"You can. You simply need to choose to stay with us."

I feel the resentment in his voice. I avoid his scrutinizing gaze and divert my eyes to the carriage window. He is right, I can choose to stay here, but I won't. I need time away from all this chaos. I need time for myself. I need to console myself and rethink all the choices that have led me to this point. I want to redeem myself. I need to clear my mind. I want to give myself space and enough time to understand my own heart.

Moments later, the carriage arrives at the spruce forest that marks the boundary between Agaptus and Puer Lunae. This is where they chose to open the gateway for me to return to the human world.

The darkness has completely blanketed the surroundings, with nothing but the pale moonlight and white snow illuminating the place, creating a very serene and peaceful atmosphere. As I step down from the carriage, my attention is captured by the sight of my husband.

He's here? But why? He never approached me after the trial, nor before it. So why is he here now?

"You're just in time. I just completed the gateway back to the human world," Nemue announces, drawing my gaze towards her.

"Great," I reply with a forced smile, then turn to gaze at my loyal butler. Samuel's eyes seem pleading, but he doesn't say another word. "I'll miss you," I tell him.

I can't hold back anymore. I close the distance between us and encircle my arms around his waist for an embrace. If there's one person in this world who has offered me real friendship and alliance, it's Samuel. He became my best friend and my best partner in crime. It's painful that he's one of the people I have to let go of as I return to the world where I belong.

"I want to force you to stay, but that would be unfair to you," Samuel finally spoke in a woeful tone. "You've been in so much pain since you entered this world. Who am I to blame you if you decide to leave this world? I won't beg you to stay here anymore, but please remember that you can always choose to come back whenever you feel like it."

Despite the pain in my chest, I look up and smile at him. I nod and release him from my embrace.

"Stay safe, okay?" I tell him before turning my attention to Zizina.

Zizina closes the short distance between us and gives me a tight hug.

"I hate you for choosing the human world, but it's okay. I can always visit you whenever I want to," she says, smiling.

"Yeah, but please, next time you visit me, don't bring any fan mail. I don't want to receive any," I joke half-heartedly, hoping to lighten the mood.

As she releases me from her tight embrace, a wave of relief washes over me. I feel a small sense of comfort knowing that my friends here have accepted my decision. I turn towards the gateway back to the human world, a swirling black mirror that beckons me towards the unknown.

This is it, the moment I've been waiting for. I can't believe I'm going back now.

I resist the urge to glance back at my husband as I take my first step towards the portal. The soft humming emanating from it becomes louder as I get closer. I can't let myself get distracted and lose the courage I've worked so hard to gather. I stare straight ahead, fixating on the black hole in front of me. It's intimidating, and the thought of what lies beyond it is daunting.

Just as I'm about to step through the portal when Atticus' voice shatters the silence.

"Don't leave..."

The sound of desperation in his voice makes me halt, and I can feel my resolve starting to crumble. My heart starts to race upon hearing his plea, but I choose to ignore it. My fists clench tightly by my sides as I struggle to resist the urge to turn around and run back into his embrace.

"Please stay," he pleads in a broken voice, and tears begin to well up in my eyes. The walls that I had built around my heart began to collapse. I take a deep breath and firmly shake my head in response. I don't have the strength to say another word.

Forgive me, Atticus.

I need this.

We both need this.

With that thought, I step into the portal, leaving everything behind me, allowing myself to fall into the dark abyss that will take me to the world where I truly belong.

EPILOGUE

Naya

The light passing through the glass window of the room forces me to open my eyes. The first thing that welcomes me is a yellow flower placed in a vase above the bedside table, just beside the window. I can't help but smile as I take in the beauty of this morning, a beautiful daffodil on the bedside table and the lively chirping of the birds from the outside. A great start to a promising day indeed.

I rise up from my bed with my heart fluttering in happiness and contentment. Life has decided to smile at me upon my return to the human world. It has been a month since I left Puer Lunae, and since then, I have been working hard to solve one last case before submitting my resignation to my boss.

Being a detective is an amazing job. It taught me a lot about the darkness in the world. However, that same darkness almost devoured my soul, so I knew I needed to let it go.

I make my way towards the bathroom to brush my teeth and wash my face before heading to the kitchen. When I arrive at the kitchen, I immediately open the refrigerator and get a blood bag from it.

I am so glad that I am not a friendly person and I don't get many visitors. If someone were to accidentally open my fridge, they would surely run away from my house as far as possible after seeing my stock of blood bags inside. I am a vampire now, and I don't need coffee for breakfast. I need blood.

After emptying the bag, I throw it in the bin near me and walk towards the wrap-around porch of the house to take a glimpse of the beauty of the sunrise. Life itself is beautiful, especially for those who value it. It's mid-May now, and the grounds are blanketed with hundreds of dandelions and daffodils, my two favourite spring flowers.

My eyes unintentionally land on the ring I'm wearing. Yup, I haven't removed our wedding ring. I don't have the heart to take it off. I want to keep it for life, along with our memories together. Our story probably started in tragedy and ended in tragedy, but that doesn't mean it's something that I want to bury in the dust and forget.

My gaze shifts to the car that has come to a halt in front of the gate to my house. Its door swings open, revealing my favourite human partner in solving crimes.

"Hey! Good morning to the most gorgeous detective of all time," Michael exclaims, his face adorned with an irresistible smile that effortlessly mirrors my own.

"Hey," I greet back. "You're early today," I make my way to the gate to let him in.

"This is your big day, and I don't want to ruin it by being late, so I decided to come here as early as I can,"

"I just woke up a few minutes ago, dude. You're way too early," I laugh at him. "You had breakfast already? I'm cooking for us." I walk inside the house with Michael following me from behind.

"Great! Perks of being early, I can have free breakfast with coffee," he says as he settles in my living room while I proceed to the kitchen to cook for us.

I can't help but smile as I start to take out all the ingredients needed for the meal I plan to cook. Then I hear my partner turn on my Xbox from the living room. Michael is like my Samuel in the human world. He's very reliable.

After our breakfast, I take a few more minutes to take a bath as he washes the dishes. Then, we head off on the road, with him in his car and me in my baby Sportster.

Moments later, we stop in from of a huge mansion. It's a beautiful villa from the outside, but what lurks inside is a dangerous criminal capable of killing his own colleague without a second thought. I step out of my car and walk towards the gate. I push the doorbell button twice and wait for someone to open the gate for us.

"I'm nervous that we're doing this without any backup," Michael says, following behind me.

I turn to him. Seeing the hesitation and slight fear in his eyes makes me feel guilty. But it is his fault anyway. I told him that I could do it alone, but he kept insisting that two heads are better than one. So here we are.

"You can still back out if you want," I offer proactively.

This is my problem to deal with, not his. As much as possible, I don't want anyone involved in it, especially if they have nothing to do with the case.

"Nah! You're my senior and my partner. I can't leave you here on your own. Besides, this case is long overdue. It took ten years to solve it. I can't miss the chance to witness the end of it firsthand," he responds.

A warm smile spreads across my lips. Michael is a huge fan of my father, and when he was assigned as my partner, he acted like a simp. But he proved to be a hardworking detective in the past years. It's amazing how my father inspired some youths to follow in his footsteps, including Michael and me.

The massive gate of the mansion opens, and a house helper in uniform greets us with a smile. She leads us to the waiting area of the house as we wait for Commissioner Faison to come down. We don't have to wait long, as moments later, the old man descends the stairs.

The confusion appears in his eyes for a moment as he sees Michael and me waiting for him.

"Naya, Michael, this is a surprise. I didn't expect you to visit me this early," he says. "Is it really that urgent that it can't wait until I arrive at the station?"

I smile, keeping my gaze fixed on him. "I'm pretty sure that what I'm about to tell you is something our colleagues at the station wouldn't like to hear," I say in a calm tone.

His forehead furrows slightly, but he nods in agreement and turns his attention to one of the house helpers.

"This conversation might take a while. Can you prepare some coffee and breakfast for our guests?" he requests.

The woman nods and heads to the kitchen without a word while the man takes a seat in front of us, leaning back on the sofa. Once the woman is out of sight, he speaks up.

"I'm all ears, Naya. What brings you here unexpectedly?" he inquires with unwavering confidence, deftly reaching for the tobacco on the table. With practised precision, he expertly ignites it, the ember glowing brightly as wisps of smoke curl and billow, creating an atmosphere of contemplation and gravity.

I clear my throat before delivering my speech. Each word is full of conviction. "Commissioner Mark

Faison, you are under arrest for the murder of your wife and for murdering my father. You have the right to remain silent. Anything you say can be used against you in court. You have the right to have a lawyer present during questioning,"

He looks at me with a surprised expression on his face, his lips breaking into a lopsided grin as his suspended tobacco hovers mid-air. After a few moments of shock, his amusement fills the mansion, reverberating with his echoing laughter. I remain motionless, my gaze locked on the old Commissioner.

He flicks his tobacco before extinguishing its ember in the nearby metal ashtray. "Are you certain about your accusations, Detective Naya? You're aware that I could pursue legal action for malicious prosecution if you fail to substantiate your claims in court. I implore you, Naya, to reconsider. Your talent as a detective is exceptional, and you possess immense potential."

I fold my arms over my chest, a confident smile forming on my lips.

"You said it yourself, Commissioner. I am a great detective. Therefore, I am confident that the result of my investigation is highly accurate. We managed to trap the man you hired to kill your wife. He admitted that you are also the one behind my father's assassination. You killed my father because he solved the case of your wife's murder. You killed him to make him shut up," I say, my fist tightening in controlled anger as I speak, not wanting to lose my composure in front of an enemy.

No wonder all the evidence that the police station gave me didn't match up. Some of it had been destroyed purposely to lead me to a dead end. It's hard to believe that I've worked for five years under the same man who murdered my father.

I rise from my seat and make my way toward him. I retrieve the cuffs from the side pocket of my denim jacket and speak in a low voice, "I hate to break it to you, but I'm afraid you'll be having your breakfast in jail today." And with that, I handcuff him.

He knows better than to struggle or try to escape. I am an officer on duty, and it doesn't matter if he is a commissioner or not. We have warrants for his arrest, and if he tries to harm me in any way, that could result in another offence.

"You're going to regret this," he threatens, his face dark with contained fury,

I smirk. "No, you will regret the crime you have committed," I retort and pull him towards the door.

Michael shoots me a proud smile as he opens the door for us.

Finally, after years of waiting, I managed to solve the very first murder case that was assigned to me. It took five long years to close that case, but it doesn't matter. What matters most is that I have solved the mystery behind Detective Cirillo's suicide-murder case.

That day took longer than I expected. The people at the station were shocked when we arrived with the Commissioner in cuffs. The case for the murder of his wife was reopened on the same day. Mark Faison has many connections in the higher department, but I have substantial evidence against him.

The day before his wife's death, he forwarded a large amount of money through the bank to the man who murdered Mrs Faison. The same thing happened a day after his wife was pronounced dead. The money transfer occurred again before and after the death of my father.

His greatest mistake was using a bank transfer to make the payment for the murders. With enough connections, I managed to obtain the details of those transactions from the bank.

The whole day was exhausting with all the questioning and requirements that I needed to submit for the case. On that same day, I returned my badge and submitted my resignation letter, stepping down from my position as a Detective Inspector.

It was supposed to be an emotional day for me, but I knew better than to shed tears for it after all of the things that I've been through. I loved my job. However, there were moments in my life when you needed to let go of something you loved.

That night ended with Michael and me at one of the local pubs, drinking to celebrate solving my very first case and our last night together as partners. Before we said our final goodbye, we gave each other one last hug and bid each other good luck. After years of being partners, we were now set to take two different roads.

It's almost midnight when I park my motorcycle in front of my home. I'm a bit tipsy from the alcohol, but I can manage. As I'm about to open the gate to bring my bike inside, I smell something odd coming from my house. My forehead wrinkles, and I bend down to pull out a blade hidden on the side of my boots.

Who's stupid enough to enter a vampire's cabin at 12 am? Do they want to be my midnight snack or something?

Instead of opening the gate, I decide to jump over it as silently as possible. I walk towards the backdoor and frown upon hearing the sound of my TV, which I recognize as a Forza game. My brows furrow in confusion.

Forza? Really? Wow. Someone has the guts to enter my house and play Forza on my Xbox? That's it! The person inside my house is definitely looking for trouble.

I open the back door as silently as I can and make my way towards my living room. I see the culprit comfortably sitting on my sofa, eyes glued to the TV screen, completely unaware of my presence. I quickly close the distance between us with the silver dagger in hand. I'm just a meter away from him when he finally feels me looming over him.

He tilts his head, looking over his shoulder, but before he can even get a glimpse of me, I let my reflexes take over. I swiftly throw the dagger in his direction. And that's when I recognize those warm hazel-coloured eyes. But it's too late. The man leans to his left, narrowly avoiding my blade. It grazes his cheek, drawing a small amount of blood before embedding itself into the TV screen.

I can't help but cringe as the screen goes black. Even the uninvited visitor turns his attention to the TV screen, alerted by the crashing sound it makes. I curse. Looks like I will be needing a new TV now.

"C'mon! I'm so close to winning that race!" He complains, making me turn to look at him again.

For a moment, I am unable to say anything. I am both shocked and surprised to see him in my home. I swallow hard. Suddenly, all of the emotions I had bottled up in the past month came crashing down on me.

"You... you're here?" I manage to come up with only two words, though I have thousands of questions.

Atticus turns his eyes back to me and rises up from the couch.

"Yes, I do. Or else I might end up losing my mind waiting for you to come back," he says as he starts to cross our distance. "I understand that you need time, but you've been away for more than a month already. I don't care how much time you need to recover. I can't stay away from you anymore. If you are not ready to return to our kingdom yet, I am staying here with you until you are ready to be my Queen again."

My forehead creases in confusion. He had been waiting for me to come back?

I shake my head in response, not knowing what to feel about his confession. "I am not your Queen anymore, Atticus," I reply and turn my back against him to go to the kitchen. I need a glass of water right now.

"You are my wife, my beloved. The higher council could never remove that. I miss you, Naya. Please come back to me," his voice is filled with pleading, his footsteps getting closer and closer to me.

I halt on my step when I feel his presence looming behind me. "Can't you see it? I am not Lady Naya. I am not the woman you thought I was." I mutter, my voice shaking as I struggle to regain my composure.

I miss him, I really do. Leaving Puer Lunae helped me realize a lot of things. That includes my feelings for him. I thought it was just the bond, but I was completely wrong. I love him. I truly do. Not because of the bond but because he is the man who shows me how beautiful it is to be a woman.

I showed him both my scars and Lady Naya's scars, but his feelings never changed for me. He accepted both broken Naya and fraudulent Naya without a second thought. He protected me in the best way he could. Being with someone who can accept and support you in both your weakest and strongest moments is the best thing in life.

Atticus is more than just my soulmate; he's my twin flame, my other half.

As his arms wrap around me from behind, I surrender to his embrace, feeling the warmth of his touch against my skin. The gentle pressure of his hold anchors me at the moment, and I resist the urge to break free or pull away. Tears stream down my face, tracing a delicate path down my cheeks. I can't help but yearn for the days when I could flirt and fall in love with him without any restrictions.

"I know you're not her. I'm fully aware of that," he murmurs close to my ear, his words a balm to my aching heart. "It takes a lot of time for me to accept that you are not her, that the woman I used to love is long gone. I loved Naya; she was a very sweet person. But you're different in a way that I can't help but love you for who you are. You're not a replacement; you are your own person. There are no words that I can say right now to prove that. Only our future can do that for me. Naya, I'm begging you, give me a chance to prove my love to you..."

I wipe away my tears and face him. With a smile, I tiptoe to give him a peck on his lips. It's long overdue, but leaving was necessary to sort out my feelings for him and solve my father's death. Now, I guess this is the best time for us to start over again.

If he's willing to travel this far to give our story a second chance, who am I to say no? Finding a man who's willing to cross a parallel universe just to tell you he loves you is no joke.

Atticus blinks twice, looking at me with a confused expression.

"So does that kiss mean—"

"It means I love you, asshole!" I hiss at him and hug him back.

He chuckles a bit and steps back, our eyes locking with each other. Sometimes, it's incredible how destiny works. In a graceful motion, he leans down, bridging the gap between us, and his lips tenderly meet mine. I close my eyes, allowing myself to fully immerse in the sensation of his soft, sweet kiss. The taste of his lips lingers, a bittersweet reminder of the love we once shared. Right there and then, I know that I've found my way home, inside my beloved's arms.

Reluctantly, he releases my lips, and our foreheads touch, creating an intimate connection between us. I open my eyes, gazing into his mesmerizing gaze, and a radiant smile adorns his face. His gentle touch caresses the side of my cheek, leaving a trail of warmth in its wake.

"I love you, my Queen," he murmurs, his voice filled with affection and devotion. Suddenly, he kneels before me, a gesture both unexpected and heart-stopping. My world freezes as he reaches into his pocket and retrieves a small blue box. My jaw hangs open in utter surprise.

"Detective Naya Cirillo," he continues, his words filled with sincerity and a hint of vulnerability, "Encountering you in this lifetime was an unforeseen twist, bringing a whirlwind of chaos into my life. Yet, truth be told, you're the chaos I'm more than willing to accept. You are the woman I yearn to spend the rest of my days with, standing by my side as my Queen. Will you do me the extraordinary honour of becoming my wife?"

Tears cascade down my face as I fix my gaze upon him, his outstretched hand holding the gleaming ring. This time, they are tears of pure joy, an overflow of overwhelming emotions. Unable to speak, I nod my head vigorously in response. A soft chuckle escapes his lips in response to my animated reaction.

With graceful poise, he rises from the floor, his movements imbued with quiet grace. His fingers deftly slide the ring onto my awaiting finger, nestling it beside our wedding band, a perfect union of commitment and eternal love.

"I love you," he whispers, his voice filled with tenderness, and I tilt my head upward, meeting his gaze.

"And I love you too, my King," I reply, the words resonating with absolute certainty as I close my eyes, savouring the calmness that lingers in the air. In a cherished embrace, I lift myself onto my tiptoes, bridging the gap between us, and our lips unite in a tender kiss.

Our tale may have begun in a web of lies, deceit, and the macabre stain of bloodshed, but none of that could stop our affection for one another. They say true love is a force that conquers all, and at this moment, I wholeheartedly believe in the veracity of that adage. True love endures. True love conquers.

Special Chapter

Atticus

"It has been a month since she departed. Why aren't you doing anything to get her back?" Samuel's voice interrupts my thoughts, compelling me to turn and face him.

I let out a heavy sigh and returned my gaze to the vast expanse of my territory.

The castle feels different without her presence, almost lifeless. My heart aches for her, the very essence of my being echoing her name incessantly, yet I find myself lacking the fortitude to trail her into the human world.

"I want to, but what right do I have to force her to stay here if she doesn't want to be here in the first place?" I express bitterly, draining the contents of my glass in one swift gulp. "I granted her the power of choice because I sensed she had been stripped of it upon her entry into our world. I never thought that the first thing she would do when given a chance to decide for herself is run away from me..."

The weight of the decision bears down upon me like an oppressive stone, pressing relentlessly against my chest. I want nothing more than to beg her to stay, but deep down, I know that doing so would be incredibly unfair to her. The world we live in has done nothing but traumatize her, leaving deep scars on her soul that may never heal. It pains me to admit it, but this world killed her and her sparks.

What right do I have to force her to stay? The answer, of course, is none. I cannot in good conscience coerce her into staying with me, especially when her heart may not be fully in it. That would only serve to trap her, to rob her of the freedom to make her own choices.

"But what if she truly wants to stay?" Samuel probes once more.

"I want her back more than anything, Samuel," I reply, my grip on the glass tightening. "But I want her to come back to me willingly. Not because she's trapped or has no other options, not because she's bound to me in any way. I want her to choose me because that's what she truly wants."

How many times do I dream of her returning to this world? The Kingdom feels so bleak without her presence, and my heart aches at the thought of her being so far away. I want her so badly it pains me to know that we are universes away from each other.

"You're a coward. If you don't want to make a move to get her back, fine! Have fun asking yourself a lot of 'what ifs' in the future," he snaps with impatience lacing his voice. Then I hear his footstep fading away from the distance.

I sigh and take another sip of whiskey. He's right, of course. I could stay here, wallowing in my grief while waiting for her return, or I could take action and try to win her back into the human world.

A faint smile tugs at my lips at the thought. I wish it was that easy.

After emptying the bottle of whiskey, I conclude that it is time to bring the evening to a close and retire to our shared room. Yet, as I turn the doorknob, a sinking sensation takes hold of my heart. Her memories permeate every corner of my vision, an unrelenting reminder of the void left in her absence.

Suppressing the excruciating ache within my chest, I collapse onto the bed, surrendering to its embrace.

Sleep is a great escape when everything around me feels like a mess. Since her departure, slumber has become an escape, a respite from the weight of my responsibilities, allowing me to drift into dreams where she remains ever-present.

As the night unfolds, my dreams carry me once more into her beguiling presence. Yet, this evening possesses a palpable distinction from the others. Every aspect of her being exudes vivid realism. Each tender kiss and affectionate embrace we share feels nearly tangible as if she were truly by my side once more.

"Naya..." I murmur her name, allowing it to linger upon my lips as our kiss intensifies.

Mentioning her name makes her freeze for a second, giving me a chance to regain consciousness and control.

Then, like a sudden bucket of cold water thrown on me, I realize that a woman is indeed beneath me, but it's not my beloved. The flames of desire that had consumed me mere moments ago vanish like an illusion, replaced by a surge of irritation as I gaze upon Harriet.

"Harriet, what the hell are you doing here?" I hiss at her, rising abruptly from the bed and tugging at my hair in exasperation. I look at myself and thank the heavens that I am still fully clothed, just like she is.

"What the heck were you thinking, woman?" I holler, still feeling irritated.

Harriet looks at me with a surprised expression, her eyes wide in a combination of dread and apprehension.

I take a few deep breaths to calm myself. Harriet, despite occasional moments of prickliness, is a decent woman. She's now one of my Ministers, and I don't want to hate her, but she needs to stop trying to lure me into loving her.

"Look, Atticus... I'm sorry. It's just that I've noticed how lonely you've been these past few days, and I thought—"

"You thought you could make me happy by stooping this low and trying to have sex with me?" I interject, my voice laced with both frustration and anger. Harriet falls silent, her gaze dropping as she adjusts her dress. I release a heavy sigh, my eyes locked upon her figure. "Harriet, you're a beautiful woman, and every man in this Kingdom dreams of having you as their wife. You don't need to push yourself on someone who doesn't feel the same way about you."

Harriet nervously twiddles with her hands, her gaze fixed on her palms, deliberately avoiding eye contact with me.

"She's not coming back, Atticus. Why can't you just forget her? I love you, and I'm here for you. But you chose her. She died, and now you're choosing a woman who looks like her. I can love you. I can choose you," she says, her voice breaking mid-sentence.

I rub my forehead in disbelief, feeling the weight of her words pressing down on me.

"Listen, Harriet. I don't love you, and no matter who I decide to be with or why, it doesn't change the fact that I cannot choose you. It wouldn't be fair to you or to me," I plead, hoping that she understands. "You're an amazing person, Harriet, and I don't want you to be stuck in a one-sided relationship. You deserve to be with someone who truly loves you, and I'm not that person."

Without a single word, she stands up from my bed and leaves the room, the sound of the door closing, echoing in the silence.

I slump back onto the bed with a sigh. I cannot help but admire Harriet's courage. She pursued the person she loved, even though it was as clear as a blue sky on a summer day that I did not share her feelings.

I lay down on my bed, gazing up at the ceiling of my room, and the weight of my indecision weighs heavily on me. Perhaps Samuel is right, and I am a coward. Maybe I need to take action and fight for the woman I love. With that realization, I spring up from my bed and walk towards the bathroom, determined to take control of the situation. If Naya is hesitant to come back, then I need to give her a reason to return to Puer Lunae.

Once I finish freshening up, I head over to my closet to pick out some clothes that won't draw too much attention from humans. As the midnight chimes reverberate from the church, I find myself standing at the threshold of Nemue's dwelling, resolved to take charge of the situation at hand.

I knock twice and wait for someone to answer. After a minute, the front door creaks open, revealing a drowsy witch in her nightgown.

A grin spreads across my face as her eyes widen in shock at the sight of me.

"Your Majesty! What brings you here at this hour? Hold on a moment. Let me go wake up my mother," Zizina says as she turns to leave, but I stop her before she can take another step.

"No, you are the reason why I came here tonight," I tell her firmly.

She stops in her tracks and looks at me, her forehead creasing in confusion.

"Me?" she asks, pointing to herself.

"Yes, you. I need you to open the gateway to the human world for me,"

She hesitates, her brow furrowing as she contemplates my request before a surge of excitement illuminates her expression.

"You're going after her!" she exclaims in astonishment, her eyes widening with exhilaration, prompting me to swiftly move towards her and cover her mouth.

It's the dead of night. Most people sleeping right now would have a nightmare at her shout.

"Yes, I am. Now shut up before you wake up the whole Kingdom," I hiss at her.

She nods, and I release her. Her smile never fades as she looks at me, clearly much more excited about this than I am.

"Wait for me here. I'll be back in a sec," she murmurs before dashing back into the house, displaying no inclination to invite me inside.

Moments later, I find myself deep in the heart of Puer Lunae's forest. The dense foliage blocks out the moonlight, casting a dark and eerie atmosphere around me. The forest floor is covered in a thick layer of leaves, making each step I take soft and muffled.

Zizina starts the ritual to open the gateway for me, a shimmering dark portal that almost looks like a small black hole that distorts both time and space.

I pivot, casting one final appreciative glance toward Zizina for her assistance, before venturing through the gateway into a realm entirely unfamiliar to me, driven by the determination to reclaim the woman who holds my heart.

"Go forth, my King," I hear Zizina murmur from behind me. "Bring back our Queen."

That was, without a doubt, the best decision of my life. Life can be quite unpredictable at times. It has this nasty habit of taking away the things that matter most unless one musters the fortitude to battle for them. And I'm grateful that I chose to fight for what truly matters to me.

"A penny for your thoughts?" Naya inquires as she elegantly pours wine into two glasses sitting atop the side table.

I can't help but smile as I gaze upon her stunning beauty. Dressed in a white and silver nightgown, she looks every bit like a goddess. We're currently at the royal chamber, relishing the beauty of the night in each other's company.

"Nothing, I'm just thinking how blessed I am to have you," I respond with a soft smile on my lips.

She gracefully makes her way towards me with her hands full of two wine glasses.

"I thought you were thinking about our first night together," she says with a smile, extending a glass of wine towards me. "No need to worry. This one isn't poisoned."

I smirk, unable to resist a flirtatious response. "Even if it were poisoned, I'd still drink it if it meant I could have a chance to lick that body," I tease, scanning her stunning figure. My wife is truly a vision of beauty.

She laughs softly, a playful smile dancing on her lips as she takes the wine glass back and licks her lower lip seductively.

"Well, that's not a bad idea at all," she says before pouring the wine all over her chest.

My gaze remains fixed on hers as the red liquid saturates her nightgown, revealing tantalizing glimpses of her body underneath.

My body reacts instinctively, arousal coursing through me as my beautiful wife teases me in the most delicious way. This room feels as if it is on fire with my beautiful wife teasing me like this.

"You know what? You're absolutely right. It's not a bad idea at all." I agree as I pull her towards me.

Moments later, I find myself hovering above her, showering her face with tender kisses on her cheeks, nose, and lips, all the way down to her jawline. My impatience to remove her gorgeous nightgown takes over, and I end up tearing it apart with fervour. My lips immediately find their way to the top of her breasts while my hand plays with the other, tasting the sweet nectar of wine against her skin.

The wine may not be sufficient to intoxicate me, but my wife possesses an unrivalled ability to leave me intoxicated with desire within mere seconds. My lips trace a path along her body, relishing in the taste of every inch, until an unusual sensation captures my attention at her stomach. Despite the haze of lust clouding my mind, I summon all my clarity and lift my gaze to meet hers, prepared to share the exhilarating news.

Puzzled by my sudden pause, she looks at me with inquisitive eyes. "What's the matter?" she asks.

I shrug, unable to contain the joy swelling inside my chest. "I can feel a faint heartbeat from your stomach," I reply, leaving her more perplexed than ever.

"What... what do you mean?" she asks.

"You're carrying our first child. We have a prince or princess on the way," I declare in a voice full of enthusiasm, leaning in for another breathtaking kiss.

I don't know what I did in my past life to deserve all of this— A beautiful and loving wife, a kingdom to protect, and a baby on the way. I am overwhelmed with gratitude.

Sometimes, it's easy to get caught up in life's challenges and forget about the many blessings that surround us. But if we take a moment to look closer, we'll realize that life is indeed full of wonders and gifts that we often take for granted. Life is full of blessings. You just need to learn how to count them to see it.

AFTERWORD

Dear readers,

Thank you for taking the time to read this novel. I hope you enjoyed it. If you did, I would be grateful if you could leave a review with a sentence or two in Amazon. Your feedback is extremely valuable to me as an independent author and will help me grow and improve. Your support means the world to me.

Thank you so much for your time and consideration.

Best regards,

Jeka BC

About The Author

JEKA BC

Born and raised in the countryside, Jeka has always been passionate about reading and writing. After earning a scholarship to attend college, she graduated with a degree in Office Management and a BS in Accounting Technology. Since 2017, She has been working in the customer service industry, and began taking writing more seriously in 2020.

In her free time, she enjoys indulging in her love of literature and spending time with her family and friends. She is also excited to share her writing with a wider audience and hope to continue learning and growing as an author.

Books By This Author

Bewitching Her Alpha

Bubbles is a green witch with one mission when she sets foot in the metropolis: to destroy the sinister creature that she accidentally unleashed. However, her journey takes an unexpected twist when she crosses paths with Etho, her destined mate. The sight of him is a dream come true for Bubbles, but her joy swiftly transforms into a nightmare when Alpha Etho chooses to immediately reject her for being a witch.

Etho has been through a lot because of a witch who pretended to be his mate and almost destroyed his whole pack in the past. Now he holds a deep grudge against witches like Bubbles. Determined to safeguard his pack from further harm, he plans to maintain a distance from the enchanting yet dangerous little witch until they succeed in neutralizing the creature terrorizing his pack territory.

Yes, she might have that beautiful and innocent face that can easily lure men in her direction, but Etho knows firsthand that behind that innocent beauty lies a poison capable of destroying one's mind.

Will Bubbles be able to break through Etho's defences and earn his trust? Can they find a way to bridge the divide between them and forge a love strong enough to overcome their troubled pasts and the present danger they face?

Made in the USA
Las Vegas, NV
23 June 2023